# Custom Dwarven Chocolates

## LEAH R CUTTER

KNOTTED ROAD PRESS

**Custom Dwarven Chocolates**
Copyright © 2025 Leah R Cutter
All rights reserved
Published by Knotted Road Press
www.KnottedRoadPress.com

Cover Art:
GetCovers.com

ISBN: 978-1-64470-435-6

Cover and interior design copyright © 2025 Knotted Road Press
http://www.KnottedRoadPress.com

**Reviews**
It's true. Reviews help me sell more books. If you've enjoyed this story, please consider leaving a review of it on your favorite site.

**Come someplace new...**
Do you enjoy exploring strange new worlds, new cultures, new people?

Journey into the various lands envisioned by Leah R Cutter.

Sign up for my newsletter and I'll start you on your travels with a free copy of my book, *The Island Sampler*.

http://www.LeahCutter.com/newsletter/

# Also by Leah R Cutter

**Cozy Fantasy**

*A Dragon's Guide to Killing Gods (And Other Lies)*

*Custom Dwarven Chocolates*

*The Ice Elf & The Snow Cone*

*The Ice Elf & The Fire Elemental*

**Cozy Paranormal Mystery**

**The Water Witch Mysteries**

*The Witch is Inn*

*To Scratch a Witch*

*Witches and Waterways*

*Grilled Sand and Witches*

*Witch Mirror?*

**Urban/Contemporary Fantasy Series**

**Seattle Trolls**

*The Changeling Troll*

*The Princess Troll*

*The Fairy-Bridge Troll*

*The Troll-Demon War*

*The Troll-Human War*

*The Troll-Troll War*

**The Witch's Progress**

*Stairs of the Gods*

*Cities of the Gods*

*Graves of the Gods*

**Houses of the Dead**

*Houses Divided*

*Houses Fallen*

*Houses Reborn*

**Forgotten Gods**

*A Wind Blown Torment*

*A Stone Strewn Clash*

*A Sea Washed Victory*

**The Tanesh Empire Trilogy**

*The Glass Magician*

*The Desert Heart*

*The Ghost Dog*

# Contents

# PART ONE

## Preparation

❧

# A Rose By Any Other Name...

~⚬~

Never ask a Dwarf to explain their genealogy.

Not unless you have a spare hour or three. Plus at least one keg of good ale to wet thirsty throats.

Dwarven family trees are messy. They don't start with a couple and progress nicely from there, a solid trunk with many branches.

No, you might start with something like an oak. Then graft on an apple tree. Maybe add those firs over there. And yes, some shrubberies as well. Then let the entire mash-up grow together for a few years.

The end piece takes an expert hours to detangle. If they're lucky. And all Dwarves, of course, consider themselves experts. They do love their history. Which means maybe add another hour (and another keg) onto the time it takes to explain their family "tree."

We'll start with the basics. Dwarves either use a family name that they've inherited or a name that they've earned.

Most of the time, an earned name has more prestige than a family name. So they track family history through the handed-down-name segment of their progenitors until they get to the generation where the name was earned.

However, not all earned names are worth passing down.

For example, Whirthric Pebblefoot got his name because a witch cursed his shoes so every time he wore them, he'd have to stop to remove pebbles from them. Even when he walked along a clear city street with no stones anywhere to be found, pebbles would still appear in his shoes. (Whirthric wasn't the brightest lamp in the mine, so it took him a fairly long while to realize that all the pebbles weren't just bad luck and that his shoes were indeed cursed. But that's a story for another time.)

Clearly, none of his progeny wanted such a name, not even the one who inherited the cursed shoes.

Yet other earned names, like Yarnid Opalbender, took on such prestige that they're still passed down and chosen over a mere family name.

This is a tale of how one young Dwarf earned her name and started her own messy branch of family ties.

Come along for the ride.

And bring some ale...

# Shar

Shar looked at the emerald she held and despaired.

It wasn't that she'd done a bad job faceting the gem. No, her cuts were precise. Light entered from one side of the stone, traveled across the bottom of it, then out the other side, giving the gem an inner luminescence, almost a fiery glow. No empty facet marred the emerald, that the light could escape from undirected. The buckle around the center of the stone, where it would be held by its setting, was precisely squared off, not wobbly or broken. Every angle was perfectly aligned, each point joined correctly to the next. The polish had been applied evenly, so none of the hundreds of tiny facets were cloudy.

Shar had done her mentors and her family proud with this emerald. The fact that she was allowed to work on real gems despite only being twenty was an honor. Plus, she was determined to *not* be like her brother Durziak, whom her family often threatened with the name "Gembreaker" instead of allowing him to keep their given name of Opalbender.

*Maybe* she had some satisfaction, that of a job well done.

However, the fire inside the gem lit nothing inside of her. Beautifully cut stones didn't make her soul sing.

What was wrong with her?

She was a Dwarf. She was supposed to love gems, working with them, cutting them, making beautiful things.

Right?

Shar sighed and set the emerald to the side, stretching at her workbench before standing up.

She'd earned a break. Hadn't she? She'd finished, uhm, okay, maybe only two gems that morning, and it was almost noon. Her mother, the master gem-cutter Vatdrotir Opalbender, could cut four times as many in half the time.

Well, Shar wasn't a master. Wasn't likely to ever be, given her pace.

She sighed again and took off her apron. She made sure that she had no gem dust on the burgundy sleeves of her shirt, her black pants were still clean, and her beard was still plaited neatly with beads of bright blue stones woven into it. Only then did she walk out of her workroom, into the adjoining tunnel.

Her family lived under the Kibizar Mountains, in the Gemstone District of the coastal city of Shazirakz. To her left, past the other workshops, was the grand showroom. Only the best gemstones and most beautiful settings were on display there for customers.

She was certain that none of her gemstones would ever be placed in those fine glass cabinets.

Instead of going that way, Shar quickly slipped out the back and into one of the main halls that bustled with many Dwarves going about their business.

Shar fell easily into the flow of traffic, walking along and enjoying her break, quickly leaving the Gemstone District and ending up in the Old Market, slowing and browsing the tables of the usual vendors.

She wasn't out of beard oil. However, it never hurt to stock up.

She was *not* running away from her workshop. And the gemstones that she should be faceting.

No, really.

Shar had just reached the main intersection of the Old Market district and was debating if she should continue on to the next district or head back to her workshop when a familiar voice called her name.

She smiled as her best friend Hulda came hurrying up.

"Good," Hulda said as she gave Shar a quick once over. "You look acceptable." She paused, waved her hand dismissively. "Acceptable enough."

Shar didn't roll her eyes *too* hard at her friend's assessment. Shar would have had to spend three hours braiding her long brown hair as well as her beard, not to mention the makeup she'd have to put on as well as the fancy outfit before she'd meet with Hulda's non-grudging approval. And she'd have to be wearing some monstrosity of a shoe instead of her comfortable, worn boots.

"Come," Hulda as she linked arms with Shar and turned them, rushing the pair of them up the main intersection, away from the Old Market.

"Where are we going?"

Then she noticed that Hulda wasn't wearing her guard uniform. Hulda's family—the Mineshields—were employed as security for the mine that produced the raw stones that Shar's family finished. Some of them worked as guards for rich families, or for the queen.

That day, instead of Hulda's usual leather vest covered in iron rings and thick, reinforced leather pants, she wore a pretty blouse, with thin blue ribbons tacked to it using gold thread. Similar ribbons, with gold beads, were woven into her beard. Her black trousers ended just below the knee, like Shar's did, but they flared out at the cuffs, giving them much more volume. Her shoes, of course, were better than Shar's, the black leather so shiny Shar could use them as a mirror.

"We're going to the general audience," Hulda told Shar as she hurried them along, out of the Old Market toward the Nobles' Borough. "There's a new Human ambassador from White Hall. I want to check out what he's wearing."

Shar shook her head and didn't say anything, but hurried along with her friend instead. Despite Hulda's enthusiastic tendencies to always suggest dealing with problems by thumping them (repeatedly) with her stout quarterstaff that was shod in iron, she *loved* fashion.

Queen Namnorelli Amberheart granted a general audience twice a month. While she sat on a dais at the front of the throne room, the court and other rich people gathered on the floor of the room. The people who were not so rich could come to see the queen and watch the proceedings from the balcony at the far end of the throne room. It wasn't very deep, but it went the entire width of the room.

People who stood on the balcony were expected to be respectful, and were occasionally searched to make sure they weren't carrying anything that could be dropped (or even accidentally spilled) on the nobles. It had been many years since any sort of incident had occurred, and the noble who'd been covered in blue skin dye had actually taken the name Bluebeard as a result.

The queen was popular, as queens went. And there were only seventeen years left in her reign, so no one was agitating for her to get a move on. Then the next monarch in line, the King Consort Yarnard Goldarmor, would step up to rule for the set length of forty years, then pass the title along, as Dwarven monarchy had done for a few centuries.

"Don't we need tickets, or something, to get onto the balcony?" Shar asked.

"Nah, that system was abolished a few years back. You just have to get there early enough to get in," Hulda said.

"I hate to point it out, but this isn't exactly early," Shar said. She could already feel her stomach starting to rumble in hopes of lunch soon.

Hulda just waved her comment away. "My cousin Therfog is working the door this morning. He'll let us in."

Generally, Hulda worked as a guard in one of the various market districts. It was a good starting position, since she was the same age as Shar, and it allowed her to meet many of the important merchants in Shazirakz. Hulda hoped that at some point one would hire her to protect a caravan going to another big city. She'd also stood watch outside the mine, as all guards did on a rotation.

(Dwarves weren't immune to bribes. Particularly of bright shiny gems. To allay the temptation, the guards were paid well and put into a rotation that changed frequently, making it difficult for an outsider to figure who exactly they needed to bribe to gain access to something they shouldn't. Hulda's family had earned their name of Mineshield by being one of the few groups of guards who hadn't been bribed during the latest incursion into the mine, over two hundred years before.)

Hulda led Shar to the back of the palace and quickly through one of the tradesmen entrances, past the kitchen (where Narriud Boneborn, the chef, was preparing a mushroom dish that smelled absolutely amazing and reminded Shar yet again that she hadn't eaten since breakfast), through some back corridors crowded with bustling servants, up a set of deserted stairs, then through a door.

They popped out in the corridor that led directly to the balcony for the throne room.

"Hey, Therfog!" Hulda said, greeting the guard standing at the door to the balcony. He wore a fancier guard uniform—still a leather vest with iron rings, but the leather itself was dyed blue, and the bracers he wore had been recently polished until the iron shone.

He gave her a great grin, "Hey, Hulda!"

Then he paused. Scowled.

Obviously putting two plus two together and not liking the gem count he had.

"I'm not supposed to let anyone else in," he complained.

"It's just us," Hulda said. "We won't take up that much room. Really."

Even Shar raised an eyebrow at that. Sure, they were Dwarves. That just meant they weren't tall. They weren't skinny waifs like *Elves*. Both Hulda and Shar had a nice hefty girth, showing that they were well fed and muscular.

"I don't think so," Therfog said, slowly shaking his head.

"I'll take your next mine shift," Hulda said.

Therfog at least appeared to be considering that bribe.

Shar understood that the shifts guarding the mine were the least interesting. Could Hulda really move her shifts around that way?

"The next two," Hulda offered when it looked as though Therfog was about to deny them entrance again.

Therfog gave her a great grin. "You got yourself a bargain." He opened the door and peered in, then glanced back out and whispered to them. "The audience hasn't started yet. You be quiet and respectful. Don't shame the name Mineshield."

"I won't," Hulda promised. "Thank you."

Hulda paused and grinned at Shar, who returned the smile.

Looked like they were going to have another adventure.

The balcony was hot, crowded, and full.

There weren't any lights in the balcony area. The bright lights of the throne room shone beneath them. Being Dwarves, they both had excellent night vision, and it didn't take long for their eyes to adjust.

However, neither of them was tall enough to see over the shoulders of the people already standing there. Shar rose up on her toes for a few moments, trying to catch a glimpse of the area below.

"Still can't see," she whispered to Hulda.

"Doesn't matter. I don't want to ruin these shoes by trying to get up on the toes," Hulda whispered back.

Shar did *not* roll her eyes as hard as that statement deserved.

Really.

"I've got an idea," Hulda said after a moment.

She tugged on Shar's arm and led them all the way across the back of the balcony before she tried going back down toward the front. There was a bit more room along the edges, so they could make some forward progress, getting at least three-fourths of the way to the front.

Shar might have considered this good enough—they had a view of the queen on her throne after all—but Hulda wasn't satisfied yet.

She slid sideways between another couple of groups, then very rudely pushed her way through a few more people.

Shar didn't want to follow, but she wasn't going to abandon her friend either. At least she started up with a whispered litany of, "Excuse us. Pardon us. I just need to follow my friend. Excuse us."

It surprised Shar that Hulda managed to get them all the way to the front railing of the balcony without anyone stopping them.

Then again, Hulda was much more used to working her way through a crowd, such as when she accompanied priests from the Temple of the Cricket, out of the Temple District to anywhere else in the city. Brushing against the robes of one of the priests of the Cricket was considered good luck, so they always had guards surrounding them, pushing through crowds for them.

Down below, Queen Namnorelli Amberheart sat regally on her throne. It was carved from a single purple geode, a master work. Veins of gold had been added to the polished arms, blended in so well they looked natural. The natural purple and white crystals flared out like a flower behind the queen's head.

"Do you see that dress?" Hulda whispered excitedly.

Shar didn't want to admit that all her attention had been captured by the throne.

The dress was pretty enough, she guessed. Hundreds of tiny slivers of diamonds had been sewn into the white corset, giving it a nice sparkle. Fine lacy sleeves poofed down her arms. Gold and silver rings covered her fingers, some with solid gemstones while others were filigreed. The voluminous white skirt had gold ribbons loosely attached, almost like a shimmering second skirt.

Of course, the queen's beard was immaculately braided with many precious gems, as well as some gold ribbons that matched her outfit. Shar couldn't see much of her hair, as it was tied back. Her crown, though, was what Shar had heard her mother call a "Day Crown"—a much lighter filigreed piece made primarily of gold, instead of the heavy silver-and-jewel studded monstrosity that the queen wore for important events.

"Oh! And do you see the ambassador? There!" Hulda said, pointing.

It took Shar a few moments to make out who Hulda was talking about.

A tall, white-skinned Human stood on one side of the dais. He wore a brown coat tailored within a centimeter of its life, with darts in the front and probably the back to make the stiff cloth form fitting. The high collar had gold braid around the center of it, as did the voluminous cuffs. A series of knotted buttons caught in loops closed the front of it, all done in gold as well. His pants looked plain and black, until he shifted, and they shimmered.

Shar did *not* point out that the pants resembled work of the Elves, not Humans. They weren't likely to be fashionable at any point. At least among the Dwarves.

His shoes were black and pointed, with gold buckles on top.

Of course, the Human was clean-shaven. Humans who tried to compete with Dwarves in terms of beards didn't tend to be too popular among the Dwarven merchants. He also wore his brown hair short, keeping it trimmed well above his collar. It would be cool in the summer, but cold in the winter or down deep in the mines.

The general assembly was called to order in just a few minutes by the court herald, his loud voice booming out over the crowd. He wore a brown tabard with stylized gemstones in the center of the chest, the symbol of Shazirakz and the Dwarves who lived there.

After the herald called everyone to order, the first ambassadors approached. Dwarves from the Ashveil Mountains presented the queen with their grievances about needing better roads between the two sets of mountain ranges, as bandits and brigands had been plaguing their caravans.

The queen promised to see what she could do. She made the suggestion of setting up more way stations so that travelers had more safe places to stay as they made the journey. The problem was, few Dwarves liked living above ground. They'd have to rely on Humans, probably, to run such places, and everyone knew that Humans were the most susceptible to bribes. Which might make having more way stations moot, if the bandits and brigands would just pay off the innkeepers so they could stay there.

Still, not everyone would be bribed. And it might be cheaper to found a few places like that, putting up the money to build the inns, then let someone else profit from them. (After paying back the capital expenses. With interest. They were Dwarves, after all.)

Next came a priest from the Temple of Wood, asking for permission to expand their mission and add a few buildings to their existing temple complex.

Shar nodded at the grumblings she heard coming from around her. The Temple of Wood was an Elven and Human offshoot, and didn't worship a proper Dwarven god. Who in their right minds worshiped wood? In addition, though most of the buildings in Shazirakz were made of good stone, the priests would want to expand their buildings using wood.

It was clever of them to get an audience in front of the queen, though. Particularly on a general assembly day. The queen had to be seen as caring for all her peoples.

Even the weirdos.

The queen did manage to brush the priest off, saying that he was going to have to work with the city planners on his expansion plans.

Finally, it was the Human's turn, the ambassador from White Hall, the capital city on the southern continent.

He approached the throne slowly, bowing low to the queen and giving her her due. Though technically all the races were reigned over by the king of White Hall, which meant that the queen was a vassal of the Human king, she still had a higher rank than most.

"Greetings, your majesty! I bring you news from White Hall, and the great contest, *Chocolates Galore!* I am Antonio Bagaduce, the winner of this year's contest," he said with a second bow.

Shar perked up at that. Of course, she'd heard of *Chocolates Galore!* The contest was held every other year to determine the best chocolatiers not just of the southern and northern continents, but of the entire world of Indunel.

And Shar, like most Dwarves, enjoyed sweet things.

The winners of the contest pretty much had their pick of places to go work. Kings and queens, as well as various rich families, all vied to hire the winners. They might also open their own chocolates shop in White Hall or any of the other major cities. Shar had been to one of the smaller chocolates shop here in Shazirakz, but hadn't been impressed.

So maybe this Human wasn't an ambassador? Or was he a chocolate ambassador? She'd have to ask Hulda about it later.

After the queen greeted Antonio, he continued. "I bring a sample of my work. Not just for you, though, but for your entire court!"

Another Human pulled a cart out in front of the throne. It stood about a meter on a side. It looked as though it was made from the roughest wood. Even the wheels wobbled!

How dare this chocolate maker use such a lowly, poorly made thing and drag it in front of the queen!

Grumbles came from around Shar, other Dwarves agreeing with her.

The only redeeming thing about the whole presentation was an enormous egg sitting in the middle of what looked like straw. It was at least half a meter tall, its base a deep brown but the outside of it spattered with garishly bright colors.

It took Shar a moment to realize that the egg wasn't from some monster. No, the Human had made it! Then decorated it, because Humans believed that sweets needed to look obnoxious. (At least it was better than the Elves and their prissy desserts that were barely a mouthful.)

Though the queen kept a pleasant smile on her face, Shar could tell that she wasn't impressed.

With a dramatic flourish, Antonio pulled out an iron hammer. It was a domestic hammer, the kind with a flat tapping surface on one side and a claw on the other. He made as if to strike the egg, then paused. "All this demonstrating is such exhausting work. Do you mind?" he said, gesturing with the hammer.

The queen shook her head, saying, "No, go ahead. It's fine," though clearly she was as puzzled as Shar.

"Thank you," Antonio said with a bright smile.

Then he brought the hammer up to his mouth *and bit off the claw of it.*

It wasn't made of iron. It had just been painted to that effect.

Shar gasped along with the rest of the audience.

The hammer had been made out of chocolate!

"Mmm," Antonio said. "Delicious! Here, try a bit of the cart."

He broke off a piece of the cart and handed it to the queen.

The entire cart was also made of chocolate?!?!?!?!?

What was the straw made out of?

Antonio pulled apart a piece of straw and informed the queen as well as the court that it was made out of spun sugar, flavored with peppermint.

Shar found her mouth watering.

With great deliberation, Antonio tapped a circle around the top of the egg using his chocolate hammer. Shar approved of his technique, the tool striking with great precision.

A final harder thwack broke the top of the egg right off.

Chocolates spilled out of the now open egg.

Another assistant joined the first and they started tossing the small treats out to the crowd of royals.

"Up here!" Hulda called out. Others on the balcony joined her.

Shar held up her hand when she saw one of the assistants targeting their section of the balcony.

A soft hit made her close her fingers and catch what had struck her palm.

The treat she'd received looked like half an egg, oblong with a curved top and a flat bottom. Even in the dim light she could tell the piece looked shiny. The colors weren't too garish—bright blue, pink, and gold—done in an abstract pattern. The brown of the chocolate was visible as well.

After making sure that Hulda had also snagged a piece, Shar lifted her prize up. It smelled of sweet chocolate with a tang of berries underneath.

The chocolate snapped as she bit into it, and flavor flooded her mouth. First came the sweetness of the sugar, followed by the tartness of a jam that had been encased in the shell. The richness of the chocolate lay under the brighter notes, making it a complex symphony.

As she started to chew, she realized that a crunchy layer had been hidden inside the treat as well, perhaps a type of maple candy. At first it delightfully snapped, then it melted on her tongue.

Shar blinked in surprise as she finished her first mouthful, sadly looking down at the chocolate in her hand.

There were only two bites, perhaps three more, if she was careful.

Shar took the most delicate of nibbles, reliving the experience of a chocolate created by a master craftsman, feeling her entire being catch on fire.

Gemstones didn't rock her world. Didn't make her soul sing.

This chocolate on the other hand?

Did.

# Shar

"And that cart! Amazing!" Shar exclaimed as she walked with Hulda away from the Nobeles' Borough back toward the Old Market. "I wonder what it tasted like?"

Did she really deserve such an eyeroll? She did not. Shar had spent *hours* listening to Hulda go on and on about fashion.

Hulda could at least spend a little time listening to Shar talk about chocolate.

"Why don't you go ask Antonio for a sample?" Hulda said sweetly.

"He's...he's a master craftsman! And I've never worked with chocolate! Why would he talk with me?" Shar said, flustered.

She knew what master craftsmen (and women) were like. There were plenty of them in the Opalbender family. They always acted as if they were too good for anyone who wasn't a recognized master. Particularly Shar, given her lack of enthusiasm for gemstones.

"Hey, let's stop at the chocolates shop in the Old Market," Shar suggested. "They won't be selling any of Antonio's work, but they might have something comparable."

Hulda grudgingly went along with Shar as she tugged their

joined elbows to the right. "Fine, we can go there. But you're paying."

Shar sighed but agreed. It was only fair, since she was the one who was making the suggestion.

The chocolates shop wasn't on the main drag of the Old Market, but three blocks off, down a smaller side street. Shar had always just thought of it as the chocolates shop. Now that she stood outside of it, she realized that it had an actual name: Muddy Bean Chocolates. She didn't recognize the pale yellow pod that decorated the side of the sign—did that have something to do with chocolate?

A cheery bell sounded as they pushed the door open. Shar took a deep breath, swimming in the heady scent of chocolate and sugar.

"Tell me iffen ye'd like to try any," said an older female Dwarf sitting behind the counter. She didn't even bother looking up from her knitting. "One sample per customer," she warned.

Lighted cases stretched across the front of the small store. Curved glass covered the outside of them. It felt cool under Shar's fingers: probably some magical element inside the cases, keeping the chocolates at a consistent temperature.

Little signs next to the trays told Shar what they contained, such as the various types of fudge, truffles, and bonbons. In addition were chocolates she hadn't tried before, such as things called turtles, sea foam, and chocolate bark. The bark came in three varieties: white, milk, and dark chocolate.

There were different types of chocolate? White chocolate? How could she not know this? What other types of chocolate existed?

There was so much for her to learn! To taste!

Shar didn't want to push her luck with the old woman, so she split a sample of the sea foam with Hulda. The crunchy middle surprised her, as well as how fast it melted on her tongue. It tasted of caramel, beautifully complementing the dark melted chocolate that coated it. The salt that came at the end of the mouthful livened up the tastes, making her crave more.

Shar was *not* going to spend her entire allowance on chocolate from this shop, no matter how much she was tempted to.

Instead, she limited herself to a small piece of dark chocolate walnut fudge, a peppermint truffle, and three different types of bonbons: raspberry, strawberry, and pineapple.

Hulda only got herself some fudge, the milk chocolate variety with marshmallows.

Shar tried Hulda's fudge, but while her friend enjoyed it, she found that she gravitated much more toward the darker, richer chocolates. The truffle had been rolled in chocolate powder, with a much lighter, fluffy chocolate center that had been flavored with peppermint.

The bonbons—well, if Shar was being honest—weren't that impressive. Particularly not with the memory of Antonio's chocolate still fresh in her memory. The chocolate left a greasy feeling on her tongue, and she just knew that something was missing from them, though she couldn't figure out what.

Were there better chocolate shops in Shazirakz? Shar rarely crossed the city to try the Piers' Market, close to the wharfs. And wasn't there a market near the Temple District?

She was going to have to start exploring. Learning more about chocolates.

And how to craft amazing ones, like what Antonio made.

It took Shar about a month to hunt down every single chocolate shop in Shazirakz. She discovered so many hidden secrets to the making of chocolate through talking with people, such as that to make a shell of chocolate snap, the chocolate had to be tempered correctly—a magical process that she still was unsure of. No one crafted great pieces of furniture or huge displays out of chocolate— that was too expensive both in terms of time and money. However, some shops did have showier pieces in their front windows, such as chocolate cakes with beautiful, asymmetric swirls of chocolate on top, or one for a children's party that had what looked like bubbles placed on it—white chocolate brushed with amazing colors.

Most of the shops she visited did pastries as well as chocolates. Muddy Bean Chocolates was one of the few that only worked in chocolate. As Dwarves favored buttery, crumbly desserts (the better to feed their beards with), almost every other shop offered those with only a few pure chocolates on the side.

While Shar wasn't opposed to a delicious slice of chocolate cake, or chocolate cream pie, or even chocolate tarts, they were all lesser expressions of chocolate amazingness to her.

She'd stopped by Muddy Bean Chocolates often enough that she'd learned the name of the shop owner—Basteateleen Hammer-guard—who gave Shar permission to call her Leena. She ran the shop by herself during the day while her husband worked in the mine. It was hard work, particularly as they were both older, but their daughter had gone on to White Hall to be one of the King's Guard, and their son had his own family to raise.

Shar had spent another frustrating morning faceting gemstones and dreaming about chocolate concoctions. At least that morning she'd been able to do a little work with a silver ring, ensuring that the gems she faceted fit perfectly into their buckles, the prongs holding them firmly.

Though Shar's family primarily crafted gemstones, and some people (like her mother) had magic that worked with the stones, Shar's primary magical affinity was with metal. However, at age ten, when she'd been judged by a Seer, she learned that she had very little magical potential. So her family had never put a lot of money or training into her magical abilities.

(Honestly, Shar still hoped that perhaps she had some special secondary ability with chocolate, but she wouldn't really know that until she started actually working with it directly.)

This meant that Shar could take a rough ring, fresh from a mold, and smooth it out without tools, or bend a metal prong past the breaking point and have it stay together, there wasn't a lot more that she could do with her metal magic. Her ability didn't lend itself to crafting magical hammers or armor, she couldn't shape hot metal without molds, and she had no affinity for the forge.

After finishing two rings that morning—faceting their stones as well as placing them carefully into their settings—she decided she needed a break.

More specifically, a *chocolate* break.

She slipped out of her workshop, down the hallway, and was soon out of the grand Gem Hall and on her way to the Old Market. She found herself hurrying, carried on the imagined smell of chocolate beckoning her from Muddy Bean Chocolates.

Leena wasn't in the front of the shop when Shar arrived.

That was strange.

"Leena?" Shar called as she walked toward the front cases.

"Coming!" Leena called.

A loud crash followed.

Shar darted around the counter and through the door leading to the back of the shop, that held a large kitchen that Leena had invited her into a few times.

Leena lay on her back in the middle of the floor, moaning. A tray used to hold chocolates lay underneath her, the treats spilled all over.

"What happened?" Shar asked as she reached down to help Leena sit up.

The old Dwarf scowled at the floor. "Grease over there. Or something."

Shar nodded, but wondered. Sometimes the old Dwarf's hands shook, or her head trembled. Possibly something else was going on, but she didn't know Leena well enough to suggest that she go visit a healer. It may also have been Leena's age.

The tray had been squashed by Leena's healthy weight. Shar

picked it up and showed it to Leena, who made a sour face. "Ach. Can't afford to fix another tray."

Shar held the tray with one hand and ran her other hand over the bent surface of it. It was made out of a flimsy metal, then painted gold. "I could fix it for you," she offered slowly.

"Eh? How?" Leena asked.

Shar ran her hand over the tray again, concentrating, pulling on that tiny thimble of magic inside of her, urging it to come out.

The metal smoothed out and the gold paint brightened. With just a couple of passes of her hand, the tray was as good as new.

Leena blinked, impressed. "Thank ye," she said. "But I can't pay ye for it."

Shar looked around the kitchen. There were banged up pots and pans on the shelves, knives standing in a block on the counter, trays and metal molds for chocolates.

"I know you can't pay me," Shar said. "And I can't pay you." In the past month she'd not only spent her entire allowance, she'd also dipped a little into her savings, buying chocolates. "But you could use some help here, couldn't you?" Shar continued on.

"Maybe," the old Dwarf said cautiously. "What are ye thinking, lass?"

"Can you teach me? All about chocolates? How to make them? How to temper them? All the craft that goes into them?" Shar said in a rush.

Leena paused, considering. "And what do I get? Besides yer lovely company."

"I'll clean up, every night," Shar said. "I'll fix all your pots and pans, make them shine like new. I'll keep your knives sharp as well."

Using magic was tiring, but she'd do it.

If only Leena would agree.

The old Dwarf took a deep breath, considering.

"The path of chocolate—tis a hard one, lass. Sometimes the god of chocolate—Chaa—turns his face from ye. Chocolate's fussy. Ye breathe on it wrong and it won't set up. There's a feel to it, ye got to work with it 'til ye feel it in yer bones, 'cause I don't have none of those fancy tools the bigger shops have," Leena warned.

"I'll do the work," Shar promised. "It's the only thing I think about. The only thing I dream about. Chocolate, and the things I can make out of it."

Leena gave her a sly grin. "Not gemstones?"

Shar didn't have to fake the shudder she had at the comparison. "No, not hard stone," she said quietly.

"I could teach ye," Leena said after a few moments. "But why should I? Is it just a hobby for ye?"

"No. Yes. Maybe. I don't know," Shar said. She paused, then decided to confess her biggest, brightest dream. "I told you about seeing Antonio Bagaduce at the general assembly, right?"

"Aye," Leena said. "Man does fine work. A little showy."

"He was the winner of *Chocolates Galore!*" Shar said. "I know that he took years to learn his craft. He apprenticed to a master chocolate worker when he was eight. And there are rumors that he has a magical affinity for chocolate. No one knows for certain, though."

Shar had tried to find out everything she could about Master Bagaduce from the other chocolate shop owners, but no one knew that much about the Human. She heard many conflicting rumors, and had decided that the truth was somewhere in the middle of all if them.

"I'm with ye, lass," Leena said, encouraging her.

Shar took a deep breath, then spoke her heart. "I want that. I want to win *Chocolates Galore!* I want to become a famous chocolatier and maybe get a job working for the queen. I want my family to be proud of me and the work that I do. The gemstones I facet will never be displayed in the grand Gem Hall. But I still want something. Recognition of my skill. Crafting work that I actually enjoy."

Shar shook her head and looked at the floor, at the mess of

chocolates still scattered everywhere. It was how she felt her life was going, broken and in pieces. Nothing solid holding her together.

"I know that passion," Leena said quietly. "That fire in yer belly that keeps ye warm even with everyone saying no to ye. It's why I have a store that just does chocolates, and not cakes and pastries." She gave a wry smile. "It's why we don't do as well, 'cause most Dwarves prefer to feed our beards with our sweets."

Shar snorted at that. It was a well-known stereotype—the clueless Dwarf who missed the gemstones at her feet because she was distracted by all of the crumbs in her beard.

Leena looked away from Shar, seeing some point on the far horizon. "Did ye know that I won the regional chocolate contest, when it was held here in Shazirakz eons ago?"

"No!" Shar said. "What happened? You have to tell me all about it!"

"Aye, I will," Leena said. "Because I had that same fiery passion as ye do, once. But then I met Rurfean, me husband, and I put those dreams aside, focused on me family, until I could open this shop."

The soft smile on Leena's face gave Shar pause. The old Dwarf loved her family. Shar had heard a few stories about them, how proud Leena was of her daughter in the King's Guard, the delightful visits with her son and grandchildren, the warm love of her husband.

Would Shar ever find someone who could replace her innate love of chocolate?

Doubtful.

"So I'll teach ye," Leena said.

Before Shar could do much more than bounce up and down in place, Leena held up her hand, cautioning patience. "Now, the chocolate I have here is good enough for ye to practice on. But yer gonna have to get better. I know me chocolates taint the best."

Shar instantly wanted to protest and defend the Dwarf's work. However, Leena continued. "I know it for a fact, 'cause the chocolate

I use isn't the best. Iffen ye want to do fine work, ye need to start with finer ingredients. That means better chocolate."

"Oh," Shar said, her eyes wide. That made sense. Was that why Antonio's chocolates had been so much better than any she'd tried in Shazirakz?

"So while I can use the help—and I wouldn't turn down an evening or two of work for some lessons—yer also going to have to sort out some trade with a merchant. Get yerself some high quality chocolate."

Shar nodded solemnly. That seemed fair to her.

"Let me start today," Shar said. "I'll help clean up the kitchen. And fix your pans. Then, do you know anyone I could talk with about trading something for better chocolate?"

Leena's face broke into a huge grin. "Aye, I do. He's a Human," she warned.

Shar shrugged. She'd met Humans, though she'd rarely talked with any.

But if she wanted to make good chocolates, she'd have to get the best ingredients.

# Goddess Save the Queen

The Dwarves are currently ruled by Queen Namnorelli Amberheart (known as Nori to only a select few). She's ruled for twenty-three years, and has only seventeen years to go.

No, not because something terrible is about to happen to her, some plague, poison, or Goddess forbid, political shenanigans.

A Dwarven monarch rules for forty years. Then, they step down and the next ruler takes his or her place.

As there's currently a queen, a king consort waits in the wings, biding his time until he takes the throne.

In exactly seventeen years.

And once his forty years are up, a queen will replace him.

Has this passage from one royal personage to the next always gone so smoothly? As precise as the clockwork that the master smiths tinker with?

Cue maniacal laughter here.

Of course it hasn't. There's always some upstart who thinks their rule should either start earlier or not end at the appointed time.

Fortunately, the last time that happened, about three hundred years ago, *Events Occurred*.

You see, all Dwarves worship the Goddess Erisgrungrid, an earth goddess of some renown. (Not sure what it says that all the various races of Indunel believe that the earth beneath their feet is represented by a goddess and not a god.)

So when King Hazzoum Warforge announced to the court that he was extending his reign (having already killed the queen consort and her guard) a great calamity struck.

The entire capital city of Shazirakz started to shake.

It was worse in the throne room, where chunks of granite, marble, and other decorations fell from the walls. Some people were injured, but no one was killed. (Except of course the poor queen consort and her guard, but that had happened the night before.)

Most telling, a *huge* crevice formed appeared in the throne room floor. It started at the back of the room and slowly made its way toward the dais. Every meter, a percussive *crack* resounded through the room, upending the few courtiers who'd remained standing.

King Hazzoum Warforge had seen actual war. (This was when the Dwarves and the Humans still occasionally had conflicts over land rights unreasonable enough to gather armies. However, that hasn't happened in a generation or more.) He'd stared death in the face more than once. He believed that nothing could sway him from his course of action.

No one knows exactly what happened. Some swear that the Goddess Erisgrungrid spoke to him, using words shaped like golden daggers flying toward the king's ears. Others think it was the slow, gradual pace of the crevice, and the certainty that the earth was about to swallow the king, and his throne.

Something caused King Warforge to rescind his order, to step down from the throne, before that crack reached him. What exactly, we'll never know, as he never said. Plus, he died less than a week later, falling down stairs, the step that he'd landed on mysteriously crumbling (though rumor has it that all the other stairs remained rock solid).

The queen consort who'd died had had a sister, who stepped up to become the queen instead.

As for the huge rent in the floor of the throne room, some wanted to leave the gaping crevice just as it was. Others wanted the entire marble-covered floor of the throne room to be pulled up and replaced, the rent smoothed over so no one could see what had happened.

Fortunately, a Human was there to witness the event, and his idea struck a chord with the powers that be. There was a tradition with his people, a way to fix what had been broken, but at the same time, to make it more beautiful as a result. So while the crevice itself was filled with dirt, the very top of it was patched with a thin layer of gold. The effect was striking. The craftspeople responsible for the work created a unique masterpiece.

From then on, all the kings and queens, when they take the Dwarven throne, are reminded of what happens when they try to overreach.

Now, was that crack in the floor actually the Goddess Erisgrungrid expressing her displeasure at how the Dwarves were running their government? Or was it an alliance of wizards, magic users, mages, witches, and other magical beings who all came together and agreed that they needed to scare the piss out of the king and spoil his plans? A group tired of war, tired of losing good people for no good reason?

Possibly.

Particularly since after the floor was fixed a number of magical inhibitors were placed around the edges of the throne room, so that nothing like that could happen again.

As long as the queens and kings kept their vows.

# Rafael

Rafael knew, *knew*, that his curiosity was going to get him killed someday.

It was why he ran a general shipping and merchandise firm, Curious Cat Shipping. Why he'd left the comfort of his hometown and the familiarity of his large extended family. Why he and the three ships in his hire that plied their trade up and down the west coast of Indunel, searching for the unusual.

It was why the stores he supplied carried such eclectic stock. Not everything sold in every location. Sometimes it took a while for an item to find its market.

All right. Fine. Sometimes his ideas were a bust.

Though he still thought that those boomerangs that were used by the Plainsmen would come into fashion *somewhere*.

It was why he was sitting in his office that afternoon, talking to Sharaksir Opalbender, instead of sailing to his next port.

But Basteateleen Hammerguard had called in a favor. She was old enough, and respected enough, that he couldn't just ignore her request. So he'd put off sailing out of Brightring Pier for an extra day.

It surprised him how young Sharaksir appeared. He wasn't good at judging the ages of Dwarves (and no one could ever tell the age of an Elf) but he'd still guess that she was in her twenties.

Stout, of course, because she came from a rich family. (One of the saddest sights he'd ever seen had been that one town where there'd been a famine and he'd had to help a bunch of skinny Dwarves.) The Opalbenders were one of the families responsible for supplying the grand Gem Hall with merchandise. What they sold there was too expensive for Rafael to carry—not that he couldn't afford a few pieces, but the extra guards that he'd have to get would be a headache. And how could you trust the guards? Particularly if they were Dwarves, and tempted by such goods?

No, it was better to not even enter the Gem Hall, because his curiosity might tempt him into seeing what he could sell.

Sharaksir was pretty enough for a Dwarf. Her skin was a chestnut brown, smooth and unwrinkled. She had big brown eyes, a button nose, round cheeks, and a mouth that looked like it was made for smiling. Her beard appeared soft, done in some intricate braided style that he knew better than to ask about, not unless he wanted to spend an hour learning about the various beard oils she used. Braids also held back her hair, though those were much less elaborate. She wore a sturdy workwoman's burgundy tunic, black pants that ended just below the knee, and solid black boots that had seen better days.

And she was asking about chocolate.

Seriously, his curiosity was going to get him killed at some point.

"So, why are you looking for this type of chocolate, Sharaksir? It's very high grade," he pointed out after hearing what she was looking for.

"Please, just call me Shar," she said. She reached into a bag that she'd carried in with her and pulled out a box.

Inside were a collection of fancy chocolates. They were small round shapes, decorated with white splatters.

She offered him one. "You don't have to eat it," she said. "Only if you want to, if you like chocolate. But what I want you to do is to crack the chocolate shell."

Surprised at her request, Rafael did as she requested.

"See how it doesn't really break cleanly? And there's still a greasy feeling on your fingers? That's because the chocolate isn't tempered correctly," Shar said. "It's difficult to temper lower quality chocolate. It has too many impurities in it."

She handed him a second chocolate. He noticed that it was from the opposite side of the box.

"This chocolate is shinier," Shar said, continuing. "And if you snap it, it'll break cleanly. This one was made with better chocolate."

"I see," Rafael said after he inspected the piece in his hand, taking a chance and biting into it.

The chocolate did snap cleanly between his teeth. A semi-sweet familiar flavor filled his mouth from the filling. Was that coffee he was tasting? And maybe a hint of raspberry underneath? It was surprisingly yummy.

And very craveable.

"What's in here?" Rafael asked as he popped the rest of the chocolate into his mouth.

"Coffee ganache," Shar announced proudly. "With a very thin layer of raspberry jam."

"These are delicious," Rafael said. "Did you make them?"

"No," Shar said, shaking her head. "I am not a master of chocolate. Not yet. I am newly apprenticed," she said, sitting up and seeming proud for the first time. "The chocolate we have at the shop is good enough to practice on. But to make better chocolates, I need better ingredients. Specifically, I need chocolate that is one hundred percent cacao, in bar form, not powdered. And I need a supply of cocoa butter."

Rafael had to admit that he was suddenly far out of his league when it came to these ingredients. They weren't the type of thing that he normally carried.

Shar appeared to realize that, and continued. "I know you don't generally supply the city with chocolate. But the merchants who do only bring in one type of chocolate, and it isn't adequate." She took a breath. "Leena—Basteateleen Hammerguard—said you would be the only one who might be up for the challenge."

Rafael liked the way she placed a slight emphasis on that last word.

*Challenge.*

Because sometimes, really, it was a race to see whether curiosity would kill him first, or if he'd be killed by some foolhardy challenge.

"Suppose I could get you this higher grade chocolate," Rafael said. He held up his hand at the instant excitement that overtook the young Dwarf. "I said *if*, not that I could."

He continued on this path despite her crestfallen expression. "So, *if* I agree to go looking for this better chocolate, and *if* I find it, how are you going to pay me? And no, not in chocolates."

Shar winked at him, acknowledging his tease, before she grew thoughtful. "I had two thoughts on this," she said slowly. "One, my primary magical affinity is with metal. If you had base objects that needed repair, or scuffed things that needed polish, I could work with them. I can't create enchanted items, or reforge anything. I can just fix things. Small things."

"All right, we'll put a pin in that," Rafael said. He had a container of brass candlesticks that needed to be polished before they could be sold. And once he went through his inventory, he'd bet there were things he didn't remember that Shar could fix or straighten out or something. "What's the second thought?"

"You can't tell anyone about this. At least not yet," Shar said seriously. "So I need your word that you won't tell a soul what I'm about to tell you."

Rafael wondered just how well Basteateleen Hammerguard had prepared her protege for this conversation, if she'd known that appealing to Rafael's curiosity would be the best way to get him to agree to *anything*.

"I promise that everything that we're discussing will never leave this office," Rafael said.

Shar took a deep breath. "Okay. The next regional chocolate competition is in about a year's time. Then, *Chocolates Galore!* will be held the year after that."

Rafael nodded, not sure where she was going.

"All contestants have sponsors," Shar said. "People who back them and pay some of their expenses. The contestant would then have banners advertising the business that's sponsoring them. It's a win-win, as the business gets more customers and the contestant gets the supplies she needs to compete."

Shar took a deep breath, appearing to have to work her way up to her next statement. "I plan on winning, not only the regional contest but *Chocolates Galore!* as well. Are you willing to be my first sponsor? Secretly, that is, until I can announce to my family that I'm competing?"

Rafael opened his mouth, shut it, then sat back in his chair. It had never occurred to him that Curious Cat Shipping might sponsor someone.

It *would* increase business, he was certain of it, particularly if she won. His business as a general merchant and trader was well suited to this sort of venture, while a shipping company that only dealt with a single type of merchandise wouldn't work as well.

"Do you think you can win?" Rafael asked. He'd pretty much already decided he was going to go ahead and sponsor her, but he wanted to get a better handle on his soon-to-be partner.

"Chocolate is all I think about," Shar admitted. "I dream about it. I imagine all the things I can create in it. Both the show pieces as well as the little chocolates. I'm collecting samples of every spice I can, matching them with chocolates."

Rafael nodded at that. He was no spice merchant, and he was

glad she wasn't asking him to supply that. Those people were *specialized*, and Rafael was a generalist. Mostly. Which was why a sponsorship made more sense for Curious Cat Shipping, as he had more to offer than most.

"Will I win? I can't guarantee it," Shar said. "Chaa, the god of chocolate, may turn his face away from me at a critical moment."

That impressed Rafael, that despite her age, she was being realistic about her chances.

"All I can tell you is that I'm determined to do this. I'm stubborn," Shar warned. "Stubborn as only a Dwarf can be. And I will lean into that as much as I need to."

Rafael found himself nodding along. "Can I have another chocolate?" he asked.

Puzzled, Shar nodded and dug him out another piece from the good side, that had better tempering.

"To a long, fruitful, and delicious partnership," Rafael said as he toasted her with the chocolate before popping it in his mouth.

Really, this bargain was too sweet to pass up.

# Shar

Shar hugged herself and giggled all the way from the Brightring Pier back to her workshop. Leena had been right: Rafael was driven by his curiosity. He'd even named his shipping company after that.

And he was curious about whether she could win.

She'd spoken with much more confidence than she actually felt. She didn't know if she could win the local regional contest, let alone *Chocolates Galore!* She had so much to learn.

She hadn't lied about her determination, though. Or the fact that among Dwarves, she was more stubborn than at least anyone else in her family.

How else could she have continued doing a job she hated for as long as she had?

And that she continued to do?

Temple bells rang out the hour. It was almost midday. Shar started to walk more quickly. Wouldn't do to run—Dwarves weren't really made for running. Plus, once a Dwarf got moving, well, their weight and inertia kept them moving. Kind of like a cannonball, where only a solid wall would do for stopping them.

But nothing was going to stop her. She was going to study chocolate. Practice with it every night. Win the regional contest first, then *Chocolates Galore!*

The world seemed so bright.

Everything shocked back to normal—or even darker—colors when Shar entered her workroom and found her mother standing at her workbench, looking critically at the gems that Shar had faceted that morning.

Mother wore her work apron, of course. The only time Mother didn't wear it was during the large family dinners the Opalbenders held on rest days. Her beard was done in a simple forked braid, though a few small silver rings with amber beads had been woven in. Shar got her brown eyes and skin from her mother. However, her mother's nose was much sharper, her cheeks flatter, and her forehead broad and wrinkled. Gray touched her mother's temples, her hair pulled back into a precise bun.

"He—hello, Mother," Shar said as she shoved the box of chocolates under some papers next to the door and grabbed her own apron, quickly donning it.

"I see you haven't gotten any faster in faceting," Mother said disapprovingly. She glared at her daughter. "Your brother has also been complaining that you're leaving your workshop at all hours."

Shar pressed her lips together rather than let loose with a highly inappropriate curse.

She was going to have to figure out how to bribe her brother Durzi. She couldn't facet gems for him—she was barely making her own quotas. Plus, the family would be able to tell that it wasn't his work. Shar wasn't good enough to look at a gemstone and know who'd done the cutting on it, but her mother and other members of the family were.

Did he like sweets? She didn't think he liked chocolates. He was ten years older than she was, and she had a memories of him picking pastry pieces out of his beard with relish.

Well, Leena did say that Shar would have to learn how to make pastries and other desserts if she wanted to compete in regionals...

With a start, Shar realized that her mother had just asked her a question that she hadn't heard.

"I'm sorry?" Shar said. "Could you please repeat that?"

"Where has your head gone?" Mother said plainly irritated at having to ask her question a second time. "You're still doing good enough work. But you're not paying attention. Either to your work or when you're with the family."

Shar nodded guiltily at that. The last big dinner the family had had she'd kind of stopped paying attention when Uncle Oridgrul had started going on (and *on*) about this new faceting technique that he was trying to perfect. Shar had quickly lost interest.

Instead, she'd started thinking about how to craft a faceted mold, to make a chocolate that had many sides on it, instead of the smooth round molds that Leena used.

"I'm sorry, Mother," Shar admitted. "You're right. I'm not thinking about the gemstones that I'm working with enough." Or at least, not enough for her family's pleasure.

"What is it? Have you met someone?" Mother asked.

"What? No!" Shar said immediately. "Of course I haven't. Met someone. Not like that."

Mother gave her a soft smile. "It's okay. I was young once, though you may not want to imagine it."

Shar realized that her mother had taken her adamant denial as a confession.

"I know what it's like, first flush of young love," Mother continued.

O dear gods, how embarrassing was this confession about to be!?!?

"I remember my first love, before I met your father. We shone so brightly when we met." Then her mother grew stern again. "However, loves will come and go. Gemstones will never leave you."

Shar wanted to complain that gemstones were cold, hard, and heartless. They weren't made with love, unlike chocolates and sweets and all the wonderful concoctions that Shar was planning on making.

"But I haven't met someone," Shar said. "Well, all right. Kind of." Did having a crush on a master chocolatier count?

Her mother's smile grew softer again. She folded her arms across her chest and leaned against Shar's workbench. "Want to tell me about him? Or her. It's all right, whoever you choose."

"Even a Human?" Shar asked.

Mother opened her mouth, then closed it again. She peered curiously at Shar, as if she wasn't certain if Shar was actually asking or just teasing her.

Then Mother nodded decisively. "Yes, even a Human," she said. "Though I would be sad that you would never have grandchildren." After a moment's pause, Mother added teasingly, "We'd be having a different conversation if you were interested in an Elf."

Shar snorted. "No, it isn't an Elf," she promised.

"But there is someone," Mother insisted.

Shar shrugged. "Maybe?" she said. Did chocolate count as a person? She certainly did have a fascination with it, a love of it.

And she really, *really* wasn't ready to tell her mother about her second career, or her plans.

Eventually, yes. After she won regionals, she decided. Then she could formally approach the family and see if they'd sponsor her for *Chocolates Galore!* In the meantime, let her mother think that it was some Dwarf that she was chasing.

Not dreams so very different than the ones laid out by her family, by her heritage, even her name.

"All right," Mother said, pushing herself off the workbench she was leaning against. "You need to keep up with your quota," she warned as she started walking toward the door. "I won't increase it, as long as you do what's expected of you."

"Thank you," Shar said.

After her mother had left, Shar kind of collapsed against her workbench, letting her head thunk down on the hard wood.

That hadn't gone as badly as it could have. And she hadn't had to tell her mother anything.

Yet.

And perhaps pretending to have a beau would get her out of the halls more easily, and with fewer questions.

# Shar

Tempering chocolate was certainly putting Shar in a temper.

Or something like that.

Leena had explained that decades ago a Dwarf by the name of Fostaline Crystaldelver, who had an affinity for crystalline structures, had discovered that chocolate had miniscule crystal foundations, far too small for the eye to see, but that she could see using her magic. Warming chocolate changed the basic structure. Properly tempered chocolate had an abundance of a certain type of crystal, called tempering crystals, or T-crystals for short. Overcooked chocolate turned grainy, caused by an abundance of a different type of crystal. Same with chocolate that just sat, and developed a whitish surface, called a bloom.

The trick was to get the chocolate to the right temperature, then to hold it there. In the hot kitchen with all the ovens lit, already cooking treats, it was difficult. Shar frequently overshot the mark and had to cool her chocolate down again.

She worked with a small amount of chocolate, still trying to perfect her technique. First, she heated the chocolate in a pan, just enough to melt the outside of the cutup pieces. Then she took the pan off the stove and placed it in a nest of pot holders that would maintain the temperature of the pot while she worked the chocolate. If she placed the pan directly on her marble working surface, the chocolate would cool too quickly.

The chocolate bits slowly melted. As they melted, she added more, working to get the perfect shiny consistency that was no longer runny but more like a thick cream.

So. Much. Stirring!

Finally, she got the chocolate to where she wanted it. She dipped a spoon into the pot, then smeared the chocolate gathered there on her marble slab. The chocolate dried quickly on the cool stone, but it wasn't shiny enough.

So she ladled some of the chocolate out onto her slab and worked it there, dropping the temperature down more before she added the worked batch back into the original bowl.

More stirring before she tried the smear test again.

Finally! It dried smooth and shiny. A batch she could work with!

Quickly, Shar ladled the tempered chocolate into the tray that had many indentations in it, the molds that held her chocolate. While the tray was made from a very thin steel, smooth tin coated the inside of every hollow. Leena had told her that the shinier the metal, the more sheen the chocolates would have.

Shar used molds that had rounded shapes as part of her training. Molds that had points, like stars, more easily developed air pockets that were difficult to remove.

Before now, Shar had never used a flat scraper, but it was her most used tool currently. She carefully scraped away the extra chocolate from the mold, letting it drip into a trough that held leftovers from her experiments. She'd be remelting and using that runoff again shortly.

Then Shar tapped the side of the mold with the back of her scraper. She had to be careful to not strike the mold too hard, so as not to dent it. She also had to strike it hard enough to get out the air bubbles. She carefully watched the bubbles rise to the top of the small circular indents. When she didn't see any more bubbles rising, she turned the mold over and scraped the top of it while holding it perfectly flat, though upside down. This would form the edges on the bonbons. Again, they had to be thin enough to not get in the way of eating the chocolate, while at the same time, thick enough to give a ledge for the bottom coating of chocolate to hold onto.

Satisfied that no more chocolate was dripping out, Shar turned the mold over and took a look at how well her chocolate had filled each of the hemispheric holes.

Every indentation appeared to be evenly filled. Clean edges lined the bonbons. She'd managed to hold the mold flat enough that the chocolate hadn't clung more to one side than the other.

Pleased, Shar set the mold upside down on the waiting tray. Once the chocolate had rested enough, she'd put it into the cold box for a while. After the chocolate had hardened sufficiently, she'd take each bonbon out and examine it for flaws. Only when she was certain she could make perfect confections every time would she move on to the next step, which was filling the bonbons with a jam. The last step would be to add another coat of chocolate across the top, sealing in each treat.

It didn't make sense to just go ahead and do all the steps to make complete bonbons, particularly not from imperfectly made shells.

By stopping at this step in the process, if the bonbon shells didn't work, she could melt the chocolate down and reuse it.

And practice some more.

While the bonbons were setting, Shar opened the oven and pulled out one of the trays of chocolate cupcakes she had cooking there. The tops sprang back slightly when she touched them, but not enough. They were merely close to done. She'd have to give them another few minutes.

Plus, she still had to make the filling for them. The muffins would have to cool before she could frost them, so she had some time for that.

Then there were the cinnamon rolls that she was making. Those were a yeasted dough and still rising. She took the towel off the bowl that held the dough and inspected it. It hadn't quite doubled in size yet. She had time to make the spread that would go inside of them—cinnamon, butter, sugar, and just a drizzle of chocolate ganache, that she also had to make.

There was just so much to keep track of! So much to do! At least with a gemstone she was only working with a single component, not trying to juggle multiple items, each with their own prep and cooking time.

And while some of the time, things didn't turn out perfect, and despite her frustration trying to perfectly temper chocolate every time, regardless of the heat in the kitchen, Shar was having the time of her life.

# Hulda

Hulda walked away from Shar's workshop at the Gem Hall, frustrated at not finding her friend there.

One of the merchants at the night market (which took up part of the Old Market once a week) had come in with a delightful array of new ribbons. Instead of being smooth and a single color, he'd come in with some spools of ribbons that had been embroidered! The work was simple (and quite frankly, not very good—even Hulda could have managed to make straighter lines with a needle) but it was colorful. Buying them meant she didn't need to do all that work herself, as well.

Hulda had wanted to invite Shar to the night market, to ask her opinion about whether Hulda should get some. (Not that Shar had any great sense of fashion. She still might bring up interesting points, getting Hulda to think about the ribbons in a different way.)

But Shar wasn't around, as always.

At least Hulda knew where she'd find her friend—elbows deep in chocolate and pastries in the kitchen at the back of Muddy Bean Chocolates. (Though Shar swore that she no longer accidentally covered herself in chocolate. She'd finally learned how to finagle the chocolate molds so that she only got a small bit on her fingers, instead of all over her arms. And face. And apron. Hulda had even had to point out to her friend that she had dripped chocolate on the top of her worn boots.)

(And no, she didn't want to contemplate how long it had taken for Shar to finally admit that the chocolate on her boots could *not* be reused. Or eaten. Or anything other than thrown out.)

Hulda walked around to the back of the chocolates store and rapped on the door with her staff. The iron covering on both the head and the foot of her staff gave it a nice heft and made her knock seem more impressive.

"Come on in, Hulda!" came the response.

"How did you know it was me?" Hulda asked as she walked into the sweltering kitchen.

Honestly, it was as bad as walking into a forge sometimes. Particularly since Hulda still wore her guard vest with iron rings sewn into it, heavy pants, and boots with the toes reinforced with steel.

At least Hulda looked good in her outfit, as she'd put darts in the pants to make them fit properly. She hadn't been able to put the rings into an interesting pattern, as her mother had nixed that idea, insisting that the overlapping rings needed to be defensive, not pretty.

"No one else knocks on the door with quite that much force," Shar said with a teasing grin. "Just let me get these out of the oven and I'll have a bit of time to chat."

She pulled out two trays of golden brown cookies. They smelled sweet, though if Hulda was any judge (and she would admit that she'd gotten much better at these sorts of things over the past three months) there wasn't any chocolate in the cookies at all.

"What are those?" Hulda asked, slightly surprised.

Shar slid them onto a cooling rack. "Melt Aways," she said with a grin. "I won't decorate them until they're a little cooler. Then, I have these glazes that I'll use."

At least a half-dozen small bowls containing obnoxious shades of color that Humans preferred sat on the huge workbench that took up much of the center of the kitchen.

"Really? You'll use those?" Hulda said, disapproving. Maybe she should rethink her opinion of Shar's judgment. She still pulled up a stool and sat next to the bench.

However, Shar just beamed at her. "I'll put a couple in the freezer box, so they'll cool fast enough that I can frost them and show you."

Shar quickly scuttled around the kitchen—really, she seemed so comfortable here that it made Hulda almost feel like an interloper.

"How are you?" Shar said as she came back to the workbench. "It feels as though I haven't seen you in ages."

"Me too," Hulda said, happy that her friend had acknowledged that she'd been missing for a while. "I'm doing well. I just came from the night market." Hulda continued on, explaining about her find of the ribbons. She still wasn't certain if she was going back to get a spool or not.

Shar nodded, her hands busy, mixing up another bowl of something that started with melted chocolate. "I don't know how well those would work in a braid," she mused. "I would think the hair would cover the design. You wouldn't really be able to see it."

Hulda beamed at her friend. "See? This is why I came to get you. You would understand my concern about that immediately." She didn't want to admit that she hadn't thought of that aspect on her own.

"Still, they'd be pretty tacked to a sleeve or something," Shar said, nodding. "I wonder if I could do something like that with a braided sweet bread?"

She paused, then pulled out a stained notebook. Smears of berry, brightly colored dye, as well as chocolate, "decorated" the front of it. Shar jotted a quick note, then deliberately put the notebook to the side.

"If I'm not careful, I'll spend all my time taking notes and coming up with ideas and not *doing* anything," Shar explained sheepishly. "I get kinda focused sometimes."

Hulda rolled her eyes at that. "Yes. Yes you do." She paused, then added, "But you've stayed focused on chocolate, haven't you? For four months now? Five?"

"I have," Shar said with a shy smile. "I don't have any magical ability with it. My primary metal affinity appears to be my only magical affinity. But I still love chocolate, and I've grown to enjoy baking. And it all feels magical, sometimes. Here, let me show you."

She retrieved the cookies she'd put into the ice box. "First, I coat these in white chocolate," she said, dipping the top of a cookie into a waiting bowl, deftly twisting her wrist so that the white glaze stayed on the cookie and didn't drip or get all over Shar's fingers.

Hulda was impressed. Shar had made progress. She could see the smoothness of Shar's technique. It wasn't as effortless as Master Ironshod, when he was working with Hulda on her fighting skills. However, Shar was well on her way to a great technique.

"Next, I put a couple of drops of colors into the center," Shar said demonstrating. "Then, I take my pick and drag the colors out."

Hulda was surprised at how the colors faded into something more pleasing once they mingled with the white. The design that Shar made looked like a delicate spiderweb over the face of the cookie.

"There," Shar said as she finished, before she handed her work to Hulda. "The frosting hasn't completely set, so it's still a bit moist. But you should still have the same effect."

Hulda felt obliged to try the cookie, though she really wasn't one for sweet things.

A slight taste of cinnamon, the warmth of cloves, and a touch of nutmeg greeted her tongue. (All things she'd learned about since Shar had started baking.) The soft slide of the still wet icing coated the roof of her mouth, though not in an unpleasant way. Was that lemon that Shar had mixed in with the decorations?

Then the cookie melted away. It was as if she'd been eating air, or a dream.

Puzzled, Hulda took another bite. The deliciousness of the baked cookie lasted for just a couple of chews, then everything dissolved again.

"Wow," Hulda said. "That's so different!"

Shar gave her a great grin. "I know, right? It's why they're called Melt Aways. They just dissolve in your mouth." Shar paused, then continued more seriously. "As I said, there isn't any magic in what I'm doing. But baking, cooking, making chocolates? Is its own type of magic."

"Huh," was all that Hulda had for response.

Later on that evening, as Hulda walked back to her rooms, she thought about Shar and how much she'd changed since she'd discovered chocolate.

Hulda understood her friend's passion. She'd known something similar since she'd been young enough to hold a sewing needle. She loved fashion. She loved adjusting the cut of a jacket so it fell in the perfect spot on the body, or tweaking the lines of a pair of pants so they flattered the wearer. She also knew how to put together an outfit (though honestly, most of her practice in that had come from critiquing the outfits of others).

However, Hulda also really enjoyed thumping things with her staff. She liked the workouts and training she did. Standing guard wasn't always as interesting, but she frequently entertained herself by putting together better outfits for the people passing by.

Or imagining how she might thump them.

But her friend Shar, once she'd found her passion, had started to pursue it madly. Hulda could admit that she sometimes felt envy when Shar started talking about chocolates and desserts and everything sweet.

Even Shar's mother was convinced that she'd fallen madly in love with another person, which honestly, wasn't that far from the truth.

What could Hulda do to pursue her passion? Did she have a dream beyond working as a guard? Did she want to become a seamstress and make clothing? Did she want to become a tailor and fit clothing? Or did she want something else? Perhaps just to dress people, getting them to wear outfits that would be the most becoming to them? Along with the perfect accessories and makeup?

Hulda didn't know what she wanted. She didn't want to give up thumping things. Or standing interesting guard duties.

But maybe, just maybe, she could figure out a way to practice her own passion as well.

# Y'all Ain't From Around Here, Are Ye?

❧

The southern and northern continents of the world of Indunel, along with the archipelagos that run along parts of the coasts, are primarily inhabited by the three main races:

- Humans
- Dwarves
- Elves

Humans make up about forty percent of people, with Dwarves being another twenty-five percent, and Elves the remaining twenty.

The astute reader will realize that those numbers don't quite add up.

There are other races on Indunel. But their numbers are so few, their habitat so localized, that most people never even see them.

Take the Plainsmen, for example. They live in the far north, on a long band of territory that stretches from the east to west coast of the northern continent. They stand upright and have three fingers and a thumb. However, their heads are best likened to that of a ram, with a longish, fur-covered snout, vertical pupils, and horns that extend up from their foreheads then curl down to their shoulders.

Plainsmen don't have cities, per se. They're primarily nomadic. They do have a large market every summer where most of the tribes gather.

The reasons they're allowed to live on the outskirts of civilization, and can hold such a large territory, have been hotly debated by scholars for years.

It might be because they're immune to magic. Fireballs turn into puffs of smoke when tossed their direction. Lightning bolts ground themselves at their feet. Poisonous gasses just blow back into the caster's face.

It might be because they're ferocious fighters, berserkers of a sort, who won't stop killing until everyone bothering them who isn't a Plainsman has been pummeled into the mud.

It might also be because they've managed to hammer out treaties with every bordering nation, treaties that give them such favorable terms that some scholars question if the Plainsmen actually do have magic. (Of course they do. Everyone does. However, that isn't something that they discuss with foreigners.)

There are also the Maurinan, a cat-like people who live in the desert that makes up much of the northern part of the southern continent. They are also nomadic, and work as guides when someone absolutely has to get somewhere quickly across the sands. No one bothers them because no one actually wants their territory. They are skilled illusionists, and quite frankly, terrifying fighters.

Merfolk inhabit the coastal waters on both the east and west coast of both the northern and southern continents. Scholars have given up trying to assign tribes and territories to them as their genealogy is even more complicated than the Dwarves. Plus, there's the whole trying to interview people who live underwater thing, and though there are spells that help researchers do these things, they aren't great.

There are other races, of course, like the Ice Giants who live on snow-capped mountains, the Were-Badgers in the west, and the most ferocious Spiked Armadillos that anyone has ever encountered in the far south.

But still, all together, these others only make up about ten percent of the population.

Which leaves the remaining five percent for *others*.

Magical lands create magical beings at an astonishing rate. However, they do tend to be one-offs. Like the sentient vines of the southern jungle, that are extremely localized to just a few trees. Or the iguana-man who can heal a person with a flick of his tongue. There are also stories of a rat-king who could kill a person with a similar flick of his tail.

So while exceedingly exotic creatures do inhabit Indunel, they tend to be rare. And they will take offense if stared at too much, or poked at.

And the consequences are never nice.

# Shar

Shar despaired at the flavor combination that Leena had placed in front of her.

Basil. And rosemary.

How in the heck was she supposed to put those into a dessert? Or mix them with chocolate?

Still, she knew that the regional contest would possibly have this sort of challenge. It was less likely to be part of *Chocolates Galore!* though it did happen, say, once every five contests or so. Shar had been doing as much research as she could into what was thrown at the contestants every year, as well as tracking who'd won and what they'd gone onto.

Both for regionals as well as *Chocolates Galore!* judges constantly came up with different challenges, so going in with a set game plan would never work. They'd yet to repeat a contest. Shar had to be flexible, able to think on her feet, as well have a gazillion recipes memorized in order to even place. And the ability to think on her feet.

The task was daunting, but Shar was determined.

And stubborn.

One of the things that Leena had emphasized again and again to

Shar was that she needed a plan before she exploded into action. Leaping straight away into making something, then having to pivot, hadn't served Shar well at all.

So instead of racing to cool box, or running around the kitchen to pick up ingredients, Shar pulled out her notebook. She couldn't look at her old, existing notes. Those wouldn't be allowed at an actual contest. She could, however, start sketching a plan out, how she was going to use these ingredients.

The clock ticked away as Shar scribbled down ideas.

Chocolate and basil, as a straight combination? Never work. However, basil did lend itself to berries, such as raspberry. Shar could make a molded chocolate that contained a raspberry and basil jam. That would work!

Now, the rosemary. Oh, yes! Rosemary! She could make biscuits with rosemary. Then top them with cut strawberries, whipped cream, and a drizzle of chocolate.

Shar didn't have to include chocolate in every dessert for the regionals, but she still tried to do that, because for *Chocolates Galore!* it would be a requirement. Even if it was just a garnish, it had to be present.

After Shar wrote down the order of the items she'd work on, she put her notebook aside and got to work.

Tempering chocolate had to be the first thing she did, as the bonbons would take the longest. After the chocolate was perfect, she filled the mold, then set it to the side to cool down. The bonbons would have to go into the cool box after they set for a few minutes.

Making biscuit dough came next. At least that was quick, not a yeasted dough that had to rise.

After the biscuits went into the oven, Shar pivoted back to her chocolates, putting the molds in the cool box. Then she started on her basil and raspberry jam. She kept tasting it, making sure that the flavors were balanced, that you could taste both the berries as well as the basil. She ended up adding thyme and additional salt as well, because those rounded out the flavors nicely.

She set the jam aside to cool and checked on the biscuits. Not done yet. Time to make the whipped cream. Though she was tempted to flavor that as well, she thought it might be one taste too many. Better to have something more neutral with all the rest of the contrasting flavors. So she whipped that up by hand—because Leena insisted that everything Shar did had to be done by hand instead of spending money on fancy magical equipment. (Shar felt as though she'd developed muscles like a miner over the last six months).

Then Shar pulled out her sharpest small knife and started cutting the strawberries neatly. Knife work counted, particularly when chopping fruit. It wouldn't do to have squashed or uneven pieces. She put the strawberry pieces in a bowl with a sprinkling of sugar on top, to macerate the berries and draw out more of the flavor.

It was at that point that Shar realized her mistake.

She should have checked on her biscuits again before she'd started on her strawberries.

She opened the oven to find that while her biscuits weren't burnt, they were a bit too brown. They'd be fine if she were serving her family.

They weren't professional level, though.

Things fell apart from there.

She discovered next that she'd made the whipped cream too early. It had melted in the hot kitchen, turning into a soupy mess. She tried to beat the cream into shape, but it wouldn't hold its form. She had to start over.

The strawberries were perfect, but she didn't have time to drizzle any chocolate over them. That might have taken away some of the bitterness of the over-baked dough.

The chocolate she'd used for the bonbon shells hadn't been as perfectly tempered as she'd originally believed. The chocolates didn't want to pop out of their molds when she tapped them on the table.

They did taste lovely, and she was going to have to remember this combination of flavors because they worked together so well. But the tops were a bit messy from where she'd had to force them to come out.

When Leena called time, Shar felt like collapsing onto the floor and weeping.

Instead, she held her head high and presented her plates to Leena who was acting as the judge.

Shar had needed to create five perfect plates.

None of them were up to either Shar's or Leena's exacting standards.

Leena examined one of the bonbons, then took a taste. She kept her face inscrutable, neither smiling nor frowning.

Shar feared the worst.

The biscuit had so many issues! The insides were baked, but the outside was just too brown. And the whipped cream was still a bit runny.

She forced herself to stay standing, proud and strong, to show as little emotion as Leena was.

"Well," Leena said when she'd finally sampled everything Shar had produced. "Yer ideas were good, lass. Very good. The combinations ye came up with were creative. And flavorful. The execution though..."

Shar sighed and nodded. "I know. My timing was off. I should have pulled the biscuits sooner."

"And let the chocolates rest more," Leena said. "The jam is a wee bit too salty. Ye have to remember that salt gains strength as it melts. Yer jam probably tasted fine when ye pulled it from the stove, but as it sat there, the salt concentrated."

Shar hung her head. She *knew* better. She'd just gotten so flustered while trying to finish everything up on time, to make it all as perfect as she could.

"We only have five months left to train ye up," Leena said slowly.

Shar felt her entire body grow rigid. Was Leena about to throw in the towel? Was she going to tell Shar that she couldn't get ready in time? What could Shar do to convince Leena to keep going?

"Yer gonna have to come in and do the speed cooking more than just once a week," Leena finally said.

Shar let out a sigh of relief. "That's it?"

"That'll be a lot," Leena warned. "Because yer gonna have to keep up with the rest of the chocolate and pastry making."

Shar nodded. Since she'd started working with Leena at Muddy Bean Chocolates, they'd expanded their menu, selling Shar's baked goods to cover the costs of all the ingredients she was going through. While Rafael's sponsorship definitely helped defer some of the expenses, it wasn't enough.

Maybe she could just sleep an hour less a night. She was already getting up before the rest of the hall, sneaking out and working in the kitchen, providing all the baked goods for the morning rush. Then working at her gemstone workbench all day, faceting gems and placing them in settings. As soon as Shar had made her quota, she took off again, spending the rest of the afternoon and every evening, frequently late into the night, making chocolates as well as trying and to perfect new recipes.

If she got up earlier, maybe she could cook more? Or try recipes in the morning? The problem was that Shar was far from a morning person. Working late at night suited her so much better. It was only after she'd started spending all her time at Muddy Bean Chocolates that she'd come to realize how different her clock was from everyone else's in her family. They were all early to rise, early to bed.

Shar wanted to spend her evenings coming up with new delights, not sleeping.

"I can do it," Shar finally said, realizing that Leena was waiting for her answer. "I'll come in earlier to learn, so that I can do more practice cooks at night."

Leena slowly nodded. "That might not be enough," she warned. "Ye do need to rest sometimes."

"I know," Shar said. She was already pushing herself hard.

However, as she'd told Rafael, she was stubborn, as only a Dwarf could be.

She could do this.

"All right," Leena said decisively. "I have a new plan. Work hard during the work week. As hard as ye can. But when a rest day comes, ye *rest*. I know, I know, cooking comes from the heart. The head needs a break as well. Ye need to refill and refuel."

Leena held up her hand when Shar was about to protest, cutting off the words boiling up inside her like overheated milk.

"Ye have the skill," Leena said softly. "And I think yer gaining the knowledge. Ye could be great one day. But ye know what happens when ye overwork a dough. Or overbeat a cream."

Shar sighed and nodded. She didn't feel any relief being told to take more time off.

She would listen to her mentor, though, and relax. Not work. At least one day per week.

"So go on. Get out of here," Leena said dismissively.

Shar froze. "But the mess—"

"I can clean up for once. Goodness, me dear, I taint scrubbed a pan in months!" Leena chuckled. "Might forget how with ye here. Now, git."

Shar nodded, slowly taking off her dirty apron. When had she spilled jam on it? And flour? At least there weren't any chocolate smears she could see. She was getting better, and more careful with that expensive ingredient. Then she realized that the ties of the apron had chocolate coating on the ends of them, where they'd been tied behind her back. When had that happened?

Leena was right. Shar was trying to move too fast, do too much, and wasn't taking the time to execute to her fullest ability.

At the start of every challenge, Shar had learned to write down her gameplan. The problem was that she wasn't executing that plan well enough.

Maybe she needed to check her notebook midway through a cook? Just to make sure she was on track?

Shar nodded to herself and kept her feet moving back to the Gem Hall, her mind on cooking and timing and all the things that could go wrong and how she was going to adjust.

# Shar

Shar was not, *was not*, about to pull out her notebook to jot down another idea while sitting with her gathered extended family that rest day.

No, she was going to *rest* as Leena had said.

Her mentor had promised that she'd feel better after taking a day off.

Shar wasn't so sure about that.

"So how's it going with your not-beau?" Mother asked as she came sidling up to where Shar sat off to the side, away from most everyone.

"Fine! Fine. Everything's fine," Shar said. "We're just taking a break. Just for today." Shar wasn't certain if she was assuring herself or her mother more.

"I see," Mother said. She wasn't wearing a work apron for once, but instead, was dressed in a pretty maroon tunic over a white shirt with brown pants. She'd even taken the time to braid the front pieces of her beard in a simple but elegant design, instead of her usual, practical, split braids.

Shar hid her smile when her mother went to put her hands in the pocket of her apron and found she couldn't, that her hands slid down the outside of her tunic awkwardly.

"So, why do you feel you need a break?" Mother asked.

"Because I need to rest," Shar said honestly. "I've been getting up so early, and working so late. I just need a break. Or so I've been told."

"I see," Mother said, though it was obvious that she had no idea what Shar was talking about.

"Do you ever take breaks?" Shar said, peering intently at her mother.

"From your father?" Mother said, sounding puzzled.

"No, from working with gemstones," Shar explained. "Or do you think about them all the time? The way you could facet them, the settings they might go into?"

"I used to," Mother said with a smile. "Your father would complain that sometimes my hands twitched when I was sleeping, as if I were still holding a hammer, tapping at a gem."

Her mother nodded, then shot Shar a sharp look. "I have learned, though, that family is also important. Like you. And Durzi. So we implemented these family dinners, on rest days at the end of the work week, to give me something to do, something to think about, other than my work."

"Really? Huh," was all that Shar had to say.

"I resented it at first," Mother said. Her eyes looked at something far away, possibly in the distant past. "But after a while, I realized I needed the time off. I came back to my workbench refreshed."

Seemed that Leena might be onto something, insisting that Shar take some time off.

"All right," Shar said, nodding. She stood up. "Tell me who's doing the best molds in the family," she asked. She wanted to start crafting some of her own chocolate molds. She'd made improvements to the ones at Muddy Bean Chocolates; however, they just weren't good enough. She needed excellent ones to make finer chocolates. And she couldn't expect Rafael to provide her with those along with the high-quality chocolate he'd found. He wouldn't know what to look for, the difference between a good mold and a bad one. Shar herself was just learning to feel the difference.

"I think that would be your cousin Algruzlea," Mother said, still puzzled.

"All right. I'm going to go talk with her," Shar said, standing.

Or that had been the plan. Until her brother came up and her entire world fell apart.

# Durzi

Durzi looked at the amethyst in his hand and despaired.

It wasn't that he hated gemstones. No, in fact the way they sparkled and shone always delighted him. He loved the fire he saw in cold stone, the difference between the unyielding surface and the brilliance within.

However, Snazalgrid, the god of not just gemstones but gem cutters, had turned his face away from Durzi.

Durzi tried. Oh, how he tried. He studied patterns of faceting. He practiced on worthless crystal all the damned time. He visited his uncles, his aunts, his mother, sat in their workshops and observed every minute detail of their technique. He took notes (So. Many. Notes.) about how to properly hold a hammer, the correct angle to strike a gem, the different chisels and grinding stones and polishes. He could *teach* a master class in how to facet gems.

He just couldn't do it himself.

His fingers fumbled. Or despite all his care and checking, rechecking, verifying against his checklist, then checking one last time, he still made mistakes.

Like this poor amethyst. The points weren't straight, where one connected to the next. It gave the entire gem a lopsided feeling. He hadn't noticed his error early enough. Then he'd tried to correct it, but had overcorrected instead.

Durzi put the gemstone down on his bench and heaved himself up. He wasn't about to take a long break, not like that lazy sister of his. He was going to master gem cutting if it was the last thing he did.

(Sadly, he sometimes suspected it would be the last thing he'd do. That he'd die at his workshop with a perfectly cut gem in his hands, his first, last, and only successful attempt.)

Speaking of that lazy sister of his, though...did he have any more of those delicious pastries that she'd found for him? He'd tried to throw a twist at her, asking for crumbly rolls that had not just cinnamon and the usual flavors, but chocolate as well.

He still had no idea where she'd gotten them. She must be scouring the entire city, stopping at every little bakery and pastry shop, just to score his latest obsession.

He found his napkin-wrapped deliciousness over in the corner. (It would never do to scatter crumbs on his workbench. He might not be able to cut a gemstone correctly, but he could clean his beard adequately so as not to get his work dirty.) The pastries were the ultimate combination of flaky dough, warm spices, and earthy chocolate.

He unwrapped his last one, marveling at the golden sheen on the top. He wasn't sure how the baker had achieved such a rich, perfect crust. It practically snapped as he bit into it, the richness of butter coating his tongue. Then came the sweet spices, the cinnamon rising up, supported by the cloves and nutmeg. The chocolate came last, just a hint of deep richness that underlay all the other tastes and carried him forward to the next bite. And the next.

He looked down at his suddenly empty hand, surprised at how fast he'd made that pastry disappear.

Where was she getting them? They always appeared in his workshop like magic, wrapped in a napkin. No identifying bag. No way of tracing her steps, not unless he wanted to stalk after her when she disappeared from her workshop. (And quite honestly, she was gone so often, he was surprised that she managed to get any work done at all.)

Sometimes, early in the morning, the pastries were also still slightly warm, as if fresh from the oven.

She must know some baker.

Oh, that was it!

Mother had mentioned that Shar had a beau somewhere. She must have met up with the owner of a bakery. That had to be where she was spending all her time!

He'd have to ask her the next time he saw her. Demand to know where she was getting these delicious pastries.

He knew that she'd scored a bargain with him—that he wasn't to harass her or to complain to Mother about her being gone in exchange for the delicious treats.

But at some point, their bargain would end, and she'd either break up with her beau or move in with him.

And Durzi would be without a constant supply of delectable treats.

Nope. Wouldn't do.

While he might despair when it came to faceting gems, he could secure a constant supply of deliciousness.

He had to have some sort of delight in his life.

Durzi saw Shar talking with Mother at the family gathering during the rest day that week.

Perfect opportunity for him to ask her about where she was getting her baked goods!

He strode over to the pair of them, just as Shar stood up and appeared to be going somewhere.

"Hello, Shar. Hello, Mother," Durzi said as he came up.

He must have imagined the sigh that Mother gave, as if preparing herself for an arduous task.

"Now, I know I'm not supposed to bother you regarding your beau," Durzi said. He gave what he believed to be a sly wink to Mother. (Because really, why else had she told him about Shar's mysterious disappearances?)

"Yes," Shar said slowly, looking at him as if he was about to quiz her on some faceting technique. (Which he totally could.)

"But I have to know where you're getting your pastries from!" Durzi said. "They're amazing. The crunch on that last set of baked treats was perfect. And the taste! Divine! You have to tell me what shop you're going to."

"Uhm," Shar said, looking from her mother to Durzi.

"What is this?" Mother asked.

"Shar's taken up with a baker. Or shop owner. She's been giving me some of the most amazing treats," Durzi explained.

"Really?" Mother said.

Was she pleased? Or exasperated? It was so hard to tell with Mother sometimes. (Most of the time.)

"He must be who's supplying her with all that deliciousness," Durzi said, being totally reasonable. "But I have to know who it is, before you move on."

"Uhm," Shar said again.

"Now, dear, I know I said I wouldn't interfere," Mother said, turning on Shar. "But really? A baker?"

"Not just an ordinary baker," Durzi said, trying to help Shar out. "He's absolutely amazing. See, I've been asking for some special treats," he confided in Mother.

"I can see," she said dryly, her gaze going from his face to his waist and back again.

Or did he still have crumbs in his beard?

"And she's been finding them for me. I thought at first that she must be scouring the city for these pastries, but then I figured out that it must be this beau of hers, who you told me about," Durzi said. "Now, I'm not asking about his name. But he is the baker who's been providing me all those treats. Right?"

Shar's gaze darted between Mother and Durzi and back again.

"Is that why you were asking about molds?" Mother said. "Because your beau needs some better ones? And about taking a break for a day? Refreshing your artist's soul?"

Shar gave a deep sigh. Then a second one.

"Kind of?" she said eventually.

"You'll have to bring him—or *her*—" Mother said with a pointed glare at Durzi, "to meet the rest of the family. Maybe the next rest day?"

"Could I just bring some desserts?" Shar asked.

Mother appeared to think about that for a few moments, before she shook her head. "No, I've been quite reasonable for long enough. I'd like to meet this beau of yours. Even if it is a Human."

Durzi heard his own gasp. "A Human? Really, Shar?" Then he paused and considered. "Though, if he can bake like this, I can see why you might."

"At least it isn't an Elf," Mother muttered.

Durzi nodded. That would have been one step too far.

"All right," Shar said, seeming to have come to a decision. "Next rest day, I'll come with an assortment of desserts. And chocolate. And you'll get to *meet* my beau."

Durzi wasn't certain why his sister gave such an emphasis on the word meet. It was like there was going to be a lot more to meeting this individual than anyone expected.

Mother didn't appear to notice though. She just gave Shar a huge smile, then said, "We were just going to talk to Cousin Algruzlea about her molds. Want to come along?" she said, inviting Durzi.

He nodded dutifully. Though he couldn't necessarily facet gemstones, he was always up for learning more technique about all the steps in the process of making beautiful jewelry.

# Half Nothing

I know, I know! There are so many stories about half-Dwarf, half-Human. Or half-Elf, even. There are also not-for-polite-company stories of even half-Plainsman, half-Human.

Now, while it's true that a Human will copulate with anything that stands still long enough for them to mount, nothing ever comes of such a union. (Which honestly? Is probably best for everyone. Or the Humans would be out-populating every other race by a factor of ten.)

It isn't that the Humans are particularly randy compared to the other races. Every group has its own wide range of acceptable behavior, from mating once a year to as often as they can get it. (Hey, how *you* doing?)

The truth is that Humans are just not particularly picky about Tab A or even Slot B. Not all Human individuals, but certainly a large percentage of them as a race. Even the Merfolk, who have city-wide orgies once a month on the full moon, are more choosy when it comes to mating.

It's why Humans are the only ones who have come to realize that the Plainsmen who show up in town when they go walkabout are more often than not female. There aren't any outward physical characteristics that distinguish a female Plainsmen from a male. However, their society as a whole is actually a matriarchy. (They've never bothered trying to get the name for their people changed to something more accurate in the Common tongue because it amuses them.)

There are, however, stories of centaurs. And there are the Merfolk. Some of the Ice Giants appear more Human than not. So perhaps at one point, some sort of melding did occur.

But the gods (Yrthria, the Great Emperor, whoever) have turned their face against such unions and they haven't been fruitful ever since.

Gods know, though, the Humans keep trying.

# Shar

〜

"And what am I going to do?" Shar wailed as she finished pouring out the entire ridiculous story to Hulda. They sat in the overly warm kitchen of Muddy Bean Chocolates. Shar had just put another tray of pastries into the oven. "You wouldn't happen to want to pretend to be my beau, would you?"

Hulda rolled her eyes. "First of all? Eww." Before Shar could build up any resentment, Hulda explained, "You're like a sister to me. I don't want to even pretend to date my sister."

Shar had to nod at that. She hadn't really thought it through. No, pretending to date Hulda would be awful, actually, now that she came to think about it.

Particularly because to make it work, Shar would have to allow Hulda to dress her. And *not* in comfortable work clothes.

"Second, I don't bake. You couldn't possibly pretend that I was the mysterious person providing all your goodies," Hulda pointed out.

"You're right," Shar said with a sigh. "But I don't know anyone else."

"Rafael?" Hulda suggested.

"No," Shar said. "While he's Human, and I've hinted that I might be dating a Human, he isn't here. He just left for his next trading venture." He was going to be hunting down a few specialty ingredients for Shar while he was gone. The chocolate he'd been supplying her with was amazing. She was slowly but surely emptying out all of her savings. She would never stoop to stealing gems from the family, but maybe she could get a third job, doing adequate enough faceting on gems for some other family?

At least Rafael kept finding things for Shar to either mend or polish, so she didn't feel as though she was taking that much of an advantage of him. She still worried about it sometimes.

"So obviously you need to just tell your family what you're doing," Hulda said.

"I can't!" Shar said, the idea filling her with panic. "I'm not ready!" There were still so many things she had to learn! So many recipes to master! Her chocolate work was getting much better, but she still had difficulties with the challenge bakes that Leena set up for her. And regionals were only three months away.

"This is your family you're facing," Hulda said firmly. "Not some fancy judge. They won't know the difference between competition-level pastries and things that just taste amazing."

Shar opened her mouth then closed it again.

Muddy Bean Chocolates had seen a huge spurt in business over the last month as Shar had perfected more of her baked goods. She'd found the exact right combination of flavors—in part, due to the requests from Durzi—that appeared to appeal to most Dwarves. They constantly sold out of some of her pastries. Leena had had to hire help out front, as she couldn't handle the business all by herself. Particularly in the mornings, when the pastries were fresh from the ovens. Sometimes the line went out the door!

At least the popularity of those pastries meant that Shar was paying Leena back for all the materials that she'd been using. Doing the mock cooking challenges used up a *lot* of expensive ingredients.

"All right. Fine. You're right. They won't know the difference," Shar said. "But I don't think I'm ready to tell them yet. What if they hate the idea?"

Hulda shrugged. "Would it really stop you?"

Again, Shar opened her mouth and closed it again. "Uhm. No," she said. She hadn't been lying when she'd told Rafael that she was stubborn.

"And if your mother does something stupid like forbids you from pursuing your career, you can come and stay with me," Hulda offered.

Shar shook her head. She really, *really* didn't want it to come to that. "Where would you put me?" she said, more out of curiosity than because she was planning on such a future.

"I've, uhm, well, I've acquired a second room," Hulda said, suddenly shy.

What in all the names of the gods did Hulda have to be embarrassed about?

"Okay," Shar said slowly. "And?"

"It's a closet, all right? Full of clothes and finery," Hulda said.

"That doesn't sound big enough to sleep in," Shar pointed out. She was a Dwarf. She wasn't that tiny.

"No, it's as big as my other room," Hulda said. "But all that's in there are a miraculous sewing machine that my mom bought for me, fabric, and accessories, like ribbons and lace. And rack upon rack of clothes."

"Really?" Shar said. "That sounds amazing! For you," she added hastily. "You've always been so into fashion."

Hulda gave her a brilliant smile. "I knew you'd understand! I'm not really a good seamstress. I mean, I can put an adequate garment together. I've learned that I need to leave the fine detail work to the professionals. However, I'm really good at coming up with designs. And dressing people."

She paused and looked Shar up and down. "You're going to have to start dressing the part of a fancy baker, one of these days."

"What does a fancy baker wear?" Shar asked, puzzled. "Besides flour, chocolate, and smears of jam?"

"You need an outfit for regionals," Hulda announced.

For a third time, Shar opened her mouth, this time to object, but then snapped it shut again with an audible click.

Hulda was right.

"What are you thinking?" Shar asked, still hesitant.

"Don't you worry," Hulda assured her friend. "I'll have you all fixed up in no time."

"Remember, I have to move. This has to be a practical outfit," Shar warned. "I have to be able to use my arms, walk quickly from one place in the kitchen to the next. I need a pocket for my notebook. I need some sort of apron, to protect my coat. I need to look at least vaguely presentable after a bake so I can go in front of the judges."

Hulda nodded. "Got it. I'll make you something that you'll look and feel amazing in."

"All right," Shar said slowly. She was still worried, but if Hulda had decided to pursue her passion, Shar was going to support her friend.

"Good," Hulda said. "Now that that's settled, what are you going to make for your family the next rest day?"

Shar groaned. At least Hulda had distracted her for a few moments. "I don't know!" she wailed, dropping down and banging her head on the workbench of the kitchen.

"Come up with the perfect menu," Hulda said firmly. "You're getting good at those, right?"

Shar raised up her head and looked at her friend. "You think so?"

"I know so," Hulda said. "You said that you're getting a lot less frazzled at the quick cooks, right?"

"That's true," Shar said, nodding. "What do you think my family will like?"

"What ever is your most popular seller here at the bakery," Hulda said. "They are Dwarves. And a *lot* of Dwarves like your pastries."

"You're right," Shar said. "It's the chocolate work that I'm most worried about."

"Again, these aren't finicky judges. This is your family. They won't be able to distinguish good chocolate from bad."

"But *I'll* know," Shar said. "I need to be proud of my work. Particularly if I'm presenting it to my family."

"So make it good," Hulda said. "You got this."

Shar took a deep breath in, then let it out.

Hulda was right.

She could do this. She could make chocolates and pastries and a showpiece cake that her family would love.

And if they didn't?

She'd be sleeping on the floor of Hulda's closet.

# Shar

Though it took some persuading on Shar's part, she managed to get Hulda to help her deliver all the baked goods and other treats to her family's gathering the next rest day.

There were cookies. And pastries. And fruit tarts. And hand pies. And truffles.

The two-tier cake was chocolate-raspberry, with an additional third tier just of fancy chocolate work, swirls of perfectly tempered chocolate reaching for the ceiling. She'd done a classic buttercream frosting, adding just a touch of chocolate to it so it came out a very light brown, then decorated each layer with raspberries.

Then there were the bonbons. Shar still hadn't built her own molds, and had had to use Leena's. So while the shapes weren't as fanciful as she would have liked, the tastes ran the gamut from more traditional chocolate to thyme-berry jam mixed with hazelnut paste. All of them had some sort of lovely crunch layer in them as well.

It took both Shar and Hulda several trips to carry all the goodies in. In the meanwhile, Shar's family gathered in front of the table that was practically groaning by the time Shar finished properly setting it all up.

"Well, that's quite a display," Mother said.

Shar grinned. Hulda had helped her back at the bakery do a mock setup, finding boxes so Shar could display the desserts on different levels. Then she'd loaned Shar a black velvet cloth to cover it that had a discreet shimmer to it. (Nothing like what an Elf would use, but possibly a little shinier than traditionally used by Dwarves.)

Hulda stood behind the table, dressed in her finest leathers (and yes, she'd rearranged the rings on her leather jerkin to be a more pleasing pattern, dying them so they started black and went to the brightest silver, creating an interesting ombre effect that Shar wanted to try with a layered bar or cake sometime). Hulda glowered at Shar's family, playing the part of a strict guard, not allowing anyone to sample Shar's work until she was good and ready.

"Thank you, Mother," Shar said with a nod. "These are the treats that I promised you for this rest day." She walked from one end of the table to the other, describing the dishes.

Despite having just finished their midday meal, Shar could see the hunger building in the eyes of her family, particularly her brother.

When she reached the end of the table, she took a small bow, then gestured her guests to come forward. "Enjoy!"

"Just a minute," Mother said, derailing the rush forward. "I told you that we expected to meet this mysterious beau of yours today. Where is he? Or she?"

Her eyes darted over to Hulda, then back to Shar.

Shar looked down for a moment, taking a deep breath in and out, before she defiantly raised her head.

"I am the maker of all of this," Shar said. "I haven't been seeing a person, Mother. I've been pursuing a second career."

"What?" Mother asked, not pleased. "What do you mean by that?"

"Gemstones don't bring me joy, Mother," Shar said. She kept her voice deliberately low.

Her uncles and aunts grumbled at that. As did her cousins. Even her father, standing toward the back of the crowd, shot her a frown.

"How can gemstones not bring you joy?" Mother asked, completely confused. "They're in our blood. They're what we do."

Shar shook her head. "Not me. I find joy in baking. In sweet dough and delightful confections. But most of all," she paused, and pointed to the cake with all the fancy chocolate work on the top of it, "in chocolate. Working with it. Creating beautiful things using it."

Mother's eyes narrowed. "So you don't have a beau?"

"Only if you consider chocolate to be the love of my life," Shar said. And it kind of was. She and Hulda had discussed it, and had decided that bringing up the master chocolatier Antonio would just confuse matters.

"An Elf might have been better," Mother muttered to herself, shaking her head and looking down.

Everyone waited while Mother contemplated what was before her. No one would make a move until the matriarch had decided what to do with her wayward daughter.

"What do you intend to do with this, uh, *love*?" Mother finally asked.

"I've been practicing, doing cooking challenges, so that I can compete in the regional cooking competition held in Anthus this year," Shar said. "And once I win regionals, then next year, I'll compete at *Chocolates Galore!*"

Surprisingly, Mother started chuckling at that. "Oh my dear, you don't dream small, now, do you?"

Shar shrugged. "I want to do you proud," she said. And honestly, she did.

"What should I try first?" Mother said. Her tone had grown cool again.

Shar had tried to take all the various preferences of her family into account when preparing her feast of desserts. Mother had been the hardest to figure out, as she didn't really have strong food preferences. Her head was always thinking about gemstones.

Shar really, *really* needed to make herself a mold that made chocolates that looked like gems.

She still picked up one of the rounded bonbons using the fancy tongs she'd borrowed from Leena, put the chocolate on a plate, then brought it over to her mother. She'd used dark chocolate for the shell, with gold and white cocoa butter splatters across the top of it. It wasn't as fancy as what a Human would make (or as gaudy). And it was possibly bigger than the bite-sized desserts preferred by Elves. However, the chocolates did have a restrained elegance to them that Shar liked.

Hopefully Mother would like it as well.

She picked up the piece and looked at it critically.

"The chocolate's been tempered," Shar explained. "So it won't instantly melt in your hand. When you bite into it, it'll have a pleasing snap. I used eighty-eight percent dark chocolate for the shell."

"What's on the inside?" Mother asked.

"Try it and see," Shar said with a shy smile.

Mother did as instructed. Her eyes widened at the taste. Ah. There came the crunch layer as well.

"So what's in it?" Mother asked again after swallowing.

"Strawberries that have been soaked in vinegar, then made into a jam, with a hazelnut crunch layer," Shar said proudly. It was her newest flavor combination and simply divine.

"I've never tasted anything like that before," Mother said, her voice and face still neutral.

"Is that a good thing?" Shar asked after a moment.

Mother broke out into a huge grin.

"Of course it is! These are exquisite. But you need better molds," Mother added seriously.

Shar nodded. "I do. I want to start an entire line of bonbons done in the shapes of various gemstones."

"I think we can help," Mother said. She nodded. "I'm not pleased that you don't want to follow in the family's footsteps. I wish that gems actually brought you joy. I understand why you didn't want to tell me, though."

Shar waited, the moment stretching out long as Mother made up her mind.

"However, I'm not going to stop you," Mother said. "I'll allow you to continue to make these amazing desserts. As long as you keep up with your quota on gemstones."

"And you'll let me compete in regionals?" Shar said.

"Yes, you can compete in regionals," Mother said. "The family will help you in that."

"And if—I mean when—I win? Will the family sponsor me to *Chocolates Galore!*?" Shar asked, the words tumbling out before she could catch them.

Mother narrowed her eyes. "*If* you win, then yes, the family will sponsor you. And at that point, you'll no longer have a gemstone quota."

"Thank you, Mother! Thank you!" Shar said. She impulsively darted forward and gave her mother a hug. Though the Opalbenders weren't really a touching family, Shar felt certain that this occasion rated it.

"You're welcome, daughter. Now, I expect you to do us proud," Mother said firmly. Then she looked around at the rest of the relatives still just standing there. "What are you waiting for? There are desserts here! Waiting for you to taste. And judge."

Shar stiffened slightly at that. She knew her family had strict criteria when it came to gemstones.

Hopefully she'd survive their critiques on her pastries.

# Shar

Shar collapsed on her bed, her head still whirling. After presenting her family with all those desserts, they'd come up with so many ideas (So! Many! Ideas!) of things she could work on, what she could do to improve her already amazing treats.

She'd also spent time speaking with Cousin Algruzlea about making chocolate molds. Her cousin had agreed to come up with some rough designs to show Shar later that week. They'd come to the conclusion that a classic emerald cut—rectangular in shape, with an edge around the top—would be the easiest to start with.

While Leena had been great at guiding Shar along her journey, having input from other Dwarves really had opened Shar's eyes as to what they were looking for in terms of taste.

Plus, Shar had always thought that being a master gem cutter just meant that the Dwarf in question had more than adequate faceting techniques. Now, she was realizing how much artistry was involved.

Spending the afternoon talking about the small touches that made something beautiful had really opened her eyes.

She couldn't wait to get back to the bakery the next morning.

Even her father, who generally stayed in the background and let his wife take the lead on everything, had come over at one point and told her that he was proud of her.

The next morning, Shar had a mission.

She'd learned so much by having Dwarves comment on her food.

Now, it was time to expand her audience.

The judges for both the regional as well as *Chocolates Galore!* were from the three main races of Indunel: Human, Elf, and Dwarf. Very rarely did anyone else join in, like a Plainsman or Maurinan. (In fact, the Maurinan were slightly allergic to chocolate.)

The city of Shazirakz lay on the west coast of the southern continent. It was conveniently located in the center of the great Kibizar mountain range. Dwarves made up the vast majority of the population. Still, Elves also made the city their home, as well as Humans, though each generally stuck to their own enclaves.

The Elves primarily lived in the Temple District, close to the Temple of Wood. According to Leena, they liked small, fussy desserts. She'd said the Elven judges were the most difficult to please.

Humans could be found close to the piers and Warden's Wharf. While the main corridors leading from the piers to the various market districts and to the Nobles' Burrough had high enough ceilings to accommodate a Human (or an Elf, for that manner) most tunnels weren't comfortable for the other races.

So how could Shar get her goods to them? How could she start judging the quality of what she was making based on their individual tastes and preferences?

Shar walked slowly to the bakery, musing over this concern.

When Leena walked into the kitchen a couple of hours after Shar had started, it was the first thing Shar asked about.

"Ach, I wonna worry too much about it," Leena said after a few moments of thought. "Ye can't please all the crowd. Tastes vary too much, ye know?"

"But I want to make sure that what I'm creating will at least be well received by the other races, even if it isn't their preference," Shar said.

"Ye got a point," Leena acknowledged. "Let me give it a think."

Shar continued with her baking, finishing up soon afterward so she could rush back to the Gem Hall and start her day faceting gemstones.

She brought pastries for her brother, of course, and asked him if he had any friends outside of Dwarves who she could bring treats to. He didn't, but he did suggest that she reach out to Mother, as she had contacts with a lot of different people.

Mother, in turn, directed Shar toward her Uncle Unstomi, who ran the Gem Hall, as he was always taking in jobs from various people, custom work for customers.

However, it turned out that Uncle Unstomi just dealt with agents, who were all Dwarves, and it was they who had contacts with the Elves and Humans.

So Shar was back to square one.

She brought her plight up to Hulda the next night when she came to visit the kitchen. (All right, possibly Shar complained about it. A lot. How was she going to meet her potential audience?)

Hulda looked down at the great work table in the center of the area as she replied. "I, uhm, I might have an idea," she said softly.

"Really?" Shar said. "I'm all ears."

Strange. Hulda wouldn't look up or meet Shar's eyes. What was going on?

"Have you ever heard of a pop-up store?" Hulda asked in a rush. "Instead of having a set location, like here at the shop or a stall in a market, you just show up. Once. For like, an afternoon."

"Where?" Shar asked. "Like, in the middle of a corridor?"

"On the edge of a corridor, yeah. Or in some market. Sometimes you can get someone else to let you take over their stall for half a day. Or sometimes you just put up your own stall," Hulda said.

Shar considered. "That might work," she said, thinking about the layout of the Temple District. Could she find a small market right outside of the Temple of Wood? Or maybe a shop that would allow her to set up a table outside their door?

"I've been thinking about doing one to sell some of my clothing designs," Hulda said very softly.

"That's a brilliant idea for you!" Shar said. "That way, you wouldn't have to worry about a store or anything. And you could close down once you sold out!"

"You have a much higher opinion of what I make than I do," Hulda said wryly.

"You've always had a good eye for fashion," Shar said seriously. "I think you'll be able to have very successful pop-up."

"And what about you?" Hulda asked. "Do you want to go in with me some afternoon?"

"Oh, I see," Shar said, nodding. "So we would work a pop-up together? With desserts on one side and clothing on the other?"

Hulda nodded, still trepidatiously keeping her eyes downcast.

"I think that's a great idea!" Shar said enthusiastic. "That way, we'll have each other and aren't alone, working a booth. You're brilliant!"

"Thanks," Hulda said, finally looking up and smiling at her. "Do you really think it could work?"

Shar shrugged. "I have no idea if it would work or not. Remember, the reason I'm doing this is so that I can get a better feel for what people other than Dwarves like in terms of desserts. So I might fail at first, trying the wrong combination of flavors."

Hulda nodded. "Could we start in one of the Dwarven markets, though?"

"We could," Shar said, though she really didn't see the point. She already knew what Dwarves liked to eat.

"That way, I can better judge what our people like to wear," Hulda explained.

"Of course!" Shar said, ashamed that she'd been so selfishly thinking of just herself. "I'd love to help you with that! Draw them in with a sweet treat, then get them to browse your goods."

"Thanks," Hulda said. "I'm sure you'll be a success."

"Don't sell yourself short. You'll be a success as well," Shar said.

Or at least she hoped so.

# Hulda

Hulda carefully re-arranged her hats and scarves across her half of the booth. She'd covered the rough wood with a beautiful purple cloth that wouldn't stain easily. (That had been a serious misstep on her part when she'd loaned Shar the black, shimmery cloth. Though Shar had done her best, the jam and chocolate stains hadn't ever fully come out.)

The stall had been built by one of Shar's uncles, though he complained about having to work in wood instead of proper metal or stone. But he'd come up with a clever design that folded in on itself, which made the stall easy to assemble and take apart. It had a broad table resting between two upright pieces that were connected at both the bottom and the top. It also had extra poles rising a few feet above their head, where they could hang a banner. Eventually.

All that Shar had done for now was to add a little stuffed cat to her side of the booth with the words Curious Cat Shipping underneath. She carried business cards for Rafael's company as well, and planned on telling people about him to pay him back for the chocolate he'd been supplying her with.

Hulda had talked with Shar about what type of clothing she

should sell for a long time. She eventually decided that having something that people could easily try on would be the best for their first event. Hence, hats and scarves.

The hats were the type of flat cap that miners wore, with a front brim that could hold a lighted gem if necessary. They were primarily to keep dust and dirt out of hair and eyes, and were frequently made of some dark material to hide the fact that they were covered in coal dust.

Hulda had taken that design, made the brims a little smaller, and used brightly colored cloth. Not Human levels of garish, no, but still much more colorful than what was traditionally used.

These were for fashion, not for work. She'd also brought a hand-held mirror in a brass frame that people could use to see how they looked wearing their new accessory.

The scarves came in all sorts of length, from barely going over the shoulders to draping down to the bottom of one's beard. Some of them matched the hats, some of them could be sold separately.

If anyone bought any at all.

Hulda had no doubt that Shar would sell out of everything that she baked. She was absolutely *amazing* when it came to making pastries and chocolates.

And she wasn't above using her friend as a lure to get people to stop at their booth, because she was certain her wares wouldn't be as captivating.

"It's going to be all right," Shar told Hulda as she started to reach for the scarves again, adjusting one just so.

"I know," Hulda whispered. "I'm just...nervous."

It had surprised her how anxious doing this pop-up had made her. She was *never* nervous like this. She thumped people for a living! (Though, quite frankly, most Dwarves were rather well-behaved and she rarely actually had to use her staff on anyone. Still. She was always ready to give someone a good thumping!)

"I know," Shar said, giving Hulda's shoulder a gentle squeeze.

She was dressed in an all black outfit, though she wore one of Hulda's caps. Bright red, because it was like the cherry on top of something called a parfait, a dessert that Hulda had yet to try.

"It's going to be fine. And even if we don't sell anything at all, at least we'll learn something. And we'll have the whole afternoon to chat!" Shar said, obviously trying to find the positive things in their venture.

Hulda did manage to give Shar something she was sure was a wavering smile at best.

"And here comes our first customer," Shar said as an older, matronly Dwarf started to approach. "Remember, be friendly! Smile! Don't threaten to thump anyone!"

Hulda gulped and nodded.

She could do this.

And she wouldn't threaten anyone.

She promised.

Hulda had suffered through long workouts in the past. Had spent hours attacking and defending with her staff. Had trained for months in many different fighting styles, on the mat every day. Learning how to perfect a punch by repeating it three hundred times every morning.

None of those activities had left her as exhausted as standing all afternoon behind a wooden booth, talking to potential customers and selling things.

At least Shar appeared to be equally taxed, yawning as she carried her end of the stall. Hulda was surprised that her friend's face didn't crack in two, between the yawns and the excited grin.

Of course, Shar had sold out of all her treats. Once people realized that this was the baker behind Muddy Bean Chocolates, the news spread quickly.

Hulda had sold fifteen caps out of the twenty that she'd made, so she counted it as a win. She'd only sold three scarves though.

Dwarves were just not that stylish.

They trundled back to the bakery and stashed the stall in the back storage room, then dragged themselves into the kitchen, where Shar immediately started making a strong cup of something for each of them.

"How do merchants do it?" Hulda said from where she was stretched out across the top of the center workbench. "Talking with people shouldn't be that tiring. Should it?"

Shar just shrugged. "I didn't mind it as much," she said. "Then again, I was mainly filling orders. I wasn't having to talk people into buying things. Plus, telling people about Curious Cat Shipping. I think I scored Rafael some business as well."

Hulda nodded. Just filling orders would be less tiring.

Still. Talking was a lot more tiring than she'd expected.

Shar set the steaming mug in front of Hulda who finally found the strength to raise her head. She sniffed.

"Is that hot chocolate?" she asked. She pulled the mug closer and looked into it. "It seems...thick."

"It's a type of drinking chocolate," Shar said. "And yes, it's a lot thicker than usual hot chocolate. I also put some peppermint into it. Take a taste."

Hulda raised her mug. The liquid flowed over her tongue, hot and velvety. Then the peppermint rose up, dancing across the roof of her mouth. She felt the rich chocolate coat her throat, the heat seeping into her bones, strengthening and fortifying them. By the time she'd finished her first few sips, she was already sitting up straight.

"Wow," Hulda said. "That's amazing."

"Thank you," Shar said. "It's a recipe I came up with. It isn't easy to make, because I start with melted chocolate, but I prefer it so much to regular hot chocolate that people usually serve."

"I do too," Hulda said. She took another bracing sip, then looked at Shar. "All right. What's next?"

"We find a place near the Temple of Wood to set up the next pop-up," Shar said.

"Will the Elves buy anything I make?" Hulda mused.

"I'd stock up on scarves in neutral colors for them," Shar replied. "I don't think they'll buy hats, though."

"You're right, I don't think Elves wear hats," Hulda said, feeling defeated again.

"Maybe you could weave together some ribbons, and make a few head wreaths?" Shar suggested.

Hulda considered the suggestion. "That might work nicely," she said after a few minutes.

Her fingers already hurt from the amount of work that she was going to have to do.

But Hulda would do it.

If Shar could follow her passion, so could she.

# On the Utterly Sacred Nature of Beard Oil

All Dwarves have beards. Male, female, and everything in between that declares themselves a Dwarf.

Children start growing their beards around their tenth year. Some start coming in as early as eight, or as late as twelve. But from then on, until a Dwarf dies of old age between one hundred and fifty to two hundred years later, a Dwarf has a beard. Always.

Dwarves in different parts of Indunel have various customs when it comes to the maintenance of said beard. For example, the Dwarves from the mountain range of Grizrond trim their beards so they fall to mid-chest, while maintaining a soft, silky, feel. (There's a beard oil for that.) The Dwarves from Bautanzar also trim their beards, even shorter, but the mark of a good beard for them is how full and fluffy it is. (There's a beard oil for that.) Whereas the Dwarves of the Kibizar Mountains grow their beards as long as they can, while frequently braiding in beads, ribbons, or rings. (No, they do *not* add glitter. They're Dwarves. Not Elves.) (And yes, there's a beard oil to help the hair stay in nice, neat braids.) There's even a flame-retardant bead *paste* favored by smiths, though they've never been able to convince anyone that it's a step up from any sort of oil.

It's honestly something of a complaint that non-Dwarves have about Dwarven markets. At least half of every Dwarven market is taken up with row upon row of various beard oils. Everyone has their favorite brand. Or brands that they mix together to come up with the perfect formula for them and their family.

After genealogy and tracing their family's history, a Dwarf's second favorite topic is always beard oil.

Bring another keg if you happen to ask about it sometime.

# Shar

The priests at the Temple of Wood actually allowed them to set up their stall just inside the gate, in the front courtyard of the temple complex. Shar tried not to be too bothered by all the wood surrounding her.

After all, once she left Shazirakz, most every place she went to would be enclosed with wood. So it made sense that she try to get used to it. At least a little bit.

Her back still itched, though, as if the wood were trying to infect her or something.

Hulda, on the other hand, didn't seem to notice or care that their surroundings were so very different. Instead, she was focused on watching the parade of people going in and out of the courtyard gate.

"Do you see that hair style? I could copy that. Oh, and those robes! I'd look silly in them, but maybe I could shorten the waistline..."

Shar just rolled her eyes and tried to beckon people over with the promise of good chocolate.

Instead of her usual fist-sized pastries, she had mini versions of everything. Tiny little tarts that could only hold two blueberries on the top. Cinnamon-sugar rolls as small as a thumb ring. Even little squares of cake perfectly glazed and decorated that could be eaten in a single bite.

The bonbons were normal sized, all half-rounds. She'd cut out different colored cocoa butter stars and put them into the bottom of each mold, so when she flipped the chocolates over, the stars would be on the top. The light purple chocolates were filled with lavender, the gold ones with hazelnut, and the white ones with peppermint.

Eventually, they managed to catch the eye of an Elf maiden who strolled over to see what these two ridiculous Dwarves were doing in the temple courtyard. Her face was beautiful and her white skin flawless, with black hair cascading in soft waves, held back with filigreed butterfly hairpins. Glacial blue eyes glared at them. She wore what Shar believed to be formal robes (though she was certain that Hulda could tell her exactly the type of robe, the material, and if the cut was fashionable that year or not). The color was sage green, and under them she wore an off-white blouse that had pretty green ribbons tying the cuffs.

Hulda explained the concept of a pop-up, and first showed off her wares, then Shar's.

The Elf maiden sniffed after glancing at Shar's work. "I suppose I could try one of the rolls, though they aren't very elegant."

Shar handed the Elf a roll, and gave her a free bonbon (the hazelnut version) as a thank you for coming to see them.

The Elf's eyes widened slightly after she took a bite of the chocolate. She stayed where she was, delicately sampling both treats. Then she turned her attention to the scarves. "Do you have anything that might match this color?" she said, pointing to the off-white shirt that she wore under her sage-green robes.

Shar could tell that her friend could barely resist rolling her eyes at the request. The shirt had no color at all. *Anything* would go with it.

"This would make a nice contrast," Hulda said, pulling a gauzy dove-gray scarf out from the bottom of the pile. "It will add a touch of somber elegance to your entire outfit. Try it on!"

The Elf maiden rubbed the cloth between her fingers, looking displeased at the quality of the material. She still wrapped the scarf around her neck, throwing one end over her shoulder, then glanced at the results.

Shar couldn't see any difference, but Hulda immediately said, "Try it knotted. Here, may I?"

The Elf maiden nodded, looking slightly confused, as Hulda reached across the stall and unwrapped the scarf so it just hung from the maiden's neck. Then she quickly tied a complicated knot in the front of it, making the scarf more like a necklace.

Cautiously, the Elf maiden accepted the mirror from Hulda, looking at herself with a neutral expression.

After a moment's consideration, the Elf maiden blinded them with a cheery smile. "That will do," she said.

Shar managed not to roll her own eyes at that proclamation of okayness, when, in fact, the girl appeared to be delighted.

She quickly paid them and went off.

As soon as she was out of sight, Hulda hung a scarf around her own neck and tied a knot into it. Though Shar could tell that the knot was different than the first one Hulda had done, she couldn't have repeated either of them. Not even with really thin strips of dough. Though it did give her an idea about doing some sort of braided bread...

More Elves came up. The knotted scarves appeared to be a hit. Hulda put simple knots in some and more complicated knots that were at least the size of a fist in others.

Shar learned that peppermint was the most successful flavor in terms of her bonbons, followed by the hazelnut, then the lavender. Though that last ingredient appeared to be polarizing: while some of the Elves loved it, most wouldn't eat it.

They didn't seem as interested in a Human shipping company,

though they did listen politely when she told them of Rafael's business, and that he'd supplied her with much of the chocolate she used.

She heard many comments about the lack of refinement on her tiny pastries. The rolls needed to have more decoration on them, possibly a glaze on the top. They'd been brushed with butter and had an appealing (to Dwarves) sheen, but weren't shiny enough for the Elves.

The blueberries on the tarts needed to either be identical in size, or else two completely different sizes, so that the choice of berries looked deliberate instead of haphazard.

And while the tiny cakes were delicious—she had Elves who came back for seconds of those—the decoration on top needed to be more elegant. Perhaps a curl of chocolate, or a tiny piped flower, or even a some sort of standing coin design. Someone had suggested a half-moon shape. Shar could see the appeal to that, particularly for the Elves whose magic frequently worked better in the moonlight.

Though it was nice that Shar sold out of all her treats (which surprised her, given how slow their afternoon had started) the feedback had been invaluable.

Hulda was having the time of her life, as she'd sold all but one of the forty scarves she'd brought. She'd managed to sell six of the ribbon head wreaths, all to children who'd dragged their parents over. Seemed that mature Elves didn't wear such things, even though she'd had many customers who tried them on, then reluctantly put them back down.

All-in-all, the pop-up was a huge success, which led them to make plans for their next venture: a pop-up in the Human section of Shazirakz, near Warden's Wharf.

# Shar

~~~~~~~~

The pop-up close to Warden's Wharf was *not* going well.

They'd struck a bargain with the owner of The Tiny Giant Inn and Tavern: Shar given the owner a large selection of her best sweet rolls, the kind that both Durzi and her family liked the most, in exchange for setting up their stall in the corridor just outside the inn.

There was excellent foot traffic. So many people went by! While there were some Dwarves, and the occasional Elf, the vast majority of the crowd were made up of Humans.

But none of them were stopping.

Not even for the offer of a free sample of chocolate.

Hulda had changed up her offerings again, this time making caps in the outlandish colors that Humans preferred (at least in their desserts) as well as patterned scarves. She had a few solid colored ones that she'd knotted, to see if Humans would like those.

But everyone merely glanced over at the stall as they kept walking.

"What are we doing wrong?" Shar asked Hulda quietly.

"They all seem busy," Hulda said after a few moments. "Like, they're all on their way somewhere and don't want to stop."

Shar watched the crowd for a while and had to agree with Hulda that appeared to be the case. The vast majority of people were all leaving the wharf, heading into the city. None had come the other direction.

"Maybe after they finish their shopping they'll be more interested in picking something up?" Shar proposed.

Hulda shrugged. "Possibly. Or perhaps this is just the wrong location. Maybe we need to be closer to one of the markets, instead of the wharf."

"Do you want to pack up and move?" Shar asked after another tedious half hour had passed and no one had stopped.

"Let's wait until the tide turns," Hulda proposed. "I want to see what happens when people start to return to their ships."

Shar nodded and agreed to wait. She didn't rearrange her goods (yet again) or fidget. Much.

She'd prepared some chocolates that were obnoxiously decorated, with many colors on them, as well as some more demure ones, to see if Humans preferred those types of decorations or not. As for pastries, she'd focused on chocolate desserts, like small chocolate hand-pies, chocolate cream tarts, and chocolate-chunk cookies. The latter had absolutely no design on them. However, Shar had been told by Rafael that cookies should only rarely be decorated. They'd seem too fancy to a Human if all of them were glazed.

After three hours of not a single customer, an older Human woman finally stopped at their stall.

"So whatcha got here, girlies?" she said in a sing-song voice.

"All manner of sweets, as well as caps and scarves to delight you," Hulda said, her refrain well practiced from the first two shops.

"Would you like a free sample of chocolate?" Shar said as the woman continued to peruse their goods.

"Ah wouldn't say no ta that," the old woman replied.

Shar handed her one of the fancier bonbons. The woman ate it without comment, neither proclaiming it great nor terrible.

"Can you tell me where everyone is off to in such a hurry?" Hulda asked as the woman seemed about to turn away.

"Market day," she said, sniffing. "Ye should be closer ta there." Then she paused. "And yer on the wrong street."

"What do you mean?" Shar asked, surprised. This had seemed the perfect street. The inn keeper hadn't been lying about the amount of foot traffic that they'd seen go by.

"Eh—there's streets that lead ta the market, see?" the old woman said. She looked at her empty hand where the bonbon had been, then back at Shar.

Shar nodded and placed one of the cookies into her palm, getting a huge grin in return.

"Then there's the streets that ye follow leaving ta market," the woman continued.

Shar and Hulda exchanged a puzzled look.

"So people won't come down this street after they finish with their shopping?" Hulda finally asked.

"Nope!" the woman proudly proclaimed. She took a bite of her cookie and finally showed more expression, chewing it with relish. "A whiles back, there was too much traffic. Congestion, ye know? So peoples were asked to use this corridor ta go *to* the market, then use Sea Way, over yonder, ta come back." She shrugged. "Became a habit. There'll be some who wander by after the shopping, but lessen yer here all the time, this taint the right place for ye."

She held out her hand again, and Shar gave her a chocolate hand pie. "Thank you," she said earnestly.

The woman wandered off, nibbling at her treat.

Hulda sputtered at Shar as soon as the woman was out of hearing range. "I've never heard of anything so stupid as one-way corridors," she said. She looked as though she wanted to thump whoever had come up with such a notion.

"What do you want to do?" Shar asked. "Do you want to stay here for the rest of the day? See if anyone comes by? Try to find a new location and move there today? Or close up now and come back some other time?"

"Can you sell your goods at the shop?" Hulda said. "My hats and scarves won't spoil, whereas your cakes and desserts will."

Shar nodded. "You have a point. Why don't we see if there's someplace close to the nearest market where we could set up the stall again?"

"Do you think the owner of the tavern knew?" Hulda asked softly, looking over her shoulder.

"Probably not," Shar said. "I had no idea that a new store was going in just down the street from Muddy Bean Chocolates, that started selling coffee and tea. Not until the owner came down and introduced themselves. I was always too busy in the kitchen to go walk around the immediate district." The two shops had done a deal, with Shar providing them with a few baked items that they could sell. In return, Shar got all the coffee and various teas that she wanted to flavor her desserts with. Bonbons and truffles with coffee-flavored ganache had become best sellers.

The two Dwarves quickly disassembled their stall, loading it onto a cart that one of Shar's uncles had built for them, then trundled up to Bell Market, which turned out to be not that far away. A tall tower stood at the center of the sprawling open area, where a huge bronze bell hung, ringing in the hours. It was manned by the Forward Shadow Temple, whose main prophet declared that evil shadows were dispersed by noise—in particular, bells. (Other markets and places throughout Shazirakz had similar towers and bells. The Gemstone District had their own clocks and bells maintained by the Dwarves.)

The two girls took a little time to verify which road most people took leaving the market before they set their stall up. There was competition for space along this road, as many merchants had figured out the same traffic flow, so they had to set up a little outside of the market.

This proved to be fortuitous, as they were told by one of the Humans who stopped by that setting up a stall in the market involved fees. And paperwork. And possibly even getting a seller's license.

Why did Humans insist on so much paperwork? It was something Shar didn't understand, though Rafael had tried to explain it to her once.

Luckily, with their pop-up now in the correct location, the pair of them were able to sell most of their goods. The caps were Hulda's most successful product, particularly the ones patterned with bright colors. Shar sold out of the cookies first, followed by the hand pies. Humans wanted food they could carry with them and eat one-handed, as they were usually carrying bags filled with market goods in the other hand.

The most colorful bonbons were a big hit as well. Humans didn't mind lavender, at least as much as the Elves. Coffee and hazelnut-flavored ganaches appeared tied in preference.

Shar wasn't certain how successful their pop-up had been when it came to determining Human flavors. These probably weren't the people she should be targeting. Still, as far as Hulda was concerned, the pop-up had been great for her business. More than one Human had commissioned her for additional hats, scarves, and even a pair of matching gloves. Plus, a few people had seemed interested in Rafael's shipping company as well.

The regionals were less than two months away. Leena insisted that Shar spend all of her spare time doing the challenge bakes instead of more pop-ups after this. Shar reluctantly agreed, though she did sneak away and help Hulda set up and tear down the stall on more than one evening.

After all, Hulda had supported her all this time. It was only right that she support her friend's passion as much as she could.

Shar would never feel as if she'd learned everything she needed to know. All she could do was her best.

Hopefully, that would be enough.

# PART TWO
## Regionals

# Chocolates and Truffles and Bonbons, O My!

❧

Just as you should be wary of asking a Dwarf about their genealogy, you should also be aware that asking a Dwarven baker to define what exactly makes a chocolate, or a truffle, or even a bonbon, will involve at least one cask of ale. Possibly a flavored ale, so that the baker can go into detail about the various pairings that she has already thought up to match the flavor.

First, for the casual eater of sweet things, is the distinction between *chocolate* and *chocolates*.

Chocolate is that yummy substance that has cocoa butter in it. (Except for those purists who insist that chocolate must contain not only cocoa butter but also the cocoa solids. These ~~overly-picky~~ discriminating connoisseurs do not include white chocolate in their lists of the various types of chocolate.)

(They are wrong, of course. Chances are, they've never had actual *good* white chocolate, but only that commercial crap that's mostly composed of cheap oil and not cocoa butter.)

(Their loss. That just leaves more for the rest of us.)

*Chocolates*, on the other hand, are those delectable delights that are made of chocolate of some form or another. It's a catch-all category that describes most sweets that are primarily composed of chocolate.

(And no, chocolate cake is not a chocolate. It's cake. Bring more ale if you need more details.)

Then there are truffles. Originally, truffles were composed of a ganache that's solid enough to hold a shape, then rolled in cocoa powder.

That's it.

Whereas traditionally, a bonbon is a molded chocolate with a non-chocolate center (fruit or jam, for example). There can be more things accompanying that delicious, sweet filling, such as a gelée or a layer of crunchy stuff.

Now, the terms have spread, like untempered chocolate melting in the sun.

Truffles can have a nut coating.

Bonbons can have a chocolate ganache center.

(Cake is still not a chocolate.)

Truffles can also be done as a type of bar, with more than one layer of ganache slightly hardened and cut into smaller pieces.

Or you can take your ganache and enrobe it in tempered chocolate (a sticky, messy, delicious procedure).

How you define your sweets is kind of up to you.

Just don't ever ask a true baker if you're doing it right.

# Shar

"What do you mean, you're coming with?" Shar said with amazement when Hulda appeared with a travel bag the morning Shar was heading out to regionals.

Anthus was a good week's journey away. Shar and Leena were leaving ten days before the contest began, both to give themselves time to recover from their travels and in case any delay occurred while they were on the road.

Hulda beamed at Shar. "Now, I'm not supposed to tell you anything about who's paying for me to guard you while you're on the road," she said. "However, let's just say there's a family member who's concerned about you and wants to make sure that you get there and back again safely."

Shar found herself swallowing down a lump of emotion that appeared to have blocked her throat. She'd been prepared to leave Shazirakz on her own, with just Leena as a guide, to get to the city of Anthus.

"Was it my mother?" Shar asked when she could finally speak again.

"Can't say," Hulda said, shaking her head no.

"My father?" Shar said, certain that he would never take such initiative on his own.

"Still can't say," Hulda said, again shaking her head.

No matter what family name Shar threw out—Durzi, her uncles, her cousins, her aunts—Hulda continued to shake her head no.

"Eh, we best get cracking," Leena finally said, interrupting Shar's interrogation.

"Fine," Shar said, happy that she had an unknown benefactor, though still puzzled as to who in her family might be helping her.

Officially, the family wasn't involved in this contest. She had to win it before they'd sponsor her for *Chocolates Galore!* the following year. Mother hadn't given her any time off to prepare for the regional contest, but she had given Shar a month of time to go compete. (Durzi had complained about it, of course. Then again, Durzi was likely to complain about most everything, particularly since Shar would no longer be bringing him sweets on a regular basis while she was gone.)

The three Dwarves were dressed for the road and changeable spring weather. Each wore pants that actually went down over their boots instead of ending at the knee, to better protect their legs. Heavy-duty work boots covered their feet. Shar wore a light-weight unbleached shirt with a beaded vest, and had a jacket in the huge pack she carried.

She'd been told by more than one concerned member of her family that layers were key when it came to the great outdoors.

Hulda wore her fancier leather vest, with the colored iron rings sewn into it, and carried her stout staff, of course. Leena had even fewer layers, just a vest with no shirt, saying that outside would be too warm once they got there.

Anthus was east and north of Shazirakz. They'd opted to go the land route, instead of finding a ship to carry them up the coast, then a second boat to take them along the river to the city. Both paths took about the same amount of travel time.

So instead of walking out of Shazirakz by the piers and wharf, they went east through the city, to stairs that led to the surface. (There was a fancy elevator that could take them up. However, it was usually reserved for merchants and their carts. They'd have to buy a ticket in advance as well, which Shar had discovered far too late.)

It was a good jaunt going up the stairs. It would take them at least half of the first day to climb them. Hulda was well familiar with them, as part of her training involved regularly running up and down them.

Shar thought her thighs and calves were going to strangle her by the time she reached the surface, despite the fact that the three of them had taken many breaks, primarily for Leena's sake (though Shar had never complained anytime they'd stopped).

A stone shelter built specifically for travelers stood at the entrance to the stairs, along with other shelters that were for the Dwarven guards.

Shar took one look at the open sky above her and raced over to the shelter, breathing deeply and relaxing again when she felt good stone above her head.

Leena nodded at her as she also reached the shelter, though she didn't appear to be having the difficulty breathing that Shar did.

Of course, Hulda didn't appear to notice that their surroundings had changed. Maybe she'd come up here before, as part of her guard duty?

Shar hadn't thought about the fact that not only would she not be surrounded by stone, there'd be open sky above her head.

Other buildings were scattered around the entrance, including what appeared to be a huge structure that held animals. Since very few horses, mules, or oxen were allowed in the city itself, merchants stabled them up on the surface. An inn was attached to it, a place where Humans and Elves might stay if they didn't want to go down to the city.

Evidently being underground was a problem for some people.

"You okay?" Hulda asked after a few moments.

Shar nodded tentatively. "I think so." She looked out over the vast open plains in front of them. "It's just...so exposed, you know?"

"I know," Leena said, patting her arm. She slid out a paper parasol that had been attached to the side of her pack. "Here, this might help."

Shar opened the parasol. The underside of it had been painted with the appearance of stone.

"Thank you," she said gratefully.

After taking a few deep breaths, Shar finally talked herself into stepping out from beyond the stone shelter, out into the open.

She could do this. She *had* to do this. Going to regionals was just the first step in her glorious career.

She only had to get used to the open sky.

Other Dwarves had done so.

She would too.

Eventually.

The road leading east along the river had many people traveling on it. Caravans as well as individual carts passed them as they plodded along. Shar looked enviously at the Dwarves traveling in comfort on the back of a cart, then shook her head.

She couldn't afford such a contrivance. Not yet. Her own two feet would just have to do.

It was late spring or early summer (Shar wasn't exactly clear on the distinction) so the days weren't too hot and the nights weren't too cold. Shar marveled at all the different colors of green grass, how the pretty wild flowers bobbed their heads at any breeze, how loudly the insects buzzed when darting between them.

The three of them would be walking along grasslands and farmlands for most of their trip, with only the occasional grove of trees.

The inns spread along the road were set up both for people who would be traveling greater distances (with carts) and for those who were on foot, so at least Shar wouldn't have to be sleeping on the ground every night.

She and Leena had talked about it, but Leena had firmly vetoed the idea. Sure, it would save Shar money (and she had been steadily draining her savings already). However, Shar also needed to be ready to compete at the end of this journey. That meant that despite the walking all day, every day, she needed to comfortably rest.

Besides, Leena had an idea for how to offset the costs of the inns. And no, she wasn't about to tell Shar what she had in store.

That first night, they stayed at the Tiny Great Hall Inn. Leena instructed Shar to dump her pack outside and for Hulda to watch it, then she dragged Shar inside.

Even though the structure was wood, Shar still took a deep breath being under a roof at least. And the floor was made out of solid flagstone, not wood, unlike the walls and the rest of the structure.

The main hall was open, with dozens of tables. Travelers were already gathered around them, sipping ale, mead, or hard cider. An empty hearth took up the front half of the left wall. It must be very cheery during the winter, with the fire going. A long counter stretched the length of the room at the back. Shar assumed it was the innkeeper standing behind it. The sounds of cooking came from behind him.

The innkeeper was a stout Dwarf whose magnificent beard was intricately braided and falling down to his waist. His shirt looked worn and frayed at the cuffs. Shar was glad Hulda wasn't there to judge him. At least the leather jerkin he wore over it fit him well.

After Leena organized their beds (the three of them in a four-person room) she asked, "Do ye have a dessert on the menu tonight?"

The innkeeper scoffed. "People won't spend their coin on sweets when there's good ale to be had," he said.

"But ye have sugar? And flour? And some spices?" she persisted.

"I do," the innkeeper said cautiously. "What do you have in mind?"

"This here is me protegee. She's off to compete at the regionals, the big baking contest in Anthus," Leena said proudly. "Ye supply the ingredients, she'll whip ye up something delightful for tonight."

Shar wanted to protest. She was exhausted, first from the arduous climb up the stairs, then the long walk. Her soul ached from being outside all day. The parasol had helped, but she wasn't okay, not by a long shot.

However, she managed to give the innkeeper a firm nod when he looked at her, as if asking how she felt about this.

"You got yourself a bargain, then," he said. "You all will eat dinner for free, and breakfast, too, if your dessert is a hit."

"Thank ye!" Leena said, beaming. "Now, ye go make me proud," she instructed Shar, waving her off to follow the innkeeper back behind the counter and into the kitchen.

Shar managed to keep her sigh to herself.

She reminded herself just how stubborn she was, despite her legs feeling wobbly.

She could do this.

She would make her mentor proud.

No matter what.

The kitchen in the inn was totally foreign to Shar. She had no idea where anything was, and had to either scrounge around for ingredients or ask the innkeeper's wife, a lovely Dwarf by the name of Lutgramora Chaosbrow, who insisted that Shar just call her Luta.

It wasn't until Shar was elbows deep in flour that she realized what Leena had done for her. By getting Shar into the kitchen, doing something that she was familiar with and loved so much, Shar was finally settling back into her skin.

Tricky old Dwarf.

The inn didn't have any chocolate, so Shar improvised, making a sweet orange-flavored glaze for an almond quick bread. Luta's eyes grew wide at the first taste.

"My heavens!" she exclaimed. "That's tasty! And you're going to compete at regionals this year?"

"I am," Shar said, feeling proud of what she'd accomplished so quickly in a foreign kitchen.

"If I was gambling on the winner, I'd place all my money on you," Luta said with a nod.

"Thank you," Shar said. "That means a lot to me."

"Now, you go eat some dinner," Luta said. "I'll serve these as the time comes."

"All right," Shar said, though she felt a little strange. Shouldn't she be serving dessert as well?

However, she did as Luta suggested (though honestly, it was more of a demand) and went to join her friends out in the large open area of the inn.

Most of the tables were full at this point. The innkeeper and two other Dwarves (perhaps his children) went from table to table, serving drinks.

Food started coming out shortly—a delicious chicken soup that Shar had helped Luta with, along with a baked veggies casserole and bread (that again, Shar had had a hand in). The food was simple, but filling.

Then came Shar's sweet quick bread, one slice per person. She would have served it more elegantly, perhaps reserved some of the glaze to pour on top.

Still, the dessert was well received. Shar kept glancing around at the diners, seeing who ate what. The Dwarves, of course, ate their entire slice of the quick bread and asked for seconds. The Elves picked at it (but their desserts were always so small and delicate). The Humans ate the top of the bread, where the glaze had been drizzled first, before digging into the rest of it.

The innkeeper (who Shar had learned was called Raizemere, or simply Razi for short by his wife) stood up as people were finishing up and called everyone's attention to him.

"Now, as you regulars know, I don't go in for fancy sweet treats after a meal. What we serve here at the Tiny Great Hall is hearty enough to fill you up. Am I right?"

"Hear, hear!" more than one of the patrons said, raising their mugs up in a salute.

"But tonight, we had a special treat, baked by none other than Sharaksir Opalbender, a contestant on her way to winning the regional baking contest in Anthus!" he proclaimed proudly.

At Leena's urging, Shar stood up and took a bow while the rest of the patrons applauded.

It seemed that some people did appreciate what she'd baked, as more than one of the merchants came up and asked where the group was planning on stopping the next night, to see if maybe their schedules could match up and they could have more of Shar's baking.

Shar had to depend on Leena's knowledge of the road, as she had no idea.

Finally, a rather gruff looking Dwarf came up. He stood silently looking at the three of them at their table for a moment. He was dressed in a nice burgundy-colored vest with a fancy embroidery on it and an off-white shirt underneath with puffy sleeves, tied at the wrists with red ribbons. His beard had bits of silver and bronze braided into it. Overall, he looked like a wealthy merchant.

"What is it?" Hulda asked in a challenging tone.

"There's three of ye, yes?" he asked after a moment.

"There are," Leena said. "Hulda is with the city guard in Shazi-rakz. I'm leading this group, and Shar is the baker."

"Hmmm," the Dwarf said, considering. "I'm a just thinking that

I could use another guard. And some more fancy treats. What about ye?" he said, his voice growing more challenging as he shifted his gaze to Leena. "Iffen I give ye all a ride, all the way to Anthus? What can ye bring?"

She gave a cheery laugh. "Don't you worry about me, ye old coot," she said, her voice sounding affectionate. "Ye want someone ta talk with, doncha? Tell tales along the road? Someone who knows more than coal dust and gems?"

The Dwarf stroked his chin as he considered. "Aye. Ye got the right of that." Suddenly, he grinned at them. "Me name's Kraugorn Hammerbrew. I'm a carrying some of ta finest hard cider yer likely ta taste."

Leena nodded. "So we'll be riding? Not walking?" she persisted.

"Aye," Kraugorn said, nodding. "Me guards have ta be ready ta fight. Not be tired from walking along beside the three carts."

Leena beamed at the Dwarf. "We might have a deal. I want to see yer carts, first."

"Mighty high-brow of ye," Kraugorn grumbled.

Leena just shrugged. "Comes from experience, ye old coot."

"I see," Kraugorn said. He stepped back from the table when Leena rose.

Shar and Hulda stayed where they were. The exhaustion that Shar had felt earlier came crashing down on her. The cooking and the eating had relaxed her. Now, she could barely keep her eyes open.

"Do you think she had that planned all along?" Hulda mused. "Get you into the spotlight, so we could get a ride?"

Shar shrugged, yawning greatly.

"You don't have to wait for her to get back," Hulda said gently. "Why don't you go crash in our room? Sleep while you can?"

"That sounds lovely," Shar said. She got up and slowly made her way to the staircase that was located near the back of the room, next to the long counter. She would have gone more quickly, but people wanted to thank her for the dessert she'd made.

Eventually, Shar got up to the room, then to her bed, only pausing long enough to take off her boots, too tired to change out of her travel clothes.

The morning would come soon enough. And she'd have to do it all again.

Wondering how Leena was faring, Shar closed her eyes and let sleep catch her and drag her all the way down, unaware of anything until the morning.

# Shar

While riding in the back of a cart was certainly easier on her legs, Shar had decided that she didn't like traveling all that much. The sky was still too open above her. Instead of the gods turning their faces away, she felt as though every eye was on her.

Plus, the traveling itself made Shar feel tired. She tried listening in on the stories that Leena spun to Krau (as he'd insisted that they all call him). However, she found herself nodding off, dreaming of pastries dotting the blue sky, and her trying (but failing) to reach them, just so she could have a taste. Plus, Hulda traveled on the last cart, keeping an eye behind them, so she didn't have her friend to talk with.

That night, when they reached The Sickle Moon Inn, word of their arrival had already reached the innkeeper. He was more than happy to have Shar bake, this time, in exchange for not just their food but for their room as well.

Shar found herself in yet another foreign kitchen. The inn lived up to its name, as it was built along the curve of the river, and so the kitchen, instead of being rectangular or square, was actually a long, curved room. Shar found herself racing from one end of the galley to the other, grabbing ingredients from the far pantry and dumping them on the worktable.

The two other Dwarves grumbled at her taking up space on their bench, but grudgingly helped her when she asked where things were located.

The inn had some powdered chocolate—not good for making actual chocolates from, but Shar used it generously to flavor not only the chocolate mousse hand-pie that she baked, but the special cocoa that she made for herself and the staff. A cold wind blew in from the river, and the Dwarves kept the windows open so the kitchen wouldn't grow too stuffy.

After getting their personal treat, the two Dwarves (Snari and Dori, a brother and sister who'd been hired by the innkeepers to cook) were much more accommodating when Shar asked for anything.

The hand pies turned out lovely—the flaky crusts produced adequate crumbs to feed the beards of the various Dwarves. The colors were too muted for the Humans, but Shar had insisted on pouring out extra glaze for the ones served to them, so that they tasted sweet enough.

There was no pleasing the Elves. The pastries were just too rustic and not elegant enough. Still, Shar tried by cutting theirs up into smaller portions and arranging them beautifully on a plate, with extra decorations on the plate itself to make the dessert seem more refined.

She got her meal at the very end of service. However, Leena had saved her an overly-large portion of the baked cheese, tomato, and meat casserole that the cooks had baked up. It was referred to as *lasagna*, something Shar had never heard of before.

(She had to admit that while she'd watched Snari and Dori bake up their portion of the meal, she'd started to wonder if she could do a sweet version of the dish, using pastry dough to replace the noodles, a red jam to replicate the tomato sauce, and possibly shaved white chocolate to mimic the cheese.)

The innkeeper didn't announce that Shar had made the dessert that evening, but enough of the travelers who'd seen her the night before had recognized them, and came over to express their thanks again.

At least that night Shar was able to keep her eyes open for about an hour after the meal, sitting and chatting with her fellow travelers, before she finally took herself up to their room, yawning the whole way.

The rest of the week passed in a blur, the days long, traveling on a cart, the afternoons busy as Shar found her way around yet another strangely laid out kitchen, the evenings passing peacefully until Shar dragged herself off to bed.

They saw the city of Anthus in the distance early the next morning, though Krau announced that they wouldn't arrive until much later that afternoon.

Shar saw why as they drew up behind a long line of carts snaking along the road.

Turned out that Anthus sat between two large rivers, one in front of the city and one behind it. As part of their defenses, they kept the river bridges narrow, and had guards posted at each of them, ensuring that not too many merchant carts tried to cross at the same time.

There was also a ferry service, but Krau's cart was too wide (and too heavy) for one of the little boats. The people who traveled on foot were able to bypass the lines going over the bridges and arrive in the city long before the merchants and their carts.

Shar hopped off the cart after a while and walked back to where Hulda usually sat. The four guards had gotten off their cart and claimed some space in the road for themselves, then had gotten into some sparing matches.

Guards from the other carts had walked over to watch, give

colorful commentary as well as occasionally stepping in and taking their turn.

Currently, Hulda sparred with an Elf. They both had long staffs that they flourished, seeking to find weaknesses in each other's defenses.

Brudrick, one of Krau's guards, leaned over to talk with Shar as they watched. "He's got reach on her," he commented, talking about the Elf. "But she's got a lot more power. They're pretty evenly matched."

Shar nodded, thankful for the pointer on what to watch.

Hulda did swing her staff with a lot more emphasis. Shar had always believed that to just be her friend's nature, but now she wasn't so certain. Maybe it was a deliberate fighting technique that she'd been taught, specifically for taller opponents.

The Elf had an edge on Hulda not just for his longer reach, but also with his quickness. He nimbly skipped out of the way, or side-stepped, most of her blows.

That was when Shar noticed something.

The Elf always moved out of the way rather than block a blow.

Could he actually survive a direct hit?

On the other hand, Hulda was always able to shake off any blow that he landed. Shar guessed that he probably wasn't putting all his strength behind his swings. Still, it was very interesting to watch, now that Shar knew what to look for.

They eventually called a halt to their spar and bowed to each other, both of them grinning.

Shar was transformed by the Elf's expression—that lighthearted grin that changed the stoic warrior into a happy person.

That was what she wanted to bring to people, to all people. That level of joy.

Perhaps that particular Elf wouldn't like her desserts. But her goal was always to bring happiness to folks with her baking.

Much refreshed, Shar chatted with Hulda for a few moments before making her way back to her usual seat.

She had things to plan. A menu to prepare.

And a contest to win.

# Hulda

While the core of the city of Anthus was built up on earthworks, the shacks in the shanty town that had grown outside of its wall were all built on stilts. Brudrick explained that the rivers that surrounded the city regularly flooded, so any house built directly on the ground would be carried away.

"Couldn't they prevent that?" Hulda asked as the line slowly crept over the final bridge and approached the city gates.

Brudrick shrugged. "Don't see the point. Keeps the riffraff down. Only the poorest of the poor build on the ground around here."

Hulda nodded, a bit puzzled at the guard's cavalier attitude. Why wouldn't Dwarves help other Dwarves?

As they passed through the shacks (which weren't built that close to the road) she realized that the majority of people that lived in the shanty town were Humans, not Dwarves.

There was probably paperwork to file, as well as fees to pay, in order to build a proper house out here on the outskirts. And people just barely making a living couldn't afford that.

The sun was close to the far horizon when they finally reached the gate. The guards there didn't bother looking inside their carts, just checked the license and papers that Krau had and waved them through.

Krau let them off at a merchant's inn, the three of them saying goodbye to their traveling companions as Leena marched them away, heading toward a different inn.

Though Anthus was bigger than Shazirakz, it was difficult to judge the size by just wandering the streets. Not until Hulda looked up. While most Dwarven homes and halls in Shazirakz were only one to two stories tall, the bigger houses here were easily four or five. The streets felt more crowded as well, though Hulda had assumed that was because they were narrower than the Dwarven corridors.

No, there were just that many more people living here.

Leena went first, as she was the one who supposedly knew the way to the inn, Hulda walked beside her, glowering at anyone who dared get in their way. She didn't have to use her staff to make a path through the throng, though she was tempted more than once.

They finally arrived at the Rusty Nail Inn and Tavern. Leena stopped on the steps and turned back to Shar. "No cooking tonight, or any night before the contest," she warned. Though they'd had a wagon to travel on, they hadn't gained any time. It had still taken seven days to reach the city, and so they had three days before regionals began.

Shar looked relieved.

"I'll git the lay of the land, first, before we talk of anything important," she continued. "No mention of contests or chocolate. Not yet."

Hulda and Shar exchanged a puzzled look, but they both nodded.

"So what are we supposed to do for the next few days?" Hulda asked.

Leena gave them both a big grin.

"Go shopping, of course."

Though Leena and Shar had wanted to start out at the baking supply stores, Hulda managed to talk them out of it.

If they weren't supposed to advertise Shar's involvement in regionals, they shouldn't give the game away by heading immediately to a cooking store.

Instead, Hulda got her way and led them first to her idea of Heaven: a fabric store.

Stepping inside, Hulda paused and took a deep sniff. The scent of dyes, trim, cotton and silk filled her soul.

All right, so perhaps no one else would register those scents. But Hulda would swear that she did—acidic and dry, sparkling and soft.

She wore her re-designed leather armor that day, with the ombre of rings. Her black pants were fashionably short and flared out around the cuffs. There wasn't much she could do about her stout work boots, and she wasn't about to exchange them for something that didn't have steel protecting the toes.

The other two looked like regular Dwarves, with plain blouses under colorful vests and short pants.

Hulda headed directly toward the silks. They were hard to come by in Shazirakz, and just what she needed for scarves that she could sell to the Elves.

A Human clerk came out from the back of the shop. She wore a set of mismatched plaids, the top yellow and black, while the long skirt was a sea-green and blue.

Hulda wasn't certain that the outfit worked. However, the woman moved with so much confidence, as if she wore the most beautiful gown in the world, that Hulda was mostly convinced.

"How may I help?" the woman asked, her tones light and friendly.

"How much for a meter of the blue silk?" Hulda asked, though she wasn't certain of the color. It might not be light enough for an Elf, and no Dwarf would wear either the silk or the color.

The woman quoted a price that made Hulda blanch. But only on the inside. On the outside, she still wore a pleasant smile, as if she was stepping onto the sparring grounds and certain she was about to win over her opponent.

"How about that red-orange one?" Hulda said, switching things around in her head quickly. The Elves might like it, claiming that it matched their fall colors, while the color seemed rich enough that she could probably use it to line a fancy embroidered vest for a Dwarf.

Again, the cost was so far outside her usual price range that Hulda couldn't imagine ever justifying the cost.

And while Shar's mother had put quite a lot of coin in Hulda's purse, to go along and protect her daughter, Hulda wasn't about to splurge all of it on half a meter of cloth.

"There is a discount if you buy more than a meter," the woman explained. "There's also the remainders bin."

"What are remainders?" Shar asked.

Hulda silently blessed her friend who was willing to appear uneducated when Hulda wasn't.

"Not-quite meters of left-over cloth," the woman explained. "It's all last year's fashions as well as pieces and scraps. Not enough to make an entire outfit."

Hulda nodded. As she was still focused on hats and scarves, that actually sounded perfect.

The woman led them to the back of the shop, where an overflowing barrel stood.

The clerk hadn't been kidding when she said it contained merely scraps of some cloth. Hulda held up a piece of absolutely lovely cotton, with a beige background and beautiful orange and red stripes running through it. There wasn't enough to even make a scarf from it.

Though she could fashion it into the brim of a cap...

Hulda spent the next hour happily digging to the bottom of the pile of scraps. She'd found several good bargains, even some silk that Elves wouldn't turn their noses up at.

She didn't bother looking for trim, ribbon, or fringe. She knew that she would never afford such notions here.

By the time she left the shop, Hulda had put a rather large dent in the purse that Shar's mother had given her.

However, she'd be able to fashion all of what she bought into usable—and more importantly, sellable—items.

Shar wasn't the only one with big dreams.

# Mushrooms and Other Edibles

❧

Dwarves prefer to live underground. There's a good portion of the Dwarven population who will boast about never having taken a single breath above the ground. There are other Dwarves who do spend most of their time outdoors, and they aren't considered complete weirdos. (How they're perceived of generally depends on the area of the world in which they live. Dwarves living in big cities tend to be more forgiving of such eccentricities than those from small villages isolated in the mountains.)

This is all well and good—except for one thing.

What do all those Dwarves who live strictly underground eat?

They aren't growing cattle down there. Or a lot of vegetables. (They do grow an impressive amount of herbs. And no, not just so they can flavor their ale [or chocolates] with them.)

Fortunately, at least for the Dwarves, no other people work with gemstones, or can produce jewelry, like they do. So they are easily able to import about half of their food. (This is one of the main reasons why the Dwarven new year traditionally starts when the first markets open and all the fresh food comes available.)

Dwarves are masters at preservation. Anything fresh can be pick-led, frozen, or made into alcohol to last them throughout the long winters. (And remember, *to pickle* is a verb. It can be done with salt, sugar, alcohol, or vinegar.)

The rest of their food? They grow themselves.

Deep in special caves, Dwarves grow mushrooms.

While there are more varieties of mushrooms than you can easily count—and yes, their genealogy is as tangled as a Dwarf's—speaking in the broadest of terms, there are really only two types of mushrooms.

The first has been bred to be hearty, healthy, and tasteless. The other type comes in an amazing array of flavors and textures.

The tasteless ones (and really, they're like eating nothing) are used as a base for other dishes.

Feeling like having some goat meat? There's a sauce that some Dwarf along the line developed that you add to one of the tasteless mushrooms, and voila! You have something that's the taste and consistency of goat meat.

Maybe you'd like a hamburger. Again, add a different group of very specific herbs to chopped up mushrooms and you won't be able to taste the difference between the burger made from mushrooms and the one made from beef.

The Dwarves use mushrooms in almost everything, from stews to savory pies to appetizers to the main course.

However.

Dwarves do *not* add mushrooms to their desserts for the most part.

A mushroom does not have the right crumb to feed one's beard. Sure, they can be added to a jam to thicken it. But why bother? Flour or butter (or just about anything else) works better.

Sure, there's at least one Dwarven baker in every major city who specializes in imitations, trying to do mock versions of all the sweets that Dwarves tend to love ,using nothing but mushrooms.

These places are novelties at best, and don't last too long. Dwarves prefer their sweets a specific way.

# Shar

It chaffed Shar that she couldn't talk about baking or chocolate or *anything* that she really cared about while they were in the public areas of the inn. Seemed that a couple of her competitors were also staying there. Shar had spent some time studying the crowd in the main room while they were eating but hadn't been able to pick them out as they, too, were keeping a low profile.

She supposed she'd meet them soon enough.

At least they now could visit one of the larger baking supply stores. Like Hulda the day before in the fabric shop, Shar blanched at the prices.

However, there were so many *amazing* cooking and baking tools there!

Thermometers that told you the precise temperature of boiling sugar for making hard candies. Magical marble slabs that changed colors when the chocolate spread over them was tempered correctly. Spoons that kept stirring even after you released them (Shar was the most tempted by these). Pots that kept the contents within at a consistent temperature (very useful for tempering as well).

Shar knew that none of these implements could be used for the contest. All cooking utensils were provided. That would include some of the high-end magical blenders and stand mixers, things that Leena had never allowed Shar to use.

Leena did have Shar bring a few chocolate molds, that hopefully she'd be able to use. In addition Shar had brought a few special ingredients, for the later cooks, when hopefully they'd be allowed to use the things they'd brought.

No personal magical ability was allowed during a bake. Too many of the contestants didn't have magic that related to cooking. Therefore, to make it fair, no one could use it.

The shop also had knives. So. Many. Knives! All with beautiful handles and wickedly sharp blades, many of them enchanted so they'd never dull. Sets of bowls going from giant-sized to so ridiculous small that even an Elf would find it challenging to handle. All of them gorgeously colored, of course.

Shar did sniff at the quality of the chocolate molds she found there. There was a single tray that she would even consider getting, but that was only due to the shape of the impressions, little crowns would sell well on royal holidays or the queen's birthday. The tin wasn't nearly shiny enough, and with her magic she could feel the lack of smoothness around the corners. If she bought this mold she could improve it, but she wasn't sure she wanted to take the time or effort.

The molds she'd brought with her were so much better. Plus, they'd been made specially for her by her cousin, to her own exacting standards.

Finally, the first day of the contest arrived. Leena had already registered Shar, returning with a shiny metal disc that marked her as a contestant.

She wore the token around her neck, over her new outfit that Hulda had presented to her that morning.

The top was a coat, all in black material with red piping along the seams, standing collar, and cuffs. It fit Shar perfectly but also gave her freedom of movement. The matching apron was a burgundy red with black trim. There was even a cap to go with it, though Shar had decided not to wear that on the first day, as she was worried about the heat in a strange kitchen. On the left side of the coat Hulda had created a black cat, outlined in yellow, with "Curious Cat Shipping" carefully stitched underneath.

Hulda had also produced matching ribbons, then had rebraided Shar's beard with them in it.

The three of them walked to the grand plaza that stretched in front of the government buildings at the center of the city. A crowd had already started gathering around the space. Guards kept the audience away from the group of contestants gathered at one end.

"Ye'll be fine," was all that Leena said as she gripped Shar's arm before letting her go.

Hulda at least gave her a hug, whispering in her ear, "You got this."

Feeling less confident than her friends, Shar walked over and joined the line of contestants that the guards were letting through.

Shar had to turn her token in to the guard as she passed into the open area. A table marked one end of it. While some of the other contestants appeared to know each other and were chatting together, most of them, like Shar, stood to one side and waited.

The wait wasn't long.

A tall Human wearing a green tabard with a gray heron embroidered on it stepped forward. Shar recognized that as the symbol for Anthus, like gemstones were the symbol for Shazirakz. He put a short brass horn to his lips and blew a short tune, calling everyone's attention to him.

"Hear ye, hear ye!" he called out, his voice magically amplified to carry over the crowd. "Welcome to the first day of the regional sweets bake off!"

The crowd gave a half-hearted cheer.

Would the crowds grow bigger, and possibly more enthusiastic, as the contest went on?

"Let me introduce to you your judges!" the man enthusiastically went on.

Shar nodded, as did several of the other contestants. Though the final judging panel was always kept a secret, from her study of previous contests she knew that there was actually a relatively small pool of people that the contest relied on.

Three people marched out of the crowd and found their places at the table: a Human, an Elf, and a Dwarf.

"You know her pastries, you love her cookies, and her advice is priceless! The mother to us all, Cyna Whitely!" the herald proclaimed.

Shar studied the old Human woman. According to the reports that Shar had read about the previous contests, Cyna had been judging the regional contest for years. She lived in Anthus because that was where her grandchildren lived, though she regularly traveled to White Hall and made desserts for the king, particularly on the holidays.

Cyna was dressed in a bright blue and white shirt that Shar was certain Hulda would have strong opinions about. She wore her white hair very short, teased up into spikes all around her head. The makeup she wore (bright blue eyeshadow that matched her outfit, as well as rouge on her cheeks and lips) didn't try to hide the fact that she was old—instead, it appeared to celebrate the fact. She smiled out at the contestants, a sparkle in her dark brown eyes.

"Next, we have Yazgrak Goldenberry, the master of cakes! He's forgotten more decorating tips and tricks than most ever learn!"

The herald was referring to the Dwarf and master baker, of course. Shar was thrilled (and yeah, okay, maybe a little intimidated as well) to be baking for him. He was stout, even for a Dwarf. His coloring was a little darker than Shar's, both his skin and his hair. Though his beard was rich and full, the hair on his head was definitely thinning. The brocade vest he wore was dove-gray with gold embroidery on it. His smile lit up the area, and he seemed truly pleased to see them all.

"Last but not least, the newcomer to our panel! A rising star in the baking community! The one, the only, Erwel Leodras!"

The Elf Erwel had only judged one other contest before, so Shar didn't know much about her preferences. She appeared to appreciate bold flavors, though. She'd won the regional contest the second or third time she'd competed, though she hadn't won *Chocolates Galore!* merely placing third.

She wore muted colors, of course, a pale yellow robe that set off her black skin, with voluminous sleeves. The blouse underneath was an off-white. Her black hair grew long and had gentle waves, pulled back behind her pointed ears with bronze clips.

Shar gaped for a moment before she remembered where she was.

Those clips were in the shape of whisks!

Erwel would look good in one of Hulda's scarves. Maybe one out of that sky blue remnant of cloth that Hulda had found...

"Greetings fellow bakers and culinary wizards!" Erwel said. Her voice was melodious, and naturally carried over the crowd. "We're glad that you're here!"

The crowd gave a louder cheer at that.

Obviously, Erwel was a fan favorite.

"There will be several challenges that you'll have to win to prove that you should be the regional champion," Cyna warned. "We've arranged for you to be working in several of the kitchens of nearby businesses, that are our sponsors for this contest. This first bake will be staggered, with five groups baking at the same time."

Shar blinked, then tried not to grin too widely.

Was that part of why Leena had had Shar do so many cooks in inns along the way? So she'd get used to baking in strange kitchens?

"This first bake you'll be paired up with another competitor," Yazgrak said. "You'll each come up and pick a card. On it will be a color and a number. The color matches with the sponsored kitchen that you'll be working in. The number tells you which heat you'll be competing in. There will be five heats."

Shar nodded. This was what generally happened, group and team challenges at the start, when there were so many contestants, until the end when they'd be competing individually.

"However, the person you're paired with is not your teammate," Erwel warned. "They are your direct competition. This is a head-to-head baking challenge. Each pair will receive one ingredient for their bake. Whoever utilizes that ingredient the best will be the winner. For the loser, well, that's the end of the line for them."

Shar felt her eyes grow large. They were eliminating *half* of the competitors in the first round? Her beard trembled and her heart started pounding.

She had this one chance. *One chance*. To get it right. To move on to the next round in the competition.

But not only that, she had to do better than whoever she was paired with.

Shar joined the slowly shuffling line of competitors walking up to the table, picking up their cards.

She really didn't want to be in the first group. She wanted time to watch the judges, see what they liked and didn't like.

She also didn't want to be last, at the end of the day, when the judges were likely to be tired and their palettes overextended.

Second or third would be best.

Shar felt as though Chaa, the god of chocolate, was smiling down on her when she drew her card and saw the number three across the top of it.

The color purple had no significance, as it just represented the kitchen she worked in. And Shar had already proven to herself that she could work in pretty much any kitchen.

The herald had the contestants group together by color. As there were five kitchens, there were five groups with ten people in each.

Fifty contestants total, and down to twenty-five by the end of the day.

Shar didn't like her chances, but she was determined to do this.

Then she learned the name of the Dwarf she'd be cooking against.

Kigora Goldenberry.

A relative of one of the judges.

She was so screwed.

# Shar

"So you have purple too, huh?" Shar asked Kigora.

"Oh. I'm competing against you?" Kigora asked.

Though the other Dwarf was the same height as Shar, she still managed to look down her nose. She wore an outfit similar to Shar's, though the coat was a very pretty blue with black trim, and her apron was red with blue trim. Her beard held nuggets of gold and silver instead of ribbons. Shar judged them to be about the same age, in their early twenties, given Kigora's clear gray eyes and lack of general wrinkles in the smooth tanned skin of her face.

It appeared that her family, the Goldenberrys, were sponsoring her. Many of the other contestants had sponsors, but not all.

"I am!" Shar said, determined to be friendly. "Do you know which kitchen is purple?"

"I don't," Kigora said. "But I don't really care. I can bake anywhere. Can you?" Her tone held a challenge.

Shar gave her a smile. "I think so. On the way here, my mentor had me bake in all the kitchens of the inns we stayed at. Reduced our costs on the road."

"That's...thrifty," Kigora said, as if that had been a bad thing and something far below her consideration.

"I'm assuming that Goldenberry means you're related to Yazgrak?" Shar had to ask.

"Yes, I'm one of his nieces," Kigora said coolly. "I won't be getting any favors from him, though. He'll probably judge me more harshly so he won't be seen showing favorites."

"Oh," Shar said. She hadn't thought about that. "What's your favorite dessert?" she said, still trying to have a discussion with her competition.

Particularly since she'd be sending this person home.

"Anything chocolate, of course," Kigora said.

"Same here," Shar said. "Antonio Bagaduce came to see the queen, and I got to try one of his chocolates. That was amazing!"

Kigora just sniffed at her. "I've had private lessons with him."

"Really?" Shar said, excited. "What's he like? Did you learn amazing things?"

"I'm not about to tell you what my lessons entailed," Kigora said frostily. "You're my competition. And I intend to win."

With that, Kigora turned and walked away, going to one of the Human bakers and deliberately starting a conversation with him. They both glanced over at Shar, then laughed.

Crap.

Kigora was going to be almost impossible to beat. She was a relative of Yazgrak. She'd probably started baking as soon as she could hold a spoon. This was her profession, what she'd started off doing. She'd even had *lessons* with Antonio Bagaduce!

How was Shar going to be able to compete with all that?

Another peal of laughter came from over in the general vicinity of Kigora.

Shar felt herself stand up taller as her spine stiffened.

It didn't matter who her competition was. How long they'd been cooking.

Shar was just going to have to be stubborn about this. To dig into her Dwarven soul and pull out something amazing. Something that the judges would adore. Something that would set this contest alight.

She wasn't about to go home on the first challenge, unlike half of the people standing around her.

She paused, then took a good look around. There were Elves, Dwarves, and Humans all competing. Some of them looked to be about her age, but many of them seemed older. (Though who knew when it came to Elves?)

It didn't matter what experience they had. How long they'd been cooking.

She had so much more to lose than they did.

She was going to beat every single one of them.

The kitchen was at the back of a large, five-story inn that catered to all the races. There were underground tunnels for the Dwarves, gaudily decorated rooms for the Humans, and the top floors had gardens and trees for the Elves.

Despite that, the kitchen itself was only about twice as big as Muddy Bean Chocolates. Alred Kyney, the Human official who brought them to the kitchen, gave them a few minutes to familiarize themselves with where everything was.

Alred lived up to his name, with bright red curls and a silly looking, equally red mustache that curled up on the ends. (He probably used *wax*, not beard oil. Shar shuddered at the thought of it.) His skin was as pale as white chocolate, with a smattering of freckles across the bridge of his nose. Green eyes peered intelligently out at her, and he always seemed to be smiling. He wore a tabard like the herald, the gray heron decorating his chest. Over that hung a large crystal that gave off a slight purple glow—probably something magical, though Shar had no idea what.

Shar knew that she'd get lost in the kitchen, forget where things were. She also knew that she wasn't about to get any help from Kigora.

Erwel floated into the room.

Huh. Though those robes of her looked solid, they were a lot more gauzy than they appeared, as they drifted behind her.

Shar and Kigora introduced themselves to the Elf, who smiled cheerily at them.

"You're related to Yaz, right?" she asked Kigora.

*Yaz?* Oh, to be so familiar with one of the masters of baking!

"Yes, he's my uncle," Kigora said stiffly. "I don't expect any favoritism, though."

"Oh, no, child, Yaz has more integrity than that," Erwel said. "I would never doubt his judgment. He'll be fair. You don't have to worry."

She turned to Shar. "And you! Coming all the way from Shazirakz, right?"

Shar nodded, suddenly shy in front of one of the judges.

"Who have you been studying with?" Erwel said, obviously very curious. "We haven't had someone from your city compete in decades."

"Basteateleen Hammerguard," Shar said proudly.

"Basteateleen," Erwel repeated. "Where do I know that name from?"

"She won the regional contest the year she entered," Shar said.

"Yes! That was my first competition! She beat me," Erwel said with a surprising grin. "She was always so kind, so giving of her knowledge. It's a shame she never went on to *Chocolates Galore!* She quite possibly could have snatched the title."

Shar beamed at the Elf, suddenly feeling herself settle in even more.

She might not have Kigora's family name, but her own heritage was just as good. At least for someone like Erwel.

"So, I'm here to give you your instructions, as well as the secret ingredient for this bake."

Relief flooded Shar and she felt herself relax slightly. Though the rules had been explained, it was good for Shar to hear them again, because she was so nervous she might have forgotten something.

"You will have two hours to make the dessert of your choice. Show us who you are as an artist!" Erwel exclaimed. "You must produce six identical servings: three for the judges, and three to be auctioned off to support the contest. This is your chance to really shine as an individual, because the next few bakes after this will be team challenges."

Shar nodded. That was generally how these contests were run.

At least she wouldn't have to worry about being paired with Kigora in any of coming challenges, as Shar was determined to send her competitor home.

"Now, remember, no magic. Alred's necklace here will instantly detect it if you try."

Shar gave Alred a smile and got a nod in return. That was what the purple crystal around his neck did! She wasn't about to break the rules. Besides, her magic was only metal related.

"And your mystery ingredient is!" Erwel paused dramatically as Alred fetched her a large tray covered with a purple silk napkin.

"Ginger!" she said as she plucked away the napkin.

Shar grinned. Fortunately for her, ginger and chocolate paired together beautifully.

"And your time starts now!" Erwel continued.

A large hourglass suddenly appeared on the wall, the sand already sliding from the top globe into the bottom.

Shar got out a clean, never before used notebook and walked back to the workbench that she'd claimed, while Kigora rushed frantically to and from the other.

What could Shar make with chocolate and ginger?

She decided on a Dwarven specialty that was only served during the winter solstice. It had other warm spices in it, like cinnamon and nutmeg. However, ginger was the focus.

Was that enough, though? Just a plain spice cake? How could she elevate it? Make it elegant enough that even Erwel might be impressed?

She could make a ginger tuile—a light and golden colored cookie, artistically bent into the shape of a cone—to offset the heaviness of the cake. Plus maybe a sauce to go with...

Plans in place, Shar began her own rush around the kitchen.

Even though she'd started later than Kigora, she was pleased that her competition hadn't stooped to taking all the ingredients or hogging all the cooking pans. Leena had warned her about that, that with some of her competitors, the time she spent thinking at the start of any bake might be used against her.

Despite Kigora's attitude, she was at least honorable enough to share.

After Shar had gathered all her ingredients together, she paused for another moment, going over her list, making sure that her plans still held water.

Yes.

And she was off, shredding fresh ginger, chopping candied ginger, then measuring and mixing together ingredients for what was certain to be an amazing cake.

# Shar

Shar used the tip of a clean napkin to wipe off the last of the crumbs from one of her plates, making them all as neat as possible just as Alred called time.

Shar stepped back, shaking her head.

Her cake hadn't turned out how she'd wanted it to. Not at all.

It was a little crumbly, not perfectly moist and firm. The tuile had turned out great, so an elegant cone decorated the top of every cut piece. She'd made a spiral of a mixed berry jam to decorate the plate and to give the judges a bit of acidity. She hadn't had time to make a dipping sauce, but hopefully, her plate wouldn't suffer from that.

She had nearly despaired, though, looking over at Kigora's dishes.

Her competition had managed to make beautiful chocolate curls that decorated the top of her chocolate-ginger mousse pie. Each slice was perfectly proportioned, the crust flaky, the mousse certain to be delicious.

Kigora's plates looked like something that could be served to Queen Namnorelli Amberheart, while Shar's was best given to family alone.

Shar still held her head high as they made their way back to the judges. She had done her best. And if she didn't win her round against Kigora, well, she could always come back and compete in two years' time.

Though that would mean two years of extra baking practice, it would also mean two years of doing a job she hated, her fingers fumbling with cold, hard gemstones as she dreamed of soft, delicious dough.

Kigora presented her dessert to the judges first, detailing the ingredients and the process she'd used for her chocolate-ginger mousse pie.

"This looks so pretty!" Erwel exclaimed.

"And this crust is perfect," Yazgrak said. He used his fork to flake it apart. "Really, just textbook. And it's baked all the way through, too. Good job."

Kigora couldn't help but preen at the praise.

Then they tasted.

Cyna peered at Kigora, then sighed. "It tastes amazing, of course. The flavors are great. But I'm not getting a lot of ginger, honey."

"I agree with Cyna," Yazgrak said.

"Now there's a shocker," Erwel teased.

Yazgrak just rolled his eyes. "I can tell you put a lot of powdered ginger into this. There's a slightly grainy aftertaste. But that isn't enough when it comes to creating great ginger flavor."

Erwel sighed. "Your dessert is beautiful. Absolutely picture perfect. And if this wasn't a ginger challenge, you'd handily carry away the win. But this *is* supposed to be all about the ginger. And girl, you just don't have it."

Kigora held herself well. "Thank you for your feedback, judges," she said as she bowed her head and stepped back.

It was Shar's turn. Amazing how suddenly her palms started sweating and her beard trembled.

"What I've made for you is called a *Barazir Bake*. It's a traditional

Dwarven cake that's served at the winter solstice. It contains warming spices, as well as ginger. I've decorated it with a ginger tuile and a mixed-berry jam. Enjoy."

Shar felt her entire body want to start shaking, but she couldn't allow herself that privilege. Not until after she got back to the privacy of her room at the inn and had started packing her bags, getting ready to go home.

Yazgrak held the cake up closer to his eyes for scrutiny. "What type of flour did you use?"

"Finest cake flour I could find," Shar said.

"That's the problem," Yazgrak said. "This cake is generally made with bread flour, not cake flour. See the way this crumbles? Your proportions were probably off, and you added too much cake flour because it isn't as dense or as weighty as bread flour."

Shar swallowed against a suddenly dry mouth.

Rookie mistake, and she knew it.

She was better than that, but she determinedly kept her smile.

"And while the tuile and the swirl add a certain flair, your desserts need to be a lot cleaner," Erwel added.

"But I'm sure it will taste good!" Cyna added, giving Shar an encouraging smile. "I can't wait to try it!"

Shar nodded and awaited judgment.

The three judges were silent after their first bite. They exchanged glances with one another, their eyes wide.

Shar felt her heart sink into her boots.

It wasn't that bad, was it?

Erwel broke the silence. "Girl!" she said, drawing out the syllables. "I don't know how you did it, but you managed to pack an amazing amount of ginger flavor into this."

"Uhm, thank you," Shar said, a little confused.

"This is so good," Cyna said. "I'm not sure that I can limit myself to a single bite!"

"You did Dwarves everywhere proud," Yazgrak said. "If I got this in a shop? I'd be back the next day to buy out their entire stock. Tell me how you got the ginger flavor in here."

"You have to use more than one type of ginger to get the taste right," Shar said, spouting the wisdom she'd learned from Leena. "Powdered, dried, fresh, and candied."

"That's exactly right!" Yazgrak said excitedly. He looked past Shar's shoulder at the other contestants. "I hope y'all are taking notes. 'Cause none of the rest of you have even come close to this amount of ginger flavor in what you've given us."

Shar gulped. That was high praise from Yazgrak.

Had she really done that well? Was it possible for her to win this contest and beat Kigora?

Only time would tell.

The judges weren't telling anyone who won or who lost until after they'd tried the rest of the dishes from all the contestants.

The morning had been spent with Shar listening to every bite described by the judges. Every heat of contestants had had a different secret ingredient. The first group had had rose. The next group, peppermint. The last two groups had cranberries and lemon.

Each was an ingredient that one wouldn't serve on its own, not as a dessert. It had to be manipulated, somehow. In addition, all of them had different forms that could be added to a baked good: candied, powdered, dried, and so on.

Finally, the contestants finished their bakes. One at a time, the heats were called up and the judges announced their decisions. Shar couldn't remember who'd baked what by that point, as forty-eight dishes were a lot to try to comprehend.

But the judges did their job quickly, and there didn't appear to be any grumbling from the audience scattered behind them, most everyone agreeing with their decision.

Shar's palms were sweating again as she stepped up with her heat.

The judges quickly went through the other ginger contestants, knocking out half of them, until only Shar and Kigora remained.

"Now, we're going to do things a little differently at this point," Yazgrak warned. "I need you two to stand to the side for now."

Shar glanced over at Kigora, but the girl had her entire being focused on Yazgrak.

Without a word, Shar stepped over to the side. When Kigora didn't move, Shar reached out and tugged at her sleeve, breaking whatever spell Kigora was under.

Kigora glared at Shar but fell into place beside her.

Though Shar knew better, she still whispered, "Do you know what's going on?"

"I have no idea," Kigora replied, also in a whisper. "And I don't like it."

Shar didn't care much for what was going on either, but she was willing to wait.

Particularly since she could still pretend that she was going to go on in the contest and reach the next round, at least until she was told otherwise.

The judges went through the next heat quickly, then the last heat was called up. Finally, just two contestants stood before the judges, both Humans.

Shar vaguely remembered these two. The judges had seemed disappointed in both of them. Neither of them had made food that either tasted good or was well displayed.

The judges asked Shar and Kigora to come and stand in a line with the other two.

"Now, as I said, we're going to do things a little differently from here," Yazgrak warned again.

"Chefs Otwick and Taburn. You both failed at this challenge, producing desserts that were neither plated well or tasted good."

Erwel piped up. "Now, you know I like a good pucker. But your lemon desserts were far too sour."

Yaz continued. "Chefs Opalbender and Goldenberry. You both had minor flaws in your bakes. Goldenberry, your food was delicious and your tart crust was perfect. It was one of the best plated desserts of the day. However, you didn't meet the ginger portion of the challenge. Opalbender, your dessert was delicious. Our favorite bite of the day, quite frankly."

Shar felt her breath catch in her throat. She'd made something that delicious right out of the gate? That was amazing! Maybe she did have a chance.

"However, it lacked refinement," Yazgrak went on.

Cyna added, "It wasn't a looker, but it sure was a taster."

"We have to eliminate two people," Yazgrak went on. "That's the nature of this contest. We need to get the number down to twenty-five people. The original plan was to eliminate one person from every competition cook. However..."

The Dwarf paused dramatically, his eyes darting from one chef to the next.

"By unanimous decision, we've decided to eliminate both chefs from one of the cooks. Chefs Otwick and Taburn. Neither of you are continuing on. While Chefs Goldenberry and Opalbender, we will see you both the next round."

Shar felt herself gasp, as if she hadn't been breathing for the last few minutes.

She'd made it through? Just on taste alone?

Erwel caught her eye. "You make sure to give us something beautiful next time," she warned.

"I will. I will!" Shar promised. "Thank you judges. Thank you. I won't let you down."

The only thing marring her relief was the look of pure hatred that Kigora shot her.

It wasn't until Shar was leaving along with the rest of the chefs, released for the night, that she finally felt herself coming back down to the ground.

Crap.

This meant that Kigora was going to be in the group challenges, and there was a very good chance Shar was going to have her on her team at some point.

# In The Beginning...

Everyone knows how the world Indunel was created.

Right? The great god Omatusoni carved out a space in the darkness, made it whole with His word, then fiddled around a bunch to make it livable.

That isn't what actually happened, though.

According to the Plainsmen, the brother of the great goddess Yrthria tried to rebel against his sister's rule. She put down the insurrection with prejudice, not only killing her brother but throwing him out of Heaven, casting him far beneath her. His body became the earth that all walk on now.

Then there are the tales of the Elves, and how a chorus of celestial beings followed a brilliant light from one end of the universe to the other, creating worlds from their songs, the greatest and bestest place of all being Indunel.

Humans have a tale of the Great Emperor who took the top off an egg. Inside the egg, the yolk, is the world Indunel. The stars are all the shimmery bits contained in the white of the egg. Sometime, the Great Emperor will cook the egg, and a new world will be born from the next day's breakfast.

(This story is actually closer to the truth than you might realize. There are actually millions of eggs in a carton, each containing its own world and universe. It's tricky to travel between them, to pierce through the shell of one in order to leave without destroying it, then enter the shell of a second without destroying *that* place. Let's just say that the Great Emperor frowns on that sort of travel because mistakes get made more often than not.)

So of course, everyone knows how the world of Indunel was created.

And now you do as well.

# Shar

Shar and Hulda sat in the main room of the Rusty Nail eating their breakfast. Shar only had a little time before she had to be back at the main area, ready for the next bake. Leena had had some tea, then scurried away, telling them to eat without her.

Though Shar had looked at everyone already in the main room when they'd come in, she still didn't see any of the other contestants. Maybe they were breaking their fast in their rooms. Leena had mentioned that was an option, but for now, she wanted Shar visible, eating in the main room.

Leena came bursting into the room just as Shar and Hulda were finishing up, grinning from ear to ear.

Shar had seen that smile on her mentor's face a few times, but not often.

Generally when she had something devious planned for the next challenge bake for Shar.

"What's up?" she asked as Leena hurried over to sit with them.

"I suspect yesterday was kinda a blur for ye, yes?" Leena asked Shar.

"Yeah," Shar admitted. She remembered that she'd been allowed on in the contest based on the taste of her food alone, as the design hadn't been enough.

"So, ye made six portions, right? Three for the judges, and three to be auctioned off," Leena continued.

Shar nodded. She vaguely remembered that as part of her setup.

"Ye'll be pleased to know that yer dishes brought in the most money at the auction last night," Leena said, looking proud.

"What?" Shar asked. "But there were so many other beautiful desserts!"

"Aye, but ye had the best bite of the day. And most of the folk in the audience, while they appreciate something that looks good, what they really want is something tasty."

Shar opened her mouth then closed it again. "Really?" she had to ask again.

Hulda reached over and twacked her arm.

"Ow," Shar said reflexively, though the punch hadn't really hurt.

"Told you," Hulda said. "You always do an amazing job in terms of flavor."

"But I can't win the entire contest on flavor alone," Shar warned. "Hopefully it will be enough to get me through the next few rounds, though."

Now, Leena reached over and slapped Shar's other arm.

"What was that for?" Shar asked.

"For defeatist talk," Leena said sternly. "Ye can outbake the best of 'em. Ye can win this. Ye can't git in yer own way. Ye got to approach this knowing that ye can win. All of it. Ye start thinking ye just need to get through the next round and yer sunk."

Shar sighed. Her mentor and her friend were right. She had to keep thinking that she could win regionals. It was the only way forward for her.

"I'll do it," Shar said. She'd nearly said that she would merely try, but that wasn't good enough. Not for her, or for her mentor.

"Tha's right," Leena said, nodding. "Yer gonna do this."

"And I'm happy to thump you anytime you start thinking or talking otherwise," Hulda promised.

"Thank you," Shar said. With friends like this, she knew she could go far.

~

The next challenge was a team challenge, as everyone had suspected. Again, there were cards, each with a number and a color, randomly dividing the bakers up into five teams of five.

Shar didn't really breathe until she realized that Kigora was on a different team from her.

Good.

She'd be happy to compete against her nemesis. She didn't want to have to cooperatively bake with her. Not at this point. Despite the peptalk that her friends had given her this morning, Shar still didn't feel as if the ground under her feet was completely solid.

At least this round, it wasn't half of the bakers leaving. Instead, it was a single team. So they would go from twenty-five contestants down to twenty by the end of the day.

Shar assumed that would be the case for the next few bakes, that large groups of people would be winnowed down until they got to the individual challenges. Only then would just one person at a time go home.

Her team got the color green, and was composed of two Humans (male and female), two Dwarves (Shar and another female), and one Elf (male).

The challenge? To make a cohesive dessert flight, one of each of the types assigned by the judges: a hot dessert, a cold dessert, a cake, a baked confection, and chocolate.

After the teams arrived at their kitchen, the judges gave them five minutes to discuss their strategy and to come up with a team name.

"Green is a good color," Golodhon the Elf said seriously as the group gathered around the large work table in the center of the already sweltering space. He was dressed in shades of green and yellow that offset his tanned features well. The other Elves were all pale compared to him. His hair, also, wasn't the pure black of the other Elves, but a pale gold instead, that trailed down to the middle of his back, held in place by bright green clips in the shapes of leaves. (Shar didn't learn until much later that he was a mountain Elf, not a wood Elf, and lived high in the hills of the Ashveil mountains.)

"Should we go with that as a theme?" Golodhon suggested. "All spring and summer desserts? Then we could call ourselves *Zöld Mystique.*"

Shar wasn't sure about that. As a Dwarf, she lived under the Kibizar Mountains, and so she didn't experience the seasons as fully as those who were at the mercy of the weather. At least the name was somewhat clever, as everyone knew that the Elvish word for green was *zöld.*

Frori, the other Dwarf, was equally uncertain about the theme. She'd also come from the Ashveil Mountains, though from a small village deep underground.

However, before either of them could express their misgivings, the Humans chimed in.

"I think that's a great idea!" Ames, the male said. "I'd be happy to go first, with the hot dessert. Something to warm you up after the chilly winter. Maybe a berry cobbler with a heated sauce."

"Be sure to put some alcohol in it," Frori said. "You know how Cyna likes her liquor." They all nodded at that. Not only had Shar learned that through her previous research, it had become evident while watching the judging the day before.

"Aye," Bela, the female Human piped up. "And I can do some-thin' cold. That brisk morning air. Clean. Fresh. Peppermint, proba-bly. Maybe ice cream. Right?"

Golodhon beamed at them. "That sounds amazing," he said. "If you wouldn't mind, I'd like to do the cake portion, and to decorate it appropriately."

Shar nearly rolled her eyes at that. Of course the Elf wanted to do the flashiest piece of the set.

Frori nodded slowly. "I've got a good recipe for a baked pistachio crumble. If you do it right, pistachio bakes up brown on the outside, but will be bright green on the inside."

Everyone turned expectantly to Shar. "You want me to do chocolate? I got you covered," she said.

This was going to turn out so well! Chocolate was the course she'd really wanted to do.

Plans set, the five of them awaited the official timer to start.

And they were off.

The challenge was *not* going well at all.

Shar had ended up having to help the two Humans find their way around the foreign kitchen. Turned out that this was the second time they'd had to cook someplace other than their own bakeries (the first time being the day before).

Then Frori needed help chopping up the pistachios, as the kitchen didn't come equipped with the sort of magical grinder that she was used to at home.

Fortunately, Shar had managed to get her chocolate properly tempered and into the molds provided so she was able to take a break from her own cook to help.

She wasn't just going to serve bonbons, though. The judges had looked askance at the contestant who'd done that the first challenge, saying that they hadn't done enough.

She did have three types of chocolates that she was preparing: milk chocolate with a lavender berry filling, dark chocolate with mint, and white chocolate with pear.

In addition, Shar planned on doing a more formal version of a browned-butter chocolate cookie. She'd drizzle white chocolate across just half of each cookie, then decorate the other half with candied versions of her three flavorings: lavender, mint, and pear.

It was a lot (A. Lot.) of elements on a single plate.

However, if Shar could pull this off, she'd be a shoo-in for the next round.

If only the rest of her teammates would get their act together!

Golodhon also helped once he got his cakes in the oven, taking over chopping for Frori, his knife moving so quickly it was almost a blur.

(Shar glanced at the official who stood by the door. He was there to make sure that no one bothered them as well as to check for magic. However, the purple crystal necklace he wore hadn't started to glow. Huh. Golodhon wasn't using magic. He was just that fast.)

Shar rushed between simmering berries for her jam, making ganaches, and candying various ingredients.

The one advantage that a team challenge had, at least with a group that was cooperating, was that they all got to taste each other's food. Mint was a common ingredient in every dish, to make sure that the dessert flight had a cohesive element.

Shar didn't have time to be embarrassed or cautious when people asked her opinion, though she was surprised at how often her teammates sought her out to taste their desserts. (It wasn't until later that evening when Hulda reminded her that according to the judges she'd had the best bite of the day from the first bake that she understood why they valued her taste guidance.) She advised more mint to Ames, as his berry cobbler wasn't quite there, as well as less mint to Bela when she offered a taste of her ice cream. (The woman decided to add in a swirl of chocolate, which created the perfect balance of flavors.)

Golodhon's cake was amazing, of course. It had the perfect crumb, and was firm and moist. Both mint and vanilla flavored it, the combination delicate but not overly sweet. He used a buttercream dyed green for the frosting then made a bunch of pink flowers out of a sweet paste for decoration. Shar helped him create some branches using chocolate that had been melted, combined with a simple syrup, then worked until it became a stiff dough.

The cake really was a show stopper when it was finished, the molded chocolate branches with the flowers stuck on them taking on a lifelike appearance.

Frori's baked confection turned out amazing, the brown crust being perfectly golden while the inside was shocking green. She'd used mint and raspberry jam as the filling.

The team all loved Shar's bonbons. She had to agree that the flavor combinations worked well, both individually as well as together. The colors also worked: the dark chocolates had tiny leaves of green icing on them, to represent the mint; the milk chocolates had a miniature purple flower also done in icing to represent the lavender; while the white chocolates had tiny pieces of actual candied pear topping them.

Her cookies weren't as elegant as she'd originally imagined them. They tasted absolutely amazing, and Ames had already asked her for her recipe. While the white chocolate drizzle done on half of each cookie did dress them up some, the dark color on the other half of the cookies made the plate feel heavy, even with the candied elements on top of the cookies.

Golodhon helped her with that. At his request, Shar melted some chocolate that Golodhon put into a paper cone. He then used that to pipe designs on her plate. He arranged the three bonbons on each plate, drew circles around each of them, connecting them to a stem that sprouted a few leaves, making each collection of bonbons look like a flower.

The cookies were perfectly round, so they didn't need shapes drawn on the outside of them. Shar arranged four cookies on each plate so that the white drizzle was on the outside, while the darker part was in the middle, like the center of a flower. Then Golodhon drew another stem and leaves connecting them.

All in all, Shar felt proud of what her team had produced. She didn't know if they'd done enough to win. However, she didn't think they'd get sent home, as everything tasted amazing.

It was all up to the judges, now.

# Kigora

Kigora had initially been excited about the team she'd been assigned.

First off, that annoying country bumpkin Sharaksir wasn't on it. Next, Kigora was the only Dwarf on the team, which meant that she didn't have to share ideas or flavor profiles with anyone. Plus, not one but *two* Elves were on her team, which meant that the team's decorations should be great.

She hadn't anticipated that the two Humans would be such egomaniacs who both demanded that things be done their way and wouldn't listen to anyone else.

The desserts had to be cohesive and the team needed to work together to achieve that. Kigora had listened to Uncle Yaz complain often enough about a team challenge being the downfall of more than one brilliant baker. (Uncle Yaz regularly worked as a judge not just on the prestigious regional contests but on smaller affairs as well. He'd even been paid well enough once to judge a grudge match between two sisters who each proclaimed that their crumble cake was the best in all of Anthus.) (He'd pronounced it a tie, partly in an effort to bring peace to the family.) (It hadn't worked.)

However, the two obstinate Humans had their ears stuffed with rocks and just wouldn't listen.

Their team color had been orange, so at least they'd come to a quick conclusion to go with all citrus: oranges, lemons, grapefruits, limes, and an Elven specialty, erorets. They chose an appropriate team name as well, *The Citrus Coalition*.

As far as Kigora and the two Elves were concerned, that meant that the color palette should also be filled with brighter colors: oranges, yellows, and greens. It was important to signal to the judges what they were getting. Making a baked good anonymous, or misleading as to the flavor, frequently backfired. (Unless that was the challenge: making a food impostor, that is, something that looked like one thing but tasted like something else. Kigora had PLANS if that turned out to be one of the challenges.)

The Humans wanted to prove themselves though, and kept advocating using darker colors than what Humans traditionally used for their desserts so that they would be seen as playing against type.

Kigora rolled her eyes at their explanation.

"I understand your point," she told them. "But given our choice of theme, now isn't the time."

One of the Humans—Mel? Mac? some name that started with an M that Kigora hadn't bothered learning, as he'd be gone out of the contest soon enough—shook his head like a stubborn miner intent of following a vein to the end while getting less and less return on his investment. "I want to do elegant work that isn't brightly colored," he insisted.

"How about we do an ombre?" Nerwyne, one of the Elves, suggested. "Start with the brighter colors and work down to the darker ones? That does mean, though, that you'll have to do the baked confection and the chocolate."

The two Humans, after much cajoling, finally agreed to the plan. (One of them, not Miki [or whatever his name was] had had her heart set on making the cake, but finally agreed to make the baked confection instead.)

Kigora agreed to make the cold dessert, while Nerwyne made the hot one.

However, instead of an ice cream (which she was certain all the other teams would do, as that was the easy choice given the special Dwarven magical ice cream machines that every kitchen now had installed) Kigora decided to make a sorbet out of her chosen fruit, which was the Elven eroret, a bright-pink fruit that tasted like a combination of sweet grapes and sour oranges.

And no, she had *not* been taking notes about using different forms of an ingredient to get the most taste out of it that Uncle Yaz had pointed out at her first judging. She already knew that. She'd made an error and not used enough of the other types of ginger in that last bake.

A mistake she wasn't about to make a second time.

So not only did she make candied eroret and add that to her sorbet, she also pickled some of the fruit with both vinegar and sugar, to use as a topping for the iced treat. And she added a baked granola made primarily out of almonds to add a crunch element to her dish.

Nerwyne baked a beautiful lavender cake that he then cut into tiny, elegant pieces and was planning on pouring a steaming-hot lemon and berry sauce when serving the judges.

Ethodrel had made a two-tiered cake, with a lime curd that Kigora thought tasted amazing, being sweet, sour, and silky, with just a hint of salt at the end that was perfect.

The female Human (Constance?) took grapefruit for her baked confection, and made a creampuff with a dark orangish crackling on top. The patachou dough that she used turned out light and fluffy, with the exact amount of crunch and chew to it.

The problem was that her pastry cream was too sour. However, Constance refused to change it, claiming that she didn't have time to rework her vision. (Kigora just shook her head at that. Constance hadn't even decorated her own plate! Nerwyne had taken over and done that for all of them.)

The other Human—Mesym, Kigora had finally learned—had taken orange, as that was one of the few types of citrus that actually went well with chocolate. Fortunately, his chocolate eclairs had risen well and tasted divine. Nerwyne had drizzled white chocolate dyed orange over them to make them look less like brown turds on the plate. (Seriously. Kigora was so disgusted by the end of the cook that she was willing to throw both Humans under an oncoming rockfall.)

The dessert flight looked cohesive enough, the idea of an ombre at least noticeable once it was pointed out.

However, no one was completely happy with their work as they trudged out to see the judges.

Kigora knew that they wouldn't win this round. She hoped that they weren't bad enough to get sent home, though.

She just had to survive the next few team challenges and get to the individual rounds. Then she could show everyone exactly what she was made of. Do the Goldenberry name proud.

Show up that upstart Sharaksir, if she even made it that far, which Kigora doubted.

# Shar

As Shar had suspected, *Zöld Mystique* didn't win their round. They did come in second, and part of that was based on flavor. Shar was dinged again on presentation, though Golodhon had at least helped make her plate acceptable. She learned that she should have used white chocolate or cocoa butter dyed green for piping the leaves and stems on her plate, instead of the dark chocolate.

Next time, she'd do better.

Everyone on her team was praised for their flavors. The judges assumed they'd worked well together, and they had.

Shar worked to keep her face passive when Kigora's team came under some fairly harsh criticism. Seemed that they hadn't modulated their flavors well enough.

Cyna didn't like things that were too sour, as every contestant should have learned from the first day. Even Erwel made the comment, "Girl, you know I like a good pucker. But this grapefruit cream is too much."

Kigora's team made it through to the next round, though.

The eliminated group were composed of bakers Shar hadn't really met or talked with. Their team had two Dwarves, two

Humans, and one Elf. The judges seemed sad to say goodbye to the Elf in particular, but the rest of the group had let that person down.

The team had also admitted to fighting amongst themselves, and no one had tasted all their dishes, ensuring that they were cohesive.

Shar nodded at the judgment. She'd read the reports from previous contests, listened to Leena's guidance about such things, but it was something else to actually hear the judges say that the teams must work together or they'd all be going home.

She resolved to herself that even if she ended up on a team with Kigora that they would both be professionals and do their job together.

And then there were twenty of them left, down from fifty after two days.

The next round was different than any of the previous rounds. Shar hadn't ever read of a challenge like the one facing them.

The remaining bakers were split up into five teams of four.

Shar was pleased to see Golodhon on her team again. The other two—both Humans—were people she hadn't met before.

Once they were all in their groups and arranged in front of the judges, Yazgrak went on to explain the rules.

"Now, see those people standing next to you?" he asked.

Everyone nodded.

"They are both your teammates as well as your competition," he warned.

Erwel picked up the instructions from there. "Each group will be assigned a single type of dessert: cakes, cookies, chou pastries, pies, or baked confections. Then, each member of the group creates one of your assigned type of dessert."

Cyna concluded with, "You will be judged as a team, at the judges' discretion. Either you will go head-to-head, and two members of your team will be eliminated. Or," she paused dramatically, "your team will do well enough that you'll all go forward, and some other team will lose more members."

Yazgrak added, "No two people on the team can choose the same flavor. Be sure to work together, though. You need to ensure that everyone does well enough so that you're all here tomorrow."

Shar caught Golodhon's eye. He nodded. The two Humans seemed more skeptical about it, but hopefully they'd cooperate as well.

They'd all make it to the next round if Shar and Golodhon had anything to say about it.

∾

Unfortunately, Shar's team was assigned patachou, that is, chou pastries. She hadn't worked often with that sort of dough, as Dwarves preferred things that crumbled more and fed their beards. However, she had baked with it a couple of times, as Leena had insisted that she learn this type of baked confection as well.

Once they got to their kitchen, they were given five minutes to come up with a gameplan before their bake started. Alred stood at the door and gave Shar a big smile when she glanced over at him.

The encouraging gesture meant a lot to her.

Particularly given the temperament of the two Humans who didn't want to work together as a team.

"Look," Wyneful said, explaining her point of view. "Shar, you admit that you've rarely made chou dough. Same with you," she added, glancing at Golodhon. "We have," she said, indicating the other Human, Mesym, standing next to her. "We'd rather take you out then try to support you and lift you up."

Shar shook her head. "Weren't you listening to the judges? They value team work over individual work, at least in the team challenges.

You making the decision to go on your own and not help anyone else will be used against you during judging."

Mesym shook his head. "My creampuffs and flavors will more than make up for any negative critique I get from working on my own."

"We can help each other," Golodhon said. "Shar is amazing at flavors. I can elevate your decorations. If we work as a team, we'll be much more likely to all succeed."

Wyneful and Mesym glanced at each other, then both of them shook their heads. "You two help each other," Wyneful said. "I don't need your help."

Shar rolled her eyes at that. "People always need help, whether you admit to it or not. I will still be available if you change your mind," she added.

"I choose blackberry," Mesym said, deliberately moving forward rather than continuing their argument. "I'm making a creampuff with a blackberry crackling and filling."

"I'd like to do a fried chou dough, with chocolate," Golodhon said.

Shar nodded. Though chocolate was what she was most comfortable with, she knew that she needed to branch out, to show the judges other flavors.

Wyneful chose strawberries and eclairs, which was fine with Shar, as she decided that she'd do a cheese and apple profiterole.

The main difference between a profiterole and a creampuff was that a creampuff was left whole and filling was piped into it, while a profiterole was cut in half and then filled. This would give her the opportunity to add the cheese and melt it before adding the sweeter apple filling.

Everything decided, the bakers started rushing around the kitchen gathering their ingredients. Shar decided to start her apple filling first as that would take the longest to cook down.

Making patachou didn't actually take that much time. The

dough was pretty simple: flour, water, chilled butter, and eggs. It didn't have to rest or rise. The cooking of it was more challenging, as the oven temperature had to start high and then be lowered, to give the outside a hard shell first and to dry out the insides. Fortunately, the ovens in the kitchen they'd were using contained a magical heating element so the temperature was much easier to control.

After cutting the apples and starting to simmer them, Shar began her first batch of patachou dough.

The number of eggs that one added to a chou dough was based on feel, rather than a specific number. Eggs came in different sizes, so it was impossible to know the exact number necessary. Plus, she was only making a few of the desserts, and had had to adjust her recipe down from working in the Muddy Bean.

So Shar ended up tossing out her first batch of dough as she'd added too many eggs, not paying careful enough attention to how the dough was stiffening. (Or didn't firm up, as in her case.)

The second batch turned out much better, and Shar put it into the oven with enough time to make a third batch, just in case.

That turned out to be a wise decision, as she didn't turn down the temperature in the oven in time, and the tops of her second batch were too brown.

She watched the third batch like a cat watching a suspicious hole, just waiting for a mouse to pop out. The dough turned golden brown and the crust had a nice crunch, while the inside was moist and chewy.

After shredding a small amount of a sharp hard cheese that she'd found, the profiteroles went back into the oven for just a few minutes, melting the cheese. Then she added her hot apples that she'd cooked not just with cinnamon and nutmeg, but also with a good amount of ginger, to give the spices additional warmth.

Shar shared one of the completed profiteroles with Golodhon whose eyes grew wide at the taste.

"Though these are a bit big and messy," he said. "The taste is amazing."

"Your dessert also tastes divine," Shar said. She'd never had fried patachou before. Golodhon had fried long pieces of it, each about the diameter of her thumb, then rolled them in cinnamon and sugar and dipped them in chocolate.

Though Shar might have been tempted to use the fried dough whole, he cut each into small pieces and arranged them artfully on a plate.

For Shar's decoration, she sprinkled sugar and spices onto a few apple slices then quick broiled them.

She knew that her plate left much to be desired in terms of design. Hopefully, though, her flavors would carry her through.

When the bakers were all assembled in front of the judges again, instead of getting right to it, the judges stopped to talk with them.

"We may have forgotten to mention one tiny detail for this challenge," Erwel said with a teasing grin. "How we're going to choose which desserts will go head-to-head on a team."

"What you didn't know was that your watchers were part of today's challenge," Yazgrak continued. "They reported to us which teams worked together, which teams didn't, as well as which individual bakers advocated for teamwork. And who didn't."

Shar felt her eyes grow big.

She *knew* that teamwork during the team challenges was actually important.

Cyna added, "What was strange was that on *every* team, it was evenly split between those who wanted to cooperate and those who didn't. There were no teams who worked together one-hundred percent."

Yazgrak gave a shrug. "At least you made it easy to figure out who each of you will be judged against."

That told Shar that she wouldn't be put against Golodhon, but one of the two Humans instead: either Mesym's blackberry cream-puff or Wyneful's eclairs. If the judges decided to pair the two desserts that most resembled one another, they'd put her against Mesym and Wyneful against Golodhon.

Which turned out to be exactly the case.

Their group was third. Shar felt hopeful because the judges were being particularly harsh on the people who hadn't cooperated. It wasn't easy gold—just because a person was willing to work with others didn't guarantee that they'd go forward in the contest. At least three-fourths of them did, though.

Mesym, like Shar, had put some of the fruit he'd used—blackber-ries—on the plate in a decorative design with the creampuffs. Shar had to admit they looked amazing. He'd made his individual puffs a lot smaller than she'd made her profiteroles. She had put only one profiterole per plate, whereas he had three.

Yet another things she'd have to remember for her next bake: smaller desserts were perceived to be more elegant.

She was a Dwarf. She didn't automatically do things that were Elf-sized.

But she was going to have to start making smaller portions.

Mesym bragged about his use of spices in his filling, the blackber-ries cooked in ginger, the purple crackling he used as decoration for his creampuff, the blackberry compote on the plate.

The judges tried his and seemed slightly disappointed with his patachou dough. The bake had been inconsistent, as Yazgrak's was still doughy inside though both Cyna and Erwel had perfect creampuffs.

Then Shar presented her plate. "What I've made for you today is a profiterole. The filling is sharp cheddar and apple, with broiled apple slices on the side. Enjoy!"

"What's this on the top?" Yazgrak asked. "Is this shaved white chocolate?"

"Oh! No," Shar assured him. "It's melted cheese."

Cyna looked at her plate, looked at Shar, then sighed. "I'm certain this is going to be delicious. It smells amazing. But you can do better than this in terms of decorating."

"I know you're a Dwarf," Erwel said. "But you still need to channel your inner Elf, and give us something more elegant next time, if you're still here."

Shar nodded. "Noted," she said. And she would.

The judges dug into her dessert.

Yazgrak heaved a huge sigh. "This is a problem," he said.

Shar's heart sunk and she felt her throat grow dry. What had she done wrong?

"I can't finish this. I have all these other desserts to judge. But honestly? I'm going to be thinking about this dessert, right here, for the rest of this session," he said.

Cyna snorted. "I'm just going to eat it anyway," she said as she took another bite.

"Girl," Erwel said. "I cannot believe that this isn't some sort of magic. The flavors are truly amazing. This is going home with me so that I can finish it later."

"Done!" Cyna announced, showing Shar her clean plate.

"Clean plate club! Clean plate club!" Erwel called out to everyone.

"Thank you, judges," Shar said.

Now, she was aware that other races, Humans in particular, blushed when they grew embarrassed. Dwarves usually didn't blush. They might stammer a bit, and their beards might tremble from all the contained emotions.

Shar felt her cheeks grow slightly flush, and her beard definitely shook some.

Of course, she was pronounced the winner over Mesym.

Golodhon handily won his round over Wyneful as well, the judges praising both his elegant plating as well as his deliciously fried dough. Wyneful, on the other hand, had turned in an éclair. Yazgrak called it *expected* and *pedestrian*. The bakers needed to do more than what everyone usually did with an ingredient.

The next group contained Kigora. Shar kept her face neutral as her nemesis was scolded, particularly by Yazgrak, for not working with the other bakers on her team. However, her pie turned out amazing, with the best crust of all of the pies baked that day, so she was moved forward.

By the end of the day, they were down to ten.

# Shar

Shar celebrated that night with Leena and Hulda at the Rusty Nail. There had been three other contestants staying at the inn. Two had been sent home, and had already packed their bags and left. The Dwarf Hazzoum Oakenbowl was the other remaining contestant staying at the inn. He seemed nice enough, but kind of shy. He came from a family of bakers and was incredibly skilled at baked confections. Shar had really wanted to try a couple of the dishes that he'd presented to the judges.

They waved to each other across the busy eatery, but before Shar could invite Hazzoum to their table, he was shepherded upstairs by his companion. Possibly his mother, based on her similar appearance, their beards being almost the same auburn color.

"So, ye know that they'll throw an individual challenge at ye next, right?" Leena said.

"After all that talk about teamwork and helping each other out?" Hulda said, curious. "Really?"

"Exactly," Leena said. "There's ten of ye. Individual next, so there'll be nine. Then, a team challenge. Three teams of three. They'll want ta see if ye can remember, take their lessons ta heart."

"That may be the case," Shar said. "But historically, once they start the individual challenges, they don't go back to team challenges."

Leena nodded. "Aye. That has been the case in the past. But remember, the judges are always switching things up. They may do things differently this time."

"So how do I know?" Shar said. "How do I prepare?"

Leena grinned at her. "Ye don't know," she said. "But yer already prepared. I know it, ye know it. Ye just got to keep trusting what ye know. What ye can do."

Shar sighed. That didn't seem like enough. She'd really, *really* like to feel more confident going into the next bake.

Sure, her flavors had won over the judges every time. However, presentation was going to matter more and more. Plus, if she screwed up even once, she'd be going home.

"You know what the other contestants are calling you?" Hulda asked.

"No," Shar said cautiously, not sure she wanted to know.

"The flavor assassin," Hulda said cheerfully. "No one can match you there."

Shar shook her head. "I can't start thinking that way," she warned. "I have to keep pushing myself, keep striving to do better with every bake."

"That's me girl!" Leena said, raising her mug of mead and toasting Shar. "Ye'll go far with that kind of attitude. Because it's just getting harder from here."

"That's what I'm afraid of," Shar said. "The challenges are getting trickier."

"What do you think the next bake will be?" Hulda asked Leena.

"As I said, an individual challenge," Leena said. "Ye'll all be making something similar, and it will be fancy. Like a minotaur bun. Or a thousand sheet cake."

"What about a fancy Elven dessert? Like *Kényes Sütemény*?"

Shar asked. It was similar to a regular cake, though it used whipped egg whites instead of some other rising agent, the desired consistency being very light and fluffy. The thin layers of cake were stacked, cut into small, bite-sized pieces, then individually glazed using a very shiny frosting, with beautiful delicate decorations on top.

Shar knew that she could make the cake element of that dish. The other parts required a lot of skill that she wasn't completely comfortable with.

The three of them spent time talking about what might be the next challenge, explaining the various technical difficulties to Hulda.

Shar knew her flavors were good.

However, she suspected she was about to fall on her butt.

"As you may have guessed, today is the first individual challenge," Cyna said.

Shar grinned. That was what Leena had said. When she'd been waiting with the other bakers in the park that morning, they'd discussed that as a possibility. Some insisted it would be another team challenge—in particular, Ames and Phury, two of the four remaining Human bakers. Most everyone else believed it would be an individual challenge.

It hadn't surprised Shar that the judges had equalized the representations of the races in the remaining ten bakers. Three Dwarves, three Elves, and four Humans.

"This is going to be one of your most technical challenges," Yazgrak warned. "Presentation is really going to count for this bake."

While the judge didn't glare at Shar, she still felt as if that comment had been directed toward her.

Erwel grinned at them. "We'd like you to make *Krepp Torta*. As this is an Elven delicacy, I have high expectations of you."

"And all of your *Krepp Tortas* need to be at least ten centimeters tall," Yazgrak said.

Shar gulped. She'd done a few *krepps* in her time. Leena had insisted that she learn how to make the paper-thin pancake like wrappers. But it wasn't something she practiced with regularly.

A *Krepp Torta* was basically a cake made out of potentially dozens of layers of *krepps*. Between each layer needed to be some sort of filling, whether a jam, a frosting, or a ganache. The taste had to be balanced as well: *krepps* didn't have a lot of flavor to them, but the dessert couldn't just taste like the filling.

Plus, as Shar thought about it, she would need to add a crunch layer, for texture.

Was there anyway that she could surprise the judges? In flavor, texture, or design? She knew they'd want something special.

How could she elevate hers?

What surprised her was that all the bakers were brought to a single kitchen. It looked like a gathering hall that had been turned into a bakery, ovens with magical heating elements stuffed in along all sides.

It was yet another new baking location. And all the bakers would be cooking together. Shar would bet that the bakers really needed to help each other out in this new location. Or their dessert would be dinged by the judges.

They weren't given any time to think once they arrived at the kitchen. Evidently, all their thinking time needed to occur on the walk from the field that held the judges to the hall.

Shar mostly had a plan. She was going to concentrate on making her *krepps* first, as that was the most difficult part of the challenge for her. That meant she could continue to think about flavors as she cooked them.

They had all been supplied with special pans for making the *Krepps*: a domed pan that was specially oiled so the dough wouldn't stick.

Shar created her *krepp* batter, whisking it hard to make sure that it was light and foamy. Then she dipped her pan into a bowl with the batter and set it on top of the stove.

The first few *krepps* that Shar created either tore or burned. After asking her neighbor's opinion—a Human baker named Marger—Shar added more flour to her watery dough and finally managed to get a usable product.

How many *krepps* would it take to get to ten centimeters? A dozen? More? Shar didn't want to have to stop midway through her assembly to make more, so she made thirty *krepps*, knowing that was more than she needed but she wanted the extra just in case.

She trimmed her *krepps* as she made them, using a round cake pan as her guide. She knew that some people—like Golodhon—would be able to make their *Krepps* perfectly round and wouldn't need to trim the edges. However, as at least half the bakers were doing the exact same thing she was, she figured she was probably safe.

After Shar finished making the *krepps*, she turned to cooking her three fillings. First, she heated some maple syrup, then tossed hazelnuts and spices in. Once that had caramelized, she baked it, turning the concoction into something like a brittle, for her crunchy element.

She made apricot jam spiced with cloves primarily, to keep the flavor earthy.

Then she melted some milk chocolate. While she herself preferred the dark chocolate, this dessert needed the sweeter, lighter flavor of the milk.

Finally, it was assembly time. She crafted two paper cones to use for drizzling out her fillings between *krepp* layers instead of using the cloth bags.

First a *krepp*. Then apricot. Then another *krepp*. A layer of the brittle that she'd pounded into very fine pieces. One last *krepp*, and a drizzle of the milk chocolate.

Repeat.

In the end, Shar only ended up using twenty of her *krepp* to achieve the desired height.

Glancing around the room, she noticed that two of the Elves, of course, had built much taller *Krepp Torta*. Then again, they'd made this dessert before—it was an Elven specialty—and she hadn't.

For the top of her *Torta*, Shar thinned out her remaining milk chocolate, then poured it over the top, making sure to drizzle it down the sides of the cake. This was more tricky than it sounded, because the drips had to look intentional and not as though she'd just spilled chocolate everywhere. She piled some of the apricot jam in the center of the top, then sprinkled a bit of the brittle around it.

She didn't have time to do much else in terms of decorations. Hopefully it was enough.

It turned out that it was a blind judging that day. The bakers put their desserts side-by-side on a long table. Shar couldn't help but compare her dish to the others.

Only two of the three Elves had gone big, creating *Tortas* that were twice as tall as what had been required. One of the Humans had as well. The rest were all roughly the same height, and at least ten centimeters tall. Half were trimmed, while half weren't.

Shar decided that she liked the clean edges better. That way, you could see all the beautiful layers and the different types of filling.

"I'm happy to have learned that you helped each other out during this bake," Yazgrak said as he came in. "I'm hoping that the *Krepp Tortas* we have reflect that cooperative spirit."

"Oh, I'm sure they will," Erwel said. "Just look at these!"

Cyna seemed pleased as well. "I can't wait to taste them all!"

One by one, the judges tried each *Krepp Torta*, pointing out technical or flavor flaws of some, as well as praising others. Some baker's *krepps* had been too thick. Others were uneven.

Shar had made so many *krepps* that she'd been able to choose the ones that were the same thickness and consistency. She was pleased that she'd taken the time to do that.

Erwel spoke up when the judges reached the first of the trimmed cakes. "You know, it isn't traditional to trim the edges. That's where the texture is supposed to come from, with those slightly crispy ends."

"You know, I don't mind that some of these were trimmed," Yazgrak said. "I like being able to see all the layers."

Shar couldn't help but grin as she'd already come to that conclusion.

Of course, all three Elves made a *Krepp Torta* that the judges loved. The Human *Torta* that was so tall got dinged because the flavors hadn't been balanced with all those layers and the judges could only taste the fillings.

Shar's combination of tastes were praised, as usual. The flavors she'd used had just worked, and the addition of the crunch layer had also been very pleasing. Plus, while her decorating hadn't been perfect, it had still been better than her previous attempts.

For the first time, the judges ranked all the contestants. The winner of the first individual bake was the only remaining female Elf, Ithrellas. Shar ranked fifth, and tried not to giggle when Kigora was placed two ranks below her.

The bottom two were both Humans: Ames, one of the first Humans she'd baked with, and Kater, one of the females.

The judges made much of the struggles that were apparent on their plates. It turned out that Kater had gone too far helping other people, and hadn't reserved enough time for herself and her bake.

In the end, Ames went home, both because of his inconsistency when it came to the layers, as well as a lack of balance with the flavors.

The judges had one more surprise for the day before the bakers were dismissed. All of the *Krepp Tortas* were cut into small pieces and the remaining contestants got to taste each other's work.

The number of unusual flavors amazed Shar. And different combinations as well! Some of the tastes were unfamiliar to her, such as the mango and coconut *Torta* that Phury, one of the remaining

Humans had made. And he'd added such a nice almond crunch layer to it.

Kigora's had a rich mixed berry jam spiced with thyme, plus a whipped chocolate cream layer. Part of the reason why she'd ranked so low was because she hadn't remembered to include a crunch layer with her trimmed *Torta*.

The other bakers came up to Shar afterward and praised her for her flavors. She actually got into a nice discussion with Hazzoum about why she'd chosen the milk chocolate—he'd used dark for his, to contrast with the bright ginger and strawberry flavors that he'd included.

Shar found it delightful to be able to talk with the other bakers for a couple of hours after judging, to hear about their choices of flavors and their skills. There was so much she had to learn!

However, she knew that this congenial get together wasn't done by chance.

No, the judges were up to something.

But what?

# Shar

The next morning, Shar tried to be prepared for anything. Most of the remaining bakers assumed that it would be another individual challenge, as they'd done the same research as Shar and knew what had happened historically.

Golodhon agreed with her, though, that it was likely to be a team challenge.

"You remember your rankings from yesterday?" Yazgrak asked after the judges were seated at their table at the edge of the clearing.

The crowd of onlookers had really grown in the last couple of days. It made sense to Shar: the remaining group of contestants were the best of the best.

The bakers nodded, and the top three came to stand before the judges as asked, in the order of their ranking: Ithrellas the Elf first, Marger the Human, then Mionare, another Elf.

"Now, I know we don't traditionally do this, but who wants to always live by tradition?" Cyna asked.

Shar glanced over at Golodhon and nodded.

Yup. Team challenge.

"So you're going to be cooking in teams again," Cyna continued with a great grin.

"You top three are the team captains," Yazgrak said. "Instead of the teams being randomly assigned, you get to choose your teams."

"You need to choose wisely," Erwel warned, "because quite frankly, we don't know how we're judging this yet." Then she glared at Yazgrak, who just shrugged.

Was she really angry at him? Or was this all playing to the crowds?

"Either there will be a team who's clearly in the bottom, and we'll chose one of those three to leave. Or," Cyna said, pausing dramatically, "we'll select a bottom baker from each of the teams and then chose one of them to leave."

"The choice is kind of up to you," Yazgrak said. "Elevate the dishes of everyone on your team so that you can remain. Because you might end up baking with these people again. You never know."

Erwel rolled her eyes at that. "Just help each other out, people. That's all we're asking."

"When you get to your kitchen, you'll find out what you'll be baking," Cyna said. "You'll have a few minutes to plan before your time starts."

Shar didn't envy the three team captains. They were having to make blind picks, not knowing what they'd be baking that day. They might end up picking a baker who didn't have any knowledge of that particular dessert. At least they had been able to taste everyone's *Krepp Torta* the day before, so they had some idea of what the bakers preferred in terms of taste.

But did the captains go with superior flavor combinations, which Shar had already proven herself with, or with a baker who had a wider range, like Hazzoum or Kigora? Or quite frankly, anyone else? Shar had learned the day before that she had the least experience of everyone there, as she'd really only been baking for about a year at that point.

Shar had assumed that the captains would pick balanced teams, with one Human, one Dwarf, and one Elf on each. So it surprised her when Ithrellas, who had first choice, immediately picked Golodhon.

He *had* been ranked fourth by the judges, and he was really good at decorating. Then again, so was Ithrellas. Shar had no idea what her strategy was.

Marger went next, and she picked Shar. "Come on over here, you little flavor assassin."

"Flavor assassin?" Yazgrak asked.

Shar looked down, a little embarrassed, and shrugged. "I guess?" she said.

"I like it!" Yazgrak pronounced.

Her team ended up having two Humans: Marger and Kater, all three of them females.

They chatted a little as they scurried off to the kitchen they were to use for the day.

"It's got to be some sort of dessert flight," Marger said. "With each of us baking different elements."

"They've already done that," Shar pointed out. "And they're not about to repeat themselves. Maybe a flight of pies, though. That would have to be not similar in flavor, but instead, would show a progression?"

"How about a decorative cookie wreath?" Kater suggested. "We'd each have to bake our own types of cookies, then come together to make sure that they were all decorated cohesively?"

That sounded much more like what Shar thought they'd have to do. "But is that complicated enough for the regionals? Just cookies?"

"Maybe instead of cookies, it would be cupcakes?" Marger brought up.

They all turned out to be wrong.

The judges had assigned each team a three-tier cake. Every tier had to have at least three layers, and each team member would be responsible for one tier. The judges hadn't said anything specific, but all the bakers knew that the flavors of all three tiers had to complement one another. In addition, each tier should display different decorating techniques. However, the cake as a whole needed to look as though a single person had done the entire thing.

Shar volunteered to do the bottom tier. She knew how to pipe buttercream flowers and branches, and she'd do a dark chocolate crumble around the base. That way, their cake would look as though it was growing out of the ground.

Kater did the middle layer. She had a recipe for a thin paste that would harden quickly, so she could cut out little houses and possibly some people and do a village scene.

Marger would do the top layer in an ombre, going from the blue background of Kater's to a black top, representing the night sky, with flicks of white scattered across the top of it, like stars. She'd also do tempered chocolate disks then cut them to represent the phases of the moon passing over the top of the cake.

There was some debate about cake flavors. Did they all do the same flavor of cake with different fillings, or three different types of cake with similar fillings?

They eventually listened to Shar and flavored each tier differently. She advocated for each tier to be representative of the level they were on. So her level would be a hearty, walnut-spice cake, Kater would make a standard vanilla cake, while Marger would make something like a *Kényes Sütemény*.

Shar's cake would have an orange flavored filling, with candied walnuts in between the layers for more crunch. Kater would use a bright berry compote with candied almonds, while Marger would use just whipped cream and strawberries, with cashews.

Then, it was a mad rush to get everything accomplished. They tasted each other's cakes, making sure that the flavor and the crumb was correct. Kater ended up brushing on an elderberry soak to each layer of her cake because it came out a little dry. Shar was amazed at how perfectly her own cake turned out, and Marger's was amazing as well.

They'd agreed to each decorate their own tier first, then assemble them into a whole. Shar made buttercream, then more buttercream, then even more, dyeing each batch a different color. (So. Much. Whipping!) Then she filled cloth piping bags with the various colors and started piping as fast as she could.

She knew that she wasn't as fast as an Elf. She still did her best to make her cake appear beautiful. She started with grass along the bottom edge of the tier, above that, some buds, then open flowers rimming the top.

Kater commented on how steady Shar's hand was while she piped her frosting.

"I'm already starting to feel the pressure, and my hand is shaking!" the Human commented.

"I was taught from a young age how to have steady hands," Shar admitted. "If you're faceting a gemstone, just one slip, and you've ruined not a cake, but a really expensive piece of jewelry."

"That's a serious advantage," Kater said. "It will serve you well throughout this competition."

Shar looked around the room, making sure that no one else was watching her before she said to her teammates, "Tap your foot if your hand starts shaking. That energy needs to go someplace."

Her teammates looked a little confused, then tried it, giving Shar smiles and thumbs up after a bit. She could tell that their control wasn't perfect, but if they practiced that technique enough, they, too, would have a leg up in the competition.

There were a few moments of panic as they tried to assemble the cake, as Kater nearly dropped her level instead of sliding it smoothly onto the top of Shar's tier. Then, Marger had made the mistake of putting on her chocolate décor before adding her tier, knocking over a few of the standing crescents as she added her tier to the others.

So there were things they were still trying to fix and cover up when the watcher called time.

Shar knew that the judges would see every mistake that they'd made. However, the flavors were sure to be a hit, and they'd worked really well together as a team.

Hopefully, someone else's team had bigger mistakes.

The judging went in reverse order, starting with Mionare's team. They were the only team to do a more abstract design, as both Ithrellas's and Marger's teams had done somewhat realistic images. Their cake had a beautiful ombre effect, going from a deep, rich purple at the bottom up to a white top. The bottom tier had large paisleys piped on in white butter cream, the middle tier had white flowers that edged into lavender, while the top tier was just dots that also went in an ombre from lilac to dark purple, contrasting with the color of frosting.

The effect was striking, and the judges praised them for how their cake looked, though Yazgrak did question their time management, because while it was beautiful, it also seemed a bit simplistic, particularly compared to the amount of work that had gone into the other teams' decorations.

The tastes, though, evidently made up for how it looked, because everyone was praised for how well the lemon, strawberry, and raspberry went together. Like Shar's team, each tier was a different flavor. And they'd remembered to give a crunch texture for all the tiers, though they'd used the exact same almond brittle in each. Again, Yazgrak questioned their time management as well as their creativity, as the cakes seemed pretty mundane to him, though Cyna and Erwel disagreed.

Next up was Shar's team.

"What a beautiful cake!" Cyna exclaimed as it was brought before the judges.

"I really like that though each layer has distinctly different design elements, the cake as a whole is very cohesive," Yazgrak said.

"And there's a story there," Erwel said. "You don't have to tell me anything. I already see it. And that's some high-level baking there, that story-telling element. Good job."

"However, I can see where you struggled as well," Yazgrak added. "The top tier of the cake isn't as clean as you'd like, am I right?"

Marger nodded. "The moon crescents fell over at the last minute and we had to tried to fix it."

"Those things happen," Yazgrak said, nodding. "And that bottom layer—Shar, right?"

She nodded.

"Your buttercream needed to be slightly colder when you piped it," he said. "The edges are starting to blend into one another."

She hadn't realized that, but now that he'd pointed it out to her, she could see it.

"Still, overall, it's a stunning cake and I can't wait to try it!" Cyna said.

Shar stood, trying not to let her beard tremble as she waited for the judges' critique.

"Okay, so while the outside of the cake was cohesive, the inside isn't," Yazgrak said.

Shar swallowed hard, her throat suddenly dry. She hadn't even considered that the inside needed to not just taste cohesive, but to look similar as well! They'd deliberately chosen styles of cake that matched their tier, rather than working together.

"However," Erwel said, then took a dramatic pause, "the flavors are outstanding. Both on their own as well as when taken together."

Fortunately, Cyna and Yazgrak agreed that the cakes, while so different, complemented each other well.

Then came Ithrellas's group. Their cake was decorated to represent a forest, with bushes and flowers at the bottom, trees with cute forest animals on the middle tier, the branches reaching up to the sky on the top tier, with an orange chocolate disk that represented the sun as a topper.

It was very cohesive, and looked like a single baker had done the work. They did question Kigora about her contribution to the design, or if the Elves had done all the work.

She appeared affronted by the question. "Of course I did my own decorating!" she huffed. "Mine is the bottom tier, and I piped on all those bushes and flowers." Then she paused and added, "Though Golodhon did add some of the tree trunks after we put on the middle tier. That way they'd be connected. We worked together on it, though."

"It's okay," Erwel said. "That sort of work is tricky, and kind of does need to be directed by one person."

The inside of the cake was a revelation to all the bakers, the judges literally gasping at the sight: all nine layers were done in an ombre effect, starting from a dark green, going through a yellow color and up into a white.

That was so clever! Shar wished their group had thought of something like that.

The judges seemed split, though, about the taste. While they loved the color, all three bakers had made the exact same cake, just with different fillings between the layers. In addition, the crunch texture that they'd added was the same for every tier.

Yazgrak wanted to have something more similar to Shar's group, with different cake flavors on every tier, while Cyna didn't mind the cohesive whole. Fortunately, the fillings all went well together.

The bakers were escorted to the far side of the clearing while the judges debated. All of the bakers knew that Mionare's group was in the bottom, that the other two teams were probably safe, as all of the groups worked well together, and the judges didn't have that much to say about the individual bakes.

"I'm the one going home," Mionare told the group. "I was the team leader. Everyone knows that on this sort of challenge, it's generally the leader who goes home."

Though the bakers expressed regret, no one really argued with him. His logic was sound. Golodhon did point out that the judges hadn't necessarily been following with tradition so far, so it might not be the case.

However, no one was really surprised when it turned out that Mionare was the baker leaving them that day.

What did surprise Shar was that her team had won the challenge, despite the mistakes that they'd made. The judges appreciated that they'd put more effort into their cake, making three distinct tiers, that even though they didn't have a cohesive look, the flavor combinations did work.

Finally, the bakers were dismissed.

The three Humans invited everyone to come to their inn later on that evening to share some drinks and stories. Shar was hesitant at first, but eventually agreed.

While she wasn't working the long hours that she had been before the contest, she still found herself more drained and tired. Maybe it was the focus that she had to bring to the challenges, the exacting details the judges demanded, or the standing and waiting for so long before and after each bake.

Still, she was looking forward to meeting with and talking to her new friends.

# Hulda

Hulda had always liked the expression about a Dwarf whose head was so filled with rocks that they didn't hear anything, or were too dumb to notice anything going on around them.

She'd never before thought about someone whose head was so full of *chocolate* and baked goods that they didn't notice things.

However, that expression really seemed to fit Shar at this point.

Hulda understood just how important this contest was. Shar had to win so she would be automatically qualified to the *Chocolates Galore!* contest the following year. (There were some rules about other top bakers also qualifying, but they changed every year. It was much easier to just be granted a place.)

And while Hulda would admit that Shar had a lot of confidence when it came to her passion, she didn't appear to realize that she was the front runner in terms of the current contest.

"You know you're going to win this whole thing, right?" Hulda had asked as she escorted Shar back from the gathering of bakers that she'd gone to that night. Honestly, Hulda had just looked at the outing as if it were a type of guard duty. She wasn't there for herself. She was there to make sure that Shar was all right.

Fortunately, Anthus was fairly quiet, especially at night. Magical lanterns kept the major street lit, and the watch patrolled regularly.

It hadn't taken Hulda long to figure out which parts of the city were more sketchy and which weren't. However, she'd been impressed that even in the poorer areas, the guard took their duty seriously and those blocks were also patrolled diligently.

"I can't think that way," Shar said, shaking her head. "I know, they're calling me the flavor assassin. But my decorating skills are always getting dinged by the judges. I have to get better at those. And quickly."

"You're the underdog," Hulda said. "And the crowd always loves a rags-to-riches story. Plus, the judges are loving your flavors."

"Yes, but I could fall. I could make a mistake. I could be assigned something I don't know how to bake. There is still so much for me to learn!" Shar exclaimed. "Plus, the others are so good. So talented."

"Even Kigora?" Hulda teased. The two Dwarves had barely acknowledged each other's presence at the gathering. However, their eyes had always drifted over, and they'd watched each other a lot from afar. Like, A Lot. She'd seen it.

Shar sighed. "Yes. Even her. She's been baking forever, and has tricks I haven't learned yet."

"You know, someone who didn't know your history would assume that there was some sort of relationship between the pair of you, based on how you danced around each other," Hulda said.

"We kind of do have a relationship," Shar pointed out. "She hates me."

Hulda nodded. "And do you hate her?"

Shar sighed. "She's everything I'm not," she said softly. "She's a baker by trade. She's Yazgrak's niece! She's not just allowed to follow her true passion, her skills fall in line with her family expectations. She's talented and smart and cute and I have a feeling that she'll be there in the end, and will beat me."

Hulda didn't comment on how Shar had mentioned that Kigora was cute.

Kigora also quite possibly thought that Shar was cute, given the speculative looks that she'd shot the other Dwarf.

However, Hulda also recognized that it was far too soon to try bringing the pair of them together. They were both too stubbornly focused on the contest at this point.

Maybe afterward, though...

"What have you and Leena been up to while I've been baking?" Shar asked. She sounded guilty.

"Don't you worry about us," Hulda said. "I've been working with some of the guard, training and sparring. When I haven't been browsing the mercantile for cheap fabrics."

So far, she hadn't had much success. Everything here was just so expensive! On the other hand, there was a much larger array of materials to choose from.

She hadn't been able to borrow a sewing machine, so everything she'd done had been handstitched.

Fortunately, she'd had plenty of time to do handwork. "And Leena has been catching up with old friends of hers. She knows a lot of the mentors of the other bakers, and so they've been getting together for tea most every day."

"That's how she knows everyone who's competing!" Shar said. "I'd wondered about that."

"She's a good mentor," Hulda said. She honestly didn't know about how Leena cooked, but she really had been looking out for Shar the entire time they'd been there.

"She has been," Shar said. "I hope you find someone as worthy."

Hulda gave her a great grin. "Don't you worry about me. I'll keep working on my skills, just as you have been. I'll make you proud."

"I'm already proud of you," Shar said seriously. "And in case I haven't said it often enough, thank you for coming here with me. I know we haven't talked or hung out much. But I really appreciate you being here."

"Don't worry, I know," Hulda said, though it was good to hear it. "And you'll get your fill of me on the journey home. When I have to guard the winner of the regional bakeoff."

Shar just snorted. After a few moments, as they turned the corner and the Rusty Nail Inn was in sight, she paused and added, "Seriously, though. Thank you. For being here. And for believing in me."

"You just keep knocking them over with your flavors," Hulda said. "You'll be fine."

Shar nodded, but didn't look convinced.

Hulda knew that Shar wouldn't really believe it until she won the whole contest.

Which Hulda just knew that Shar would.

# To Turn One's Face Away

～∞～

All the different people living on Indunel have their various gods, goddesses, spirit animals and sacred spas.

How can you tell that this particular pile of rocks is holy?

You can't.

This is particularly the case when it comes to the Elves, who make what could generously be called an altar by piling three stones on top of one another, then placing a leaf on top of that. (Elves, ya know?)

The thing is, though, that leaf never ages. It never gets dried up or brittle. It stays green and supple despite possibly lying on top of the same three rocks for centuries. It generally doesn't blow off, either, though it isn't affixed in any way. And if you're some fancy Human with a spell that detects magic, these altars don't register.

There's an ancient myth among the Elves that takes place when the three-rock-and-leaf combination altars were rare. However, for one particularly devout Elf's altar, the leaf didn't stay green. Instead, when the Elf came to sprinkle dew drops on it one morning, she found that the leaf had turned to pure gold and now held three seeds. Those seeds were planted in distant forests and grew into the famed

213

Arwenbraneas trees—those golden leaf splendors—that make up the heart of each of the Elven forests.

(As there are more than just those three trees, and those three forests, chances are this is a very mythical story.)

The Humans tend to build little houses for their gods, filled with rich furnishings. They'll put out tiny dishes of food and thimble-sized cups of drink. Of course, which god gets the biggest house depends entirely on the area. Coastal regions favor Jamarte, their god of the seas, while inland people tend to build bigger houses for Arior-thyne, the goddess of the earth.

The representations of the Plainsmens' gods are long, intricately carved wooden totems that they carry with them as they follow their nomadic routes. (No one had ever stolen one, due to its sheer size and weight.) The Maurinan, on the other hand, subscribe to the belief that any image of the divine is sacrilege. To properly worship, one must dance. So every morning, they do a quick little jig, not just to get the body moving but also to express their gratitude to their primary goddess.

Dwarves work in stone, of course. Ancient temples contain images of Erisgrungrid, Snazalgrid, and Malamoragrid (goddess of earth, and gods of gems and the forge, respectively) that are four to five stories tall. They sit on their thrones, looking down on all. (How the ancient temple in the Ziramunz Mountains came to be lost is yet another long tale of betrayal most foul [mostly by the Elves] that would involve at least three kegs of mead and several hours. Tack on yet another hour to learn about how the temple was rediscovered. Possibly a couple more to hear about the restoration efforts, and the arguments between using ancient methods of carving verses modern techniques.)

What's interesting about these ancient representations of the Ewarven deities is that while they all have a single head, they also have between four to eight faces, each facing a different direction. The expressions on the faces may or may not be identical.

For modern temples, the figures of the gods and goddesses are shrunk down. They're bigger than Humans—eight to ten feet tall—but possibly not as tall as an Ice Giant. There are no altars, per se, in Dwarven dwellings. Instead, every Dwarf you meet will have some stones that have been blessed by a priest or priestess that are strewn on their bedside table, and in their workshop as well.

So when a Dwarf comments that a particular god or goddess has turned their face away from them, this is an act that's almost impossible for a deity to do.

It means the Dwarf's luck isn't just bad. It's awful. The situation might be hopeless.

And the Dwarves have no Lady Luck, willing to step in and help.

# Shar

⤜∞⤛

The next challenge was *not* going well. First of all, Shar was having to bake cupcakes, something she wasn't bad at but wasn't that good at either. Dwarves preferred crumbly pastries over something as doughy as a cupcake.

Next, while the baking was fairly easy, the decorating was not. The cupcakes were to be smooshed together, with the tops of them frosted into a cohesive whole.

The bakers had each been assigned a woodland creature that their pull apart cupcakes were supposed to be decorated to represent, such as beavers, raccoons, bears, skunks, bobcats, and so on. Shar had been assigned a deer.

The flavors had to represent her animal as well. Instead of easy things like berries, all the bakers had been given various plants that grew in the forest to use.

Shar had been given a grass that she'd never even considered cooking with: clover.

The leaves tasted fairly grassy, but they weren't as bitter as she'd thought they'd be. The clover flowers were surprisingly sweet. Still with that green, grassy taste underneath, though.

It was a challenge that the Elves were certain to excel at, as they regularly used all of the various plants that had been given out. Fortunately, the lessons the judges had imparted meant that for the first few minutes of the bake, the Elves had gone through every grass and talked about its characteristics, helping the bakers tremendously.

In addition to coming up with something that went well with clover, Shar also had to use marzipan—a sweet almond paste—to make a figure of a deer to decorate the top of her pull-apart cupcakes.

Shar knew she had to rush. The cupcakes *had* to cool down before she could decorate them, or the buttercream would melt and slide off everywhere.

However, she had to take her time with the batter, to get the right flavor combination, to make sure that the clover wasn't disguised but also not disgusting. Pistachios appeared to be the right combination that enhanced both flavors. Then she was going to use a clover-honey sweetened chocolate for her filling.

She was one of the last bakers to put her two dozen cupcakes into the oven as she started her filling and whipping her buttercream.

When Shar pulled her cupcakes out of the oven, she realized that while the outsides had baked, the insides were still raw. Turned out that the clover had added too much moisture to the batter.

For this bake, Shar hadn't made any extra cupcakes. However, she'd also learned to never throw out the remains of her batter. She adjusted her ratios and put a second batch into the oven as quickly as she could.

While she waited, she started in on her marzipan deer. Since she was going to have so little time to decorate, she decided to sculpt a rather large deer head to cover most of the cupcakes.

The problem was that she was no sculptor. The deer looked more like a horse. Or a cow. The nose was too wide, the nostrils too prominent. She was able to do some nice shading with some brown-tinted cocoa butter. But honestly, it was a pretty homely creature.

Her cupcakes tasted really good. The grassy notes of the clover underneath the milk chocolate were further mellowed by the pista-chios. The filling—a clover-honey mixed-berry compote—brought in some lovely bright notes and acidity.

Honestly, it was a delicious cupcake.

They just weren't cooling fast enough. She was going to have to start frosting them before they'd cooled.

At first, she believed that maybe it was going to be all right. Then she watched the frosting start to melt.

Nope. This was a disaster.

She could only hope that someone did worse than she did.

Otherwise she was going home.

Judging went about as well as Shar expected.

With the exception of the Elves, everyone else struggled with the grasses and unusual flavors they'd been assigned. Kigora had managed to make something vaguely edible, but the Humans in particular had all done poorly.

Maybe Shar could squeak by?

However, her buttercream was a blobby mess by the time her cupcakes were brought before the judges.

At least the marzipan head hadn't slid off? If that was a good thing, given its general shape...

Yazgrak looked at the thing in front of him, then up at Shar.

"Is this supposed to be a horse?" he asked.

"No. It's a cow, right?" Erwel said.

Shar sighed. "It's supposed to be a deer."

"I'm not reading deer, dear," Cyna said. "Plus, this isn't a forest. The grass and sky have all melted together. It looks like an under-water scene. Nothing is distinct."

Shar gulped and nodded. "I had to make a second batch of

cupcakes, and they hadn't really cooled by the time I started decorating."

"You made a second batch of cupcakes?" Yazgrak said, spearing her with a look.

"That way the flavors would be right," Shar said. "The first batch was too wet, due to the clover. They were raw on the inside. And I wasn't about to serve you raw cupcakes."

"Your flavor was clover, right?" Cyna said.

"Yes, ma'am," Shar said.

"Are these going to taste good?" Yazgrak asked.

"Better than they look," Shar promised. "They're a milk-chocolate cupcake with clover and pistachios, filled with a berry compote that's been sweetened with clover honey."

The judges all took the smallest of bites. (Seriously, some of those cupcakes that had gone before hers had tasted pretty awful.)

Yazgrak smiled and nodded. "That's really unusual. I'm not sure I like it. But the flavors work really well together. This is more balanced than most of the desserts we've tasted today."

Erwel shook her head. "He has no idea what he's talking about, girl. You made the clover sing. Sing!"

"I disagree," Cyna said. "They're still a bit grassy. And while I believe you, that this batch cooked better than your first batch, they're still a bit gooey inside."

"They do taste better than they look, though," Yazgrak added.

"Thank you, judges," Shar said as she stepped back.

Maybe she'd made it through? Hers did look the worst, though.

Shar withdrew with the rest of the bakers to the far side of the grassy open area. The judges appeared to be having a heated debate. A magical barrier prevented the contestants from hearing anything they said.

The onlookers who'd bought a ticket to the proceedings that day were able to hear them, though.

Golodhon came over to speak with Shar. "I'm sure you'll get through," he said softly.

"You will, at any rate," Shar said. "The judges really loved your flavors. And your design."

He'd been given a duck pond grass, and his animal had been a beaver. Shar had learned during the cook that while the green stems weren't edible, the white roots were tender and sweet. (Evidentially most grasses were the same. Who knew? Besides the Elves, of course, and they didn't really count.)

In addition to a beautifully sculpted little beaver out of marzipan, Golodhon had made a little dam out of chocolate to sit on top of the cupcakes. He'd used almonds as the buck teeth in his creature, and had used those as a crunch element in his cupcakes. Shar had tried the sample he'd given her and been surprised at how delicious it was. The vanilla cake had an unusual sweet undertone that evidently came from the grass, and paired well with the spicy swamp-berry jam he'd made.

This contest had really opened her eyes to all the new flavors that were out there, things she'd not only never tried but frequently had never even thought of.

"Thank you," Golodhon said. He gave her a beautiful smile. He was wearing his usual green and yellow robes, though his hair pins were bright blue butterflies that day.

"So if I don't see you again after this, I'll have to come visit you in the Ashveil Mountains someday," Shar volunteered.

"You're not going anywhere," Golodhon said. He looked around, making sure that no one was listening in. Then he lowered his voice almost to a whisper. "You're the crowd favorite—a fan favorite. And while that won't always save you, I think it will this time. You just have to wow the judges with something next time."

"Crowd favorite?" Shar said. Nowhere, in any of the official documents or news reports about the contests was that written about. However, Leena had mentioned it as a possibility, that sometimes a person was so popular that the judges kept them around. She hadn't seen it happen during her contest, but talking with bakers from previous contests they all believed it had happened. Plus, the judges also had some pressure from the sponsors to keep certain individuals as they still auctioned off plates of dessert.

Fan favorites brought in a lot of money to the contest.

Still, Shar's beard trembled when the judges finally called the bakers back.

"This was a tough challenge for most of you," Yazgrak announced. "Though we had one star. Golodhon, you were the clear winner today. Congratulations."

Shar beamed at her fellow baker. (Friend? Maybe. Though it was strange to think that of all the other bakers here, the one she'd become most friendly with was an Elf.) (She couldn't wait to tell Mother, just to see her reaction.)

Then the judges called Shar and Hazzoum up.

Crap. This was it.

"Hazzoum, your pull-apart cupcakes were beautifully decorated," Yazgrak said.

Shar nodded. She'd seen them. He'd had a skunk, and had done amazing minimalistic black-and-white themed decorations. Instead of trying to do the full animal, he'd just done the skunk's tail in marzipan. The design had been elegant.

"However, child, those cupcakes of yours were inedible," Erwel said.

"Whereas Shar, your decorating was a disaster," Cyna said. "It more resembled an underwater scene than a forest, with the buttercream all melting together. And your deer head looked more like a horse."

"Or a cow," Erwel added, nodding.

"Now, this decision wasn't easy, and it wasn't unanimous," Yazgrak said, glancing over at his fellow judges.

They nodded in agreement.

"But at the end of the day, do we want something that merely looks good? Or something that tastes good?" Yazgrak said. "This *is* a design contest as well as a baking contest."

He shot the other judges a hard look.

Cyna shrugged, while Erwel gave him a big grin.

Yazgrak didn't roll his eyes at the Elf, but Shar believed that the impulse was strong in him.

"So we're sending Hazzoum home today," Yazgrak said.

Shar felt her jaw drop, then snapped her mouth back shut.

She wasn't going home?

After saying goodbye to Hazzoum, Yazgrak caught Shar's eye. "This is your last save. You need to bring it next time."

"I will," Shar said. "I promise. Thank you, judges."

"Thank these two," Yazgrak said honestly. "They're the ones who argued for you. I would have sent you home."

Shar gulped and nodded.

She had her work cut out for her.

But she'd prove to the judges that their faith in her was warranted.

No room for any more mistakes.

The pressure was on.

# Shar

Shar gathered with her fellow bakers in the bright morning light. A large crowd already surrounded the meadow, possibly bigger than the day before. Leena had warned her that might be the case—that every day the contest went on, more people would come to see them.

Particularly since Shar was considered the fan favorite. She saw a couple of homemade banners that had her name on them. One even proclaimed, "Shar, the flavor assassin!"

Other people also had their well-wishers. A group of Elves had signs that proclaimed Golodhon and Ithrellas as the champions. Kigora had a large contingent of Dwarves chanting her name. Even the Humans had their cheering section.

Shar suspected that it would only get more crazy from there on out.

Cyna started the proceedings that morning. "I've been pointing out to the others that since we favored Elves in this last bake, that for this bake, it should be time for the Humans to shine. Am I right?"

The crowd behind around exploded into applause, though the group of Dwarves bearing signs for Kigora did boo a little.

"This isn't my favorite challenge," Erwel said. "But I've agreed to it because we have such talented bakers this year. Don't let me down," she warned.

"The challenge is to take an ingredient that's primarily used by Human bakers and make it shine in your own desserts," Yazgrak said.

Shar glanced at Golodhon, who had a resigned look on his face.

What were the judges up to?

"Chilis!" Cyna announced, uncovering a tray that was in the center of the judges' table.

"Some of these chilis are really hot," Erwel said. "You better not be burning out my tastebuds."

Shar gulped. Leena had mentioned once that she should learn to cook with spicier ingredients but there just hadn't been time.

The judges labeled all the chilis that the bakers had access to: tiger cane, ivory flower, yellow dragon, silver flame, and demon root. Each baker had to use at least one of the chilis in their dessert. They weren't each assigned a chili, but rather, got to choose which one (or ones) that they wanted to use.

The Elves had helped everyone out during the bake the previous day, explaining the various forest ingredients and their properties. One of the three remaining Humans decided *not* to help—Phury— while both Kater and Marger did, quickly ranking the chilis in terms of heat and warning people to wear the gloves that had been provided when handling the hot ingredient.

The ivory flower evidently was the spiciest, despite its mild-sounding name. Shar did know that white flames burned hottest in a forge, and she supposed that might be the reason why the innocent-looking yellowish-white pepper had that name.

Both Shar and Golodhon took the yellow dragon—called a *citron sárkárny* in Elvish. It wasn't the mildest—that aspect surprisingly belonged to the demon root. Shar was determined to show the judges that she could do something not just flavorful, but showy as well.

Most people were doing chocolate, as Kater and Marger had explained that chocolate and chilies went really well together.

Shar decided not to buck the trend, and put together her simplest (but most delicious) chocolate cake. It would have two tiers, with two layers of cake for each tier. Once the cakes came out of the oven and had cooled, she brushed a chili-infused simple syrup onto the tops, letting the flavor soak in.

While the cakes were baking, Shar simmered chopped up yellow dragon chilis in her cream, then added the cream to her melted dark chocolate to make a chili-flavored ganache that turned out surprisingly delicious. Once the cakes came out of the oven and had cooled sufficiently, in addition to the ganache, she used an orange compote between the cake layers as all three tastes combined well. Then she added an almond brittle that again had been flavored with the chilis for her texture.

Because Shar had baked this cake so often, she was able to start decorating long before most of the other bakers.

That was good, because she was going to need every minute.

If Shar had had a week or more to prepare for this challenge, she might have worked with Cousin Algruzlea to design a mold that produced pepper-looking bonbons. As it was, she had to make do with some oblong rounded molds that she stuck together, then added little caps to, to make them look a bit like the peppers she'd been using. While the shells of the bonbons were dark chocolate, the inside contained more of her chili-flavored ganache, and she drew lines of a yellow glaze down the sides, again, to make each bonbon look more like the chili it was supposed to represent.

Part of why she'd chosen the yellow dragon peppers was because of the color. She decorated the outside of her cake with a smooth yellow buttercream, a plain canvas for the rest of her chocolate decorations.

Shar decided to go all out and do something fancy, instead of anything whimsical, like shooting stars.

The bakers had access to a special paper that wouldn't absorb the chocolate spread over it, but could then be shaped. She did chocolate swirls on this—spreading a thin layer of tempered semi-sweet chocolate, then carefully rolling the paper into a log shape. Once the chocolate had set, she was able to gently pull the chocolate off the paper and have beautiful swirls that she could use to decorate the top of her cake.

When the watcher called time, Shar was able to step back from her cake with a smile. It was beautiful as well as tasty. The bonbons told the judges what they were getting in terms of flavors, and the chocolate decorations made her piece look elegant.

Hopefully, the judges agreed.

"Chocolate. How surprising," Yazgrak said in a flat voice when Shar presented her cake to the judges.

She withheld her sigh. Maybe she should have bucked the trend and done something other than chocolate for the judges?

But what? She'd have to ponder that at some later point.

"I'm glad to see you pulled out all the stops with this," Erwel said. "It is beautiful."

"And you said these bonbons are all filled with a chili-flavored ganache?" Cyna asked.

"Yes, ma'am," Shar said. "I tried to make them look like little chilis."

"If I hadn't known that this was a chili challenge, I'm not sure that I would have realized that these are supposed to be chilis," Yazgrak grumbled.

"Oh, hush. You know you love this," Erwel said.

Leena had explained the night before that Yazgrak couldn't be seen choosing favorites, so he was likely to be judging both her and Kigora more harshly. Then again, the other judges couldn't be seen to be favoring their own races, so it worked out.

Shar cut open the cake and served the judges each a slice, along with a couple of the chili bonbons.

This time, when the judges' eyes all grew wide, Shar felt confident, not afraid.

Cyna sat back and started making dancing motions with her hands.

"Have you ever cooked with chilis before?" Erwel asked.

"No ma'am," Shar said.

"I hope you wrote down this recipe," Yazgrak said. "Because I want it."

"I want to take this home with me," Cyna said. "Do you have any more of the bonbons?"

"I do," Shar said. She plucked off the rest of the bonbons and brought them over on a plate for the judges.

Cyna grabbed the plate before the others could take any. "Mine!" she said.

"Oh, come on. That's not fair," Yazgrak complained.

"We know where you sleep," Erwel threatened.

"Fine," Cyna said, putting the plate down so the other judges could each help themselves to a couple more bonbons, though she was able to keep the majority of them for herself.

"Now, I have a challenge for you," Yazgrak said after the judges had finished squabbling. "I know you can make delicious desserts. We have proof of that. But you need to bring your decoration skills up another notch."

"He's right, child. This is beautiful work, but you need to take it to the next level," Erwel said, pausing for a moment before she continued. "This was decorative. But there's no soul in it."

"Exactly," Yazgrak said. "You gave us pretty on a plate. And I'm not upset with that. However, if you expect to win this contest, you need more of *you* in your decorations."

"Thank you, judges," Shar said when she realized that was all they were going to tell her.

She had *no idea* what the judges meant by that. What wasn't her? She made all the chocolate herself. She'd done the hard work. How could it not be her?

She was so confused.

In the end, one of the Humans, Phury, went home. He'd been too aggressive in his spices and Erwel complained that her throat was still burning even after trying all the other dishes.

Despite the judges' critiques, Shar was still proclaimed the winner.

Though the other bakers were going to have a little party that evening, Shar declined.

She had a lot of thinking to do about her decorations.

Hopefully Leena would have some clue as to what the judges were talking about.

# Leena

Leena couldn't help but feel her heart sitting wrong as she listened to her poor lass wail.

It was hard to be told that what ye loved weren't right. Or weren't good enough.

Leena sat and listened, patting Shar's hand until she wound herself down. The contest was taking a toll on the poor thing, as Leena well knew. Always coming up with new delights. Pushing yerself past what ye thought ye could. Working and scheming and trying ta please the judges while listening to yer own soul.

Tough place.

But her Shar could do it. Leena had faith.

"So why's ye baking here?" Leena asked eventually.

"To prove to my family that I can do this, that I should be allowed to continue this path, so that I *don't* have to go back and facet more gemstones."

The girl's full body shudder at that made Leena grin.

"Now, that's all well and good," Leena said, patting Shar's hand again. "But that's all out there," she said, waving her hand to the side to encompass all those things Shar had listed. "What's in *here* that's driving ye?" She actually poked Shar in the chest, not letting herself be distracted by just how soft her beard was.

Girl had some serious beard oil, that was for certain.

"I love chocolate?" Shar said, uncertain of herself. "I love the taste of it. The different types of it, how it can go from something with the perfect snap to something that melts as you bite into it, like that ganache I made the other day. I love how malleable it is, how I can form it into shapes."

"Now, ye remember that group challenge ye did? With the three-tiered cake?" Leena asked.

Shar nodded.

"One of the things the judges commented on was how it told a story," Leena pointed out.

Shar nodded.

"Ye need ta start thinking of the stories ye want to tell in choco-late," she continued. "Personally, I think Yazgrak was being a little harsh on ye this round. Those chilis ye made did tell a story. But that fancy part on top? How was that connected?"

Shar opened her mouth then shut it again. "They weren't," she said after a moment. "I was just showing off," she added looking down.

"That's what the judges felt, too," Leena said. "Ye were decorat-ing. Not story telling."

"What should I have done?" Shar said plaintively.

"I don't know," Leena said with a shrug. "What were the chilis telling ye?"

"They were warm. Spicy," Shar said. "They were different. Unusual. New."

"So what kind of decorations could ye make to reflect that?" Leena asked.

Shar sat and thought for a moment before she gasped. "Shooting stars!" she said. "I'd thought about that as a possibility, but discarded it. I didn't think it would be elegant enough for Erwel."

"Why shooting stars?" Leena prompted, though she had a good idea what her lass would say.

"The brightness of the flavor of the yellow dragon chilis. The discovery of new tastes. The pushing myself to new heights, learning and doing and growing more than I ever could have thought possible," Shar said, sounding breathless.

"How would ye have done the stars?" Leena said.

Shar started talking about how to stand the stars up on her cake, the chocolate tails that she could have trailing behind them, how they would have been bright yellow outlined with dark chocolate.

Leena interrupted about halfway through Shar's brainstorming session.

"Ye feel that passion? Welling up inside? How it bubbles and burns?" Leena said.

Shar nodded, her eyes wide.

"That's what the judges are looking for. Not the fancy, though they do like that. They want te see yer story. Told in yer decorations. In yer cakes and cookies and bonbons. How are ye going to bring *that* to yer next bake?"

Shar grew thoughtful before she nodded. "I need to think more before I fall into my usual patterns of decorations," she declared.

"No," Leena said, her hand falling hard on the table between them, making Shar jump.

"Ye need to *feel* more," she said, poking Shar again, this time in her gut. (Again, what in the names of the various gods did the girl use on her beard? Leena had never felt something so soft, yet always so well contained in braids!) "Thinking is what got ye into trouble this time. *Feeling* is what yer doing now. Relating that new experience, telling yer story in chocolate."

"I think I understand," Shar said. "But this is going to make the challenges so much harder."

Leena tilted her head from side to side. "Maybe so. But maybe not. Ye cooking from yer heart should help in some ways."

"No, I get that," Shar said. "It means figuring out what my heart wants to say, though. That's the challenge."

"Exactly," Leena said. "Ye can do it. I've seen ye. It's the reason why the challenge times are all so short. Ye don't have time to over-think what yer doing. Ye got to go with yer gut. So don't overthink. Just do what yer heart says. And ye'll be fine."

Shar didn't look completely convinced as she toddled off to bed.

Leena had faith in her lass. Would she win the whole thing? Leena had her private doubts sometimes.

But if Shar could find that fire, then bring it out, show it to the world, no one would stand a chance against her.

# Shar

Shar was still thinking about what Leena had pulled out of her the night before as she faced the judges in the morning.

There were six contestants remaining, two from each race. Shar knew that wasn't deliberate on the judges' part. Previous contests had been very unequal by this time, more than once with three Humans, three Elves, and no Dwarves. With the exception of Kigora, Shar approved of the remaining six. Though as she hadn't had to work with Kigora again, at least she hadn't had much close contact with the other Dwarf's unpleasant attitude.

"I know that normally, it's all individual challenges at this point in the competition," Cyna said. "But we're doing another partner challenge! And you get to pick your partner."

Shar's head immediately whipped to the side and she looked at Golodhon. He rolled his eyes at her but nodded, walking over to where she stood.

Ithrellas and Marger smiled at each other and stood together, which left Kigora and Kater together.

"So we've been talking about traditions, both with ingredients as well as recipes," Yazgrak said. "I'm sure you're both familiar with making *Krumzkag*," he said, nodding at first Kigora, then Shar.

Shar nodded, internally sighing. *Krumzkag* was a flaky, layered pastry, swirled with cinnamon and sugar. It took forever to make because in order to achieve those flaky layers, the baker had to roll out the dough, fold it, cool it, then roll it out again, shave ice-cold butter on the dough, fold it again, cool it, and so on. What was called the thousand-layer dough went through a similar process, though it was then baked in sheets, puffing up beautifully to at least twice its height if done correctly.

"I love the delicate, crumbly layers of *Krumzkag*, how the butter glaze browns, the sweetness of the fillings. Done right, it's one of my favorite desserts," Yazgrak said.

"Me, my favorite is the *Kichit Süto*," Erwel said.

Shar didn't hear Golodhon's groan, but she felt his lack of enthusiasm.

The *Kichit Süto*, which basically translated into *small oven*, was made from a very delicate cake that was layered, sliced into small squares, then covered with a special type of icing that had to be cooked then poured at the exact correct time over the tiny squares. If the icing was too hot, it melted the cakes and the ganache between the layers. If it wasn't hot enough, it wouldn't pour smoothly, and the baker would get a dull icing with lumps, instead of shiny and smooth.

"I love how such a small bite can have an amazing array of flavors," Erwel continued. "Plus the decorations on it need to be elevated and elegant."

Shar nodded. She didn't envy Golodhon at all having to make something like that.

"Then we Humans, of course, have our rainbow cake!" Cyna said. "Soft, moist cake, with colorful sprinkles and sticky frosting."

Shar had heard about this dessert, but she'd never made it. It consisted of a white cake that used egg whites instead of some other leavening agent, and didn't contain butter. For the recipe she'd read, it called for at least three layers of cake, each colored differently. Not in an ombre, no, something where the colors practically clashed. (Humans. So gauche.) The icing was sticky and would hold swirls that the baker added as it set. Again, as it was a cooked icing, it was difficult to judge the correct temperature.

The hardest part of a rainbow cake was making the sprinkles. They had to be mixed, spun out, then dried, before they could be added to the batter of the cake. They also needed to go on the top of the cake as part of the decoration.

"Of course, it would be too easy for the bakers who are familiar with these desserts to be the ones to make them," Yazgrak said.

Shar heard the crowd gasp. She felt her beard trembling with anticipation.

"So remember how we urged y'all to work together?" Erwel said. "We decided to give you yet another opportunity to do so!"

How could she sound so pleased with this challenge? It was going to be absolute torture!

"Shar and Marger, you'll each be making a *Kichit Süto*," Erwel continued.

That made sense to Shar Though they weren't Elves, they each had an Elf as their teammate.

"Golodhon and Kater, you'll be making a *Krumzkag*," Yazgrak said with a huge smile. Again, their teammates were Dwarves.

"And that leaves Kigora and Ithrellas making me rainbow cakes!" Cyna added.

"So you understand the challenge?" Erwel asked. "Though you're in teams, you'll each be making your own dish. Your team member is who decided what y'all have to do."

Shar nodded. She was having to make an Elven dessert because Golodhon was her partner, whereas he was having to make a Dwarven dessert.

"Listen to your partner. Heed what they say," Yazgrak warned.

"You won't be able to physically help each other, so each of you will have to describe everything to your partner accurately."

Shar wasn't exactly certain what that meant, but the judges weren't providing any more guidance. When she glanced at Golodhon, he had a determined look on his face.

They could do this. Shar could help Golodhon make the best *Krumzkag* she knew how. And she felt certain that he would help her every way he could.

They might not win, but they were two of the best bakers here.

They could do this.

Together.

Two drastic changes had been made to the shared kitchen overnight.

The first was that the space had been rearranged, with six cooking stations on one side, while the other side had been opened up and an audience sat there.

Shar gulped. The crowd was behind a barrier, so they couldn't shout or otherwise distract the contestants. However, they'd be watching intently. A couple had spy glasses so they could see everything.

It took her a moment to realize the other huge change.

Namely, that large black barriers had been raised between every one of the cooking stations.

Shar gasped when she realized the implications.

The judges were ensuring that the bakers couldn't physically help each other. They could only *talk* to their partner through the cook. Not look at the dough, not feel how it was turning out. No, Shar would have to describe every aspect of the dough while Golodhon worked it.

And he wouldn't be able to make suggestions to her when it

came to decorating—she could ask for help but he wouldn't be able to see what she was doing.

The difficulty of this challenge had just grown exponentially.

Shar looked over at Golodhon as they listened to the last-minute instructions from the watchers.

He gave her a serious nod.

They could do this.

Together they'd either rise or fall.

Surprisingly, the two who appeared to be having the most difficulty were Ithrellas and Marger. Shar had always found Marger to be reasonable. She liked the Human's dry wit. As the pair had actively chosen each other, not just been the left-overs like Kigora and Kater, she'd expected them to work better together.

Yet, Shar kept hearing raised voices to the left of her. (Shar and Golodhon had the center two stations, with Ithrellas and Marger on her left, and to the right, past Golodhon, were Kigora and Kater.) It seemed that Ithrellas had her own ideas about the rainbow cake, and the sprinkles, that Marger didn't agree with.

Shar tried to ignore the pair of them as she focused on her own bake. Fortunately, between her and Golodhon, they'd been able to time things well.

In between layers, while Golodhon waited for his dough to cool, he could guide Shar in her baking. They'd agreed that Shar shouldn't do chocolate this time, as that was only one of the traditional flavors of the *Kichit Süto*. Instead, Shar went with hazelnut, using a hazelnut liqueur. She wanted to add chopped, candied hazelnuts to the batter as well, but Golodhon warned against it. The cake itself needed to be soft and tender. She could add crunch between the layers of the cake, though that wasn't necessarily traditional.

Her cake turned out well. She started cooking the frosting as

Golodhon rolled out his dough again. She couldn't see it, but she had him describe the texture to her.

"How well does it pull apart?" Shar asked.

"It's stretchy, but then it breaks," Golodhon said. "It also feels a little greasy with all the butter I've been adding."

"Has the butter melted? Or is it layered in?" Shar asked, concerned.

"There are still chunks of it," Golodhon said with obvious distaste.

"That's good," Shar said. "You don't want all that butter to melt until the dough is in the oven. That will help with the light and crispy texture. You probably only need to chill it one more time after this."

"Good," Golodhon said. "How is your frosting?"

"Not hot enough," Shar admitted. "I'm taking the temperature up slowly."

"Do you have a couple of test pieces of cake?" Golodhon asked.

"I do," Shar said. While the rest of her cake wasn't cool enough yet to frost, she'd made three pans worth of cake, just so she'd have extras. She cut some of the still warm pieces out to use for testing, to make sure the chocolate frosting that she was making had the right consistency and temperature.

Then Shar turned to the decorations. Traditionally, bakers would place a delicate tuille cookie on top of each *Kichit Süto*, or perhaps a sliver of perfectly tempered chocolate. Occasionally, the most delicate of berries were used. She could also pipe a tiny design on the top.

However, Shar wanted something to represent herself on the plate, to make this dessert her own version of it. It wasn't possible to make rock candy in such a short amount of time, though she could see in her mind's eye just how striking that could be—tiny structures of elegant sugar crystals.

Instead, she went with melted sugar that she drizzled over ice cubes. As the ice melted, the sugar wrapped around it in interesting shapes. (She'd seen other people use it to make sea coral, as well as spindly trees.) She was able to pick out a few that looked similar enough to crystals that she was pleased.

Shar guided Golodhon in adding the cinnamon sugar and berry mix to the dough before folding it together one last time. While the berry taste wasn't traditional, he wanted to put his own mark on his dessert as well.

He then sliced the dough into small squares and placed each in a muffin tin, brushing melted butter on the top. His design would include tiny raspberries that he'd use to decorate the top, three on each of the *Krumzkag*. Shar had approved of the added berries.

When the watcher called time, all the magical barriers disappeared. Loud applause rolled out across the kitchen from the onlookers, the wave of noise startling Shar.

She glanced over at Golodhon's *Krumzkag*. They looked perfect, the browned butter and berries bringing an elegance that the rustic dessert normally lacked.

Golodhon smiled at her own offering. The frosting had flowed off the cakes beautifully, and she really liked the crystal-like sugar decorations.

Now, it was up to the judges.

Before the bakers were called in front of the judges, they were given the opportunity to slice up the extras they'd made and to serve them to the audience. Shar didn't blush—Dwarves don't blush—but she did feel a weird floating sensation in her stomach as people from the audience praised her baking and gushed over how impressive her performance had been.

Each station had a long line in front of it, with audience members eager to try the cooking of their favorite.

Shar told herself that it didn't matter that her line was longest.

The others baked just as well as she had and she could still be sent home.

Probably not today, though.

She served Golodhon a taste and he gave her a hearty thumb's up approval. She got to try his *Krumzkag*, and had to admit that while the berries wouldn't go over with all Dwarves, they were sour enough that they made a good contrast with the sweet, buttery dough.

What else could she do with the *Krumzkag* when she got home? Could she start a new trend? She'd have to ask Leena about it.

Shar tried to remember to tell the audience members about her sponsor as she talked with them. Maybe her popularity would rub off on the merchant as well. More than one person promised to look him up. Shar really hoped they would. She was going to be relying on him so much more in the year before *Chocolates Galore!*

Judging went how Shar assumed that it would. Kigora and Golodhon were the top two. (Not that she'd assumed Kigora would shine at this challenge, but according to the judges her rainbow cake was the best of the day.) (Whatever.)

The judges seemed pleased with her design, particularly when she explained the concept, that she was trying to emulate rock crystals. While the cakes weren't perfect, she felt much better about what she'd done in terms of decorations.

The two bakers who'd been arguing were in the bottom. Ithrellas was sent home.

And then there were five.

# The Taste of Childhood

Ask a group of five Dwarves what their favorite baked treat is and you're likely to get twelve different answers.

Ditto with Elves and Humans.

Everyone has their personal favorite, their own taste of childhood that brings them fond memories.

That being said, most adults in a region are all going to have certain tastes that take them back to their childhood.

For example, adults who grew up in the city of Shazirakz (and to some extent, the Kibizar Mountains) will remember the brightly colored gelatin squares they had. (As well as possibly being yelled at by their parents to eat the jellies and not play with them, to not press them between their fingers in such a way that they went shooting across the room.)

Elves may remember as a teenager getting up early (or possibly staying up late) and racing through a field, competing with their friends to see who could collect the most dew drops on leaves before the sun evaporated them. Then sharing the dew drops, that faint hint of moonlight still prevalent on the tongue, cool and tingly.

Humans usually remember their first cookies. Not the chocolate ones, no. But the marshmallow ones, that were sticky. After you took a bite, you could stretch white strands out between your mouth and the cookie if you were careful and moved slowly enough not to break them. (With again the usual adult admonishments to eat their treat and not play with it. Spoilsports, all of them.)

Then there are holiday treats, and each race has their specialty. For the Dwarves, it's heavily spiced, dense cakes (that are frequently soaked in a brandy of some sort). For the Elves, it's *ünnepi palacsinta*, a holiday pancake, that's served with fresh fruit for the children and fruit that's been soaked in some sort of liquor for the adults (usually pear or cherry brandy—*pálinka*).

Humans do pies. Hand pies, cream pies, double-crust pies, pies with amazing decorative tops. These are frequently served with a hard sauce, that is, a sauce that hardens after it is made and is served with hot desserts, so it will melt. This type of sauce also contains a good amount of alcohol. Why limit yourself to just brandy, when you can also add rum, sherry, whiskey, and whatever else you might have on hand?

Which leads us to the conclusion that while a childhood memory of a holiday treat may or may not contain alcohol, the adult version? Usually does.

# Shar

"So, we've done challenges that featured Elvish ingredients, and Human ingredients," Yazgrak said. "I think it's time for us Dwarves to shine. Am I right?"

The crowd behind Yazgrak exploded with noise. Shar still felt unsettled by all the attention. At least she had Hulda to walk her through town, getting her from the field where they were judged and back to the inn. So many people now wanted her to stop and talk with them! Leena, Shar and Hulda now always had to take their meals in their room, because if they ate in the common room downstairs Shar spent the entire time talking with fans and not eating. And answering questions, like why she didn't have a cookbook (yet) and where they could buy her chocolates and desserts.

As Kigora had family in the city, she stayed with them and they walked her to and from the field, so she didn't have to deal with crowds. Golodhon also had people to stay with and who protected him. The two remaining Humans had decided to bunk with each other in a different inn, and didn't seem put out with the disruptions of their fans. (Then again, they were both much more gregarious than Shar.)

"And pray tell, what ingredient would the Dwarves favor?" Cyna asked with a twinkle in her eye that Shar didn't trust.

"Ale!" Yazgrak exclaimed excitedly.

"Oh Goddess, here we go again," Erwel said, rolling her eyes.

Shar rocked back on her heels.

Ale?

Crap.

She'd never cooked with ale.

She knew a recipe for a savory bread that called for ale and garlic. She'd never even considered using it in a sweet. It was too bitter and hoppy. Particularly the ales that her father and uncles drank. Mother preferred an even harsher whiskey.

Shar had never developed a taste for ale. She never advertised the fact, though, as it made her stand out as an odd Dwarf.

Right up there with not liking to facet gemstones.

"To help you out, we've brought in some flavored ales, as well as the more hearty, traditional kind," Yazgrak said. "Kigora, as you were the winner in yesterday's bake, you get to choose your variety of ale first."

Cyna excitedly picked up the thread. "We have raspberry ale, citrus ale—which is both lemon and orange flavored—peach ale, apple ale, and traditional ale." She paused, then beamed at the bakers. "They're all my favorite. I can't wait to see what you do with them!"

Shar was certain that she wasn't the only baker to roll her eyes at that. It had been well established that Cyna liked any dessert that had alcohol in it.

Erwel piped up. "I don't drink alcohol usually. So make sure that your flavors are balanced, not overwhelming."

"But remember, we still need to be able to taste the ale as well," Yazgrak warned.

Shar nodded. That balance was going to be difficult, finding the right level that pleased all the judges.

Kigora stepped forward and pondered her choices. Shar nearly rolled her eyes again as Kigora deliberated. Sure, it was a difficult decision. But this waiting was just for dramatic purposes, playing to the crowd.

Still, Shar hoped that Kigora chose anything other than the raspberry ale, as she thought she could make something with that.

"I choose the raspberry," Kigora said finally.

Of course, that was what her nemesis would pick.

Golodhon got to choose next, and he picked citrus, which had been Shar's next pick.

Kater chose apple, which left Shar with either peach or traditional.

As Shar had started to get a vague sense of what she'd cook—something like a *Barazir Bake*, heavy with warm spices—she went with the traditional variety, leaving the peach for Marger.

The bakers could choose whatever they wanted to make for this bake. Shar walked silently with the rest of the bakers to the collective kitchen as they all thought about what they wanted to make.

She didn't have a lot of time for a yeasted dough—merely ninety minutes. But if she could pull this off, it was going to be amazing.

The first thing Shar did when they got to their stations was to start the yeast. She dissolved sugar in the water before she added the yeast, giving it a lot of food to start with. She kept the bowl with the yeast covered with a towel in her oven to keep it warm while she sifted together the rest of her dry ingredients. Finally, she added the beer and the yeast, figuring that they'd feed off each other.

Then she set the dough back into the oven to rise as she prepared her toppings.

First, she made an ale- and maple-syrup glaze that she set to one side while she cooked up some bacon. Once it was crispy, she added the glaze, cooking it a little more before taking it off the stove, letting all the flavors steep together.

She punched down her dough, starting it to rise a second time while she prepared the cinnamon, ale, butter, and sugar spread that she'd put on the inside of her rolls once the dough was ready. She left the butter as ice-cold chunks to add more richness to the rolls as they baked.

Finally, the dough was ready. She rolled it out thin, sprinkled on her spread and chopped up pecans, then rolled it back up into a beautiful cylinder. She sliced the roll into five-centimeter-wide disks, making two pans of the rolls, one for the judges and one for the audience. (She'd decide which was which after the bake.)

She used a bright red pan, as she planned on serving the rolls in the pan, and it would be part of her decoration.

All the other bakers were already in the oven by the time Shar put hers in. However, she believed her timing would be correct and that she'd finish before the watchers called time. The rolls didn't have to completely cool before she added the glaze to them—in fact, it would be better if they weren't, so the icing would melt after she added it.

It was finally time to prepare the glaze that would top her rolls. It was a pretty simple recipe, just sugar, water, and ale. She debated adding some chocolate to it, but decided against it. White chocolate would be too sweet, and dark chocolate would be too brown. The white of the icing against the golden brown of the rolls would look better. Plus, she didn't want to risk compromising the flavors that she'd built up.

Shar was rushing at the end, waiting until the last possible minute before glazing her rolls, then sprinkling the chopped-up bacon on top.

The look was decidedly rustic. Shar had known that going in, knowing that she was taking a risk by not doing much of a design. Then again, this was a Dwarven type of dessert. It didn't need to be pretty enough for an Elf.

The rolls did look amazing. Once time was called, audience members got to sample what the bakers had made. Shar also got to try what her competitors had done, as the bakers made a point of giving each other a taste.

Though Shar hated to admit it, Kigora's raspberry, chocolate, and ale cake was to die for. All the flavors blended so well together, with the deep richness of the chocolate hitting her tongue first, followed by the smoothness of the ale, then the brightness of the raspberry kicking in. Kigora had used a white glaze on her practically black cake, with tiny pieces of raspberry on top as decorations.

However, Shar didn't understand the story that Kigora was telling. The decorations just seemed...pretty. Her nemesis had gotten to choose her flavor first. Had she made her choice solely on flavor, and because it would be one of the easier things to cook with? Not because she was passionate about it?

Shar would have to wait to hear what the judges said, but she wasn't convinced that Kigora would win, even though her flavors were amazing.

Kater's apple crumble was a hearty, rustic-looking dessert, similar to Shar's. The Human had added apple slices poached in ale to the top of it as decoration, but honestly, that was the only place where Shar got the flavor of the ale. The rest of the crumble, while delicious, only tasted of apples and cinnamon, not of her chosen ingredient.

Marger's peach frangipane tart was both elegant and tasty. The top was covered in almonds and peaches that had been poached in her ale. The rich flavor went well with the peach, ale, and almond filling. Her crust was perfect too. Shar figured that Marger was a contender for the win that day.

Golodhon had used his citrus ale in a couple of different ways. He'd made creampuffs as his base. Then, he'd filled them with a ganache that had been flavored with the citrus ale, along with a beautiful dipping sauce that Shar honestly wanted to bathe in, it was so good. In addition, he'd made very pretty spun sugar "clouds" to decorate each of the creampuffs, that was also orange flavored. It melted on her tongue when she tried it. (She was seriously going to have to have to train harder in sugar making if she wanted to win *Chocolates Galore!*)

He, too, might win that day.

Shar was the first one to be judged. (Their names were drawn out randomly by the watcher, as to the order of judging.)

"It looks delicious," Cyna said as Shar presented the pan of rolls to the judges.

"I want all of that in my mouth and dribbled down my beard," Yazgrak added. "But there's no design here."

"I actually made the conscious decision to do a rustic presentation," Shar said. "I used a red baking dish to highlight that. Plus, ale is a Dwarven ingredient. My dessert doesn't have to be fancy enough for an Elf."

Then she realized what she was saying, and to whom she was saying it. "But I still think an Elf would like it," she blurted out, glancing at Erwel.

The Elf just shook her head. "Girl," she said, pausing. "It's not pretty."

"But it does look delicious. See how that icing has just melted over the edges?" Cyna said. "And the ooy-gooey filling that bubbled up?"

Shar nodded. She would stand behind how her dessert looked. It was exactly how she'd envisioned it.

The judges all got that wide-eyed look again as they tasted the rolls.

Shar tried to keep her smile to herself at that. She probably failed miserably, though.

"I forgive you for the lack of design that would be appropriate for an Elf," Erwel said after a few moments, "'cause this right here? Is worth it."

Yazgrak was nodding. "This is another recipe that you should offer in your bakery," he said seriously.

"That was one of the reasons why I chose the traditional ale," Shar admitted. "So that if this worked, I could continue to use it."

"Smart," Cyna said. She paused, then asked, "And this is a yeasted dough?"

"Yes," Shar said. "Part of why I went rustic. I knew I wouldn't have a lot of time at the end to cool the rolls down before I decorated."

"You're learning," Yazgrak said, approving. "And I think this dessert is more closely aligned with who you are as a baker. Am I right?"

"Yes," Shar said with relief. "I like doing the fancier desserts sometimes. It's a way to stretch myself. But this might be a bit closer to who I am. A little rustic with amazing flavors."

The judges dismissed Shar and brought up the next baker.

In the end, the judging went how Shar believed it would, with Marger and Golodhon on top (the Human winning) and Kigora and Kater in the bottom, with the Human going home.

That left four.

The judges congratulated them all for having made it to the semi-finals.

There were only two bakes left before the end of the contest.

Shar walked back to the inn in a daze, barely hearing the people calling her name as Hulda led the way through the crowds.

She'd made it so far, so *very* far, in this contest.

Though she'd always told herself that she was going to win the whole thing, there was a part of her (okay, possibly a large part of her) that hadn't believed it.

Yet, here she was.

So close.

And yet so far.

# Kigora

Kigora had decided very early on in the contest that she would have a small get together with the other bakers when she reached the semi-finals, and there were only four of them remaining. She had assumed that she'd at least get along with the finalists.

They had gathered together in the front greeting hall of her cousin's house. The front half of the house was built with high enough ceilings that all the races would feel comfortable, unlike the bedrooms that were smaller and much more cozy, with rock walls. This room had light blue-green paint on wood, the ceiling painted a bright white, making it seem much more airy than Dwarves were normally comfortable with. There was a collection of over-stuffed couches to one side, but everyone was still standing over next to the bar, sipping on the delicious fruit punch that Kigora had whipped up (with the perfect blending of sweet and sour, of course), as well as nibbling on the small bites of meat and cheese.

Kigora had *not* anticipated that that upstart, Shar, would be there. Invited along with the others to the home of the cousin that Kigora was staying with.

Nor that Shar would have gotten such praise from the judges.

It wasn't fair!

Okay, so maybe Kigora had tasted her ale a bit while she'd been cooking.

Then continued to drink more of it after the judging, particularly when she'd been on the bottom with that Human.

Her cake had tasted amazing! Everyone had said so! Why hadn't the judges liked it? Particularly given the horrible "design" that Shar had used. If you could even call it that.

Uncle Yazgrak had said more than once that you could only get away with a rustic design if everything else was done perfectly.

Was that what Shar was doing? Was that why she'd receive such high praise?

What was Kigora doing wrong?

And speaking of her nemesis, there she was, chatting quietly with Golodhon, with Marger standing to the side just listening. Of course, Shar would make friends with an Elf. She was foolish that way. (Kigora knew that Elves made perfectly fine bakers. And were really good people. But why wasn't Shar making friends with the Human? At least Marger made garish things. Like Shar.)

Kigora drank a bit more of her ale, growing more angry every second, before she brazenly walked over to where the others were standing. "Why are you still here?" she blurted out, glaring at Shar. "Your desserts aren't pretty!"

Shar glanced at Golodhon, then at Marger, before she stepped forward, into Kigora's space. "And yours are too pretty," she said.

"What—what—what do you mean by that?" Kigora sputtered. "There is no such thing as too pretty. Ask any Elf."

Shar rolled her eyes and took Kigora gently by the arm, leading her back to the other side of the room, away from the other two.

"I can tell you're upset," Shar said quietly. "But let's try not to alienate everyone. Okay?"

Kigora was torn between wanting to defy what Shar had said and being grateful for her thoughtfulness.

"But why are you still here? You haven't been cooking for that long. You don't have some sort of magical ability when it comes to tastes—the judges would have disqualified you if you had. How are you so good? What are you still doing here?" Kigora demanded.

All right, so maybe she'd been stewing about this for a while.

"Why?" Kigora asked again when Shar remained silent, hating how plaintive she sounded, as if she were begging, but she still had to know.

Shar sighed and shook her head.

For a moment, Kigora thought Shar wouldn't answer her, but then she did.

"I may not have been cooking ever since I could reach the top of a stove, but I have been very focused this last year, doing challenge bakes and pushing myself to learn absolutely everything I could," Shar started off with.

Before Kigora could complain how that shouldn't be enough, Shar continued.

"I also am baking with my heart," she added.

"What does that even mean?" Kigora wailed. She'd heard the judges say something like that about her own bakes. She had no idea what they were talking about.

"Take your latest bake," Shar said. "Why did you choose the raspberry ale?"

"Because it would be the easiest to work with," Kigora said honestly. "Plus, I didn't want you to have it."

Shar nodded, not upset, but approving. "Smart. But what about the taste spoke to you? Once you had it, what made it good?"

"It matched what I had in mind?" Kigora asked, confused.

"What do raspberries remind you of? What's one of your first memories of raspberries?" Shar asked.

"Standing on a stool in the kitchen with Grandma Gabritz, going through her pail of raspberries, picking out the prettiest ones," Kigora blurted out. "For her tarts."

She really should have stopped drinking a while ago. She was saying too much. But now that memory had ahold of her, of standing in that solid rock kitchen, with the warm stove behind them, working side by side with her grandmother at the workbench in the middle of the room. Of the soft smell of cinnamon and other warm spices that her grandmother always exuded. Though Kigora's job had been to find the pretty raspberries, quite a few of the berries had also found their way into her mouth, as she removed the ones that weren't pretty enough. Or at least that was the excuse she gave, the one that always made Grandma Gabritz smile.

Then, the beautiful raspberries tarts that her grandmother had made, using those few delicate berries that Kigora had picked out to decorate the tops.

"So why didn't you make those tarts?" Shar said. "It would have come from your heart. That's a dessert that means something to you. And what you did for decorations would have meant something, and not just been pretty."

"But the judges want pretty!" Kigora said. "Which is why you shouldn't still be here."

Shar rolled her eyes. "The judges don't just want pretty. They want more than just that. They also want you to cook things that are meaningful. That tell a story."

"So I should have made my grandma's tart?" Kigora said. "I wouldn't want to change her recipe, though!" Adding ale to her grandmother's recipe felt wrong to her. Grandma's raspberry tarts were special. Even Uncle Yazgrak thought so.

"Come up with your own version of them, then," Shar said. "Something that suits you, as well as pays homage to your grandmother."

That didn't make any sense to Kigora. Then again, she had had a lot to drink that night.

She shook her head, then paused, and shrugged. "Maybe," she said, Shar's point finally penetrating the thick rock wall surrounding her thoughts. "Maybe I need to think about what's important as well as what's pretty."

"Exactly!" Shar said. Then she sobered. "I...I still want to beat you. To win regionals. But I hope that this helps you be a better baker. Because I don't want to win while you're not at your best. I want to beat you when you are doing your greatest work."

Kigora nodded. "Same," she said. "You should take some lessons from an Elvish baker sometime. That will help a lot with your decorating skills. Because they're practically nonexistent."

Shar didn't take offense at the recommendation, and instead, gave a surprising laugh. "Oh, I know it. And I need to work on my sugar making. And my chocolate sculptures. And so many other things. But I think, I hope, that I know enough at this point to win."

Kigora gave Shar an appraising look. The other Dwarf was nothing special. Her beard, while soft-looking, was braided plainly, with black and red ribbons, which matched the coat she wore at the cooking contests. Her brown eyes were soft as well, and her smile made Kigora a bit warmer.

Nothing about Shar screamed that she was special. She was just an ordinary Dwarf.

Maybe that was why she'd become the fan favorite, because she was plain and rustic and yet so talented.

"May the best baker win," Kigora said with a nod. She stuck out her hand and Shar gave it a firm handshake, along with a smile.

"Aye," Shar said. "Think you can join the others and not regret it in the morning?"

Kigora didn't flush with embarrassment. But she did feel her beard shake a little when she thought about what she'd just said.

"I think so," she said after a few moments.

Kigora marched straight over to the Human and the Elf, apologizing for her previous behavior. She deliberately started playing the role of the ideal hostess, then, something that all the bakers in her family had also been taught from an early age.

She couldn't think about what Shar had just said about cooking things that meant something to her. It took too much of her focus (and willpower) just to be pleasant and to stay standing, instead of starting to tilt a little as the amount of alcohol she'd consumed let itself be felt.

Her guests didn't stay too long after that, and Kigora was left alone with the start of her hangover.

As well as too many things to ponder, even as sleep claimed her.

# Shar

"So, as y'all have figured out, we've had a theme this year of cooperation," Erwel started the next morning as the four remaining contestants stood in front of them.

Shar nodded, happy about that year's theme. It hadn't been something that the judges had announced at the start of the contest, but it had been a constant thread running through the challenges.

She'd have to go back and look at the official reports of the past regional contests, to see if the theme had been announced at the start or at the end. She suspected that it was probably half and half.

"However, that doesn't mean another team challenge," Cyna said.

Shar felt herself release her breath, not realizing that she'd been holding it. She really, *really* hadn't wanted to have to work with the other bakers. Sure, she got along with all of them. She might have even reached some sort of understanding with Kigora, as strange as that sounded. However, she wanted to shine on her own.

"So instead, we're going to ask you to bake with a pair of ingredients," Yazgrak said. He held up four colored cards: off-white, green, red, and pink. "These all represent the sweet element of your next challenge. Maple syrup, honey, chocolate, and berries."

The colors didn't make sense in terms of the ingredients that Yazgrak had just listed off. Were those to do with what would be matched to them?

"Marger, as you were the winner of yesterday's bake, you get to choose your flavor first," Yazgrak continued.

The Human chose the off-white card with maple syrup, as that was an ingredient that was made close to where she lived. Golodhon took honey, which surprised Shar, as she assumed that he'd take either the berries or the chocolate.

Shar's turn to choose was next, and she decided she'd just go with what was predictable, and take the chocolate, which left berries for Kigora.

None of the sweeteners were too bad. Whatever the judges wanted to pair with them wouldn't be too horrible, right?

Wrong.

"Marger, you'll find a little circle at the bottom of your card. Tap that twice to reveal what your partner is," Yazgrak instructed.

The look of shock on Marger's face made Shar's blood freeze and her beard tremble.

"Fish paste," Marger announced in a hopeless voice. "I have to pair fish paste and maple syrup?"

The crowd gasped while the judges all smiled and nodded.

They really did like to torture the contestants, didn't they?

Golodhon went next. His combination was dill pickles and honey.

Shar wasn't sure if she regretted picking chocolate or not. Particularly when she read her ingredient. "Red onions and chocolate," she told the crowd.

A few people hissed at that.

Shar was still in shock at the ingredients she'd been assigned. She had no idea what she was going to do with such an unlikely pairing.

"Garlic," Kigora said, her voice completely deadpan. "Garlic and berries."

"I do not envy you bakers," Cyna said. "But I do have faith that you'll all create something unique and delicious!"

"Remember, we need to be able to taste both ingredients, yet at the same time, they need to be in balance with each other," Yazgrak said.

"Good luck!" Erwel said. "Remember to work with each other solving this puzzle. Y'all can do this."

The four bakers tromped across the field, heading toward the group kitchen. The crowd behind them cheered them on.

Shar ignored the well-wishers, her head spinning. She went through idea after idea, rejecting them all.

What was she going to do? Onions did *not* pair with chocolate, despite the fact that chocolate went well with everything.

What would onions go well with?

Shar actually stopped walking when the idea came to her.

"Hey! I think I have it!" she said excitedly as she caught back up with the other bakers. "The two ingredients don't match, right? Even though the sweet we have will go with practically anything."

"Oh, we know," Marger groaned as the bakers walked into the kitchen. They all gathered around her worktable as Shar continued to explain.

"So what might go well with the 'odd' ingredient?" Shar asked. "I have onions. If I caramelize them, make them sweeter, I think I can make them work in a mincemeat filling, and make a pie."

She turned to Kigora. "What else do you add to a typical garlic sauce?" She knew that Kigora had made all sorts of food, not just sweets, in her time as a baker.

"Flour, white wine, lemon..." her voice trailed off. "I could do a lemon cake! And cook the garlic in lemon! Then that would pair well with the cake and the berries!"

"Exactly," Shar said.

"What do you make out of fish paste?" Marger said, still looking distraught. "I've never even heard of it before."

"Oh," Shar said. Huh. But then again, she'd grown up on the coast and had a lot of fish and fishy things. "It's actually more of a sauce than a paste. It has a lot of salt in it. What can you mix with the salt to carry it over to the maple syrup?"

"Salted taffy? Salted chocolate? I know! Salted caramels!" Marger said. "They have that deep richness that would go well with the maple syrup as well."

Shar nodded. She wasn't sure if that would work, but it certainly was along the right track.

The group turned to Golodhon who shrugged. "I got nothing," he said. "I've used dill before, but in a salad. Or to pickle vegetables. Not for anything sweet."

"I have an idea," Kigora said. "There's a fish dish that we make using it, actually."

"Want to trade?" Golodhon said. He held his hand up when one of the watcher in the kitchen—their usual watcher Alred—took a step forward. "Kidding." He sighed, then asked, "So how do you make this fish dish?"

"It's fresh water trout that we poach in white wine with dill," Kigora said. "Do you think you could use white wine as the bridging ingredient?"

"Maybe," Golodhon said, his eyes focusing suddenly on a distant point. "I can make dill, white wine, and honey work. Figs, perhaps?" he asked himself as he wandered off to his own station.

Shar knew that she had to get started on her mincemeat right away. While traditionally the dessert was made with chopped meat, to save time, she was going to skip that and substitute in roasted walnuts. But before she started chopping, she measured out her brandy and added coffee beans to that, letting the flavors steep together, adding the liquid to the pot once she got everything going. Lastly, she caramelized her onions and added those to the pot.

The taste was surprisingly good. The bright tang of the onion paired well with the dried fruit and brandy.

Normally, a good mincemeat filling sat for a while, so the flavors built up and melded together well. Shar didn't have the three days that took. Maybe thirty minutes, instead. So she left her filling simmering on the stove and turned to making her pie dough next.

She needed for her crust to be as crumbly and flaky as she could, using frozen butter and shaving it into the flour and other dry ingredients while the mincemeat simmered. She didn't fully bake the bottom crust, just browned it slightly before she filled it.

Traditionally, a mincemeat pie had both a top and a bottom crust. However, Shar only made enough dough for the bottom layer.

She had other plans for the top crust.

While the pie crust was baking, Shar got a tasting spoon and took a sample of the mincemeat over to Kigora to taste.

The other Dwarf's eyes went wide as she tasted it. "That's amazing," she said. "You might start a trend with that flavor. Here," she said abruptly, grabbing a spoon, dipping it into a yellow sauce and thrusting it at Shar.

The tartness of the lemon curd made Shar's mouth pucker slightly, followed by the sweetness of the sugar that Kigora had added. Then came the sharpness of the garlic. It was a complicated, sophisticated mix of flavors.

"That works," Shar said, nodding. "Though I might tone down some of the bitterness of the lemon, as the berries, while bright, will also bring some sourness."

"Got it," Kigora said seriously.

Shar turned to go back to her station when she heard the very soft, "Thank you."

Shar took out the crust, filled the pie, then put it back into the oven.

Now, it was time to temper some chocolate.

All throughout the contest, Shar had worked with dark or semi-sweet chocolate.

This time, she planned on using those, but the bulk of her design was going to be white chocolate.

She tempered a large amount of the white, spread it thickly over a sheet pan, then put it into the freezer to cool. Onto a second sheet pan she put a much thinner layer of the white chocolate. Then she added splashes of the dark and semi-sweet chocolate to the pan, so the three chocolates overlapped each other.

That pan set more quickly than the one in the freezer. Shar cut out a multitude of disks, each about three centimeters across. Then she took a wide knife, heated the edge of it, and cut into her disks. She didn't slice the disks into two pieces, but instead, just made a slit that went from the bottom, almost to the top edge.

The pie came out of the oven. It needed to cool before Shar could do anything to it. In the meanwhile, Shar continued with her chocolate decorations. She fit the disks together, aligning their slits, so they each formed a little cross, like the skeletal structure that would support a sphere. The different colors of chocolate streaked across the disks, making each one unique.

Finally, the pie was cool enough and her thicker white chocolate was ready. Shar cut out a circle that fit the top of her pie perfectly. She had a couple of heart-stopping moments while she lifted it up and gently placed it on the pie. However, the chocolate was firm enough that she could lift it and move it without it cracking into two (or more) pieces.

Though the pie was still warm, it wouldn't completely melt the thick disk of white chocolate. Instead, it would make the bottom of the disk a little sticky and gooey, which would be an awesome mingling of flavors.

Shar then took a dollop of her perfectly-tempered white chocolate, spread it out on her marble slab, then began to over-tempered it. She used her spatula to work the chocolate, back and forth, agitating it hard, until the consistency changed from a cream to a thick paste.

Small dabs of the over-tempered chocolate "glued" the little spheres that she'd made to the white disk, holding them upright and steady. She arranged the disks into a spiral pattern. The design represented her journey in this contest, always feeling as though she was spinning, until she got to the center and her prize.

Okay, so it was a little abstract. It looked beautiful, but the judges might not know what it represented until she explained it to them.

When time was called, Shar felt pretty good about what she'd done, how well she'd paired her flavors, as well as her design.

This time, the audience wouldn't get to taste the bakers' desserts until after judging.

Shar supposed that was wise, in case one of them bombed.

Plus, she figured that a fan of the show had to be really hard-core to want to voluntarily taste these unlikely pairs.

At the start of judging, the judges all praised the bakers for working together to come up with their flavor combinations, and that Shar's idea of finding a bridging element was exactly what they had needed to do.

Shar's pie was last to be judged that day. She really wasn't sure where it would stand compared to the others. Evidently, Kigora's garlic-lemon-berry tart was delicious. She'd told the judges the story she'd told Shar, about working with her grandmother, and so had decorated her tart with little pink meringues used to represent the garlic, along with the most perfect, delicate raspberries that she could find.

It was a dessert that both tasted well and had heart.

Shar was reconsidering how happy she was to have talked with Kigora about her issues.

Except that yes, she wanted to beat all the other bakers when they were at their peak. Not when they were handicapped and not capable of doing their best work.

Golodhon's white wine cake creation was elegant as always, decorated with a stringy green frosting to represent the dill. The judges were amazed at how much wine flavor he'd managed to get into his ganache and his cake. The dill wasn't as well paired as the judges would have liked, though.

Marger had a different problem. The sticky, salted-caramel bread pudding that she'd made didn't have enough of the fish paste flavor. The judges were searching for it, though the flavors she'd developed were evidently amazing.

Shar was declared the winner of the semi-final bake. Kigora came in second, and Golodhon was also promoted to the top three.

Marger went home, but with her head held high, as she'd done some amazing bakes during her time there.

Shar's head swam as a large part of the audience was allowed into the circle where the bakers stood. Other people served very small tastes of the day's cook to the braver audience members. All Shar had to do was to stand and talk with fans, let them gush over her, tell her how she was such a shoo-in for winning the whole thing. She remembered to tell more people about her sponsor, Curious Cat Shipping, when she could.

Later that night, Shar found her head was still spinning as she laid in her bed, awaiting sleep.

She'd done it.

She'd made it to the final three.

All of the bakers in the top three were eligible for *Chocolates Galore!*

The winner qualified automatically. The bottom two would have to win a couple of challenges that took place before the contest before they'd qualify.

Shar knew that she could be satisfied with what she'd done so far. She'd come out of nowhere, with no training to speak of.

Just a burning desire to prove herself, not just to the other bakers but to her family.

And the world.

She could do this.

She could win the whole thing.

Whatever the judges threw at them in the morning, Shar was ready. Her heart and her mind were aligned.

Bring it.

# You Get Magic! And You Get Magic! And You, And You, And You!

Every sentient being in the world of Indunel has magic.

Let me repeat that.

*Every sentient being in the entire world has magic.* (As do many of the non-sentient beings.)

That being said, not everyone has tons of magic to just fling around.

The best way to think about it is that everyone is born with a thimbleful of magic hidden inside their heart. (Not literally inside their heart, or cannibalism would be rampant instead of tucked away in just a couple of odd corners of the world.)

It takes skill, patience, discipline, training, and above all, luck, for a person to first access their magic, then to grow it, until it goes from a mere spoonful to a gushing stream.

The ability to do magic is traditionally divided into two parts: affinity and will.

Everyone has some sort of magical affinity. What exactly that entails depends on the person and their race. Frequently, a person might have a strong affinity—called a primary affinity—for one thing, as well as a much weaker secondary affinity for another.

Dwarves traditionally have mostly craft-based affinities, such as metal work, stones and gems, or brewing. Elves are proficient at woodworking, some sorts of farming, and weaving. (All right. Fine. Elves are *better* at weaving than everyone else, magical affinity or not. Even Dwarves, though they hate to admit it.) However, some Elves can manipulate air and water.

Things get weird when it comes to Humans. (Of course.) Instead of craft-based, they're primarily element-based. But not just fire, earth, air and water. No, they also have offshoots into lightning, ice, gravity, and so on.

How does a person figure out their magical affinity?

Rich families pay a trained seer to peer into their darling offspring's heart to tell them what aspect their sprout should focus on, though only their primary aspect. This must occur between the ages of eight and eleven—old enough that the child has some knowledge of the world, young enough that they haven't gone heavily into puberty.

A trained seer is right about seventy percent of the time. And despite the strict regulations and severe penalties of the Seers' Guild, seers are occasionally bribed by unscrupulous enemies of a family to lie about a child's potential.

Poor families go to the Temple of the Cricket. There is one in every city and most every town. Villagers traditionally go on an annual pilgrimage with their appropriately aged children to a temple to get them checked out. (Tales of how the temple came into being occasionally refer to a regular cricket named Jiminy who ascended to godhood with the assistance of a mouse god. The Temple of the Cricket does not recognize such stories and considers them apocryphal.)

The process is fascinating. The child is seated before a large piece of cloth that has many squares drawn on it, each one representing a specific affinity. A special cricket is brought out and released from its cage at one end of the cloth. The priest hums, or sings, or waves their fingers in the air, and the cricket jumps from one square to the next, finally landing on the square that contains the primary magical affinity for the querent.

Crickets tend to be accurate ninety percent of the time.

When the process works.

Sometimes, the cricket won't move from in front of its cage. The parents have to come back either the next day, or the following year, depending on their means. This happens about half the time.

Every once in a while, a cricket goes from one end of the cloth to the other, never settling on a square, and eventually comes to rest on one of the margins of the cloth.

This means the process actually worked. However, it also means that the child has a non-standard magical affinity and they're just going to have to figure it out for themselves. About a quarter of those with magical power have a non-standard affinity. At that point, luck plays a large role, because the person just has to stumble upon their affinity.

For example, the Elf Nelesar Imroth, who had an affinity for raising sunflowers. Any other plant she tried to grow died. She eventually figured out that sunflowers were her thing, and single-handedly cornered the market selling sunflower seeds, sunflower oil, sunflower nut flour, bright yellow and deep green sunflower dyes, and so on, utilizing every part of the plant.

Why would a parent choose the seventy percent method over the ninety percent method, taking their child to a seer rather than the Temple of the Cricket? Many parents use both, comparing the results of one to the other. (This is frequently how unscrupulous seers are caught.)

However, a trained seer can also judge the *potential* for magic, whereas a cricket cannot.

Remember, magic takes both affinity and *will*.

A trained seer can determine if a child's thimble is capable of growing into a cup, a bucket, or a river, with about ninety percent accuracy.

Then it's up to the individual to do the work.

It's frequently a self-fulfilling prophecy. Those who are expected to have great amounts of magic are given training early, so they can grow. Those who don't have the potential aren't given training, so they don't gain more magical ability.

What does training involve? It depends. Magic is an art, not a science.

One individual will perform a bit of magic by wiggling their fingers and waving their hands in the air. The next person will be able to perform the *exact same* bit of magic by doing a little jig. Whereas the third person must recite some doggerel that is both sing-songy and rhymes.

Which bit of the process will work for which individual?

No one can predict that.

The good news is that there aren't that many ways to transfer the magic that is deep inside a person's heart to the external world. And once a person finds their path, pretty much all of their magic is performed the same way.

They might get very good at dancing jigs as they learn.

The more a person uses magic—that is, wrings out every single drop they have inside, completely drains it—the larger their bucket grows. It's an exhausting process, physically, mentally, and spiritually.

It does come down to will at the end of the day.

There are always stories of a Hero or Heroine who has an affinity for one thing, such as air, who, in the middle of a crisis, discovers their ability to blast fire in order to protect their children. Some schools of magic try to mimic these critical events as part of their training. However, the results are frequently fatal for the student.

What's important is that everyone can easily do small magics, such as clicking their fingers (or clapping their hands, or humming, or doing a quick two-step) to heat a stove, ignite a magical gem to light a room, or activate a pump to bring water to a sink.

These mundane-seeming acts are actually all magical.

Don't you agree?

# Shar

Shar stood before the judges for the last time. Golodhon stood beside her, and Kigora stood at the far end of the line.

The three of them had all worked so hard to get there. Then again, so had all the other bakers.

Shar had learned *so much* in terms of baking and decorating. As well as just how much she still had to learn! She had a lifetime to get there, though.

One way or another, she was going to get to *Chocolates Galore!* Maybe win that as well...

The judges all looked happy to see them.

Never a good sign.

What sort of torture lay before them?

"Good morning bakers! Welcome to the finale!" Cyna said.

The cheering from the crowd took a few moments to die down.

"You made it," Yazgrak said. "Each of you should be so proud of yourself, for coming this far, for achieving this much. And as you know, though the winner of this contest will automatically be entered into *Chocolates Galore!* the other two can also apply for entry. I hope to see all three of you there!"

"Now, we've been focused on cooperation, on working with each other. You know another time when people get together, though? The holidays!" Erwel said.

Shar blinked, surprised. She felt as though the analogy was a bit of a stretch, but she could see it.

"Though all the different people on Indunel have their various holidays, we decided to pick one that everyone celebrates," Cyna said.

Erwel nodded. "Yes, in their own unique, different ways."

The three judges paused dramatically, glancing at each other before speaking together, saying, "The longest night!"

Shar started busily thinking about what sort of dessert she could make that would be appropriate for the longest night and the gifts that Dwarves gave each other that night.

"It is called different things by the different peoples," Erwel said. "We Elves call it *Téli Napforduló*."

"And us Humans call it the Winter Solstice," Cyna added.

"But regardless, everyone has some sort of celebration or rituals that they do when the longest night comes around," Yazgrak said.

Shar nodded. It had never been her favorite holiday, what with all the scary stories meant to keep kids away and out of the dark, to keep them in the light. They were bribed with presents that they were given when the sun set, but not allowed to open until the next day, after the sun had risen.

"We Humans dance the night away," Cyna said. "There are ritual dances performed by the priests of Idite, the earth goddess, to help wake her up, let her know that winter has passed."

Shar hadn't realized that, hadn't ever thought about how different people would celebrate the longest night.

"We sing," Erwel said with a fond, soft smile. "Choirs are formed in and under the trees in the great woods and amazing songs are sung all night long."

Golodhon had the same soft smile on his face, remembering something special, Shar was certain.

"And Dwarves, we give presents. Surprises to each other. They're given at sunset, but not opened until the next day, to lessen the temptation of the dark calling to us, tempting us into the deepest, most dangerous parts of the mines," Yazgrak said.

"So today, for the finale, you'll have five hours to make us a three-tiered cake that represents the longest night, and how it's celebrated by the various peoples," Cyna said.

Yazgrak held up three cards, each with a caricature on it: a Dwarf, an Elf, and a Human.

"Shar, as you were the winner of the semi-final, you not only get to choose which people's holiday you want to represent, you also get to assign the others to your fellow competitors," Yazgrak explained.

"Choose wisely, but be fair," Erwel warned.

Shar nodded and walked forward to the judges' table. "I'm going to pick the Dwarf for me," she said. "I think I have the perfect thing for it."

She picked up the other cards and turned toward her fellow bakers. "I take it you'd love to do the Elves?" she asked Golodhon.

His eyes widened and he nodded seriously, looking shocked when she handed him the celebration of his choice.

"Are you okay with dancing?" Shar asked Kigora before she handed her the card.

Kigora nodded seriously. "I am. I can make this work," she said firmly.

Shar gave her a big smile.

Sure, they might be competitors, but possibly, maybe, after all this was done, they might be able to be friends?

Maybe.

"So why did you give your competitors things that they can work with?" Yazgrak asked.

"I don't want to win because another baker is handicapped," Shar said seriously. "I want to beat them while they are at the top of their game."

"Bold," Erwel said. "I like it!"

"Now, each of you were allowed to bring a special ingredient, as well as equipment, to use on this last bake," Cyna said. "Let us know what you're going to use today."

Shar went first. "I brought a type of gelatin as my ingredient," she said, "along with chocolate molds that I made." She wasn't about to go into more details. Let it all be a surprise.

That was part of the longest night's tradition, at least among the Dwarves.

"I brought gold and silver leaves for decorating," Golodhon said. "They are a delicacy among our people." He nodded at Erwel who nodded back. "And I brought a magical rolling pin that will thin out whatever you're working on to the perfect consistency."

Shar sighed. She wished she had access to something like that. It would make her life so much easier! Then again, it was probably better that she had never gotten used to magical tools, as they weren't generally allowed in the contests.

"I'm going to be using a crackling candy," Kigora said.

Shar had never heard of that before. She was going to have to figure out what Kigora had.

"And some specialized, magical cookie-cutters," Kigora added. "They'll form into the shape I want, then cleanly cut through any dough."

Again, such a handy item when it came to decorations! Shar always baked everything by hand, from scratch, without relying on magical spoons or special bowls.

She was just going to have to prove, once again, that she could do this, even without such advantages.

"All right, you have five hours after you get to your kitchen," Erwel said. "And we'll be coming to check on you as well."

Shar gulped.

Crap.

Previous contests had reported on the "twists" that the judges threw in at the last minute, making the bakers scramble to get everything accomplished on time.

Shar was just going to have to make sure to do everything perfect, as well as quickly, to account for whatever else the judges were going to throw at them.

She'd never made a three-tiered cake like this before, not by herself. But she knew exactly what she wanted for the top tier, at least, and that would have to be her focus.

"Good luck!" Cyna said. "Be sure to make me something tasty!"

Shar wondered if that was a clue to their twist. Everyone knew that Cyna really liked her liquor. And that was something that the Dwarves always had in abundance during their longest night celebrations.

"There's going to be a twist," Golodhon grumbled as the three bakers headed toward their shared kitchen.

"I know," Kigora said. "But what?"

"Do the Elves drink alcohol or spirits of some sort during your longest night celebration?" Shar asked.

"We do," Golodhon said solemnly. "The sweetest dew wine, made that spring."

"Do either of you know if the Humans drink something special?" Shar asked.

Kigora nodded. "I've been here, in Anthus, that night, a few times. The Humans were drinking and dancing in the streets, everywhere."

"That might be the twist, then," Shar said quietly, looking over her shoulder to make sure that the watchers couldn't hear them. "Some sort of liquor to add to your dessert."

"Good idea," Golodhon said, nodding. "I'll plan for it."

"So will I," Kigora said. She paused then said, "Thank you. You aren't going to win, but I'm glad you're being fair about it."

Shar snorted at the presumption of the other Dwarf. "You look to your own bake," she said. "And I'll look to mine."

Surprisingly, Kigora gave her a great grin at that. "I will," she said proudly.

Shar rolled her eyes.

Whatever.

The audience at the far end of the kitchen was huge this time. Over one hundred people were watching them cook. However, they were still behind a magical barrier so that they couldn't disturb the bakers.

Shar didn't want to repeat herself, particularly not with the three-tiered cake that she'd done as part of the group challenge. However, elements of it were going to be the same. She'd just have to make sure that it was different enough for the judges.

Each tier would be made up of three layers of cake. She made her richest, darkest chocolate cake for the bottom tier. Those would be used to represent the mines that the Dwarves worked in. She'd frost the outside of it with a smooth black buttercream, then decorate it with gray ghosts and other spirits, to represent the temptations that might trick souls.

The middle tier was a walnut cake with dried stone fruit, to represent the halls that the Dwarves lived in. She had learned Kater's recipe for the thin paste that set quickly, and she used that to decorate the middle tier. The background was a yellowish buttercream and she dyed the paste black. That let her do silhouettes of Dwarves, and she didn't have to worry about all the pesky details that were beyond her. (At this point. She foresaw drawing as well as sculpture classes in her future.)

She made the top tier both her present as well as her surprise. The cake itself was pretty simple—a light vanilla cake, which she felt was appropriate after all the heaviness of the lower tiers. It was the only layer that she'd already planned the filling for. She had ideas about the fillings for the first two tiers, but wanted to wait until the judges came through before making her final choices. However, for the top tier, the ganache would be milk-chocolate with coffee and vanilla: you needed that pick-me-up after being up all night, as Dwarves tended to do on the longest night.

If she had time, and it set up correctly, one of the layers between the cakes on her top tier would be a mint gelée—a thicker layer of jelly. If it didn't set up (or she didn't have time) that would be all right. She might end up using it inside her bonbons instead.

However, those were just extra places for her to use her special ingredient. She'd brought it for making frosting—something called a mirror glaze because it was so bright and reflective.

Leena had done scouting in those first couple of days after they'd gotten to Anthus, discovering that gelatin wasn't common in the city. She'd warned Shar that it would be much more common in White Hall and everyone would be using it. For now, it would work as her special ingredient. (If gelatin had been more prevalent, Shar had also brought golden chocolate—a type of white chocolate made with caramelized sugar—which was perfect for making chocolate caramels.)

The mirror glaze wouldn't work without the gelatin. Shar was excited that she got to use it.

Everything was going according to plan: her cakes were already cooling, she was whipping up her buttercream for frosting, when the judges came in.

As her station was the first one in the kitchen, they walked over to visit with her first.

"Tell us what you're making," Erwel said gently.

Shar wondered if she looked as scared as she felt.

So she told the judges about her decorating plans in general terms, not really going into specifics.

"And the top tier?" Yazgrak asked. "What surprise do you have in store for us?"

"That's a surprise," Shar said in a mock scolding voice.

"I like surprises!" Cyna said brightly. "Make sure it's a good one."

"It will be," Shar promised. She'd already decorated her emerald-cut molds with different colors of dyed cocoa butter, as well as added the dark chocolate for the shell. She was planning on stuffing her top tier with the chocolates so that they'd spill out when the cake was cut as yet another surprise.

Shar took a deep breath after the judges left her station. She found herself unfocused for a bit, trying to remember what she was working on.

Oh. Right. Buttercream.

Shar was just getting back into the groove of things when Yazgrak called out, "Bakers! Can I have your attention, please?"

Shar sighed and turned toward where the judges were standing.

"You know what else goes with the longest night?" Yazgrak asked.

"Booze!" Cyna announced happily.

"Yes, that's right," Erwel said. "Even though I'm not a drinker, we're putting spirits into this challenge. Don't you make me regret this."

"Spoilsport," Cyna said. "But you need to include enough for me," she pouted.

"The flavors should be balanced," Yazgrak said, trying to bring peace between the two judges. "You can choose from any of the liquors on this cart." He nodded at Alred, who trundled in with a wooden cart filled with bottles.

Shar rushed from her station and got to the cart first.

Crap.

The names had been removed from the labels! All that she had to go on were pictures.

Badly drawn pictures.

She'd been hoping for a flavored Dwarven ale. That would have been perfect.

Instead, she picked the bottle that might have been a peach? Maybe an apricot? The liquor inside was a golden color. It shouldn't be too powerful.

She hoped.

When she got back to her station she tasted the liquor she'd chosen.

Then started coughing.

Wow.

Cyna was definitely going to taste this.

Once Shar had fought through the bitterness (and the burning of her throat from the pure alcohol) she thought she did detect some sort of fruit taste. Maybe some sort of stone fruit?

She'd use it in the ganache between the layers of her bottom two tiers, maybe as a soak for her cake, as well as to flavor the filling for her bonbons.

Now, back to work.

# Shar

Though Alred called out the amount of time they had remaining at regular intervals, Shar couldn't believe how fast five hours flew by.

Still, Shar was happy with how her cake looked. Of course, it wasn't as elegant as the cake that Golodhon had made. He had decorated each tier with the shiny gold and silver leaves as well as with notes flying up from a dark green forested bottom up to the light, a silvery moon made out of a chocolate disk, shining at the top.

Kigora's cake was also beautiful, and would appeal to Humans as it was a colorful ombre, going from black, through various shades of reds, oranges, and yellows. Evidently the priests of Idite wore bright red, so the base of her cake showed red "legs" pounding down on the encroaching darkness. The middle tier held small cookies that represented the drums and horns that Humans and priests played during their festivities. Whereas the top tier was almost golden, representing the bright sun returning at the end of the longest night. Her cake topper was also a chocolate, though a sphere, not a disk, made from white chocolate dyed yellow.

Shar's cake had turned out pretty much exactly as she'd envisioned it, with the black buttercream and spirits on the bottom, the yellowish halls of the Dwarves done in black silhouette on the second tier, and the bright shiny present on the top.

Her mirror glaze had turned out particularly well. It was primarily red with streaks of gold and white running through it. She'd decorated the top of her third tier with bows made out of white chocolate.

Comparing her cake to the other two, Shar suddenly saw her fatal flaw.

The tiers on her cake were all separate. They were each decorated differently. The cake, as a whole, wasn't cohesive. There was no obvious running theme through out. Unless you knew the story, you might not even realize it was to celebrate the longest night.

Crap.

There was nothing Shar could do at this point. She couldn't change her design.

Hopefully her cake tasted the best.

And even if it didn't, she'd still be able to compete in *Chocolates Galore!* She'd just wanted to automatically qualify, and not have to prove herself (again) and win more contests (again).

The crowd this time completely filled the park. Tents and pop-up stalls lined the edges, merchants seeing an opportunity and pouncing on it. (Shar should have mentioned this to Hulda, so that she could have done a pop-up and maybe sold some of her scarves. Then again, it would have been difficult to carry them here, as well as the folded stall.)

Shar waved as she was paraded through the corridors of people, smiling and giving them the thumbs up. The contestants had been warned to not stop and talk with anyone, to just keep moving, keep smiling and waving.

The cakes that the three bakers had made had been placed on wooden tables with handles on the ends. Human and Dwarf guards carried them. A thin blue magical bubble encased each cake so nothing would happen to it as it got walked to the judging. The crowd ooohed and ahhhed at the cakes as they went by.

Finally, the three bakers stood in front of the judges one last time.

Instead of their usual outfits, the judges were now dressed formally. Cyna wore a brightly colored red, white, gold, and green gown that emphasized her rather well-endowed chest, Yazgrak looked very serious in a red-and-brown brocade vest, and Erwel had on flowing formal sage-green robes.

Shar felt underdressed in her baking coat. There was flour on it. And streaks of chocolate. Probably a stain or two of liquor as well. Still, she wore it proudly, knowing that she'd have to commission Hulda to make her a bunch more.

"Congratulations, bakers!" Yazgrak called out. "You've made it! No matter what happens at this point, you all should be very proud of yourselves for making it this far."

The crowd behind them cheered loudly for a while before settling down again.

"Y'all have created masterpieces, that's for sure," Erwel said. "The decorating is far better than what we've seen before."

"And though it's a shame to cut into such works of art, we do have to taste the cakes as well," Cyna said, her eyes sparkling.

Shar had the feeling that while Cyna might enjoy making dessert, she preferred eating them sometimes. (Maybe all the time, now.)

Kigora went first. Cyna loved her decorations, how appropriately she'd represented the Human winter solstice. Her flavors were well received, though she'd gone a bit light on the apple liquor that she'd received. The crackling candy was a big hit. Evidently it popped in your mouth. (Shar was going to have to find some to try before they left Anthus.)

Golodhon was praised heavily by the judges for his decorations. Only Erwel had had the silver and gold leaves before. They turned out to be a favorite of all of them—slightly crispy, with a faint peppermint taste. He'd lucked out on his liquor, and had found a peppermint flavor. It had paired well with his cake. However, it turned out that he'd soaked his cakes a bit too much, and the bottom layer was soggy.

Shar's beard trembled slightly as she presented her cake to the judges. (Honestly, she was too tired to be very emotional at this point.)

Yazgrak was the only one of the judges to have made a mirror glaze before, and he explained the process to the other judges. He praised Shar for hers, how perfectly shiny it was, and how it flowed over her cake.

"But girl, you know what I'm going to say," Erwel started off with.

"It isn't cohesive," Shar said with a heavy sigh. "The three layers are too distinct, different from one another."

"Took the words right out of my mouth," Erwel said.

"Now that you see your error, what would you have done differently?" Yazgrak asked.

"Carried the spirits up, through the tiers," Shar said instantly. "Cheeky spirits hanging out on each layer. Maybe tugging at the bow. Trying to see what was in the surprise layer."

Cyna nodded. "That would have made this cake perfect," she said.

Shar nodded, sad that she couldn't win, not with such a huge flaw in her design.

Still, she made the best of it.

The emerald-shaped chocolates dramatically spilled out of the top tier as her surprise. The judges all gasped and Yazgrak in particular seemed very pleased.

"You really thought through how this cake would be presented," he said.

Of course, the judges *loved* Shar's flavors. They always had. The apricot liquor had soaked well into the sponge, giving them the taste of it without it being too much. (Sorry, Cyna. She'd just have to go have a hearty mug of ale [or something stronger] later.) All three tiers tasted great on their own, as well as together. Shar had added a baked walnut brittle for the bottom two layers, and an almond brittle for the top layer.

When the judges finished with their critiques, Shar and the other bakers were escorted to the far end of the open field while the judges deliberated.

"Congratulations," she said to Golodhon. She felt a bit bitter and hollowed out, but she could still be polite about her loss.

"What, you don't think I won?" Kigora asked.

"Maybe," Shar said. "They did like your flavors. But you didn't add enough of your apple liquor."

Kigora shook her head. "It's a minor mistake. It isn't enough to count me out," she said stubbornly.

"You shouldn't count yourself out either," Golodhon said gently to Shar. "You still have a chance."

"Not a good one," Shar said. "I missed the mark on the decorations."

"You're still eligible for *Chocolates Galore!*" Kigora pointed out.

"I know," Shar said. "And hopefully, my family will grant me the time to train this next year and compete. But they might not. I might have to stay and facet gemstones instead."

Kigora made a face at that, and Golodhon said, "I'm sorry."

Shar shrugged. She'd find the time to continue her baking and her studies without her family's support.

Even if it meant sleeping on the floor of Hulda's closet.

The three of them waited. And waited. And waited. The bell tower in the distance rang more than once, letting Shar know that the judges had taken more than an hour deliberating before the bakers were called back to the other side of the clearing.

Three tables had been brought in while the bakers were gone.

One of their cakes sat at the end of each, with servers already cutting into the cakes, ready to serve tiny tastes of them to the audience once the judges were done.

"As you might have guessed, this wasn't an easy decision," Erwel said.

"You bakers didn't make it easy on us judges. And that is a good problem for us to have," Cyna added. "Thank you for that, for presenting us with three such different masterpieces, each so well done. And tasty!"

"We did have to come to an agreement, eventually, though," Yazgrak said. "There were good things, magnificent aspects, to each of your cakes. And there were flaws in each of them as well. It all came down to which cake we'd want to have again."

Shar frowned. That meant that Golodhon wasn't the winner. His cake had been soggy, and the judges wouldn't want to eat that again. Would they?

That meant that her nemesis had won.

Shar swallowed against her dry throat, ready to give Kigora her congratulations.

"And the winner is..." Yazgrak paused dramatically, glancing first at Cyna then at Erwel.

The three of them all said the name at the same time.

"SHAR!"

The crowd erupted in loud cheering. Magical streamers appeared out of nowhere, showering all three bakers in sparkling confetti that disappeared as soon as it touched the earth.

Shar stood as frozen as a granite statue, shocked beyond belief.

Her? She won? How was that possible?

The crowd, her companions congratulating her, and all the other sounds grew muffled as she tried to process what had just happened. Her heart hammered in her chest, louder and harder than an angry smith beating on a stubborn piece of metal.

"Breathe," Golodhon said quietly as he smiled at her.

Shar took a breath and all the sound came rushing back in.

"I won?" she asked, looking first at Golodhon, then at Kigora.

"You did," the Elf said, still smiling.

"Congratulations," Kigora said, the words obviously bitter in her mouth.

"Thank you," Shar said to Kigora, then she turned to the judges. "Thank you, thank you, so much."

"You still have a lot to learn," Yazgrak said with a warm smile.

"But you're capable of learning," Erwel added. "You knew what was wrong with your cake, and how to fix it. That means a lot, and weighed in our judging."

Shar felt the tears running down her face before she realized she was crying.

"I'll do better," she promised. "I'll make you all proud."

"Girl, we're already proud," Erwel said, getting up from behind the judging table and walking over to where Shar stood. "Let me give you a hug."

The Elf bent over slightly and wrapped strong arms around Shar, holding her close for a few moments. "You got this," Erwel said quietly into Shar's ear. "Just breathe. You're the winner. You deserve this."

"Thank you," Shar said, the ground solid under her feet again.

"Let the celebrations begin!" Cyna said. She already had a full wine glass in her hand that she raised as a toast.

The crowd flooded into the area, eager to taste the cakes as well as talk with the bakers.

Leena was the first one to reach Shar, as Hulda easily cleared the path to her.

"Congratulations," the old Dwarf said, also giving Shar a big hug. "Ye did it. I knew ye could."

"Thank you," Shar said, taking Leena's old, wrinkled hands in hers as she leaned back. "I couldn't have done it without you."

"I know," Leena said with a twinkle in her eye. "And now, ye get to do what I didn't. Go to *Chocolates Galore!* And win."

Shar nodded. She had a year to prepare. It wouldn't be enough time—then again, a lifetime wouldn't be long enough either.

She could do this. She'd won the regional contest.

Now, it was time to take on the world.

# PART THREE

## Chocolates Galore!

# That Sweet Thang

〜⟶⟵〜

Though you may have heard stories of austere Elves who exist on sips of dew collected from pristine forests at dawn (weirdos) or Dwarves who do nothing but drink ale (mostly an exaggeration) or even Humans who abstain from all plant matter and who only eat meat (also weirdos), those are all extremes.

For the most part, everyone still has a sweet tooth.

Fortunately, both cane sugar as well as beet sugar are readily available. (Magic makes a lot of the harvesting and processing so much easier than doing it by hand.)

So while Dwarves may complain about the frippery and size of Elvish plated desserts, and Elves may look down their noses at the overly sweet and brightly colored desserts of the Humans, and Humans may disparage the dry scones and crumbly pastries favored by the Dwarves—as well as how so many of those crumbs end up in a Dwarf's bead, though there is a beard oil for that—the one thing they have in common is that, at the end of the day, all people like sweet things.

Pastries. Cakes. Cookies. Scones. Candies. Puddings. Danishes. Cinnamon rolls. Pies.

And chocolate, of course.

Chocolate is not rare, but it is not common either. No one has bathtubs full of chocolate that they can go swimming in. (Also? Eww. Wouldn't want to have to clean up that mess.) It primarily comes in two forms that are readily available, though for a price: powdered (which is cheaper) and bars. Not candy bars, but bars of baking chocolate.

In the larger cities, *chocolates* are available, where someone else has already gone through the hassle of making a dessert from raw chocolate. These shops tend to be rare as well as expensive.

Most desserts are built around using the powdered chocolate. It readily goes into cookies, cakes, pies, and most baked items.

The baking chocolate is for special desserts, as it takes not only a lot of processing, but a lot of skill.

First of all, a chef has to learn how to temper chocolate, which is an art in and of itself.

Then, there's the using of the chocolate once it's been tempered, as a ganache, a covering, a dip, a drizzle, what have you.

Chocolate is...temperamental. It is readily affected by heat and humidity.

Plus, sometimes Chaa, the god of chocolate (at least according to most chefs) has set his face against you, and nothing works.

However, that brings us to *Chocolates Galore!* the chocolate contest that occurs in White Hall, the largest city on the southern continent, once every five years.

Sure, there's prize money. Enough gold to fill that mythical bathtub that once held melted chocolate. Plus baking equipment, including a magical marble board that glows when any chocolate that has been worked on it is perfectly tempered.

Most important, though, at least for those who enter, is the title. Grand Champion of *Chocolates Galore!* That alone is worth the effort, the hard hours of slaving over a hot stove, melting liter upon liter of chocolate, crying and tearing out of hair when Chaa has set his face against the aspiring chocolatier.

That title means employment. Anywhere. Everywhere. It's sort of a ticket for life. Every king, queen, emperor, empress, president, tribal leader, and so on, wants to hire a Grand Champion for their own kitchens, to put that artistry to work for themselves. (This is the other reason why stores selling chocolates are so rare. People would rather have a patron than having to rely on the whims of random customers.)

Competition, as you may have guessed, to even be selected as a contestant is fierce. There are regional contests that one must win first before the big one at White Hall.

*Chocolates Galore!* isn't just a contest, though. It's a week-long celebration of all things sweet. Vendors from both continents show up with amazing goods. Trade deals are brokered. Careers are started, or ended.

Such a massive contest and festival is part of why it is only held once every other years. The sugar hangover from a week of eating sweets doesn't last more than a day or two, but the expense of the travel and provisioning takes its toll.

And people find their own excuses to eat massive amounts of sweets given their own culture and location.

After all, most everyone does have a sweet tooth.

# Shar

⤜⤛

There were days and weeks over the past year, between the end of the regional contest and the start of *Chocolates Galore!* that passed by in the blink of an eye for Shar: time spent cooking at Muddy Bean Chocolates, developing intricate cake designs and executing them, learning to do sugar work (and her first spun sugar project!), as well as exploring every market in Shazirakz, trying new spices and flavor combinations.

Sales at the shop had doubled, easily, due to her new-found fame as winner of the regional contest. She had a lot more custom orders to fill as well, with people asking her to do cakes, cupcakes, or chocolates for a celebration, like a wedding, a graduation, or a birthday.

Other times, Shar felt the grind of getting up early, baking, designing, and learning new recipes. She took different classes every night in order to get the background for making more realistic designs out of chocolate, cake, or even cookies: drawing classes, architecture classes, anatomy classes, art, color, and composition classes. Then she'd rush home to catch a few hours of sleep before getting up the next day to do it all again.

At least Shar now had her family backing her as an official sponsor. Her mother had been the one who'd opened important doors for her that Leena hadn't been able to, like the Elf who she'd studied sugar work with, the Human architect who'd pounded home the importance of a good foundation, and even the Dwarf butcher who helped her understand how creatures were put together.

Now, she was here. In White Hall, two days before the start of *Chocolates Galore!* Curious Cat Shipping had brought her, Hulda, and Leena there, carrying all their equipment and goods. Rafael was staying in the city with them, at least for the start of the contest.

As part of her "entrance fee," Shar and the other four contestants who'd automatically qualified were expected to attend and provide chocolates for one of the expositions that took place at the start of the contest. Ticket holders would choose whose goods they wanted to sample, using tokens to "pay" for what they tried.

The contestant with the most tokens at the end of the day would win some sort of advantage going into the competition.

Luckily, Shar had the stall that her uncle had built for the pop-ups that she and Hulda had continued to do, along with a brand-new banner that Hulda had sewn. It had Shar's name blazoned across the center of it and had emblems from all her sponsors lined along the bottom: Muddy Bean Chocolates, Curious Cat Shipping, Opal-bender Gems, the stylized gemstones that represented Shazirakz and the Dwarves who lived there, and even a little shield representing Hulda's Mineshield family.

The exposition hall was longer than it was wide, with the stalls of the five competitors all lined against one solid wooden wall. (Shar's was the last one, at the end of the line, the farthest from the door.) The ceiling rose up high above Shar's head—it would possibly be tall enough for a giant to stand in. Windows lined the wall the contestants faced, the glass brightened by the mid-afternoon sun. The air was stuffy, but the temperature in the hall was kept artificially cool by enchanted Dwarven stones—each pulsing a pretty blue light and about the size of her head—carefully placed along the wall behind the contestants and their stalls. (Handicapping the contestants by placing them in a hot room wasn't considered fair. At this point.)

Comparing her stall to the four others in the echoing exposition hall made Shar feel a little self-conscious. Hulda, of course, had done a fantastic job helping Shar make her display look appealing, with boxes stacked at different levels to better display the treats, little holders for cards from her sponsors as well as for Shar herself, and beautiful truffles, bonbons, miniature chocolate tarts, and chocolate-dipped baked pastries on display.

However, everyone else had *much* larger setups, some with chocolates stacked five tiers or more tall. (Then again, as Shar was a Dwarf, displaying chocolates so high meant she'd never be able to reach them without a ladder or an Elf handy.) Every other contestant came with two or three stalls that attached together.

Instead of a single color of cloth draped over most everything, the others had fancy hand-embroidered pieces, with their names and logos (logos!) stitched prominently into them. The banners over their stalls had dozens of sponsors listed.

The contest rules had stated that Shar had to provide seventy pieces of chocolate for the exposition. She thought that she'd been pushing her luck by providing one hundred pieces.

To her dismay, her neighbors had what looked like two hundred pieces. Or more.

Though she'd carefully read every report of past contests that she could lay her hands on, the expositions that took place before the contests hadn't been as well documented.

No matter how good her chocolate might taste, or her various flavor combinations, no one was going to vote for her little rustic stall. She had been careful to provide goods certain to appeal to all the races of people, so she knew that her flavors would please everyone.

Plus, she was bound to run out of treats before the audience got around to voting.

A big glass cylinder sat on one corner of the front table, where guests were expected to place their tokens.

Shar had no problem imagining it staying empty the entire time.

Watchers were employed at every stall to make sure that the contestants weren't resorting to either magic or bribery to get people to leave tokens. Shar had already offered samples to the pair standing beside her stall—a gruff Dwarven guard and a tall Human, both wearing white tabards with the outline of a hall stitched on them, the symbol of the city. They'd turned her down, though the Dwarf had taken a few moments before he'd said no, staring at her chocolate dipped pastries.

When the other watcher wasn't looking, Shar caught the eye of the Dwarf and picked up one of the pastries, putting it to the side at the back of her stall for him to take later.

He gave her a grin then turned all serious again.

Noise rushed like a wave through the hall when the doors were thrown open and ticket holders came strolling in.

Of course, everyone made a bee-line to the largest of the stalls. Not only did it have hundreds of chocolates on display, it also had a wind-up carousel that token holders could pluck their chocolates from. Though the contestant himself was Human, Shar would bet her beard hair that the mechanical device had been manufactured by a Dwarf.

Eventually, people made their way down the line to try Shar's chocolates. She tried to limit her guests to just a few, or one of each dessert she had on display, rather than allow them to grab dozens for themselves.

Somehow, she had to make what she provided last until the end of the exposition, two hours hence.

When Shar looked down the line, she could already see tokens lining the bottoms of glass jars on her competitors' stations, while hers remained depressingly empty.

Then a group of elegant Elves came up.

"Hi, sweetheart!" one of them said in a hearty greeting.

Erwel stood in front of her! She looked as gorgeous as ever, her black skin and hair setting off her elegant green-and-gold formal robes. And this time, she had what looked like tiny bonbons worked in silver filigree in her hairclips.

"Judge Erwel! So nice to see you," Shar said stiffly, bowing a little.

"Girl, none of that. Get over here," Erwel commanded, indicating that Shar come out from behind her stall.

Shar was completely unprepared for Erwel to envelop her in a big hug.

She felt herself taking a deep breath, though, smelling the faint woodsy scent of the Elf, the warmth letting her drop her shoulders and relaxing a smidgen.

"You're going to be just fine," Erwel said whispered. "I have faith in you."

Shar stepped back and gave the Elf a wobbly nod before she hopped back, safely behind her stall again. "What can I serve you?"

"Tell me about everything you have here," Erwel said loudly.

Shar complied, explaining how the tiny tart shell was made from almond flour, with a chocolate-ginger custard and decorated with artistic white-chocolate shavings, the various flavors of the bonbons and truffles, as well as the nod to her heritage with the crumbly pastry sure to please any Dwarf (and their beard). The flaky dough had been wrapped around a thick, chocolate ganache, then more chocolate drizzled over it.

"It all sounds delicious," Erwel said, and her companions, three other Elves, all nodded seriously. "We'll take one of each."

"Certainly," Shar said, gladly handing out her sweets to this crew.

After they withdrew, more people drifted toward Shar's display. They'd already gorged themselves on the chocolates from the others —so maybe they could take a gamble on hers.

Shar watched her inventory shrink. They were only halfway

through the exposition and she had maybe a handful of tokens in her jar.

Suddenly, Erwel was in front of her again.

"Girl, let me just say that you haven't lost your touch," she said as she poured a handful of tokens into Shar's jar.

The Elf behind her did the same.

Followed by the third Elf.

Instead of a line of people waiting to get chocolates and sweets, a line formed of people wanting to give Shar tokens.

She ran out of her inventory about twenty minutes before the end of the exposition. (She'd managed to sneak the one pastry to the Dwarf watcher so it wasn't sitting on her back table.) And yet, people were still coming up and placing tokens in her jar. Seemed that most of the audience had chosen to sample all the offerings before making their decision about who to give their token to.

By the end of the two hours, Shar didn't feel like a completely failure. She suspected that she didn't have the most tokens, though she hadn't been able to walk down the line to check. However, she hoped she didn't have the least, either.

Hulda was finally allowed back into the hall to help Shar break down her stall and to chat about how everything had gone.

Shar was far from optimistic. But just because she hadn't won the first advantage didn't mean that she was going to lose the entire contest.

Right?

# Shar

❦

The next day, the finalists were expected to attend the bakeoff between the runners up. There had been five regional contests that year. The other winners were standing with Shar close to the doorway of the courtyard, while the second and third place contestants stood in a group behind them. Guards prevented the two groups from talking to one another.

Nobody knew how many finalist slots were available that year for *Chocolates Galore!* The organizers changed the number from year to year.

So no one knew if there would be one bake to winnow down the runners up, two bakes, or more.

The mystery—and the speculation—were as much for the audience as the contestants. According to the people running the contest, a little mystery kept the audience engaged.

The day dawned bright and clear, though Shar had heard that there might be rain later in the week. Hopefully, they wouldn't be expected to do meringues or anything else that was sensitive to humidity. Chocolate was finicky enough.

The festivities kicked off in a very large courtyard. Comforting stone made up the walls and the ground was covered with flagstones. Bleachers had been set up at one end, stuffed with at least a couple hundred people. A long table where the judges would sit stretched along the other side. Shar stood with the other finalists just outside the entrance. They had instructions to enter the courtyard when their name was called, greet the crowd, then stand on the platform beside the judging table.

Shar waved to Golodhon standing behind her, waiting with the rest of the runners up. He gave her a serene smile and waved back. Kigora ignored Shar's wave—which honestly?—Shar was kind of expecting.

The five finalists were composed of two Humans, two Elves, and Shar, the one Dwarf. She had no idea who the the rest of the contestants would be, though part of her hoped that she'd be able to compete with (though probably just against) Golodhon.

Shar didn't have much use for Kigora and her attitude, and she didn't expect anything other than what she'd been shown.

Though the wait seemed to last forever, Shar heard the herald greeting the crowd and getting them settled down far too soon.

This was it. The start of everything.

The herald called Vincent, the Human who'd had the carousel at his stall, first. The crowd loudly cheered for him as he walked across the courtyard to the platform.

Much to Shar's surprise, she was called second. She held her head high and marched herself into the courtyard.

The cheering was *much* louder in the courtyard than she'd anticipated. She still did as she'd been instructed: waved to the crowd, nodded and smiled at them, before she walked up the provided steps to the platform, coming to stand next to Vincent.

Aiolas, one of the two Elves, was third, followed by Wulfa the other Human, while last was Penelo, the other Elf.

The rest of the contestants weren't allowed into the courtyard yet. Instead, the herald said, "Stand ready to be judged!"

Shar found herself automatically straightening up.

After the crowd had settled a bit, the herald continued. "Welcome Erde Jordey, baker extraordinaire!"

Out of a side door, a strange looking Human came striding out. His head was shaved clean of hair, as was his upper lip. Instead, he had the smallest gray-and-white goatee hanging off his chin, giving it a pointed look. He wore round spectacles and had a fairly flat face.

What was most noticeable about him, though, was his jacket. It had an abstract pattern of shiny red, white, and gold patches of cloth, each outlined with black sequins. Shar had never seen anyone wearing something so colorful and flashy. Hulda was certain to have a lot of opinions about his outfit.

Shar knew a little of Erde's history. He'd gone to all five regional contests over the course of three years, and had won four of them. Only then did he go on to *Chocolates Galore!* to sweep the title. He was married to another baker, a male Elf, who he'd met at one of the contests. (While it wasn't common for the races to cross-marry, it did happen. More so for Humans than any of the others.)

Erde waved to the crowd, calling out to them, "By the Gods! It's good to see y'all!" He danced a little jig, performing for the crowd, saying, "Well, frost my front and call me a fruit tart, I'm just so happy to be here!" Eventually, he made his way to the table and sat down.

"Now, to introduce to you a baker who really doesn't need much of an introduction. He's forgotten more about baking and technique than most of you will ever learn. The one, the only, Fenryl Elmenor!"

Shar gasped. Then the realization of who exactly she was going to be judge by sunk in and she held back her groan. Fenryl was one of the toughest judges out there. He'd been baking for over a century. He still held a monthly contest, "Slay Fenryl," where other bakers tried to outbake him. Very few won.

Though Shar had read as much about all the judges as she could, she still was surprised at how striking Fenryl looked. Not just because he was an Elf and naturally beautiful, but because he had light red hair, which tended to be rare among the Elves. Freckles dotted his pale skin, and cold blue eyes stared out at the crowd.

He waved, but didn't play to them at all, not like Erde had, before he walked over to the table and took his seat. He did shake Erde's hand and looked pleased to see him.

"This next youngster has been tearing it up not just with her cooking but also with her colorful commentary. Welcome Zignealynn 'Zigli' Chaosbane!"

Shar nodded thoughtfully as the very stout Dwarf came out. She wore a bright red brocade vest over a pink shirt, both of which set off her black skin. Her beard had tiny white and silver braids cascading from it, with diamond beads at the end of each—Shar later learned they were extensions, something she'd never even thought about adding to her own beard.

The crowd cheered even louder for Zigli, if that was possible. She walked toward them and gestured for the crowd to get louder, which they happily did.

Huh. Fenryl had gone from looking pleased to stone cold. Did he not like Zigli?

According to the reports that Shar had read, Zigli had started out as a savory chef and hadn't been doing baking for that long. Shar would have to look up whether or not she'd tried to "Slay Fenryl" at some point. And whether she'd won. (Shar learned later that not only had Zigli won, she also worked as a judge sometimes at the competition.)

"Here comes trouble," Fenryl said as Zigli finally turned back from the crowd and approached the panel.

"Don't you try me," Zigli warned Fenryl as she sat down, shaking an admonishing finger at Fenryl.

Finally, Fenryl's stony composure cracked and he smiled at her. "Good to see you."

"You too!" Zigli said, her sunny smile brightening up the entire area. "And you, Erde! How's that lovely husband of yours?"

"Oh, Darnathin's just lovely! He'll be around later on in the week," Erde said.

"It'll be good to see him," Fenryl said seriously. "We'll have to go out for dinner or something."

That just made Erde smile even more.

The herald waited for the judges to stop chatting before he made the next announcement.

"Now, welcome the runners up from the five regional contests!" the herald boomed.

The ten bakers walked in, the crowd cheering again, though it wasn't as loud as it had been. Shar wasn't surprised that each individual baker hadn't been announced. They probably wouldn't do that until the very end of this round of baking, after the contestants had been chosen for the finale.

"Every year, we do things a little differently," Fenryl said.

Zigli nodded. "It's good to shake things up. Not get as stodgy as some *old* bakers we know," throwing a glance at Fenryl.

The Elf just sighed, shook his head, and continued. "This year, we're having a single bakeoff for the runners up. There are ten of you here, and by the end of the day, there will only be five of you. However, those final five will be joining the other finalists in the *Chocolates Galore!* contest."

The crowd gasped. Even Shar felt herself take a bracing breath.

Wow. To knock out half the hopefuls in one contest? That was pretty intense.

It didn't bode well for the rest of the contest.

"Now, y'all should be proud of where yer standing," Erde said. "To have made it this far is quite an accomplishment. Can we get another round of applause for these amazing bakers?"

The crowd cheered and clapped, louder this time, with Erde smiling and nodding at them.

"Take a look at the bakers standing here," Zigli said, indicating Shar's group. "They had a contest of their own, yesterday, where they earned tokens from a hungry crowd. They're standing in the order of most tokens to least," indicating Vincent as the head of the line, and Penelo at the end.

Shar blinked, surprised. She'd received the second largest amount of tokens? Even though her display had been so rustic and small?

"These are the people you're here to beat," Zigli continued. "Are you ready for the challenge?"

"Aye!" the bakers called.

"I said, are you ready for the challenge?" Zigli asked in a much louder voice.

"AYE!" the bakers shouted.

All the judges grinned at the response.

"Our focus for this week is chocolate, of course," Fenryl said. "Every day, you're going to be testing your ability to manipulate this amazing ingredient. Today, is no different." He nodded to the runners up solemnly before he continued.

"Because y'all want to reach for the stars, yer gonna have to show us that in yer cakes," Erde continued.

"Twelve layer cakes, to be exact," Zigli said. "Not three tiers with four layers each, but a single cake, twelve layers tall."

Shar was suddenly very, *very* glad that she wasn't having to compete in this round. Of course, she had a delicious chocolate cake recipe. More than one, in fact. And she'd done what she'd considered a tall cake, before. Six layers.

Twelve layers required a lot more architecting. Possibly even a different kind of cake on the bottom for a more stable foundation. Or maybe just thicker.

"The cakes must be chocolate," Fenryl said. "But the fillings can be whatever you like."

"They better taste good," Erde warned.

"And the decorations need to be enough to get you to the next level," Zigli added.

"The city has opened its doors to us, and you will be cooking in the exposition kitchen," Fenryl said. "You'll have three hours to complete your cakes. They have to withstand not only the heat in the kitchen, but being carried from there to here, the judging courtyard."

Shar nodded. She'd already knew that from reading the various reports from previous contests. More than one baker had been sent home because their dessert hadn't been stable enough to be walked from the kitchen to the courtyard.

Special magical bubbles were always used to transport the cakes, so the contestants could never claim foul, that someone had sabotaged their goods. (A couple tried. They were all proven wrong. For every contest, the organizers hired a magical seer. Using their skills, the seer could prove that the baker's product would have fallen or melted, regardless of the circumstances.)

"Are you ready?" Zigli asked.

The bakers nodded.

Zigli sighed and shook her head. Then, using Fenryl's shoulder to support her, climbed up so she stood on the seat of her chair. Only once she was balanced there did she call out to the bakers. "ARE YOU READY?"

"YES!" the bakers shouted back.

"Then get hustling," Erde said. "Y'all need to work harder than two Dwarves fightin' over that last drop of ale."

"Follow me!" the herald said, and led the bakers out the door of the courtyard to the kitchen, which as far as Shar had been able to figure out, was just a few doors down.

Now, it was time to wait until the other bakers finished, before Shar could find out who the rest of her competition would be.

# Shar

Shar spent some time talking with the other contestants, learning their stories. All of them had been cooking for much longer than she had, of course. Still, most of them were kind, and interested in Dwarven baking. Only Vincent stood to one side, not deigning to chat with the rest of them, already convinced that he was going to win the entire contest.

Then again, he had won the first advantage. There was a noticeable trend that the baker who won the first challenge went on to win the whole contest. It happened at least half the time.

But he hadn't won the first challenge. Just the preheat, as it were. Shar (and okay, maybe the others as well) were determined to take him down a peg. Or three.

Eventually, the runners up finished their bake and cakes started drifting into the courtyard, encased in their magical bubbles. They floated over to a table that a couple of people had just set up, in front of the judges' table.

It looked to Shar as if one baker didn't do twelve layers. Or at least not twelve tall layers, as it was considerably shorter than the rest.

It had been elegantly decorated, with swirls of different colored frosting, so maybe the judges would let it pass.

The cakes all had different decorations. Some of the bakers had gone abstract, with thin twirls of chocolate and disks decorating the sides. Others had gone more literal, like the one decorated to look like a stone tower. She would bet that the cake showing a woodland scene had been done by Golodhon, or one of the other Elves. Beautiful trees with pretty flowers snaked up the sides of the towering pastry, and the topper was a silver chocolate sphere to represent the moon. She also liked the one with fireworks represented on top, with colorful chocolate stars that had sparkling trails behind them.

It turned out to be a blind tasting by the judges. They didn't know which baker had done which cake. Shar and the other bakers didn't know either.

The shorter cake turned out to have a gummy consistency, despite its elegant swirls of frosting. Erde commented on how there was no dressing up that pig, that no amount of lipstick would help.

The judges nitpicked on *everything*. Shar felt intimidated, knowing that she had to do everything perfect, every time. Though generally Shar was confident in her flavors, it appeared that even the slightest mismeasurement of salt would bring down the wrath of the judges.

After tasting and critiquing all of the cakes, the judges sat to one side and discussed their judgment. A magical bubble enclosed them so not only could no one hear what they were discussing, they were also slightly blurred so no one could read their lips.

When the judges finished their deliberations, they made a show of arranging the cakes from best to worst. Zigli and Fenryl played at moving a few cakes back and forth, as if still arguing which they considered the best.

Only after the cakes were in order did they call the bakers up, introducing the top five.

Shar wasn't thrilled that Kigora had made the stone tower, which had been chosen as the best of the cakes, putting her in first place. The better news was that Golodhon was right behind her, in second. One more Dwarf joined the finalists, which left the total at three Dwarves, three Elves, and four Humans.

The judges thanked the other contestants and sent them on their way.

"So, should we get baking?" Fenryl asked the remaining bakers.

Shar gulped. She'd expected that she'd have the rest of the day off, not that there would be back-to-back contests. Several of the runners up who'd joined the finalists on their platform paled.

"Naw," Zigli said. "You don't want *hangry* bakers with *hangry* pastries coming after you."

"By the Gods, I know we just ate a bunch of delicious cake, but I'm still starving! Worse than an Elf in a desert, with no dew drops to sup on," Erde commented. "Think they could whip us up something savory?"

Fenryl gave a lazy, yet challenging, smile to the bakers. "You up for this?"

Shar had no idea what was coming, what the judges were up to. But she gamely nodded with the others.

"So the kitchen has been restocked—" Fenryl started off, until Zigli thwacked him, *hard*, on the arm.

"Y'all going to give them a heart attack," Zigli told Fenryl. "There's *no* second contest bake today."

"But I'm still *hangry!*" Erde complained.

"I'll take care of you, sweetie," Zigli said. "How about we have a judges' wager?"

Fenryl gave that lazy yet challenging smile again, something with a smug edge to it that Zigli seemed to just want to smack off his face.

The judges decided to challenge each other to a savory cookoff, plates of appetizers that they planned on serving to the contestants.

That didn't appear to be good enough for Fenryl. "I still want to see the contestants cook!" he complained. "Get to know them a bit through their food."

"How about this?" Zigli said.

Shar didn't trust the gleam in her eye.

"Let's pick us some assistants from the finalists," Zigli said. "That way, we can get to know them better. Who knows? Might learn a thing or two about cooking from the young bucks."

"Whatever," Fenryl said, rolling his eyes. "Does that sound agreeable to you guys?"

Shar nodded eagerly. The chance to actually cook *with* one of the judges? To learn from them? Absolutely!

"I can work with that," Erde said. "Hells bells, I can work with anything!"

The judges made a show of playing slug, snake, frog, determining who would choose first.

It occurred to Shar that this was all for the audience's benefit. The judges had worked out the order—and everything else—long beforehand.

Fenryl chose first, Erde second, and Zigli third.

Of course, Fenryl chose Vincent for his first pick. The Human smugly strode over to the Elf's side.

Whatever. Shar's flavors would beat his.

"Well, by the Gods, honey, this is working out just dandy for me!" Erde said. "I'd be more than happy to take ye, Shar, iffen y'all will have me."

"I'd love to," Shar said, though honestly, she was a little intimidated by such an exuberant and outspoken judge. However, she was also certain that she could learn things from him, as he'd been in so many contests and probably had a lot of tricks up his (admittedly, glittery) sleeves when it came to winning.

Shar may have given a small jump of joy when Erde picked

Golodhon on his next round. Erde's last pick was Ryne, one of the Humans who'd been in the runners up contest.

As there were ten contestants and three judges, the last person standing awkwardly by themselves after three rounds of picks was Penelo, the Elf finalist who'd had the fewest number of tokens the day before.

Fenryl politely invited her to his team, giving him a slight advantage with four bakers, while the other teams had three. However, Shar had no idea what the stakes were, how they'd be judged.

Each baker needed to create a savory dish that would go with a flight of appetizers. It turned out that the judges wouldn't necessarily be making their own dish, but would be there to help everyone get their tasks done.

As they only had thirty minutes, and it was a savory challenge, the bakers were going to need all the help they could get.

By the time they'd walked (quickly) to the exposition hall where they'd be baking, Shar already had a plan in mind. No one talked about what they were making while they walked—that appeared to be against whatever rules the judges had decided on—so each team gathered around one of the big tables on the side as soon as they came in.

"What are y'all thinking?" Erde asked, paper and pencil in hand. "I'm thinking everything goes good with cheese."

"How about a stuffed mushroom cap?" Shar said.

"What's it got in it?" Erde said.

"Garlic and onions, browned in butter, with fried sage, rosemary, thyme, salt, black pepper, and clove," Shar reeled off. "And I can add cheese."

"Sounds mighty tasty!" Erde said, then he turned to Golodhon.

"I can do an elegant small bite—a cucumber slice, with a dill, chestnut, and cheese spread, then a carrot rosette on top," the Elf replied.

Shar grinned. Seemed that since that challenge with the unlikely pairings, Golodhon had gotten familiar with dill.

"I'll do a quick cheese cracker," Ryne said when Erde turned to her, "with a cheese, port, and fig sauce."

"Perfect!" Erde said. "I'll help you with your prep first," he added with a smile at Golodhon. "Now, I know I got all these meaty Human fingers. But just you watch. I've been known to turn a delicate peel or two."

With that, the group rushed to their stations, waiting for the bell that told them it was time to get going.

First thing Shar got going were the hazelnuts. She gave them a very light coating of oil, sprinkled salt on them, and got them into the oven to start roasting.

Then it was time to start working on the mushrooms. She was so grateful that they were already cleaned. She removed the stems, brushed the caps with melted butter, added a touch of salt, then put those into the oven as well.

After browning the butter, she added minced garlic and onions, letting those caramelize before adding in the chopped-up mushroom stems. Then she added her spices, as well as some lemon zest. She didn't have time to add lemon juice to her mixture then reduce it, so just the peel of the lemon would have to do, which would give her the flavor of lemon without all that liquid.

Erde came by at that point, tasting her filling, asking her to add a bit more of the pepper and clove. He grated the cheese that she melted into the rest of her filling, then went over to see how Ryne was doing.

In a separate pan, Shar fried the sage leaves until they were crispy. Took her caps out of the oven and stuffed them with her fried mixture. Added the smallest squeeze of lemon on top of each then the chopped up nuts. On the very top, she sprinkled the crumbled up sage. Between the nuts and the sage, she'd have some texture in her dish, and not just soft mushrooms.

Shar had just finished when the watcher called time.

To her delight, instead of being judged, all the bakers were told to grab a plate and serve themselves, to try the food made by their fellow bakers.

Shar had to admit that Golodhon's dish was not only visually stunning but his sauce packed a punch of flavor. A few others stood out to her, like Wulfa's delightful crispy fried potatoes and Penelo's tart lemon-and-walnut custard. (All right, so Kigora's was pretty good as well: a mixture of sweet and spicy peppers served with a garlic sauce in a lettuce cup. However, Kigora seemed determined to not talk with Shar, but just to look down her nose at the other Dwarf, so Shar returned the favor and didn't bother trying to chat with her either.)

The judges mingled with the bakers, talking with them, asking their opinions on the different dishes, on cooking, baking, and so on.

It made the judges seem more like people and less like gods waiting to pounce on their first mistake. Oh, Shar knew that they'd still be judged harshly. But she thought much more kindly of all of them by the time the afternoon had worn down.

The bakers also learned the story behind this cook. The judges had, at first, wanted the runners up to be paired with the finalists for their first cook, then have the opportunity to taste each other's baked goods. The people running the contest had turned that down at the last minute, but offered the judges this opportunity instead.

Shar wearily went back to the inn where all of the bakers were staying, chatting with Golodhon on the way there.

He made an effort to say something to Kigora, but she ignored him just as she'd snubbed Shar.

Shar and Golodhon shrugged their shoulders at each other, and continued catching up.

The runners up had had to bake twice that day and were pretty tired. Shar admitted to being exhausted as well, heading off to the room she shared with Leena and Hulda after telling her companions about the afternoon.

She had no idea what the judges would have in mind for them the next day.

She was certain, though, that this contest was going to be full of twists and turns.

Hopefully, she would be up for all the challenges.

# Time and Time Again

For the ease of commerce, the various races on Indunel have all agreed on similar measurements of time. This was not always the case. (Historians *still* argue whether or not Holden's Massacre—which occurred over two centuries ago, by the Humans against the Elves—occurred because those Elves were insisting on one hundred minutes per hour, as well as one hundred seconds per minute, as that was so much easier in terms of the math.)

Likewise, people have agreed on seven days in a week, with the last day being the day of rest. And that days form weeks, weeks form months, and so on.

Where the disagreement still lies is when a year actually begins.

For the Elves, who are attuned with the moon, the new year starts on the summer solstice, when the nights start getting longer and the moonlight is stronger. The Merfolk have a similar tradition, as the tides are controlled by the moon.

Humans start their year with the winter solstice, when the sun starts to become prominent again. (And as they are the most prevalent race, everyone else tends to agree on their structure of months forming years.)

Dwarves are kind of the odd race, as they prefer to live underground, and therefore don't bother with the sun or the moon as much.

Instead, Dwarves used to track years based on when the mountain passes opened and they could get their goods to market, or merchants could get to them. This meant that in Ye Olden Times<sup>TM</sup> the actual date of the new year shifted considerably, depending on how snowy the winter got and how warm the spring was.

In these decadent modern times, Dwarves celebrate the start of the new year the first week of the third month, according to the Human calendar of months.

There are still those who insist on using the older standards of time, who count Human years based on monarchies, so it would be the year 839 for them, whereas most people think of it being the year 1845.

Fortunately, those older dates are now treated as a curiosity, or the answer to a pub quiz, and no longer a fighting matter.

For now.

# Shar

Shar stood with the other bakers on a platform, next to the judging table, the following morning. The day was crisp still, promising to be bright and sunny. Over breakfast, Shar had read the sheet that described the previous day's bake, pleased (though slightly embarrassed) that she'd been singled out for her mushroom caps.

They were pretty simple, honestly. However, due to the amount of black peppers that she'd included, Fenryl had automatically assumed that she'd used chilies, when she hadn't. The cloves were what gave the dish the earthiness that chilis generally brought.

After the herald got the crowd settled down, he called out the judges. Erde's jacket had so many colors it made Shar's eyes hurt a little. This time, small ribbons were sewn into it, like fringe, not just across the front but up the sleeves. The other two wore much more mundane clothes, with Fenryl in formal Elven robes in shades of green that made his pale complexion and red hair stand out, while Zigli wore primarily white and gold, not just her vest and shirt but also braided into her beard and hair.

Fenryl addressed the bakers and the crowd. "You are looking sharp today. Everyone ready for a showdown?"

The crowd responded with loud cheering.

Shar was never going to get used to noise like that.

"Now, Fenryl, we talked about this," Erde admonished. "This week is supposed to be a celebration, not a war."

"Yeah, Fenryl," Zigli smirked. "Joyous. Not combative, old, and stodgy. Like some people I could name."

Fenryl rolled his eyes at that. "All right, then what do you two have in mind?"

"Ya know, I was thinking of celebrations, last night," Erde said. "My husband is coming home soon, and we're agonna be celebrating when he gets here."

"And?" Fenryl said, looking as though he was already regretting prompting Erde to continue.

"I was thinking that maybe we should be celebrating celebrations!" Erde said. "Now, y'all know that most Human of holidays, the first day of spring."

Shar nodded slowly. There was something about poles being set up in Human villages and towns, with ribbons streaming from them. People did a dance, weaving the ribbons around the pole.

Maybe that was why Erde's jacket was covered in ribbons?

"Why don't you tell us about it?" Zigli said.

"It's to give thanks to the Goddess Idite for all the hard work she's about to do, to bring life to the earth again," Erde said. "It's to celebrate the fecundity of the world. All the mothers are praised and praised."

With that, Erde stood up and turned, so that his side was facing the crowd.

Suddenly, a baby bump grew across his stomach. It had to be an illusion. And a pretty funny one, Erde reacting with surprise as he fondly stroked his hand across his pregnant stomach.

"So let's honor the ones who give us life by making stuffed desserts," Erde concluded.

"Stuffed desserts, huh?" Zigli asked. "But what kind?"

"There's stuffed cakes, stuffed donuts, stuffed hand pies, stuffed chocolates, even stuffed pastries, like cupcakes, cookies, and tarts," Fenryl continued.

"One of each sounds great," Erde said.

"That's too easy," Zigli said. "These bakers all know how to make a stuffed dessert."

Shar grit her teeth. Sure, making a stuffed dessert wouldn't be that bad.

"How about each baker make two stuffed desserts?" Erde suggested. "I gotta fill up my belly."

"That sounds fair," Fenryl said. "One dessert of their choosing, and one that's assigned to them. The desserts have to go together, though, and tell a story."

Shar held back her sigh. Making a single dessert with a stuffed element actually wasn't that easy, because not only did it have to bake and cool, then she had to make whatever the filling was supposed to be. And then decorate it.

Making two? And having them relate to each other? That really did make it a challenge. Particularly since they didn't get to choose the second one but had it assigned to them.

"So, everyone come up and grab a card," Zigli said, brandishing cards that each had ribbons tied to the ends of them.

The bakers filed up orderly to get their cards. Of course, the cards were blank. Shar could feel the magical dot that covered over her selected dessert name.

"Now, Vincent, we owe you an advantage," Fenryl said. "After everyone's dessert is revealed, you get to choose whether to keep the one you've received or if you want to exchange it with someone else."

Shar sighed. That would have been such a good advantage! To be able to choose what you had to pair together, so you'd make things that you knew would complement each other.

Still, she was determined to make this work.

Of course, Shar got the one dessert item she dreaded: donuts.

Dwarves made baked donuts, not fried, as they preferred their pastries more dense and chewy (the better to feed their beards with). However, she was also aware that Humans and Elves preferred the lighter, fried version.

Vincent received hand pies, which he immediately exchanged for chocolate bonbons, the card that Lambert, one of the other Humans, had picked.

"Now remember, your desserts must feature chocolate," Erde warned. "As well as be tasty enough to make any new mother proud."

Shar had to giggle as he stroked his belly again, as if showing off his own new life.

"We'll be coming by later on to see how you're doing," Zigli said.

Shar took a deep breath at that.

When the judges came to visit, that almost always meant that they'd throw the contestants a twist, some additional item or flavor that they needed to incorporate.

"Make us all proud," Fenryl added. "Because at the end of the day, two of you will be going home."

Shar gulped. She was certain that most of the other competitors did as well.

Would the judges be eliminating two competitors every time? Until there were only two left in the finale? That happened occasionally. Other times, *Chocolates Galore!* was spread out over ten days or so.

Shar decided to act as if there were only going to be five bakes before the end of the contest, and to run as hard and fast as she could (for a Dwarf) to the finish line.

Because she was going to finish on top.

Nothing else would be acceptable.

∿

Despite Shar's determination, everything went wrong with her cook. The first batch of donuts that she made didn't rise, and she had to start a second batch at the last minute. She'd chosen to make a stuffed cake along with her bismark donuts. She planned to tie them together with her decor, placing the donuts around the outside edge of her cake, decorating them to look like flower petals, while the cake itself would be the center of the flower. In addition to chocolate, she was going to highlight honey, and have bees buzzing between the donuts and the cake.

An audience sat at one end of the long exhibition hall, watching the competition. After the judges got to view the bakers' creations and taste them, the leftovers would go to lucky ticket holders. Fortunately, as before, they sat behind a magic bubble so Shar couldn't hear them.

A couple of the bakers—Vincent and Lambert—played to the crowd, holding up ingredients so they could see what the bakers were using. Shar knew that splitting her focus like that would be a surefire way for her to make mistakes.

Shar had already put her cake in the oven when the judges came in. She'd delayed as long as she dared, afraid that whatever they threw at the bakers would require her to rethink everything she was doing and have to start over. Again.

At least the illusion of Erde's pregnancy was gone.

Shar tried not to be too nervous when the judges came over to see what she was working on. They admired her ingenuity at coming up with a solution for making her dough rise. She'd taken a large pan, then put two bowls in it: one with her dough and one that she poured boiling hot water into. This gave her a warm box for growing her dough.

"Have you made fried donuts before?" Zigli asked.

"Only baked ones," Shar admitted.

"Be sure to get your oil hot enough, otherwise the donuts will turn out greasy," Erde warned.

"Thank you. I'll do that," Shar said, grateful for the tip.

Shar was planning on a whipped chocolate ganache to fill her donuts. For her cake, she made a chocolate sponge cake that was light and airy. It tied into the donuts with both of them using nutmeg as the primary spice. She was going to hollow out the center of the cake, then place sprinkles that she had yet to make, so they'd spill out colorfully when the cake was cut.

The judges were careful to just ask her about her cake and flavors. They didn't want to hear about her design.

Once they left, Shar took a deep breath, refocusing herself. She didn't want to get confused by the questions that the judges asked. She had a list of tasks to do, and she needed to get back to them.

However, Shar was stopped a second time when the judges interrupted everyone.

"While we were talking earlier, Fenryl brought up a good point," Erde said. "How are we going to know that these are spring festival cakes?"

Shar blinked. She should have thought of that! The twist that the judges were about to throw at them was obvious.

"So y'all need to make an edible pole, decorated with edible ribbons, as part of your design," Zigli added.

Crap.

How was Shar going to incorporate that into her flower design? She wasn't about to stick a huge pole in the center of her cake. That would ruin what she had in mind. Plus, the center of her cake wasn't going to be solid, not if she had stuffed it with sprinkles.

Shar's hands moved automatically as she whipped up the raspberry and chocolate ganache that she was planning on using between the layers of her cake.

What was she going to do?

Eventually, it came to her.

Not one pole, but four. Standing around the edges of her cake, surrounding the center flower. She could make them fit in with the rest of her design in terms of colors, and maybe have the ribbons floating down between the petal-donuts. And there should be a bee on one of the poles as well.

It wasn't a perfect solution, but it was something she could make that would work in the time allotted.

Shar felt like a crazy person by the end of the bake, trying to get her cake decorated, her donuts finished, make the poles stand up, dye the ribbons to be the right color, and make and place all of her bees.

Vincent dramatically fell to the floor when the watchers called time. Of course he did, still playing to the crowd.

Shar just rolled her eyes, rolled her shoulders to try to relax, then followed the floating stream of cakes out the door, to where the judges awaited.

She wasn't sure why she hadn't been expecting there to be a large crowd of people watching the parade of desserts. Maybe because it was the first bake? And there hadn't really been a crowd at regionals until the last couple of days?

Shar mostly ignored the number of people yelling and cheering as they walked by. Of course, Vincent and Lambert played to them, waving and giving enthusiastic thumbs up signs.

The order of who would be called first wasn't random, like it had been at regionals. The people who ran this contest seemed to have some sort of story arc in mind, and so informed the bakers that they would be called up in a specific order.

Strange.

Shar was judged third. She had no idea if that meant she was on the top (which she was pretty sure she wasn't), the bottom, or somewhere in between.

"So, it's your first bake here," Fenryl started off with. "And though this is good, there are a lot of places where you can improve. First off, the frosting isn't completely smooth on the cake."

Fenryl pointed to a tiny area where the frosting was disturbed.

Shar gulped.

Crap.

Were the judges always going to be that picky?

"There are fingerprints still on your ribbon," he continued. "And the glaze on your donuts is cracked."

"I'm gonna stop ye there, Fenryl," Erde said. "That glaze on the donuts is supposed to be cracked. Am I right?"

Shar nodded. That was how she'd been taught to make a donut glaze.

"It isn't very elegant," Fenryl said, glaring at the offending donut.

"Just think of it as artistic," Zigli said with a roll of her eyes.

Shar served the judges, getting ooohs and ahhhs when the sprinkles came pouring out of the center of her cake.

"You know, when we saw you in the kitchen, I was worried about your donuts," Fenryl said "But these are delicious. Crispy fried outside, tender and pillowy inside. And that chocolate ganache that you stuffed them with is perfect."

Shar blinked, surprised. Fenryl was so picky! For him to compliment her on anything meant a lot.

She ended up in the solid middle of the group of bakers, which wasn't the worst outcome as far as she was concerned. Vincent came out on top, which made Shar (and possibly a couple of other bakers) gnash their teeth. That win was just going to make him more obnoxious.

Poor Penelo was sent home, as was Lambert, the other Human who'd been playing it up to the audience. Seemed he'd been showing off more than Shar had realized, because he hadn't finished everything.

Shar knew that sometimes fan favorites were allowed to continue regardless of their bakes. She suspected that with someone like Fenryl, that wouldn't come into play. He wouldn't allow himself to be influenced in such a way.

Right?

# Hulda

Hulda sat and listened to Shar as she talked about that day's bake. They were in their room, away from the crowd that had been allowed into the bar, most of them hoping for a chance to speak to their favorite baker.

The second contest had involved a Dwarven holiday, All Spirits' Day. Various pastries and treats were made to encourage the good spirits to stay while the bad spirits were supposed to be tricked into leaving. Many of the desserts had alcohol in them, and part of the competition was to make the judges guess incorrectly which ones had spirits and which ones didn't.

Shar had been one of the bottom bakers, and felt as though she'd scraped through by the scruff of her beard.

Ever since they'd come to White Hall, Shar had appeared, well, nervous. It felt to Hulda as if Shar had been spooked and everything scared her.

Maybe even cursed.

"It's just so hard," Shar complained. "I feel like I can't breathe in that kitchen sometimes."

Hulda looked curiously at her friend.

This no longer sounded like the Shar she knew.

"Then quit," Hulda said bluntly.

"I can't—I couldn't do that!" Shar said, rocking back in her chair, her eyes wide.

"Why not?" Hulda said, still poking hard at her friend.

"Everyone is counting on me! My sponsors, my family, everyone!"

Hulda didn't roll her eyes, though she considered it.

Shar was no longer cooking for herself.

"Why is this contest important to you?" Hulda asked.

"I need to prove to my family that I'm meant to be a baker, a chocolatier, and not working on gemstones and jewelry," Shar said slowly, looking confused.

"Why do you want to be a baker?" Hulda said. "Why is that important?"

"Because I hate faceting gemstones?" Shar replied, still lost.

"I thought it was because you loved baking," Hulda finally prompted.

"I do!" Shar said adamantly. "I do?" she said after a moment's thought.

"I think you do," Hulda told her friend. "But I think that you've lost sight of that in this contest."

Shar took a deep breath, folded her hands over her beard, and leaned back in her chair, considering.

"Baking used to be all about the fun," she admitted after a few moments. "Coming up with the perfect flavors. Seeing the joy on people's faces when they ate something I made. Pushing myself to make the tastiest thing I could imagine. Then coming up with something even better."

"Exactly," Hulda said, nodding her head. "But now, you're so worried about pleasing the judges that you're no longer trying to please yourself."

"Huh," Shar said. "I do kind of need to make things that the judges like," she added after a few moments.

"But you need to bake from your heart," Hulda pointed out. "Your decorating has gotten so much better. Even I can see that. Though I still say you need more sticks to thump people with."

Shar giggled at that. Then she kept giggling.

Hulda knew that what she'd said hadn't been that funny, but she was still glad to hear her friend laughing.

"Thank you," Shar said as she finished, wiping tears from her eyes. "I really needed that."

"Besides, I can always threaten to thump the judges if they don't start being nicer to you," Hulda added.

And she would. That was what friends were for.

"I know you would," Shar said, nodding. "Hopefully, that won't be necessary." She took a deep breath and let it out with a sigh.

"So have some fun tomorrow," Hulda advised. "It's the only way you're going to do well. Better than the others."

Shar peered at Hulda suspiciously. "Did Leena put you up to this?" she asked.

"Uhm, no?" Hulda said, confused. "I'm speaking as your friend here. Not as some sort of mentor figure."

"Got it," Shar said. She suddenly gave a great yawn. "Tomorrow is going to dawn far too early," she complained as she stood up, stretched, and toddled off to bed.

Hulda nodded, sitting by herself for a while.

Shar had really been lost.

Hopefully, she'd find her way now.

# Shar

Shar was determined to find delight in that day's bake.

Only four bakers remained. Today was the semi-finals. Then there would be the finals.

Shar was happy that Golodhon had survived.

Less happy that Kigora was still there. Along with Vincent.

According to Leena and Hulda, Vincent was the fan favorite this year. The audience really liked how he played up to them. He spent every night in the main room, talking with fans.

As well as saying bad things about his competitors.

Hulda had threatened to thump him more than once. (Not to his face, but just to Shar.)

He was as obnoxious in the kitchen, but Shar had learned to ignore him. And the desserts he made were always top notch. However, he wouldn't share ingredients. He hogged them all so frequently that Shar and the others had stopped asking each other for the location of this spice or that. Instead, they went directly to his station and took what they needed. (If they asked, he always hemmed and hawed about it, wasting their time.)

All of the bakes so far had been following holiday themes. The latest had been an Elvish celebration, the fall of the golden leaves from the Arwenbraneas trees that lived at the heart of the Elvish forests.

What would be today's theme? Would they be doing more holidays? Perhaps something from the Plainsmen, or the Merfolk? Or something else?

"Welcome to the semi-finals!" Fenryl said as he came striding in. "Everyone's looking sharp today. As sharp as our contestants!"

Though the Elf was tall and snooty (and exceedingly picky about decorations) he always greeted the crowd when he came in.

Hulda had speculated it was because he knew the crowd paid his wages, came to his own cooking events, and bought his goods. He may not care too much about the audience, but he knew better than to bite the hand that fed him.

"And do we have something special for you today," Erde said. "Mmm, mmm. It's a good one!"

Shar had learned to "read" Erde's jackets, as they generally gave some sort of hint about the coming challenge. For the All Spirits' Day challenge, he'd worn a gold and red brocade. Afterward, Hulda had pointed out that the design was very Dwarven, and similar to what a rich Dwarf might wear for a vest.

For the Elvish holiday of the falling golden leaves, his jacket had been white with gold leaves embroidered on it.

Today, Erde wore a weird design. The left half of his jacket was white with the outlines of small flowers done in black stitching, while the right half was black, with white stitching.

What did that represent? Was there a black and white holiday? Shar couldn't think of any.

"Hello everyone!" Zigli said as she came out. She, too, had a black and white theme going. Not in her outfit (which was a burgundy shirt with matching black-and-burgundy vest), but the ribbons in both her beard and her hair were black and white. "How y'all doing?"

When the crowd didn't shout back with enough enthusiasm, Zigli repeated her question. The resulting roar nearly deafened Shar and left her ears ringing.

Fenryl wore his usual robes, more beige and sea-green than anything else. Nothing black and white.

"We've been noodling along the holidays," Erde said after the judges had taken a seat. "But instead of doing one special day, let's aim for two!"

"What did you have in mind?" Fenryl asked.

Again, Shar knew that this was all planned out in advance for the audience's entertainment.

"My husband arrived last night—" Erde started off with.

Zigli held up a hand and interrupted him. "Don't you push me. I don't need any details."

"There isn't enough brain bleach in the whole world for that," Fenryl added.

Erde rolled his eyes. "As I was saying, I got to thinking—"

"You were thinking after your husband arrived?" Zigli teased.

"So that's what the kids are calling it these days," Fenryl said dryly.

"By the gods, give me some patience with you two!" Erde said, trying to continue. "Darnathin and I are kind of opposites, you know? I'm a Human, he's an Elf. I'm a bit loud, he's quiet."

Shar was pretty sure that Zigli had a comment along the lines of, "You don't say," but Erde ignored her.

"He dresses, well, like you, Fenryl. I prefer a bit more style," Erde said, proudly gesturing to his jacket.

"Uh huh," was the only comment Fenryl made, but an entire page of judgment was packed into that short phrase.

"Despite our differences, we balance each other out," Erde continued. "And that got me thinking about today's challenge, and how it should be all about the balance of things. How you need equal parts of the right pieces to make the perfect whole."

"Oh, I get it!" Zigli said. "Like the spring and fall equinoxes. Something that everyone celebrates, just in their own way."

"Exactly!" Erde said.

Shar nodded. She could do that. Come up with a dessert that represented the equinox. Probably wouldn't know which one until the judges assigned them.

But there were only two equinoxes. Was this going to be a head-to-head battle?

"Just making something that celebrates an equinox is too easy," Fenryl complained.

Crap. What were the judges up to now?

"I agree," Zigli said.

Again, that evil twinkle came to her eyes that Shar was afraid she'd have nightmares about. Later. When she wasn't so tired she just fell into her bed unconscious and didn't even roll over until Leena came to wake her in the morning.

"Now, I don't think that a team challenge would be fair at this point in the competition," Zigli continued. "It's the semi-finals. Y'all should be able to live or die on the basis of your own creations."

"Still, it would be good to get some additional pressure from your fellow competitors," Fenryl said. "How about getting their desserts to reflect one another?"

"That's what I had in mind," Erde said. "Both literally as well as in the decorations."

"Two of you will be assigned the spring equinox," Zigli said. "And two will get the fall one. You must reflect each other in terms of taste and design."

"And because we want your cakes to reflect each other, they should actually *be* reflective as well. You need to do a mirror glaze on part of your dessert," Erde said.

Shar smiled at that. Fortunately, that was a technique that she'd practiced a lot over the past year.

"So you need to both work with each other, as well as compete against each other," Fenryl warned.

"We want your flavors to balance each other," Zigli said. "Plus chocolate."

"And your décor to reflect one another, as well as remind us of the equinox," Erde said.

The bakers all had to file up to the judges' table and select cards. After everyone had their card, only then did their choices get revealed to them.

Shar got the spring equinox.

As did Kigora.

She glanced over at the other Dwarf, only to find Kigora glaring at her.

Shar raised her eyebrows. Really? They were going into a competition bake with that level of animosity? When they needed to at least vaguely work together? That was a surefire recipe for disaster.

Surprisingly, Kigora appeared to get the silent message that Shar shot her, because she sighed, then nodded.

Good.

As haughty as Kigora had gotten, at least she appeared to be willing to work with Shar, at least as much as she needed to, at least for this bake.

After that, all bets were off.

# Reaching for the Brass Ring

For some, baking is an all-consuming passion, and so they're focused on baking (and chocolate) contests.

For others, though, they have different passions.

So they have different contests.

There are contests for savory cooking. The problem with these is that while the scents may be tantalizing (and with magic, can easily be spread through an entire crowd of onlookers), the dishes that the contestants create just aren't as showy as a tall, beautifully decorated cakes. So these contests tend to be much smaller, with a proportionately shrunken fanbase.

There are contests of strength, speed, or endurance. The problem is that these have to be limited to a single race. If you put a Dwarf against an Elf in a running race, the Elf is going to win every time. Ditto with strength, only with the Dwarf winning. Humans have surprisingly good endurance compared to the other two races, and will almost always take home the prize in those challenges.

Some contests have been put together that have all three elements, and competitors have to come up with well balanced, multi-race teams to have a chance of winning. The Toughie Tow is one such competition. It dumps a group of contestants out on one of the islands to the west of the southern continent and forces them to survive in a climate that they're unfamiliar with. There is additional strategy involved, as members have to vote their own teammates off the island every few days.

It's a difficult contest to win, and equally difficult to view. The audience is composed of either rich people who live for watching other people suffer, or poor people who have won the opportunity to just watch and not be forced to compete.

The prize money makes it worth it, though, so poorer people do prepare to become contestants if they can.

However, not just the Humans, Dwarves, and Elves have contests.

The Plainsmen have competitions among their youths every summer at the grand market, when all the nomadic tribes gather together every year. These contests involve archery, running, and wrestling. The tribe who gathers the most trophies for the year wins favorable conditions in the market, such as moving their stalls to the best location, as well as gathering most of their supplies at a discount. (The pressure for their teens to do well may or may not be one of the reasons why young Plainsmen leave their tribes and go out to wander the other lands instead of competing.)

The Merfolk have swimming contests, with speed, agility, and dance/performance being the top categories. (Honestly, if you ever have the chance, go see one of the latter. It's quite amazing to see the groups of synchronized swimmers popping in and out of the water, tails waving or heads appearing.)

All people have gambling contests, of course. Anything that can be raced—from rats to weasels to horses—will be bet on.

And smaller baking contests that are city wide, market wide, or perhaps just among the bakers in a particular neighborhood. Decorating contests to see who can create the most amazing house. Sculpting competitions, out of clay, butter, sand, or even toothpicks.

Silly three-legged foot races through Dwarven corridors, tree-climbing of young saplings too weak to hold much weight in Elvish forests, and pie eating (without the use of hands) in Human areas.

People are generally busy, and so they don't need much entertainment.

But during the holidays?

A good competition is sure to send the message of celebration.

# Kigora

By the gods, Kigora was *pissed*.

First off, that upstart Shar had stolen her win at the regionals. All her family (with the notable exception of Uncle Yazgrak) had told her so.

Shar didn't have any experience cooking. How she'd managed to beat all those other bakers was a mystery to Kigora.

Sure, Shar could work well with flavors. But her decorations weren't anywhere *near* what they needed to be for her to have been chosen as regional champion.

Everyone thought so. (Kigora might have only paid attention to those reports of the contest that agreed with her point of view.) As Kigora was considered a local (in the broadest sense of the term, as she had family in the area), the news sheets from Anthus were all unhappy with the upset.

Kigora had nursed these wounds and her anger for an entire year. She pored over the descriptions of Shar's entries, finding more and more fault with each of them.

And she came to a conclusion.

Shar had been the fan favorite. That was why she'd won.

Not because of her talent.

When Kigora arrived at *Chocolates Galore!* she could barely contain her disdain for the other Dwarf.

How dare she be standing there, as a finalist, when that should have been Kigora's place?

It didn't matter. She'd win back her spot.

Never mind that she was still following Shar's advice when it came to decorating, and so she'd made her initial twelve layer cake to look like a stone tower, because as a Dwarf, that was a material she was comfortable with.

Never mind that every dessert that Shar had baked during the contest had tasted amazing.

There had been that one chance that Shar would have gone home, after the All Spirits' Day bake, the day before. But she'd come back that morning, more determined than ever.

Was Shar smart enough to have put herself in the bottom, just so her story would be better? People loved a comeback story. Was that mentor of hers, Leena, that tricky?

It didn't matter.

Just as that Human Vincent's bragging was all empty hot air, so were Shar's chances of winning.

That title belonged to Kigora.

And now, this equinox bake. She was going to have to *work with* her nemesis, once again.

Could her life get any worse?

"Let's do day and night, in equal parts," Shar said as the pair of them stood at a table in the joint kitchen. The place felt empty with just four bakers left. All the cooking stations had been moved to one side and the audience now took up the opposite side of the room.

"I'll take the night side," Kigora said quickly, as she'd been thinking of the same general design.

Shar opened her mouth as if to protest. However, she didn't fight Kigora on this.

Good. Kigora would have really argued for her position.

This was *Chocolates Galore!* after all.

The night side was going to feature a rich, dark, chocolate cake. And Kigora had a divinely inspired recipe. Everyone loved her chocolate cake. Even Uncle Yazgrak had complimented her on it.

"Fine," Shar said after nodding. "What should the designs be?"

"Three smaller cakes, not a three tiered cake," Kigora said firmly. "Mine will represent the phases of the moon."

"That works," Shar said after a moment. "I'll do the day transition, from winter into spring."

Kigora felt her eyebrows rise in surprise. That was actually a really good idea.

"Colors?" Kigora asked.

"I'll do different blues for the mirror glaze, to represent the sky, with greens, pinks, and reds for the decorations."

Kigora nodded. "I'll do purples, dark blues, and blacks, for the night sky. With stars and crescents."

"I'm assuming you're doing a dark, heavy, chocolate cake?" Shar said after a moment.

"I am," Kigora said proudly.

"I'll do a lighter sponge, then," Shar said. "Should we tie the cakes together with complementary compotes?"

They agreed that Kigora would do a dark cherry filling, while Shar would do a much brighter strawberry layer. As for the crunch element, Kigora went with a hazelnut brittle, and Shar chose to work with lighter candied almonds.

"We will need to taste each other's work as we go along," Shar warned. "And the judges are sure to throw a twist at us."

Kigora sighed. The other Dwarf was right on both counts, though Kigora was already tired of working with the upstart.

"Agreed," she said. She could be a professional. Uncle Yazgrak had said it was important to be able to work with anyone in a kitchen, because sometimes one of your co-bakers would be having a bad day. (Though too many bad days and Kigora would drag them out by their beard.)

Everything planned out, the two of them started their baking.

Kigora had to admit that Shar certainly moved with confidence around the kitchen. She knew what she needed, and went to get it directly. (Of course, they both had to stop at that stupid Vincent's station as he'd stolen all the spices. As usual.)

The compote that Shar came up with to layer between her cakes was surprisingly refreshing and light. She said she'd added lime to it, which brightened it more than lemon would have. (Not that Kigora would have used lemon, though that was her go-to ingredient.)

Shar did suggest that Kigora add some basil to her jam to get more earthy tones. Trying the two side by side, the tastes really complemented one another.

Kigora sighed and tried not to allow her resentment to show.

As much as she hated to admit it, Shar was pretty good at this sort of thing.

Kigora could only grin when Shar's eyes got really wide as she tasted Kigora's chocolate cake.

"By the gods! That's amazing," Shar said. "You'll have to give me the recipe. Wow."

Kigora felt her back stiffening. She wasn't about to share something like that!

"After the competition," Shar assured her.

After pausing for a moment, Kigora said, "It's the vanilla."

"Hmm?" Shar said, as she'd already turned away, back to her station.

"I use three times the usual amount of vanilla in the cake," Kigora admitted. "Along with coffee and dark chocolate."

"It's really good," Shar said.

"So is yours," Kigora said before she went back to her own bake.

Really, there was no need for her to be friendly with Shar. Even if she would privately admit that Shar was really talented, smart, and kinda cute. No, Kigora needed to focus on her own cooking, her own recipes, her own win.

However, Kigora kept finding herself wandering into the other Dwarf's cooking station, having her taste this or that component, asking her advice for the mirror glaze, as well as offering her own when Shar started doing her almond crunch.

Maybe cooking with someone wouldn't be that bad?

Kigora had to stop doing everything when the judges came by. She explained their concept and let them taste her components: the cake, the jam, the brittle.

Shar walked over to chat as well, giving the judges tastes of her bake.

The judges appeared pleased and impressed with what they'd gotten done so quickly.

Of course, that meant that they were about to throw a wrench into the works.

"Attention bakers!" Erde called out. "It occurred to me after we gave you this challenge that there's one more thing that we want y'all to add to your cakes."

"We need something that represents your season, not just the equinox," Fenryl said.

"So for the two bakers doing the spring equinox, you need to add edible flowers somewhere to your design," Zigli said.

"Whereas y'all doing fall? You need edible fall leaves," Erde said.

Kigora tried to stop herself from panicking. Where in the names of the Dwarven mines was she going to put flowers? They had no place on her design!

She glanced over at her companion.

Shar was grinning. She leaned over and told Kigora, "I was already planning on putting flowers on the tops of my cakes," she said softly.

Kigora nearly groaned. Of course, her nemesis was already prepared for this.

"I could help you put some purple and black flowers around the base of your cakes," Shar added. "That would meet the twist as well as make our cakes more similar."

Kigora squeezed her lips together tightly to stop from automatically refusing Shar's help. They were both so pressed for time already.

A little help might not be the worst thing in the world.

Even if it came from her nemesis.

"I'll let you know," Kigora said, nodding.

"We got this," Shar told Kigora firmly. She reached out and grasped Kigora's forearms in strong hands. "We're going to beat them."

"All right," Kigora said, a little uncertain.

"We will," Shar said, "particularly that Vincent," before she released Kigora and went back to her own bake.

Kigora drifted back to her station, a little perplexed, a little bemused.

She was used to working on her own. She'd had mentors and teachers, but never a baking companion.

What would it be like, after she won the contest, to actually bake *with* Shar, instead of against her?

Maybe, just maybe, she would take a chance and find out.

# Shar

∾

Shar looked with pride at the desserts that she and Kigora had made. The mirror glaze on all six of the small cakes was perfect. The designs matched as well. Shar had tiny rose buds on the smallest of her cakes, with half-opened blooms on the second, and fully open roses on the last one. She'd done small disks of golden chocolate on the tops of her cakes, going from small to large, to indicate the sun growing stronger.

Kigora's cakes looked just as elegant in their darker mirror glaze. Shar had ended up helping her pipe some flowers around the base of her three cakes, making sure they matched hers.

She knew that both cakes tasted amazing.

Were they good enough, though?

The guys also had really nice-looking three-tiered cakes. However, Shar wouldn't say that they complemented each other, or even reflected one another.

Golodhon's cake was beautiful, of course. The top layer was the only one he'd done as a mirror glaze. It looked like a fall forest. Shar would bet that he'd already planned that, before the judges came in with their twist.

Vincent's cake, on the other hand, didn't look like much of anything at all. He'd done blacks, blues, and purples, like Kigora. He'd also pulled out every trick from his cookbook. There were swirls of spun glass, truffles, and molded chocolates decorating the tops of every tier. Mushroom caps—a fancy cookie that the Elves specialized in—were stuck to the sides of his tiers, all brushed with a glittering, pearlescent edible powder. The leaves were made out of cookies and painted brilliant fall colors.

Shar didn't know where her eye was supposed to land. All those techniques scattered her attention. Plus, where was the equinox? How was he representing that? What was his story?

Golodhon gave her a sad smile as they stood waiting for the judges.

"You okay?" Shar mouthed.

Golodhon looked at his cake, sighed, and shook his head.

Her heart ached for her fellow baker. He must not be confident in what he'd made.

Did that mean that it was going to be her and Kigora as the two finalists?

The judges finally arrived, laughing at something one of them had said.

"Let's ask the audience," Zigli said as the Dwarf marched over to face the crowd instead of going and sitting behind the table with the other two.

"Cake pops ain't chocolates," Zigli told everyone. "Am I right? AM I RIGHT?"

The crowd got the hint and yelled back, "YOU ARE RIGHT!"

"See?" Zigli said as she started walking back toward the table. "Told you."

"What about chocolate cake pops?" Fenryl asked, teasing.

"They're still cake," Zigli said.

"Chocolate cake pops dipped in chocolate?" Fenryl said, still grinning.

"They're still not chocolates, Fenryl," Zigli said. She shook her head in exasperation.

"How about—" Fenryl started.

"Don't you try me, Fenryl," Zigli growled. "I'm not putting up with you today."

"All right, fine," Fenryl said. "Let's get down to business, shall we?"

The first two to be judged were Golodhon and Vincent.

"Explain this," Zigli said, waving at Vincent's cake.

He tried. Shar would have to give him that. He did try. But it was just a hot mess, according to Erde.

Golodhon, on the other hand, was greatly praised for his design, how well it fit the fall equinox theme.

However, then the judges got to tasting.

Golodhon was aware that he'd soaked his cake too much. (Shar later learned that it had come out of the oven dry, then he'd over-compensated.) The lower layers had turned soggy. While the flavors were good, they weren't great.

And they didn't match Vincent's at all.

Vincent's cake was at least delicious, as were all his decorations. However, the judges dinged him on the lack of focus in his presentation, as well as how the two cakes didn't reflect one another.

Then came their turn.

Shar had had fun with baking that afternoon. She'd tried to help Kigora (when the other Dwarf would admit to needing help). She'd liked having someone there to bake with, to try flavors and combinations on.

Of course, Kigora was still her nemesis, but the other Dwarf had softened in her stance toward Shar. The afternoon had done much to thaw out her attitude.

The six little cakes all looked amazing together. Shar and Kigora didn't admit that they hadn't planned on there being a progression through all six cakes, but that had kind of happened, with Shar's biggest, brightest cake being a good transition to Kigora's smallest and also lightest colored cake.

"I think y'all did an amazing job not just representing the spring equinox, but celebrating it as well," Erde commented.

"Let's eat!" Zigli finally said.

Shar and Kigora each cut a slice from the biggest of their cakes, put the two slices on a single plate and handed them to the judges.

"Wow," was all that Fenryl said after tasting each.

Zigli had wide eyes and was just nodding. "Uh huh."

"By the gods, it's like a single baker did these. Did y'all mind meld or something?" Erde asked.

"We worked together," Shar emphasized.

"Sure, she's my competition," Kigora said. She paused, giving Shar a long sideline glance. "But she also makes me a better baker. Challenges me to do more."

Shar blinked, surprised. She hadn't realized that had been what she'd been doing. She thought she'd been helping Kigora.

Maybe she'd been doing both.

Though the judges hemmed and hawed and tried to prolong the tension when it came to who was going to the finale, there was never any doubt.

Shar and Kigora would face each other.

One last time.

The day of the finale dawned clear. The threat of rain had been pushed out one more day. It was slightly more humid than it had been, but hopefully that wouldn't affect their bake too much.

Shar had talked with Leena about what to expect for the final bake. They knew that it would be some sort of celebration. But what?

They wouldn't repeat the winter solstice/longest night of the regionals. It had to be something else, though something that everyone celebrated. Maybe the new year?

Except that New Year traditions were so different for all the various peoples.

Shar went into the final bake nervous but excited. She wasn't sure why the competition took so much out of her and made her so tired, but she was certain that she was going to sleep for a week afterward.

Kigora stood beside her on the mostly empty platform. They'd started with ten bakers, and now it was just them.

Kigora gave her a soft smile and a nod before turning forward and growing more stern.

Shar felt her heart race. Yes, Kigora could possibly, maybe, someday become a friend. (And more than a friend? Maybe?)

For now, each was going to try their hardest to beat the other baker. Despite that, Shar knew that they'd still help each other out in the kitchen as well, because it was always better to lift up your fellow bakers, not to try and unfairly handicap them, as Vincent had always tried to do.

The judges came in to resounding applause from the audience. Fenryl went to greet the crowd, as did Zigli and Erde. When they made their way to the judges' table, it took the herald a couple of tries to get the crowd settled back down again.

Shar tried to "read" Erde's coat as they waited, but it was similar to everything else he'd been wearing, brightly colored with sequins sewn in an abstract pattern. Nothing in particular stood out.

"We've been going through a lot of cultural holidays," Erde started off with. "But I think it's time, particularly for this last bake, to make it personal. Am I right?"

Fenryl nodded. "I think the bakers have all been cooking from their hearts, but I do agree that making this challenge more about them is a good call."

"And what could be more personal than your birthday?" Zigli said.

Shar blinked.

Birthdays?

Huh.

Everyone had one. It was kind of a matter of personal choice as to how one celebrated. Hulda always spent more time working out and thumping people, whereas her brother ordered himself a huge cake. (Shar had made it for him this past year.) That made the challenge very broad.

And that was the danger, she realized. The more specific something was, the easier it was to represent.

"Elves don't have birthdays," Fenryl said coolly. "We celebrate our name day."

"Do not tell me that there are other Elves named Fenryl," Zigli said. "Or I might have to go on some sort of crusade, to see if they're all as old and stodgy as you are."

Fenryl laughed at that. "No, I have seven names, actually. Fenryl Galadhing Celinor Aralglen Ingwer Saerhir Elmenor."

"Well, that's sure a mouthful," Zigli said.

Fenryl rolled his eyes and said, "My name-day name is Ingwer. All the Elves who are named Ingwer celebrate their name day together."

Shar hadn't realized that. She'd have to ask Golodhon what his name-day name was, and when he celebrated, so she could send him a cake or something.

"Is the Elvish name day celebration close enough to a birthday?" Erde asked patiently.

"It is," Fenryl admitted. He waved his hand and indicated that Erde should continue.

"So we want you to do a birthday spread," Erde said. "A big table filled with goodies for all the guests who're going to be coming to celebrate. Like *all* your cousins. And for a Dwarf, that could mean a lot of people."

Shar nodded solemnly. "Cousin" wasn't necessarily a blood relative. It could mean practically any Dwarf, if one was willing to spend the time (and go through three casks of ale) to trace the lineage.

"Or a name-day spread," Fenryl added.

Zigli glared at the Elf and picked up the narrative. "Y'all need to think about what your table is gonna look like. There needs to be a show-stopper on it, as well as at least five different types of confections."

Crap.

Shar's heart suddenly started pounding.

A show-stopper? Some sort of tall cake, to stand out from everything else? Plus five different types of baked goods? How was she going to get all of that done?

"You're going to have five hours to put together a birthday spread fit for the Goddess Idite herself!" Erde said. "And to make me as delighted as a Dwarf with a new beard oil."

Shar couldn't help but snicker at that.

"It needs to say birthday. It needs to say celebration. And it needs to feature chocolate," Zigli warned.

This was so complicated. Shar's head was spinning.

She glanced at Kigora, who looked determined, then lost, then determined again.

Shar would bet that her own expression was cycling just as hard.

"So get to baking!" Fenryl said. "We'll stop by latter to see how you're doing."

Crap. The judges threw a twist into the last bake only about half the time. The other half of the time, they just let the bakers do what they needed to do.

"Good luck," Shar wished Kigora as they stepped off the platform.

Kigora paused for a moment. "Good luck," she said earnestly. Then her expression grew proud. "Of course, I'll also be sending you my condolences, once you lose."

Shar snorted at that. "As if."

And they were off.

# To Have And To Hold

For the most part, people marry along race lines, that is, Dwarves marry Dwarves, Elves marry Elves, and the Merfolk and others marry among themselves almost exclusively.

Humans tend to be the most, well, *flexible* when it comes to their affections. The vast majority of them tend to marry other Humans. However, when there is a couple formed of mixed race, most of the time, one of those people is going to be Human.

Of course, there are *so many* theories about this, from hating their mothers (generally not true) to being bullied as children (also generally not true) to secretly identifying as the other race (a touch of truth in this one, but again, not common enough to explain these pairings).

No, the most common thing that all these couple have in common (beyond one of the pair being Human) is that the other person tends to be their opposite in every way. One will be a slob while the other will be neat. One will prefer chocolate while the other doesn't like sweets. (Weirdo.) It isn't a case of physical differences—the tallest Human won't seek out the shortest Dwarf, for example, or the skinniest Elf looking for a rotund Human.

It's as if the two need each other to form a whole, to balance each other out.

Or maybe the Cricket God was playing hopscotch through the ribbons known to draw soulmates together and got them messed up. Again.

Whatever the reason, despite the amount of adversity such a couple might have to overcome, they do tend to be the happiest of couples.

Maybe it's because they chose each other, and have to keep choosing the other, instead of being together is their default setting.

Maybe it's because they view their life as them against the world.

Or maybe it's because the other person does complete them, that they weren't complete without the other.

Once together, these couples almost always stay together.

To the point that they die together as well.

Even if it's a short-lived Human with a longer-lived Elf, when the Human goes, the Elf doesn't last long.

They're out of balance.

Soulmates only come along once in a lifetime.

And without them, well, it's no longer much of a life.

# Shar

When they reached the kitchen, Shar stopped and pulled out her notebook instead of rushing into baking.

There would be time enough for that.

However, instead of listing off various desserts, the timing of each, or steps she had to follow, Shar started writing down the names of the people who she'd invite to her birthday party.

Her parents, of course. Her brother Durzi. Cousin Algruzlea, who'd made her chocolate molds. Uncle Malodubo, who'd made the portable stall that she and Hulda used. Hulda!

And others. Leena, of course. Rafael, her first and most consistent sponsor. Golodhon, just because she wanted to give her mother a heart attack by being so friendly with an Elf. Maybe Erwel too, as she'd been so nice.

Shar paused.

"Hey, Kigora? What's your favorite dessert? If I invited you to my birthday party, what should I make you?" Shar called out.

Kigora seemed startled by Shar's question, stopping abruptly with her pans in midair, still in her hands. She slowly set them down on the counter as she thought.

"That chili-chocolate cake that you made for regionals," Kigora said after a few moments. "Uncle Yaz talked about it off and on all year, trying to recreate your recipe."

"You got it," Shar said. She wasn't certain that she'd have time to make that along with everything else, but she'd try.

Everyone on her list was special to her. Had helped her so much in her journey.

The big show-stopper cake was going to be for the judges.

Everything else? Was for her. Her theme? Presents for her friends.

And maybe for her nemesis as well.

The creampuffs turned out really well. They were all not much more than two bites, as she'd learned the lesson about smaller desserts being perceived of as more elegant. She'd made a black sugar cookie dough, cut out circles from it, then put a disk on each of her puffs, so it would form a black crackling on top as they baked. Once they'd cooled, she decorated each with eyes, whiskers, ears, and a small triangle nose to make them look like cats. The filling was a chocolate-rum ganache.

Those were for Rafael and the Curious Cat Shipping company. His present.

Kigora tasted the test one that Shar had made and declared it to be really good.

Then again, Kigora had also made creampuffs that were just as tasty.

Shar made Durzi's favorite cinnamon rolls, drizzled in chocolate. It had taken her a while to get her mother to admit to liking something, but eventually Shar had figured out that her mother's favorite was a truffle bar: white chocolate flavored with lemon on the bottom layer and raspberry flavored dark chocolate on the top layer. Shar left it as a whole bar with elegant white swirls through the top.

Hulda's favorites were still the Melt Away cookies. Shar put a colored white chocolate glaze on those, dragging a toothpick through the colors to make a pinwheel pattern. (Kigora had also declared those to be amazing. Kigora's "trick" dessert turned out to be cupcakes with those popping candies in them. Shar didn't say anything, but she knew they weren't as good as her cookies.)

For Golodhon, Shar made *Kichit Süto*, seven of them (one for each of his names, if he turned out to have as many of them as Fenryl did), out of a cake flavored with lemon and rosemary, topped with a delicate white chocolate glaze and decorated with the most delicate bow that Shar could manage. (Kigora's small walnut pastries were just as beautiful and as tasty, so Shar would rate that as a tie.)

Shar had been able to use her special chocolate molds for this bake, so for her cousin (who'd made the molds) as well as for Leena, Shar made chocolates in the shapes and colors of gems: emeralds, diamonds, opals, and rubies. Each had a different flavor combination. Some had more than just a ganache, and had a gelée as well as a crunch layer, showing off different techniques as well as types of chocolates.

These chocolates might also have been for Antonio Bagaduce, an homage to that first bonbon that had changed her world.

The three-tiered show-stopper cake was chocolate and flavored with chilies, as Kigora had requested. Shar put chocolate representations of fireworks all over it, shooting stars with trails of fiery color. She made a small cookie banner that she wrote, "Happy Birthday!" on with frosting, then stuck that to the top of her cake.

Then there was the sugar work. Shar hadn't done much of that before this bake. Now, she made pulled sugar ribbons and bows for every plate on her table. It was a unifying element for the dishes. Plus, she hoped it would make the table look more colorful, more like a celebration.

Though the judges had come by, they hadn't thrown a twist at them, which made both Shar and Kigora so happy. (Later Shar heard the rumor that because the pair of them had been helping each other throughout the bake, the judges had decided to leave them be. She didn't know if it was true or not, but it made sense to her. If they hadn't been cooperating, the judges might have "punished" them with a twist.)

Shar heard the countdown to the end of her time. She still rushed, adding last minute details to her plates.

When time was called, Shar leaned back, dropping back her head so she was looking at the ceiling. She wasn't about to collapse on the ground like Vincent dramatically had after many of his bakes, though she kind of felt like it.

She walked over to Kigora's display. It was elegant. Beautiful. Much more restrained than her own.

Comparing the two, her table looked a lot more, well, brown, though with pops of color. Particularly with the chocolate gems.

Hopefully her flavors would win the day.

However, as tired as Shar felt, she also was still happy. Despite Kigora being her nemesis (frenemy?) they'd still helped each other during the entire bake, tasting each other's dishes, giving tips and commentary.

Shar had even shared her biggest secret about how to keep her hands steady while piping.

The pair of them smiled at each other.

Shar's breath caught.

Wow. Kigora could really look pretty sometimes.

When she wasn't being stuck up and snooty.

The pair of them followed the tables magically floating back to where the judges awaited.

Huge crowds greeted them, cheering loudly as well as oohing and awing over the tables as they ambled along.

"Greetings!" Erde called to Shar and Kigora as they walked into the courtyard behind the tables. "Don't these look like a treat!"

The judges took some time to walk around each table, making

quiet comments on their own before finally inviting the bakers to describe what they'd made.

Kigora went first, describing how it was a river of flavor, each dessert leading to the next in terms of color and texture.

"Though I grew up in the Ashveil Mountains, I spent a lot of time in Anthus," Kigora explained. "Those rivers have always influenced me and my baking."

Now that she'd explained it, Shar could see the river flowing through the table of desserts. That also explained why Kigora's sugar ribbons had been shades of blue.

Wow. So pretty! So creative! Shar was certain she didn't stand a chance.

Zigli spoke up. "I can see the design, now that you've told me. But without your explanation, it wouldn't have made any sense."

Shar nodded. At least she hadn't been the only one not to see it. Then again, the judges weren't going to understand her table either.

Kigora's showpiece was a tall, three-tiered cake, like Shar's. It had spun sugar—again, done in blue—swirled around the entire thing. There were also edible cookies that spelled out, "Happy Birthday" across the front of the table. Kigora had made those with her magical cookie cutter that formed whatever shape she wanted.

When the judges got to tasting, Shar's heart sunk even lower. They all praised Kigora's flavors—Erde declared that her cake was so good he was gonna get up and dance like an Elf who'd just discovered glitter.

Finally, it was Shar's turn.

"When you're a kid, birthdays are all about getting presents," Shar said. "As an adult, you start thinking about giving presents, instead of receiving them. So this is the birthday spread that I'd do for all my family and friends. Presents for them all."

"I'm not sure I would have gotten that from just looking at your table, but I understand where you're coming from," Zigli said.

Shar explained her desserts, the cats for Rafael, the cookies for her best friend Hulda, the seven tiny servings of cake for the seven names of an Elf (which made Fenryl grin), the truffle bar for her mother, the pastries for her brother. Each of those desserts meant so much to her. Plus all the various chocolates, from the molds made by her cousin.

"While the decorations of the cake are for you judges, the flavor is for Kigora," Shar said, her throat suddenly dry. "Because I'd invite her too."

The judges nodded, while Zigli shot a look between the pair of them, smiling all the while.

Finally, it was time to serve her desserts. Shar knew that whatever the judges didn't eat would go to whoever bid the most on it from the audience.

Hopefully it would be worth it to whoever got to try her desserts.

After the creampuffs and Durzi's pastries, the judges tried the Melt Away cookies.

"By the gods! These are like magic!" Erde declared.

"It isn't often that someone surprises me with a baked good," Fenryl said slowly. "But I've never had something like this. They do just melt away."

"You sell these at your bakery?" Zigli asked.

Shar nodded, trying not to grin too hard.

"Good. Cause I'm ordering some," the Dwarf continued.

"I just want the recipe," Fenryl said.

The judges also made much of her various chocolates, how appropriate that they were gem shaped and colored.

Finally, they tried Shar's cake.

"I like baked goods with chilis in them," Fenryl said.

"You don't say," Zigli commented dryly.

Fenryl ignored her and went on. "This is marvelously balanced, in terms of sweet and hot."

The other judges nodded in agreement.

"Good choice, Kigora," Erde called out.

Shar saw the other Dwarf smile and nod, but it looked strained.

Eventually, Shar and Kigora were sent to the far side of the courtyard to chat with the audience while they deliberated.

"I'm sure you won," Kigora told Shar quietly as they walked.

Shar snorted. "No, I doubt it. I think you won. That river idea? Once you said it, I could only see that. My decorations weren't really cohesive at all."

"Except that they were all for your family and friends," Kigora said. "You were showing your heart. Giving presents as part of your birthday celebration."

Shar shrugged. "It's all in the hands of the judges. I think you did really well, though."

Kigora gave her a bitter smile. "But not good enough."

"You could always come back in five years. Beat everyone again," Shar said. "Though, do you really need the title? You're already an established baker. No one is going to question you, your ability, or your right to bake whatever you please."

Kigora nodded. "Whereas you need to prove yourself to your family still, right?"

It was Shar's turn to nod. "I do," she said quietly.

She didn't know if just making it to the top two would be enough for her mother, or whether she'd insist on the letter of their agreement, namely, that Shar win the contest before she'd receive her blessing to leave the family business and start one on her own.

To change her name from Opalbender to something else. Cakebender, perhaps? Or something with chocolate in it?

The tower bells tolled the hours once, then twice, before Shar and Kigora were finally called back to face the judges.

"Good luck," Shar said, reaching out to grasp Kigora's hand, give it a quick squeeze.

"Good luck to you too," Kigora said, holding on to Shar's hand, not letting it go immediately. "Maybe...we can cook together again sometime?"

"I'd like that," Shar said. "I'd like that a lot."

"So would I."

Dwarves didn't blush. But Shar felt that both Kigora's and her own beard may have trembled a bit.

"As y'all may have been able to tell, this contest was close. As close as two peas in a pod," Erde told them.

"We actually consulted with the contest runners, to see if we could declare both of you the winner," Fenryl said.

"They declined," Zigli said flatly.

Shar could still hear the anger in her voice.

"They insisted that we had to choose just one of you as the winner," Fenryl said, trying to smooth things out. "However, the one we don't choose shouldn't call themselves a loser. I will personally come to your shop to mentor you for a week."

"And so will I," Zigli declared.

"Me too! Don't leave me out of this!" Erde said.

That made Shar blink with surprise. That was an extremely generous offer. Possibly worth more than the title.

However, Shar *needed* that title.

"Thank you, judges," Kigora said. Her smile was still brittle.

Shar couldn't help herself. She reached out to squeeze Kigora's hand again.

The other Dwarf held on tightly, not letting go.

"All right then. The winner of this year's *Chocolate Galore!* contest is..." Fenryl paused dramatically and the judge looked at each other.

Shar glanced hopefully at Kigora, who gave her a smile that was finally soft and not cracking.

"SHAR!" the three judges all shouted out in unison.

Shar stood there for a moment, the words of congratulations that she'd planned for Kigora dying on her lips.

"Wait, what?" Shar said, looking at the judges perplexed. "Me?"

"Yes, you, you silly goose," Zigli said fondly.

"You're kidding. You're not kidding. Are you?" Shar said.

Kigora's hand in hers was the only thing keeping her grounded, otherwise she was certain that she'd either float away or sink into the safe earth.

"We're not kidding," Erde said. "Ye are the winner. And Kigora, we're all gonna visit you over the next year."

"Thank you," Kigora and Shar said at the same time.

They glanced at each other, still holding hands, then the pair of them burst out laughing.

Suddenly, streamers filled the air. Confetti, too. Shar was surrounded by flashing lights and color.

All the sound went out of the world as she looked around for just a moment.

She'd been working *so hard* for this moment. It didn't seem real. Didn't feel real.

Then she felt Kigora's hand in hers again, squeezing it. Concern filled her fellow baker's face. (Frenemy? Or something closer now?)

"Breathe," Fenryl said, suddenly standing beside her.

Shar took a shaky breath, then another. Her beard trembled with overwhelming, conflicting emotions.

She finally let go of Kigora's hand as she started talking to the judges. She accepted a fierce hug from Zigli, a surprisingly gentle hug from Fenryl, and a firm handshake from Erde. The other bakers were allowed into the small group. Golodhon congratulated her and told her that the seven cakes for his seven names would have been perfect.

Hulda arrived. As did Leena and Rafael.

"Aye told ye from the start," Leena admonished Shar after releasing her. "Ye had the skills. Ye just needed some training. That's all."

"Thank you," Shar said earnestly. "Thank you so much." She proudly introduced her mentor to the judges, telling them that Leena had won regionals the year she'd attended.

Hulda let Shar know that she was happy she didn't have to thump anyone, though she was ready to do so at any time.

Erwel showed up, adding her congratulations. She and Fenryl joked about how good that chili-chocolate cake was that Shar had made, and what a shame it was that it had to go to the highest bidder, that they couldn't just steal it.

So many people. So many kind words. Shar still felt as though her head was a balloon, connected to her body by the thinnest of strings.

The only thing that kept her grounded through all of this was Kigora. Shar kept seeking out the other Dwarf's eye, getting a nod of encouragement every time.

Kigora had received a great prize beyond the title.

Hopefully that would be enough that their relationship wouldn't sour. Again.

# Shar

Shar was *so very glad* that Dwarves didn't blush.

However, her beard might have trembled awfully hard as she, Leena, and Hulda got off Rafael's ship, only to realize that a parade was awaiting them. Or rather, that Shar was expected to walk through the long corridors of Shazirakz as Dwarves lined the streets and cheered her on. One of the queen's heralds would lead the way.

Shar insisted that the others come with her, that she not walk this gauntlet by herself.

It was yet another bizarre experience, the shouts of Dwarves echoing off the tall ceilings, people waving at her, celebrating her win.

Finally, the herald led her into the Gemstone District and the grand Gem Hall, where her family awaited her.

Shar's family weren't necessarily very tactile with one another. However, her mother did embrace her warmly, as did her father and Durzi. Uncles, aunts, cousins, and other various relatives all stood there as well, happily greeting her and giving their congratulations.

A meal had been planned, and Shar didn't have to *make* anything for it. Though Hulda and Leena were invited, they both politely declined, as they had their own families waiting for them.

Finally, after much talking and storytelling and far too many times that Shar had had to raise her mug of ale and accept a toast, she was allowed to go to the silence of her room to rest.

Shar collapsed on her bed, sleep claiming her almost instantly. Almost.

She did have time for one last worried thought.

What now?

Things were both different as well as the same.

Shar was still getting up at four AM to start the baking. However, Leena had agreed to sell Muddy Bean Chocolates to Shar's family, so it was now *her* bakery. Leena was getting old enough that sooner or later, she'd be retiring. Her shaking hands hadn't gotten any better, so she could no longer decorate cakes how she'd like.

However, Shar had also leased the building next to the shop, as that was the only way to keep up with the demand for Shar's pastries and desserts.

Plus, while Shar would never have gems or jewelry showcased in the grand Gem Hall, she did have her own small display in that half of the shop, where she kept her most dazzling—and most expensive—chocolates and creations.

Shar no longer primarily baked alone, or just with Leena. While they'd been away, Leena had hired another baker, who Shar kept on, as well as hiring three others. She planned all the baking out by the week, now, instead of by the day.

In addition, Shar had a lot of specialty bakes that she had to plan for. Such as birthdays, weddings, and Dwarven holidays.

Then came the order from Queen Amberheart. Fulfilling that nearly killed Shar: not because there was so much to do, but because it was *for the queen*.

And Shar was expected to present her work personally, as well as there for the entire time. Serving the queen and everybody(!)

Hulda had made her more chefs coats for her to wear, and created a special one for the occasion. She made matching ones for the rest of Shar's staff as well.

It was a night to remember. And one that Shar knew would happen again, as the queen had been *very* pleased with what Shar and her bakers had produced. Enough so that Shar signed a contract to provide seasonal treats for the royal family.

The next few months passed so quickly, it felt sometimes as though Shar was preparing again for *Chocolates Galore!* She did push back on opening up her own baking school. She was still learning techniques as far as she was concerned.

However, other bakers were happy to come and work with her, show her their techniques as she taught them more about flavor.

She didn't really stop to take a break until the *other* invitation came.

The one from Kigora.

Seemed that Zigli was going to fulfill her promise, and was going to meet Kigora in Anthus to give her lessons for a week.

And did Shar want to come?

It took a single afternoon for Shar to make all the arrangements, to cover the work that she'd be missing.

Because she wasn't about to turn down this invitation.

At least this time, Shar was able to hire a wagon to transport her (and her cooking gear, as well as some specialty chocolate and other ingredients) to Anthus. She didn't have to cook at the various inns she stayed at, though she still made the offer at a few of them. Hulda accompanied her, paid by Shar this time as a bodyguard. (Not that she needed one, but still, it was nice to know that someone had her back. Literally.)

Kigora looked much the same when Shar finally arrived. Black and red ribbons decorated her beard—which had frequently been the colors that Shar had worn.

Whereas Shar wore all different colors of blue, to celebrate Kigora and the rivers of Anthus.

They embraced silently, holding each other for a few moments. (Maybe more than just a few.)

Shar hadn't realized that she was missing this, *longing* for this.

And yes, both of them might have had trembling beards afterward.

Kigora put Shar in a nice, comforting room lined with stone, the ceilings a familiar height, with Hulda in the room right next door.

After Shar had settled in a bit, she came back out to find Kigora waiting for her in the formal greeting room. Appetizers had been put out, and Shar dutifully nibbled and commented on the flavors.

Neither of the Dwarves seemed to know what to say to one another. They spoke hesitatingly of the past few months, what they'd been doing, the treats they'd been baking.

Shar tried to describe the new chocolate technique she'd learned —pretty simple, really, just a few drizzled lines of chocolate, that gathered together, that could form a bird's nest.

Eventually, Kigora said, "Show me."

Once they were in the kitchen together, things flowed again for both of them. Shar displayed her chocolate techniques, while Kigora wowed her with the new sugar work she was doing. They agreed to collaborate on a cake, using different flavors that they'd been experimenting with recently.

It was only when Kigora cut up the cooling cake and picked up a piece for Shar that she paused.

Got a calculating look in her eye.

Then beckoned Shar over to her side.

Silently, she held up the piece of cake.

Shar gulped, then obligingly leaned forward, letting Kigora (her friend? Or something more, now?) feed her.

It was amazingly delicious. The chocolate melted on her tongue, followed by the tart and fruity flavors of the pure bean. Smooth, rich cacao pleasantly coated her mouth, and the sweetness made itself known. Spices kicked in next, that warming sensation of ginger and clove, perfectly balanced with the touch of salt at the very end.

Shar wasn't sure why Kigora hadn't won with this cake. It was complex, yet simple. So soft and moist, yet not falling to pieces.

And this was before it had been soaked, or any filling had been added to the layers.

Shar leaned back. Kigora grinned at her, delight dancing in her eyes.

With great daring, Shar picked up the other sliced piece and indicated that Kigora should take it.

Staring her directly in the eyes, Kigora wrapped one warm hand around Shar's and slowly took the piece of cake from her. The other Dwarf's tongue reached out and briefly licked Shar's finger.

A shudder ran through Shar as she watched Kigora finish eating her piece of the cake.

However, the kiss they shared after that?

Was even sweeter.

# Epilogue

Shar nearly leaned over and smacked Kigora's arm. "Stop fidgeting!" she whispered.

Kigora shrugged apologetically, then sighed. "I can't help it," she whispered back.

"I know, dear," Shar said, taking her wife's hand and intertwining their fingers together. Kigora's wedding ring—that matched Shar's own—wound around her middle finger. The rings themselves were platinum, though they'd been magically treated, so they looked like a delicate curl of chocolate.

Even through the last thirty-seven years, since Shar had placed that ring on Kigora's hand, the metal had never scratched, nor the color faded.

Shar took a moment to look at her own hand. At least her fingers were clean. No chocolate lurked under her nails. Her hands were strong, like Kigora's, from all the work they'd done over the decades, baking together.

Their two children sat on the same bench they did. After a horrible accident in the mines of the Ashveil mountains, they'd ended up adopting two kids. Malamora, the girl, and Reirbubera, the boy, had been four and three, respectively. They'd grown up in the kitchen, and were now in their late teens and old enough to start thinking about their own careers. Mora, it turned out, was more interested in gemstones than Shar ever had been, and had already started an apprenticeship with Shar's relatives. While Buba enjoyed baking, it wasn't his passion. No one was certain where he'd end up.

In front of them, King Yarnard Goldarmor led the naming ceremony with the priests from the three main Dwarven gods. (As the queen had retired after her forty-year rule, as had been expected of her.)

Being granted a new name was a serious business. Not always so serious that royalty had to be involved. But Shar had been cooking treats for the royal family for decades, and so the king had insisted on a formal renaming ceremony.

Particularly since this was a new name, that no Dwarf had ever held before.

Finally, the priests were ready and the king (the king!) indicated that the four of them should come forward.

Shar did her best to not let her trembling beard show.

The quick squeeze of her hand from Kigora helped.

After making the announcement of why they were there, the king turned to Shar.

"Sharaksir Opalbender, do you hearby renounce the prestigious name Opalbender, so that you and your family will now go by the shared name Chocolatecarver?" he asked solemnly.

"I do," Shar said reverently.

The king asked the same question of all of them—Kigora giving up the Goldenberry name, while the kids gave up the name of their former family.

"Let it now be written in all the genealogy tomes that the name Chocolatecarver is to be celebrated in all of the Dwarven kingdoms!" the king declared loudly.

The cheering of the crowd was deafening.

Shar and Kigora embraced each other briefly, gathering the kids to them and having a big, family hug.

Satisfaction flowed through Shar.

She'd done it.

Not only had she won her contest so many years before, but she'd won her love, her life, and now, her name.

Things were just going to get better from here on.

When the king turned expectantly toward Shar, she replied with the only thing she knew was left to say.

Shar and Kigora's bakery had provided all the treats and delights for the after-ceremony party.

"Let's eat!" Shar declared, leading them to the groaning tables in the back.

And they did, while living happily ever after.

Want more cozy fantasy? Check out these books!
*A Dragon's Guide to Killing Gods (And Other Lies)*
*The Ice Elf & The Snow Cone*
*The Ice Elf & The Fire Elemental*

# Drinking Chocolate Recipe

Seriously, what sort of cozy fantasy book all about chocolate would this be without at least one recipe at the end of it?

This is the drinking chocolate that Shar prepared for Hulda back in chapter seventeen, just after their first pop-up shop. Fair warning: it's rich and thick. Just a shot of this will set you right.

## INGREDIENTS

2 cups whole milk OR non-dairy substitution[1]
   4 oz unsweetened chocolate[2]
   1/4 cup maple syrup
   Pinch of salt
   Splash of vanilla

---

1. I, the author, am allergic to dairy. So I do my version with one cup of coconut milk, and one cup of oat milk. Just straight coconut milk makes it taste too coconut-y. By adding another type of non-dairy milk, it really cuts the coconut taste.
2. If you don't have unsweetened baker's chocolate lying around, you can sub in some other type of chocolate. You may have to cut down on the amount of maple syrup or other sweetener.

Optional: 5-6 drops peppermint extract

Optional: 1/2 teaspoon chai spice mix

Optional: brandy, rum, or whatever other alcohol you think will taste good

## INSTRUCTIONS

Chop the unsweetened chocolate up into small pieces.

Put the milk in a small saucepan. Add maple syrup, vanilla, salt, and anything else you'd like to use to flavor your drinking chocolate. Heat the liquid mixture until just before it boils.

Add chocolate to the heated liquid. Keep very warm, but don't let it boil.

Whisk the chocolate as it's melting, to get it to better incorporate into the liquid.

You'll know it's done when you can put a spoon into the mixture and the chocolate on the back of the spoon appears completely smooth, with no tiny flecks of chocolate remaining.

Pour into two (or more!) mugs. Top with whatever toppings you'd like, such as marshmallows, whipped cream, marshmallow cream, etc.

Enjoy!

# Afterword

As you may or may not have guessed from this book, I *love* chocolate, as well as reality baking shows.

For this book, I had to do some research. (No, really! *Had* to!) I took classes from Chocolate Man (https://www.chocolateman.com), and learned how to temper chocolate, as well as how to create a ganache and make molded chocolates.

Ever since I took those classes, I've been making classic French truffles regularly, that is, a hardened ganache rolled in something, like cacao powder, powdered sugar, or nuts. My most recent favorite was a cranberry, orange, and pistachio white-chocolate truffle. (If you make chocolates, I would recommend the Chocolate Man for your supplies. He buys high-quality chocolate callets by the ton, then sells them in bags by the pound. They're half the price of the exact same chocolate I could get elsewhere, and frequently, better quality.)

As for reality TV, I enjoy shows where the contestants have to make something. They need to show off their skills, not just whine and complain about their situation while scheming.

And yes, the judges in this book are all based off of real judges that I've watched on TV.

For the regional contest judges, I used judges that I've seen on the *Baking Championship* series. (*Holiday Baking Championship, Spring Baking Championship, Halloween Baking Championship*, and so on.) My characters are just vaguely based on the actual judges. I'm not claiming that I'm writing about them, specifically. (Please don't sue me.)

So Cyna, who really liked her alcohol couldn't wait to taste something, may remind you of Nancy Fuller. Yazgrak, who always gives the most practical advice, perhaps was influenced by Duff Goldman. Erwel, of course, is inspired by Carla Hall, in part because she's an Elf. I didn't use her signature, "Duuuude," phrase, though I did use "Girl" more than once.

Then there are the second set of judges, for *Chocolates Galore!* who I had just as much fun with.

I loosely (very loosely) based Erde on Jason Smith (Lord Honey!). I had a lot of fun first rewatching the shows that he was on, then adapting his phrases to fit this world. One of the first things that Jason says on his season of *Holiday Baking Championship* is, "Well, butter my butt and call me a biscuit!" (Seriously, that's a direct quote.) Writing him made me as happy as a Dwarf with some new beard oil.

Fenryl is loosely based on Bobby Flay, the old man of the cooking competitions. He doesn't really have signature phrases (except for greeting the audience and saying that they're looking sharp that night) but he does have an attitude.

And fried rice.

Sunny Johnson inspired Zigli. On TV, Sunny has a lot of fun poking at Bobby. She has a lot of attitude, and I've seen her pump up an audience by shouting at them. One of her sayings is that "Fried rice ain't BBQ, Bobby," which I adapted to chocolate. Plus there's the whole, "Don't try me," which she frequently says to Bobby after he's been teasing her."

One other comment: as far as I've been able to determine,

tapping your foot when your hands are shaking is a viable technique. I was listening to an interview with a surgeon who operated on brains. According to him (and I've also tried this myself) he was taught the foot tapping method. I've tried it a couple of times and it appears to work.

So if you're ever on a reality TV show, or doing something where you can't have your hands shake, try tapping your foot.

No book is written in a vacuum. I want to thank my dear husband for putting up with me, for coming up with the perfect title for this book, and for enjoying this ride with me. As well as for encouraging me to make chocolates!

I also want to thank my editor for his comments, he always makes my books better.

And I want to thank my readers. This wouldn't be possible without you. Thank for making the magic real.

Enjoy!

Leah R Cutter

Ravensdale, WA

March 2025

# Read More!

Do you enjoy exploring strange new worlds, new cultures, new people?

# About the Author

Leah Cutter writes page-turning fiction in exotic locations, such as a magical New Orleans, the ancient Orient, Hungary, the Oregon coast, rural Kentucky, Seattle, Minneapolis, and many others.

She writes literary, fantasy, mystery, science fiction, and horror fiction. Her short fiction has been published in magazines like *Alfred Hitchcock's Mystery Magazine* and *Talebones*, anthologies like Fiction River, and on the web. Her long fiction has been published both by New York publishers as well as small presses.

Find Leah's books on Knotted Road Press at (www.Knotted-RoadPress.com)

Follow her blog at www.LeahCutter.com.

### Reviews

It's true. Reviews help me sell more books. If you've enjoyed this story, please consider leaving a review of it on your favorite site.

### Come someplace new...

Are you a traveler? Do you enjoy exploring strange new worlds, new cultures, new people?

Journey into the various lands envisioned by Leah Cutter.

Sign up for my newsletter and I'll start you on your travels with a free copy of my book, *The Island Sampler*.

I will never spam you or use your email for nefarious purposes. You can also unsubscribe at any time.

http://www.LeahCutter.com/newsletter/

# About Knotted Road Press

Knotted Road Press publishes dynamic fiction set in exotic locations and unique non-fiction voices in genres such as autobiography, business, cookbooks, and how-to. Our authors cover a wide range of genres including science fiction, fantasy, mystery, literary, and poetry, appealing to all readers. We offer both DRM-free ebooks and print books for a global readership.

Knotted Road Press
www.KnottedRoadPress.com
www.KnottedRoadPress.com/Shop